Praise for
ELLEN EMERSON WHITE'S
The Road Home

★ "Inextricable from the story's anti-war theme is its fiercely compassionate loyalty to the people who served in Vietnam."

— *Publishers Weekly,* starred review

"This is an excellent account of wartime experiences in Vietnam, especially from the woman's point of view....It will appeal to any student looking for a well written, fast-paced, high interest story."

— *Voice of Youth Advocates*

"Combining action/adventure and romance, the novel...will appeal to a wide range of readers."
— *Booklist*

"White's account makes readers feel the agony of Vietnam...not just the horror of war, but the pain of knowing that those who served and suffered were despised by a large part of the society that sent them there in the first place." —*School Library Journal*

"Fast-paced...vivid and realistic." — *Kirkus Reviews*

An ALA Best Book for Young Adults

POINT SIGNATURE EDITIONS

From the Notebooks of Melanin Sun
by Jacqueline Woodson

Probably Still Nick Swansen
by Virginia Euwer Wolff

Dove and Sword
by Nancy Garden

The Wild Hunt
by Jane Yolen

I Can Hear the Mourning Dove
by James Bennett

Humming Whispers
by Angela Johnson

POINT • SIGNATURE

THE ROAD HOME

Ellen Emerson White

SCHOLASTIC INC.
New York Toronto London Auckland Sydney

ISBN 0-590-46738-7

12 11 10 9 8 7 6 5 4 3 2   8 9/9 0 1 2/0

For Sister Betty

THE ROAD HOME

Part I

THE WAR

Chapter One

On Christmas morning, Rebecca lost her moral virginity, her sense of humor — and her two best friends. But, other than that, it was a hell of a holiday.

Of course, if she looked hard enough, she could probably find someone else in Vietnam who had had an even *worse* time, but — well, during her rare moments off-duty, silent self-absorption was pretty much the order of the day. And lately, she was so damn exhausted that even *that* was more than she could manage. The Tet truce had — out of nowhere — turned into a major offensive, and as far as she could tell, the war was completely out of control.

Rumor had it, even Walter Cronkite was in a panic.

The entire hospital staff had been working straight through for — actually, after the first forty-eight hours, Rebecca lost track. She scrubbed in on a few cases, but mostly she was in triage, lurching from blood-soaked litter to litter, the overflow of casualties spilling over into the halls and out to the helicopter pad. Bodies — some alive, some not — were literally *stacked up* all over the place, a scene so grisly that even one of *her* nightmares couldn't have created it.

By the third day, they were being given amphetamines to stay awake, pausing only long enough to slug them down with cold strong coffee before moving on to the next patient. Rebecca worked on complete medical auto-pilot, starting IVs, stopping bleeding, and cutting off limbs that were only hanging by tendons to save the surgeons time. Things got so crazy that, for about a day and a half, there was a huge pile of amputated arms, legs, and feet piled haphazardly in one corner of the ER, waiting for some poor corpsman to have the time to haul the gory mess away.

The medevac choppers came, and came — and came, unloading countless wounded GIs and then taking off to go pick up more. After a while, she didn't even look at faces — unless the soldier had a facial *wound* — because remembering that the bleeding, shredded bodies were human beings made it too hard to work. If the kid wasn't breathing, she would try to get him started again; if he *was* breathing, she would check his IVs and vital signs, slap on fresh pressure bandages, and turn to the next one. Airway, chest, and abdominal cases went down to the OR first, followed by the traumatic amputations. Something as simple as a compound fracture meant that the kid went to the end of the line. Serious head injuries — forget it. All she could do was make sure the guy wasn't in obvious pain, and go on to someone else.

The hospital came under more than one rocket and mortar attack during all of this and, not taking the time to put on their mandatory helmets and flak jackets, they would drag all of the patients onto the floor, covering them with mattresses to try and protect them from any stray shrapnel. A direct hit would probably wipe out most of the room. The power kept going off, and sometimes the emergency generators would kick in — and sometimes they wouldn't, and as many staff members as could be spared would have to run to all the kids on respirators and work the machines by hand until the electricity came back on.

She had broken her ankle — during her lovely, festive Christmas, when the helicopter she wasn't even supposed to *be* on got shot down — and over the last few frenetic days, the cast had cracked off completely. Since it still hurt like hell, the fracture obviously hadn't finished healing, but she just gritted her teeth, taped it up during a few spare seconds, popped another in a series of Darvons, and slipped on the smallest right boot she could find from the pile on the floor. After, of course, shaking the *foot* out of it first.

At some point — it was hard to remember when — Major Doyle, the chief nurse, had instituted a mandatory sleeping schedule, requiring each of them to take four hours off during every twenty-four. Some people would go to the trouble of stumbling back to their quarters, but most of them just crashed out in the nearest empty space they could find. One time, Rebecca woke up to find her head resting against the shoulder of a completely unfamiliar, also sleeping, GI — and was too tired to be embarrassed. In fact, after maybe moving a little closer to him, she went right back to sleep. Never found out who he was, either.

Things began to slow down after a couple of weeks, casualties coming in brief spurts, instead of a constant flow. The staff was still working twenty hours a day, but the pace was somewhat less frantic, and they could do things like occasionally *pause* before making life and death decisions. A luxury, to say the least.

During a momentary lull, Rebecca was lugging a fresh box of Ringer's lactate out to the ER when she saw — amazingly, since the woman tended to be super-human — Major Doyle asleep on the floor in Pre-Op, huddled uncomfortably by the wall.

The head ER nurse, Captain Stockman, paused behind her, carrying a supply of syringes. ''Don't disturb her,'' she said quietly. ''It's been a couple of days since she's left here.''

Rebecca nodded, keeping her distance. Major Doyle kind of intimidated her, but Captain Stockman *really* did. She could turn a cocky, battle-hardened Green Beret into a wide-eyed altar boy in one unsmiling second. Her personality was a little difficult, but she was *twice* as good a nurse as anyone else, so ''Yes, ma'am, right away, ma'am'' was about as flippant as anyone ever got around her.

''She still has a few things to learn about leading by example,'' Captain Stockman said, even more quietly.

Rebecca didn't know how to respond to that, or even if she was supposed to — so she didn't say anything at all.

Everyone in the ER was stumbling around like zombies, cleaning and restocking, getting ready for the next, inevitable, load of casualties. Rebecca was so tired that she could barely see, and her bad arm trembled — yes, another swell holiday souvenir; this one courtesy of an enemy bullet — as she lifted the box of IV fluid up onto its shelf. But she just pressed her teeth together, thought longingly about Darvon, and turned around to go get another box.

When she came limping back in, Captain Stockman — who looked surprisingly alert and well-rested, despite being a good fifteen years older than almost anyone else — moved to block her path. "You're going to take a break now, Lieutenant Phillips," she said.

Rebecca nodded. "Yes, ma'am. As soon as I — "

"That can wait," Captain Stockman said briskly. "You're going to take one *now*."

Oh. Okay. "Yes, ma'am," Rebecca said, and put down the box. She felt so stiff and dull that she had to think for a few seconds before deciding to get a Coke. She opened the refrigerator, moving aside bags of blood — when they had run out a few days earlier, most of them had donated some; which hadn't raised their energy levels any — to get at the soda.

Then, she took the can outside and stood on the landing pad while she tried to figure out what to do next. It was light outside, which was kind of a surprise, since she had figured that it was the middle of the night, and she checked her blood-smeared watch. Just past 1500.

Not that it mattered, one way or the other. One *day* or another. Except that she still had seven and a half more months in this hellhole before she could go home.

And counting.

She was too tired to go anywhere, so she just sat on the muddy ground in the rain, leaning up against the wall of wet sandbags protecting the ER. More than a few had fresh shrapnel holes. She didn't have a church key, so she wiped off a pair of bandage scissors, and jabbed two holes in the top of the can. Messy, but effective.

Afraid that if she didn't *do* something, she would fall asleep, she reached for the little stack of letters in her back pocket. She hadn't exactly had time to read lately, and had only managed to scrawl a couple of "things are busy, but I'm fine" notes. Some idiot at HQ had screwed up the night she'd been brought back in from the jungle and sent her parents a telegram saying that their daughter was in stable condition, after sustaining unspecified injuries, in Quang Tin Province, Republic of South Vietnam. Oh, and — Happy Holidays.

She had finally managed to get a call through to them through MARS — Military Affiliate Radio Station — and assured them that she was fine, it was all a mistake, she had just had a minor accident. Broke her ankle and, oh, yeah, got a little — cut — on her arm.

It would have been more convincing if she hadn't started crying when she heard her mother's voice.

Anyway. She looked at the stack of letters. Several from her mother, one from her friend Irene, and three from Michael. Christ. He was writing her almost every day now. He had been on the patrol she ran into in the jungle, and — well, despite the fact that they barely knew each other, he seemed to be smitten. Right before Tet, his unit had come to Chu Lai for a stand down — cut short, obviously, by the damn war — and he showed up at the hospital to "see if she was okay."

Friendship and romance — in no particular order — were the absolute *last* things on her mind these days, but — well. He was completely not her type — all sunglasses and swagger and cynicism — and as stubborn as an entire *pack* of bull terriers. On top of which, he was arrogant, short-tempered, *younger* than she was — and every single time she saw a wounded, skinny brown-haired grunt coming in on a litter, her heart jumped. Lurched. Fell.

It would make sense to read the letters in order, but, unlike her mother, he didn't date each envelope carefully across the flap so she could keep track. She pulled out a scalpel, and sliced the top one open.

Dear Rebecca.

His handwriting was *significantly* better than hers was. But, then again, that was true of most of the people on the planet.

I hope you're okay. Things out here haven't been too bad, but nobody seems to know what the hell is going on. (So what else *is new.) Me, I just keep my head down.*

She had written so many lies herself that she found them very easy to recognize.

99-875

Snoopy says hi. At least, I think it was "Hi" — his mouth is full.

Snoopy was his best friend, a thin black kid from Newark — and easily the most angelic-looking grunt she had ever seen.

I'm still sort of worried that you might be mad. That I was too pushy.

Well, there was no question but that he had been *extremely* pushy. Talking his way into her room, and so forth. He'd spent one night, and part of another, but nothing much had happened beyond a couple of kisses straight out of Hollywood. One of the few things they had in common, actually, was a tremendous fondness for movies.

There was little doubt in her mind that there would have been considerable, if not total, sexual acceleration that second night, but she was on call — and she got called.

The next day, his company was sent back to the bush, and — there it was. Or, more accurately, there it *wasn't*.

I don't know — thought I might try something new, and not *be a jerk. What do you think? Good plan? On the other hand, I don't want to go and get all ambitious on myself. I'll think on it maybe, get back to you.*

He *was* a jerk, but — okay — she thought he was funny.

Snoopy says I should write you a poem. Says all *the young ladies are happy as can be, when they get a nice poem for under their pillow.*

Which was *exactly* the way Snoopy talked. Cute kid.

So, let me know. I can start looking at butterflies, and flowers, and all. (Does Vietnam rhyme with Mom, or Spam?)

For a grouch, he was not without charm.

Hearing the ER doors open, she looked up and saw Annie Carella come outside, moving in a disoriented stumble. Normally, she was all giggles and bounce, but right now, she looked like hell.

Rebecca lifted the Coke can, and Lieutenant Carella nodded, coming over to sit heavily next to her in the mud.

"Good Christ," she said, without much inflection.

Rebecca nodded, putting Michael's letter back in her pocket to finish later, and they sat there, sharing the Coke and slouching back against the sandbags. Compared to the rest of everyday life in Vietnam, rain was a very minor inconvenience.

"How's your arm holding out?" Annie asked.

Barely. But Rebecca just shrugged, and drank some Coke.

The hard drizzle was turning into a downpour, and they both looked up at the sky.

"Oh, God, Becky." Annie let out her breath. "I want to go *home*."

Rebecca nodded. No argument there.

Talking was too much of an effort, so they just sat in the rain, trading sips until the soda was gone.

"You sure you're making it all right?" Annie asked.

"I'm fine," Rebecca said, probably too stiffly. On the other hand, she couldn't help wondering how much Annie knew about what had happened. Beyond the bare facts of her having broken every rule in the book by jumping impulsively on a medevac with their friends Wolf and Spike — who had had extremely unlikely nicknames for two such sweet guys — and their being shot down. It was Christmas, there was a truce on, and when they couldn't find a medic, she had made a snap decision and gone along for the ride. A ride that had ended up with the two of them dead, and her lost in the jungle for the next day and a half. She'd been lucky enough to run into a patrol, and — that was that.

End of story.

The part where she had panicked and killed someone was one she was going to keep to herself.

Permanently.

Aware that Annie was looking at her with great concern, she got up, resisting the temptation to sag against the building as pain jolted through her ankle and up her entire leg. "We'd better go back in," she said, slowly easing her weight back onto the leg, and feeling a little reaction quiver run up her back.

Annie looked even more worried. "If you need time off, *tell* them."

Rebecca nodded, although she had no intention of doing any such thing. Lately, they had needed every single bit of help they could *get*.

When they walked back inside the ER, everyone was still cleaning and restocking. Major Doyle was up and working again, looking embarrassed and exhausted, doing drug inventory with Lieutenant Averill.

Rebecca stood at the front of the room, her mind feeling so sluggish that she wasn't sure where to jump in.

"Please relieve Lieutenant Averill," Captain Stockman said, holding an armload of gauze pads. "Tell her to take twenty minutes."

Good. A direct order. Rebecca nodded, and limped over to the glass-doored drug cabinet against the far wall. Both sides of the room were lined with supply-filled wooden shelves, and pairs of black sturdy sawhorses were set up to hold litters. The whole place was arranged so that everything they needed was within easy reach to facilitate treatment. When casualties came in, things were confusing enough without having to search around for chest tubes or whatever.

She tapped Lieutenant Averill lightly on the shoulder. "You're supposed to take a break, Cath."

Lieutenant Averill looked relieved, nodded, and handed her some penicillin to count.

"Class 1 painkillers next," Major Doyle said, not even looking up, marking figures on her clipboard.

Rebecca nodded, counting.

They worked in near silence for a few minutes, Rebecca able to feel her hands trembling with fatigue. She also had to count more slowly than usual, to make sure she didn't lose track.

Major Doyle glanced over briefly from her clipboard, her eyes so tired that the normal very bright blue color seemed somewhat faded. "If I may say so, Lieutenant, you look terrible."

What good news. "Gee, ma'am," Rebecca said, counting the morphine. "And I was just about to tell you how pert and sprightly *you* look."

Major Doyle smiled a little, and motioned for her to continue counting. "Cool it on the Darvon," she said in a low voice.

Rebecca looked up, guiltily. "What?"

Major Doyle looked right back at her, and this time, the blue in her eyes seemed to intensify. "You heard me. It's not aspirin. Don't treat it that way."

Personally, Rebecca thought she was doing pretty damn well managing with the Darvon, and *not* moving on to Demerol. "I'm doing my best, ma'am," she said, quietly. "Okay?"

Major Doyle nodded, glanced down at her ankle, and then went back to her clipboard.

The fact that the Major knew more than anyone else about what had happened — since she had scrubbed in while one of their surgeons, Captain McNulty, dug the bullet out of her arm, and had apparently sworn him, and anyone else nearby, to total secrecy — didn't mean that she should press her advantage.

"We're all whacked out on amphetamines — you should be worried about *that*," Rebecca said.

Major Doyle nodded. "I *am* worried about that."

Well — good. She should be. The entire staff was on the verge of a collective nervous breakdown. Under the circumstances, Darvon was a minor concern, at best.

When they were finally finished, Major Doyle

handed her the clipboard to give to Captain Stockman for her supply requisition forms.

"Find some dry scrubs to put on," she said. "No
point in your coming down with pneumonia along
with everything else."

Rebecca frowned at her, but then realized that
her uniform was soaked from the rain, and that
was probably why she was shivering so much.

"And check on the new kid, okay? Give him
some direction," Major Doyle said, indicating a
very young corpsman named Rosario, who had
had the misfortune to arrive in-country only a few
days earlier, during the height of the casualties, and
was, as a result, even more dazed than everyone
else was.

Rebecca nodded, and limped over to give him a
hand restocking the chest and endotracheal tubes.
He was a fairly frail kid, with wide brown eyes like
Bambi, and a uniform about three sizes too big.

When he saw her coming, he dropped at least
half of the tubes, and she bent down to pick them
up.

"How you doing, sport?" she asked, handing
them back.

"Yes, ma'am," he said. "I — I mean, fine,
ma'am."

Ma'am. Showing chief and head nurses respect
was one thing — but she, personally, wasn't all
that excited about military protocol.

"Rebecca," she said. "And don't worry, it isn't
always like this around here."

He smiled weakly.

Poor kid. Welcome to Vietnam. "It *really* isn't,"

she said. "In fact — " She stopped, hearing the sound of an approaching helicopter. After a while, it was easy to identify all of the different helicopters by sound alone, and therefore know approximately how many casualties were coming in.

The sound of the rotor blades got louder, and almost everyone in the Emergency Room froze.

"Oh, *shit*," someone said.

A Chinook — which was a *very* large helicopter — and it sounded full.

Chapter Two

Captain Stockman broke the silence.

"Let's go!" she said. "Get them in here! Mc-Cormack, Thorpe, get some IVs up! Let's move!"

As the entire room snapped into action, Rebecca rushed outside with several corpsmen and two of the doctors to help carry the litters. The Chinook would be bringing in at least fifteen wounded soldiers, and probably twice that many. What was known as a "mass-cal."

There were already several stretchers out on the helicopter pad, and Rebecca bent down over the nearest bleeding soldier, scanning his medevac tag. *GSW, T&T, upper chest*. Gunshot wound, through and through — which meant that the bullet had passed through his body. His pressure bandage had slipped down, and she tightened it to slow the bleeding.

"Where they from?" she yelled at Gomer, one of the corpsmen.

"Don't know!" he yelled back.

Damn. Michael's unit was Echo Company, 4/31,

and this was the nearest hospital in their Area of Operations. But she had to concentrate on what she was doing here, help with the triage. She snapped her fingers at Rosario, then pointed at the GSW.

"Bring him inside!" she said, and turned to help Gomer with one of the others. Open fracture, left tibia, bleeding under control. No problem. Back of the bus.

One of the medics inside the helicopter was struggling to pull out a litter by himself, and she hurried over to help him.

"Where they from?" she asked, shouting over the sound of the rotor blades.

"Up near Tam Ky!" he yelled.

Damn. Michael had been in the Que Son Valley — but they could have moved. The kid on the litter had a shattered skull, with brain tissue spilling out, and there was no way they were going to be able to save him. *Damn*. She glanced at the sweat-stained — or rain-drenched — medic as they dragged out yet another litter. "Who are they?"

"Gimlets!" he yelled.

The nickname for the 3/21 Infantry. Same brigade, different battalion.

It was absolutely obscene that she felt a little flash of relief.

The boy on the litter was struggling for breath and she pressed the plastic field dressing wrapper down more tightly against his chest, keeping her hand there as two corpsmen lifted him up onto a wheeled gurney. She ran along next to them, ripping his fatigue shirt open with one hand to check for an exit wound, and holding the plastic down with the other.

"Sucking chest!" she yelled as they banged through the swinging doors, and two of the doctors, Cole and Bergin, were instantly there as the corpsmen lowered his litter onto a pair of sawhorses.

By now, the ER had fallen into its usual organized chaos. Screaming, and groaning, and shouted instructions. Pain, and fear, and blood. Dirt, and sweat, and vomit. Clearing airways, hooking up IVs, drawing blood for type-and-cross. Telling each kid, no matter what his condition was, that he was okay, he was at an American hospital, he was going to be fine, don't worry about a thing.

The sucking chest was stabilized enough to go down to the OR, so she went to the next litter that came through the door — multiple frag wounds, mainly abdominal, but also genital. He had lost a lot of blood, and after getting an IV started, she turned her head.

"Low-titer O!" she called, and someone threw her a bag of blood.

Major Horan, the triage officer, stopped next to her. "What've we got?" he asked.

"MFWs," she said. "Abdomen rigid, diminished bowel sounds. Testicular damage, too."

Major Horan winced, and wrote a number on the kid's forehead. That way, by checking the numbers, everyone would know the exact priority for the OR. Triage was merciless in its logic, but effective. Save the ones that could be saved, let the minor injuries wait, forget the ones that were too far gone — and move on to someone else. Immediately.

"Get him stabilized," Major Horan said, capping his marker. "He goes right after the other laparotomy, and the kid over there with the throat."

Rebecca nodded, already re-checking her patient's vitals, then using some Betadine to start scrubbing him down.

"Not yesterday, not tomorrow, *now*," Captain Jessup was saying impatiently behind her. Which was *polite* for Jessup, who was by far the worst doctor on staff.

Her patient was staring blankly up at her, and she gave him a quick smile.

"Don't worry," she said. "You're fine." Except that he wasn't going to be so damn fine when he woke up without his testicles. She forced herself to keep smiling at him, so he wouldn't know how seriously hurt he was.

"Idiot!" Jessup was saying. "*Clamp* that, idiot!"

Rebecca glanced over her shoulder and saw Rosario holding a hemostat and looking panicked as a bleeder spurted up at him from a kid's torn-up arm. Quick, arterial spurts. She spun around and clamped the artery for him, guiding his hand down next to hers so he would be able to feel what she was doing.

"There you go," she said. "Don't worry, you'll get the hang of it." Then, she turned back to her patient, without bothering to take the time to scowl at Jessup. The boy's BP wasn't picking up, so she yelled for another unit of blood, pumping it in by hand when she couldn't find a pressure cuff.

"Relax," she said, smiling at him again. "You're going to be okay. What's your name?" When they found out they had genital wounds, they usually went into shock. With good reason. Once, she'd had a kid go into complete cardiac arrest when he saw the bloody gap between his legs, and he died before they could do a damn thing for him.

One of her many red-letter days since she'd gotten in-country.

Gomer and a lab tech arrived with a gurney to take the boy down to the OR, and she stepped over to replace the visibly shaky Rosario.

"Go help with the double-amp," she said, pushing him towards another litter.

He nodded, and stumbled over there.

"Ringer's!" Jessup barked.

Rebecca quickly pulled a fresh IV bottle down the wire strung above the row of sawhorses — they always set them up in advance, if they had time — and changed the almost-empty one.

"Clean him up and move him out!" Jessup ordered, and turned to the litter behind them, where another MFW was waiting.

Lieutenant McCormack appeared to help her, and they had the kid prepped and ready to go in about the same amount of time it took a corpsman to bring out a gurney from Pre-Op. Most of the critical cases had already gone down, and there were only a few kids still waiting. As always, Rebecca had no idea how much time had passed, but it had probably been much shorter than she thought. During a push, time always jumped into slow-motion, and she was surprised later when people said things to her like, "Jesus, you were so *fast.*" As far as she could tell, she was always a minute, and a step, slower than she wanted to be.

No one seemed to need her help, so she went over to the litter at the end of the row of trestles, where a kid was lying by himself, looking vague enough to indicate that his morphine had kicked in. His legs were peppered with shrapnel, but there wasn't much bleeding, so he was low-priority.

"Hey," he said, his eyes barely focusing as he swiped at one of her pigtails with a clumsy hand. He tried again, missed again, and smiled lethargically.

"Feeling any pain?" she asked, checking his bandages for staining, and then cutting off his fatigue pants by quickly slitting up each leg with a pair of hooked scissors.

"Wha'?" he asked, his voice very thick.

She checked his blood pressure, the systolic higher than she would have guessed. Hmmm. "What's your name, sport?" she asked.

He blinked a couple of times. "Wha'?"

Right. He was still wearing a couple of grenades, and she removed them cautiously. "José!" she called to the nearest corpsman, then handed him the two grenades to be secured. José looked just *thrilled* to have them.

The kid's hand was swinging out again, and this time, it grabbed at one of her breasts. Then, he looked even more confused.

"*Hey,*" he said. "Hey!"

The grunts were always so surprised to see women that they thought they were dreaming — and, inevitably, reached for her chest to see if she was real.

"It's okay," she said, putting his hand back down on the litter. "I'm a nurse. You're at the hospital."

"Wha'?" he asked.

He was *too* lethargic — stuporous, really — and she flipped out her penlight to check his pupils. Oh, hell. "Does your head hurt?" she asked, feeling his skull for obvious indentations or swellings.

He tried to focus on her, and then his eyes drifted shut.

Quickly, she started checking for deep tendon reflexes. "What's your name, pal?" she asked, extra-loudly. "Do you know where you are?"

He blinked a few times, then drifted off again.

Noticeable weakness on the left side. "Hey." She tapped his cheek sharply to rouse him out of the lethargy a little. "Does your head hurt? Do you remember hitting your head?" She looked up for a doctor. "Hey! I need some help over here!"

By the time Jessup — just her luck — came over, the kid had already gone into a brief seizure. Damn, damn, damn. There was a good chance they were going to lose this one.

"I think we've got a hematoma here," she said. The kid started to vomit and she automatically turned his head towards her, so that he wouldn't choke. "Hey!" she yelled over her shoulder. "Any Mannitol mixed?"

Captain Jessup fumbled for his own penlight. "Leave the diagnosing to the doctors, *nurse*."

José came running over with the Mannitol, which would, with luck, lower the intracranial pressure. "You need help?"

The kid had finished throwing up, and she shook her head, checking to make sure his airway was clear. "Tell them we're sending down a head injury with morphine complications."

"Why were you stupid enough to give him *morphine*?" Jessup asked, repeating the reflex checks she had already done.

Rebecca ignored that. "Tell them he needs a full skull series, and to get prepped for a probable craniotomy."

"You going to perform the operation, too?" Jessup asked.

Odds were, she'd do it a damn sight better than *he* would. "You're in my way, Doctor," she said, and elbowed past him to check the kid's pupils again.

By the time José and another corpsman came back to get him, the systolic had come down slightly, and she had the boy's head half-shaved. There was a knack to using the straight razors, which she had perfected only by long and painful practice on her own legs. Very painful.

"Think I can handle it from here, *nurse*," Jessup said, as she followed the gurney to X-Ray.

Oh. She stopped. Even though she was usually only with patients for a few minutes, it was always hard to surrender them to someone else. Especially someone like Jessup. But she just nodded, and let them go on without her. Hoped for the best.

Then, she went back into the ER, trembling with adrenaline. As if she would *ever* give someone morphine without checking pupillary reflex first. She took a couple of deep breaths, her heart feeling as though it were jumping all over her rib cage.

Okay. Okay. She looked around for someone

else to help. Schulberg, one of the GMOs — General Medical Officers — was stitching up a boy's lip, with Lieutenant Thorpe assisting him, while Annie was picking shrapnel out of a big burly kid with a thick mustache, and two corpsmen were mopping and cleaning. Captain Stockman was standing behind the desk by the main doors, filling out some of the preliminary paperwork generated by the wild flurry of activity.

She felt like going somewhere and sleeping for about ten years straight, but forced herself to head over to the litter where Annie was working.

Before she got there, Captain Stockman motioned her up front, and she changed directions, her ankle buckling slightly. Captain Stockman's expression was very stern, and a lecture of some kind was definitely forthcoming.

Rebecca stopped in front of the desk, reminding herself *not* to slump against it. "Ma'am?"

Captain Stockman frowned at her, looking like the most judgmental nun alive. "I anticipate a complaint from Captain Jessup, so would you care to give me your side of the story, first?"

Making complaints about the nurses — especially when they had at some point in the past refused to sleep with him — was a regular part of Jessup's day. "He's incompetent, and he's *slow*, ma'am," she said. "So what else is new?"

Captain Stockman did not, she noticed, disagree. "Nevertheless," she said, "he is one of our surgeons, and I want you to stop antagonizing him."

Yeah, sure. So what if most of his screwups really *did* mean the difference between life and death?

Rebecca looked down at the bloody bandages, torn uniforms, and other debris on the floor, keeping her jaw tight so that she wouldn't argue.

"We all know how competitive you are, Lieutenant Phillips," Captain Stockman said, "but — "

Rebecca looked up, startled. "*Competitive?*"

Somewhere behind them, she heard Annie and one of the corpsmen laugh. *At* her, no question.

"But," Captain Stockman went on, frowning, "I want you to remind yourself that we're all on the same team here."

Since when had her work been a problem? Rebecca could feel her temper a lot closer to the surface than she wanted it, but she just swallowed, and forced herself to nod cooperatively. "Yes, ma'am," she said.

Captain Stockman picked up a black ballpoint pen. "Which is not to say that your medical instincts were anything other than superb." She returned to her paperwork. "Now, please go assist Lieutenant Carella."

Captain Stockman's pats on the back were always a lot more like hard slaps. Rebecca limped over to the litter, taking some forceps out of her left shirt pocket.

"Dig in," Annie said.

Rebecca nodded, gave the boy a smile, and plucked a little shard of metal from his arm. One down, countless more to go.

"I am *not* competitive," she said quietly.

"Well, tell you what," Annie said. "I'll take this leg, you take the other, and let's see who finishes first."

Funny. "Go get yourself a nice drink of Phisohex,

Annie," Rebecca said, and dropped a frag into the small metal pan resting on the boy's stomach.

"Well, that *would* hit the spot," Annie agreed cheerfully.

Rebecca laughed. Annie was goofy enough so that they might not have gotten along back in the World, but here, they were undeniably chums. She picked out another frag, let it clink into the pan, then glanced up at the boy's face. Blondish hair, a large, slightly hooked nose above the bushy mustache, sunburned cheeks. Eighteen, maybe nineteen, and watching what they were doing with extreme, and detached, interest.

"What's your name?" she asked.

"Slasher," he said.

She did not, even remotely, want to know why. Any more than she wanted to know why Michael was called Meat. Although he insisted that it was because what was there was *cherce*.

"Pain okay?" she asked.

He nodded, tilting the little pan up to study the contents with apparent pride.

She dug, gently, after a piece she could just barely see under the skin. "What happened?"

"We done got chewed up, and spit out," he said.

That about summed up the current status of the war.

"*I* can do this standing on one foot," Annie remarked.

Actually, Rebecca was *already* standing on one foot, since her ankle hurt so much. "*I* can do it with my eyes closed," she said.

Slasher looked uneasy.

"I can do it in my *sleep*," Annie said.

More than one person *had* fallen asleep during the last couple of weeks — in the middle of operations, the middle of mopping, the middle of sentences.

Anyway. Not that she was competitive, but — "I can rub my stomach, pat my head, *and* do this — all at the same time," Rebecca said.

"While also standing on a tightrope?" Annie asked, pulling out a piece of metal big enough to make Slasher's eyes widen.

Well — no. "Probably not," Rebecca said.

Annie shrugged, as though the entire matter were settled, black curls flopping across her forehead. "Okay, then. You're not such a hotshot, after all."

"That is," Rebecca probed deeper with her forceps, checking Slasher's expression to make sure that she wasn't hurting him, "it would be too boring for me on the tightrope, *unless* I was wearing four-inch heels."

Annie did not look impressed. "Only four inches? And you call yourself a *professional*?"

"Well, they have to be that low," Rebecca said, easing out a long, twisted shard of metal, "because I'm balancing on top of two champagne flutes, on *top* of the tightrope, and — I don't want to break them."

Slasher shook his head. "I got a sister like you two."

Rebecca and Annie looked at each other.

"Well," Rebecca said, "you may *think* she's as skillful as we are, but — "

A call came in from another medevac, and she

and Annie looked at each other again, as Captain Stockman took it.

"Okay," she said, when she'd signed off. "We've got five more critical, all multiple trauma, and four ambulatory touching down within the next five minutes. Let's get moving!"

Rebecca was *very* sure that she wasn't the only one in the room who felt like bursting into tears.

Chapter Three

They worked straight through that load — and two more, everyone so exhausted and tense that they were all snapping at each other and losing patience over the most minor mistakes. No one had eaten in hours, and her friend Sammy and a couple of the other guys who worked in the hospital mess hall showed up with boxes of sandwiches, and cups of lukewarm, but very strong, coffee. There wasn't really time to stop and eat, but the coffee went fast. Rebecca had her hands full and couldn't get over there, but when one of the lab techs paused with his cup, she nodded her thanks and gulped half of it.

Someone put a soggy, very yellow, chicken salad half into her left hand while she scrubbed some kid down with her other hand, and when she bit into the sandwich, the mixture was so repellent that she had to gulp several times to keep it down, her hand clutching convulsively, pressing what was left into a doughy lump.

Which she ate anyway.

It went on, and on, and when the next round of coffee showed up, she took three aspirin and a Darvon because — well, the alternative was fainting. Things were quieting down a little, so she limped over to check the three expectants — as in, "expected to die" — who were still on the floor. No matter how busy the ER got, they always tried not to let the hopeless cases die alone.

Captain Stockman was already with one of them, a semi-comatose kid who was essentially gone from the waist down, and had also had his right arm blown off at the shoulder. She was holding his remaining hand, and saying something unintelligible and soothing.

The kid on the next litter — no, it was a man, actually; an older NCO — was already dead, so Rebecca bent over the third, a soldier who was moving restlessly, his head obscured by bloody bandages. She started to pick up his hand, saw that he was Vietnamese, and instantly dropped it. Then, she looked around to see if anyone else had noticed, and made herself pick it back up, his fingers limp and unresponsive. They had had a lot more civilian casualties than usual come through lately, as well as ARVNs, who were their South Vietnamese allies — and Viet Cong. Plenty of Viet Cong. She could handle the children, and women, and old people — but she wasn't doing too well with young Vietnamese men these days.

Particularly since she couldn't bring herself to *look* at them.

And holding his hand, whoever he was, whatever side he was on, was something that she just couldn't — the truth was, the kind of nurse she had become was *no* kind of nurse.

At least his eyes were hidden under the field dressings. It was bad enough when they looked up at her with hatred, or resignation — and fear was awful, but she really couldn't handle it when the eyes were full of *trust*. Expecting her to be able to help. To make everything okay.

Which was, of course, exactly the way the boy in the jungle had looked at her, after she shot him. It had been an accident — she hadn't meant to run into him, hadn't meant to have Spike's gun along for protection, *hadn't* meant to pull the trigger — but that didn't make him any less dead, did it.

Didn't make her any less of a killer.

Somehow, the fact that he'd fired first didn't help.

She hung onto the soldier's hand, her arm rigid. Penance. Her stomach — the chicken salad — was hurting, and she swallowed a few times, her hand clenching around his reflexively. His fingers felt chilly, and she could see from the depression in his bandage that most of his skull was gone. And probably a good two-thirds of his brain. His heart and lungs just hadn't gotten the message yet.

There wasn't much else going on, and she knew that sitting with this stranger was the right thing to do, but was it *really* the right thing if she hated every second of doing it? Not that *he* would know the difference, but she knew — and knew that it was utterly reprehensible to be compassionate purely out of a sense of duty and guilt. Besides, it wasn't compassion. It wasn't even *dis*passion. It was — sickening. She was sitting next to a person whose life was fading away, and the only thing she felt was an overpowering urge to run screaming out of the room.

And, on closer examination, not fading away — gone. Jesus, the man had died, and she hadn't even *noticed*. While she was sitting feeling sorry for, and disgusted by, herself, the damn war had chalked up yet another on its endless scoreboard. No, two more, because Captain Stockman was walking around supervising again.

She dropped the limp hand, and slouched forward against her raised knees for a few seconds, resting her head on her arms.

A hand touched her back. "You okay, Becky?" Lieutenant Averill.

Couldn't be better. Rebecca lifted her head. "Yeah." She stood up, even her good leg feeling weak and unsteady.

Lieutenant Averill was looking at her with the extra-solicitous concern they all showed her now, and Rebecca shrugged self-consciously, and went over to the nearest empty gurney so she could start taking the bodies over to Graves Registration. Since she'd returned to full-time duty, people always seemed to be watching her and, as often as not, exchanging glances behind her back.

She was trying, stupidly, to lift the dead — and hefty — NCO up onto the gurney by herself when Gomer and another corpsman came over to do it for her. She stood there, feeling herself swaying slightly, trying to decide what she should do instead.

Clean. She should clean. The place was trashed.

She found a push-broom and got to work, the ER almost silent, everyone too drained to speak a syllable more than necessary.

"All right," Captain Stockman said, scanning the duty roster once everything looked acceptable, if not exactly ready for the Inspector General. "Thorpe, Phillips, McCormack. You're all gone until oh six hundred hours."

None of them argued, Lieutenants Thorpe and McCormack heading towards the nurses' changing room. Rebecca was too tired even for that, so she made her way slowly to the ER doors, her ankle throbbing.

"I can stay longer, ma'am," she said to Captain Stockman, since offering was — the right thing to do. "If you want someone else to go first, or — "

Captain Stockman just looked at her.

"Really," Rebecca said. "I can — "

"Don't waste my time, Lieutenant," Captain Stockman said, and sent her away with an abrupt wave of her hand.

Right. Rebecca glanced at her watch — just past midnight — and limped outside into the still-pouring monsoon rain. She fell on the muddy hill below the nurses' quarters, and was exhausted enough to crawl a few feet on her hands and knees instead of getting up. It was raining so hard that she almost couldn't hear the outgoing artillery, and there didn't seem to be much air traffic, either. A couple of gunships, maybe. Some automatic rifle fire way off by the perimeter somewhere, electric generators humming, the ocean crashing around below the cliffs. Nothing out of the ordinary, except that it was darker than usual because they had been on alert so much since Tet that blackouts were turning into SOP.

The kid MP at the guardpost in front of the nurses' compound was slouched down — drunk? asleep? did she *give* a damn? — and she slogged past him, limping badly since there was no one around to see her.

Her hooch was almost completely dark — ten of them shared it, each with a small, wooden cubby for a room — and she did her best to be quiet, since anyone else who was there would be sleeping. Ordinarily, at midnight, there would still be music, and conversations, and drinking, but the war had put all of that on hold. Her room was the second one on the right, and she knocked aside the sheet she used for a door, not bothering to turn on the light. The bare bulb would just make her headache worse, anyway.

She took off her fatigue shirt and fell onto her bed, which was soaking wet — probably from rain seeping in through her screen window again. Every time she found someone to secure the flap for her, the typhoon winds just tore it loose again. She didn't worry much about it since there were lots of guys out in the field — like Michael — who weren't lucky enough to *have* pillows and mattresses, however sodden and mildewed.

She turned on the little mechanic's lamp she had hooked to the metal frame of the bed. The light was too glaring for her eyes, but low enough so that it wouldn't bother anyone else. There was an open can of Coke on the steamer trunk she used for a bedside table — two days old? three? — and she took a sip, tasting little gnats or mosquitoes or something. Delicious. She spit the mouthful back into the can, then folded her damp pillow in half so she could prop it up behind her head, water squeezing out as she did.

Her heart felt like it had moved up to pound between her ears — which just might have something to do with the extreme concentration of caffeine and amphetamines in her system — and she felt around on the trunk for more aspirin, swallowing two with a gulp of the insect-befouled Coke because she was too damn tired to go out to the refrigerator in the common room and get a fresh one.

It was quiet. Very quiet. She would have gone next door and woken up her friend Gail to talk, but Gail had gone back to the World ten days ago, leaving what now seemed like a *very* empty cubby behind.

Not that Rebecca would have *told* her anything — private — but they could have sat on the floor with too many cans of beer and talked about nothing in particular until they had both calmed down enough to try to sleep.

She still had friends here, but she didn't have *good* friends anymore. Dear friends.

Best friends.

She dragged herself off the bed and out to the common room, bringing back three Carling Black Labels. Enough to kill the caffeine, but not enough so that she'd wake up still drunk. The balance she always tried to strike.

Most nights, if they weren't on duty, she would have been with Wolf and Spike, sitting in the common room, or the Officers' Club, or out on top of a bunker somewhere. Spike would have told them outrageous lies about his many exploits with "the babes," and Wolf — who had been tall, and blond, and *devastating* — would have grinned a lot, stretched out those long legs, and plied her with compliments and jokes. Being with them was like being with her brother, Doug — who she *also* missed like hell — and she would have felt safe, and amused, and as though everything was going to work out all right in the end.

Instead, two guys full of life and energy and fun had been shot out of the sky by some goddamn truce-breaking bastards.

She gulped down her first beer, wondering if, in fact, three *were* going to be enough. Obliteration seemed to be indicated. Crying might be an even better idea, but — it had been a long time since she had been able to do that.

Years, actually.

She drained her first can in a few long swallows, then started in on her second. There was so much liquor in Vietnam, and it was so unbelievably cheap, that most of the people she knew seemed to be turning into borderline — or even beyond — alcoholics. Certainly, she had never thought that *she* would gulp the stuff down like there was no tomorrow. Then again, around here, tomorrow was a pretty uncertain commodity.

Which made her think of Michael, and about why she *shouldn't* be thinking about Michael. Since he was a grunt, and grunts had this tendency to — die. Especially grunts who walked point for their squads. Were first in line for — whatever.

Were most likely *not* to survive.

She finished off her second beer, and moved on to her third, hoping that the alcohol would work to anesthetize her mind, along with her damned ankle. When the can was empty, she let it drop onto the sand-and-mud-tracked plywood floor, watching it roll over to the wall.

Where it would probably stay for weeks.

After braving the rain for a swift, and imperative, trip to the latrine, she took off her wet clothes and pulled on her Radcliffe sweatshirt and a pair of cut-offs to sleep in. If she was ever going to get hit head-on by a rocket or mortar shell, she hated the idea of dying in an old flannel nightgown.

Her ankle was throbbing, and she loosened the wet laces on her right boot — no, actually some poor amputated guy's boot — and eased it off, her whole foot grotesquely, horribly swollen. Jesus. No wonder she'd spent most of that interminable shift grinding her molars into dust.

Slowly, she pulled on a dry pair of socks, having trouble even coming up with enough energy to wince. She was exhausted, but that didn't alter the fact that at this very moment — because of the time difference, back in the World, it was still yesterday — her mother was in all likelihood pacing miserably around Marblehead, counting the days even more than *she* was. And if Tet was getting as much doomsday coverage in American newspapers as they were hearing, then that wasn't helping matters any.

So, like the man said, attention should be paid. Regardless of personal fatigue.

She picked up the least-recent unread letter from her mother — dated January 29th, so right *before*

Tet — and opened it, her hands feeling clumsy. The usual heavy, engraved stationery, and her mother's elegant handwriting.

Dear Rebecca,

Please keep writing as much as you can. I'm glad to hear that you're feeling better, but I hope that you really are, and aren't just saying so to keep me from worrying.

Her mother's version of very-restrained hysteria.

Please try to get another phone call through, if you can. I wish I had an idea of what it's really like over there for you. Obviously, I was already *haunting the mailbox, but now I'm having trouble focusing on anything else.*

Haunting it, waiting for letters from her brother Doug, that never came. Christ. If he had settled in Quebec or someplace, and he was worried about the government tracing postmarks, would it kill him to go to Calgary or Vancouver or Toronto, and send them a card to let them know he was still alive?

Assuming that he was.

She was *way* too tired for this.

Please also keep trying to get a copy of your records sent back here — your father would feel a lot better.

When he'd heard that she had been hurt, there was a lot of huffing and puffing about how he wanted the X rays and all, so he and other "top people" could evaluate them, and properly assess her treatment. It *might* have been some kind of dormant parental concern for her welfare — but then again, her situation might also have sounded like a potentially interesting case study.

Not that she was mad at, or distrusted, him.

Not that she wasn't, in many ways, *exactly* like him.

He's spending so much time at the hospital lately, that I'm worried about him, *too.*

When the going got tough, her father — went to work. Let her mother handle the situation, whatever it was.

Maybe another beer was indicated. That is, if she hadn't been too tired to get up. She lowered the letter for a minute, rubbing her hand across her eyes. Seemed a fair bet that a lot of people over here who had enlisted might have done it to get away from shattered, angry families. There was more to it, but Vietnam hadn't exactly been in her original life plan.

Anyway.

I boxed up a bunch of new books for you the other day, so you should be getting them soon. A very good *Muriel Spark, and some other things. (Yes, more* New Yorkers *and* Lifes, *too.)*

Good. If they were ever given free time again, she would be more than pleased to spend *all* of it by herself, reading.

If you get a chance, you might want to drop Mary McDonough a quick letter. I know she's thinking about you.

Billy's mother. Doug's and her closest friend at home — who had died up near Phu Bai almost two years ago. Who was one of the main reasons she had been dumb enough to join the Army, and get sent to Vietnam.

Who had been yet another guy full of life, and energy, and fun.

Christ. No wonder she was losing her mind.

Please *let me know if there's anything else I can do for you — I feel so helpless.*

As far as hurting her mother went, she and Doug were *definitely* their father's children.

I know you don't want me to worry so much, but it's hard. Please be careful, and let us know what's happening. And remember how much your father and I love you.

Love, Mom

Damn. If she was already that worried, what were her *post*-Tet letters going to be like? There were a couple in her bedside stack, waiting to be read — but she just plain didn't have the emotional energy right now.

Time to dash off one of her cheery little notes. Neither of her Army-issue pens would work — naturally — so she used a rather dull pencil, writing on a piece of notebook paper. Had she always been so stupidly slapdash? Hard to remember any-more.

Dear Mom and Dad,
Just wanted to let you know that everything's fine. Things have been busy, but it's starting to slow down.

The trick to lying well was to tell as much truth as possible while doing so.

I don't know what the news reports are like back in the States, but from what I hear, they're pretty exaggerated. So, please don't worry. None of the fighting is anywhere near us.

With the exception of the mortars and rockets, and occasional breaks in the perimeter.

I'm feeling fine, and even got my cast off!

The "!" was pushing it.

Well, it's pretty late, so I'm going to try and get some sleep now. I hope you're both okay, and say hi to Jack and the cats.

Jack, being their dog.

Love, Rebecca

Another day, another prevarication. She put the letter in an envelope, addressed it, and scrawled "Free" where the stamp would ordinarily go. Army benevolence to troops in the combat zone.

She turned off the mechanic's light, and climbed under the wet, mildewed sheets. Her ankle was throbbing, her bad arm felt numb and trembly, her heart seemed to be beating too hard, her stomach was churning around, her head was killing her, and nightmares were *unquestionably* in her future.

On that happy note.

She closed her eyes.

Chapter Four

The next day was more of the same. Ham and cheese, instead of chicken salad. A bunch of weeping, bleeding children from an orphanage that took a direct mortar hit. A visit by some I-Corps bigwig who was handing out medals and orders in an equally pointless manner. Talked a lot about "stoking morale." Forging on. Prevailing.

His audience was not very appreciative. That is, the ones who were *awake*.

She got off around midnight again and once she was back in her hootch, sitting on her bed in the dark, she ate some limp potato chips, washing them down with a can of Wink. The day's casualty load had been down a little, but there were more burn cases than usual, and the stench still seemed to be with her.

Her room was stuffy and squalid, and making her extremely claustrophobic. After trying, and failing, to get to sleep, she gave up, putting on her flight jacket, stuffing a flashlight and a Schlitz into her pockets, and heading outside. As an after-thought, she went back and got her alarm clock, so that even if she fell asleep somewhere, she wouldn't miss her next shift.

The mess hall was being kept open at all hours lately, and she considered going over there for some coffee, but felt too tired and depressed to run into anyone she knew. Besides, she had eaten so many meals there with Wolf and Spike that she couldn't stand the place anymore.

She wandered along the bunker line at the top of the cliffs, able to see the ocean in the weird white light from occasional flares. She *liked* the ocean. The Atlantic, anyway.

It was after curfew, so she didn't pass much of anyone as she went further up the hill, and most of the soldiers and sentries she *did* see assumed she was male under her boonie hat and gave her nothing more than vague nods of recognition. Oh, look, another American. She got a couple of tired "Evening, ma'am"s and, from one kid, a "Hi" that was so lonely and eager that she paused to talk to him for a few minutes before moving on.

There were three guys standing behind a bunker getting high, and when one of them said, "Hey, baby," they all laughed. She couldn't help feeling a little jolt of fear — it wasn't really easy being one of the few American woman on a base that catered to over twenty thousand men — but she just said, "Hey, guys, how's it going?" in as pleasant and disinterested a way as possible. They thought it would be a *really* good idea for her to stick around and get friendly, but she just smiled and kept going, her hand instinctively tightening around the metal flashlight in her pocket. Fortunately, they didn't come after her. Not far, anyway.

She wandered along the road through Officer's Country, stopping to look at the HOLY WATER, FIRE WATER sign. Which meant that she could follow the arrow pointing left and go to the chapel, or the arrow pointing right and go to the Hilltop Officers' Club, where, if it was open after-hours, she would instantly be besieged by oversexed pilots. On the whole, she was better off going to the chapel.

There was a palm tree out front, and she was going to sit under it, but that felt too exposed, so she walked around to the other side of the stilt-raised building instead. She could always go *inside*, but she wouldn't want to disturb anyone who might actually still have some faith left. Hope. Trust. All that good stuff.

Despite the artillery, occasional radio transmissions and air traffic, it was quiet enough so that she could actually hear crickets. Of all things. Maybe nobody had told them there was a war on. She'd stitched up a kid once who carried around a cricket in a C-rat can — either for luck, or just for a pet — which he had shown to her with great pride. She had assured him that she was suitably impressed.

A lot of people had pets here — dogs, and monkeys, and snakes, and so forth — but she loved animals too much to have one herself. Had seen too many being casually mistreated and killed. It was the *casual* aspect of the callousness that bothered her the most. The war made it too easy to stop giving a damn.

The war made it easy even when you *did* give a damn.

She was just about to sit down and open her beer when she heard a sound and froze, getting ready to use the can as a weapon instead. She saw the small orange ember of a cigarette, and heard someone exhale.

"Hello, Lieutenant," the person said.

Major Doyle. Rebecca let out her own breath. "Hi." Her eyes were getting accustomed to the dark, and she could see her sitting on a muddy board, looking out at the living quarters below the chapel. Well — okay. Why not. The Major was so intensely private that, when she was off-duty, they almost never saw her. She wasn't exactly one to hang around the hospital Officers' Club and chat.

"I've always *heard* the phrase, 'walking time bomb,'" Major Doyle said, "but this is the first time I've ever seen it in action."

Rebecca looked at her uneasily, not sure what that meant.

"You *are* aware that you're ticking, Lieutenant," Major Doyle said.

Oh. Right. Rebecca pulled the alarm clock out of her pocket. "I didn't want to take a chance on missing my shift." Especially with 0600 looming ever closer.

Major Doyle smiled slightly, and pulled in on her cigarette. "Such pragmatism."

"I, uh, I'm sorry to disturb you, ma'am," Rebecca said. "I was just — walking around."

Major Doyle nodded. "Looking for privacy."

Exactly.

"Not too easy to find around here," Major Doyle said.

"No," Rebecca agreed, and took a step backwards. "And I certainly didn't mean to, uh — "

"So, have a seat," Major Doyle said, gesturing towards the muddy ground.

Rebecca hesitated. "Well, I — "

"Take a seat," Major Doyle said, and there was enough of a note of authority for Rebecca to sit down. Immediately.

The Major was a subject of regular fascination and constant speculation among the staff, many of whom found her significantly less than human. And yeah, she was, okay, about as reserved and formal as a person could be, and still be breathing, but when Rebecca had been on the ward — as a patient, for the first time in her life — she would open her eyes at strange hours of the day and night, and invariably, the Major would be in a metal chair by the bed, keeping an eye on her. Other people took turns, but more often than not, Major Doyle seemed to be the one sitting there, her face tight with worry, paperwork ignored on her lap.

Not something Rebecca was going to forget anytime soon.

It meant a lot then, and it meant a lot now.

There were a few bursts of M-16 fire off somewhere near one of the rifle companies, and they both glanced in that direction, without much alarm or interest. Kids on the perimeter shooting at shadows.

"So nice and restful here," Major Doyle said, and released a large cloud of smoke.

Oh, yeah. Always. She couldn't think of anything to say, so she opened her now-warm beer, drinking some. It tasted lousy.

They sat on the rickety board, in silence, Rebecca looking up as a gunship cruised overhead and away. She was about to make a mumbled excuse and leave, when Major Doyle sighed.

"Sometimes I get very tired, Lieutenant," she said.

Rebecca nodded.

"And the burden of command," Major Doyle said, very quietly, "is that you have nobody to talk to."

And, sometimes, the burden of personality. "You know, there's a level, ma'am," Rebecca said, just as quietly, "at which you and I are very good friends."

Major Doyle nodded. "I'm aware of that, actually."

She might not be a C.O.'s dream, but for some reason, she and the Major had really clicked — right from the start. In fact, some might use the word "favoritism." But people might also use the phrase "get away with murder," and since that was, of course, *literally* the truth, it wasn't so damn funny. She stopped smiling, and concentrated on her beer.

"How's the ankle?" Major Doyle asked.

Indicating that their thoughts were heading in the same general, and unpleasant, direction. "Fine," Rebecca said. "No problem at all."

Major Doyle looked at her for a minute. "Other than the pain, weakness, and constant limping."

Bull's-eye. Rebecca shrugged, feeling a familiar, and undesirable, twisting in her stomach. These

days, she was an ulcer waiting to happen. "I, uh — "
She let out her breath. "I never really got a chance
to thank you properly."

Major Doyle shook her head, looking uncomfortable.

"I don't just mean for — well, you know," Rebecca said. For covering up. "What you did officially. I mean, for taking care of me."

Major Doyle looked, if possible, more uncomfortable.

"For the record," Rebecca said.

Major Doyle looked very acutely uncomfortable,
and lit another cigarette from the stub she'd just
finished. Just about everyone at the hospital — in
fact, almost everyone in *Vietnam* — smoked constantly, but the Major was an ambulatory chimney.
Rebecca, for one, never had more than a puff of
someone else's, just to be polite. People seemed to
find the fact that she didn't smoke terribly amusing — and somewhat peculiar.

She couldn't think of anything else to say, so
she held out her beer, but Major Doyle shook her
head, taking an old silver flask from her shirt
pocket. A secret vice, apparently. Once — *once* —
back in November, she had shown up at the O
Club, gotten smashed, and been both convivial and
hilarious. Once, and *only* once. Considerable gossip
had resulted from this.

"So, how are you?" Major Doyle asked.

Friendly conversation, or a probing question?
Rebecca shrugged, feeling her free hand clench
a little. "Same as anyone," she said. "We're all
wasted."

"Okay." Major Doyle took a quick, and practiced, slug from the flask. "How are you, *specifically*?"

Rebecca shrugged, watching a parachute flare make its slow bright journey to the ground out over the waterway.

"I feel — " Major Doyle spoke in even more measured tones than usual — "a bit, uh, out of my depth on this one, Rebecca. I'm not sure how to — I assume you're talking to your friends?"

Since she *was* the Chief Nurse, it would be politic to say yes, and leave it at that. But — despite the fact that she did it a lot, she hated lying. So, she just shrugged.

Major Doyle looked at her sharply. "Aren't you?"

Rebecca tried to think of a remotely honest answer. Without success.

"Rebecca, I — " Major Doyle stopped, uncomfortably. "That is — " She stopped again. "The level at which we're complete strangers interferes with the level at which we're friends," she said finally.

In a word — yeah. Rebecca nodded, and drank some of her Schlitz. It tasted sort of rusty.

"Which is not to say that anything you told me would *ever* go any further," Major Doyle said.

Everyone was being so goddamn nice to her. If they only knew. Then again, it was a good thing that they *didn't*.

"Nothing to tell," she said aloud, and was glad that it was dark, and she didn't have to meet those penetrating blue eyes.

The crickets kept chirping away, out in the underbrush, above the hootches, the sound somehow eerie. Threatening. And she was *kicking* herself for not having just stayed in her room and gone to sleep.

"I know they're all treating you differently," Major Doyle said.

Yeah — with kid gloves. Present company included. "They should just let me do my job," Rebecca said stiffly.

Major Doyle nodded. "Probably. But — well, hell, Rebecca." She finished off whatever was in the flask. "Nobody likes to see the cheerleader go down."

Rebecca frowned at her. "Is that really what you think?"

Major Doyle frowned back. "You haven't noticed the precipitous drop in morale?"

Could have a lot to do with the fact that Wolf and Spike had been *extremely* popular. Tet hadn't helped any, either.

"Everyone misses them," she said, with her teeth set. "Of course they're upset."

"No question," Major Doyle agreed. "But they're *also* adjusting to the fact that one day, you're singing and telling jokes and keeping everyone's spirits up, and then, suddenly, you're this silent little wraith."

They were much too close to being strangers to have this conversation. Rebecca moved her jaw. "So, what are you saying? I should just cheer up already?"

Major Doyle shook her head. "I'm saying that people want to help, but they aren't sure how."

Leaving her alone would be a nice start.

Major Doyle sighed. "I guess I'm just sorry. It's

my fault that you ended up in the situation in the first place, and — I'm sorry.''

Which was rather out of left field. Rebecca frowned at her again. ''*Your* fault? You weren't even around.''

''I shouldn't have to have been,'' Major Doyle said. ''If I'd been more strict with you, right from the beginning, you would have been appropriately *afraid* of me, and the repercussions, and you never would have gotten on that damned chopper in the first place.''

That was just stupid. ''I got *on* it all by myself,'' Rebecca said. ''It's my responsibility — *I* made the decision.''

''My point, exactly,'' Major Doyle said, sounding quiet, and sad. ''Second lieutenants don't *make* decisions — they follow orders.''

Lifer logic. Lifer *horseshit*, more accurately. Rebecca shook her head, but didn't say anything.

Major Doyle looked over at her, and even in the darkness, Rebecca could feel those eyes. ''You never would have pulled a stunt like that on Ruth Stockman,'' she said.

Well — no. But, since it was Christmas, Captain Stockman had been off in Saigon, presumably with her much-rumored, never-seen lieutenant-colonel boyfriend. Rebecca shrugged, feeling a mix of guilt and annoyance.

''So, I feel *terrible*,'' Major Doyle said, tightly, ''and it's also hard not to be mad at you.''

They were both tired, and it was very late. Time to call it a night. ''Look,'' Rebecca said. ''This isn't going to be a productive conversation, ma'am. So — let's not have it.''

"Right. Fine." Abruptly, Major Doyle got up, lighting another cigarette. "See you in the trenches, Lieutenant."

Laughing at the Chief Nurse was very poor strategy, but Rebecca did it, anyway. "That's a pretty low flash point you have there, ma'am," she said.

Major Doyle's stiff posture relaxed a little. "At least I come by it honestly," she said.

Right. Rebecca grinned. "I'm only *half* Irish. That's why I'm able to demonstrate such control."

Major Doyle laughed, too. "Come on," she said. "I happen to know that you have a very early shift."

True enough. Rebecca pulled herself up, careful *not* to wince — or limp. She gulped down the last of her beer, then dropped the can in a nearby sand-filled oil drum and put her hands in her pockets, keeping her weight on her good leg.

"Are, uh, things getting better out there?" she asked.

Major Doyle nodded. "Except for Hue and Khe Sanh."

Both of which were in Northern I-Corps, so the casualties were more apt to end up in Quang Tri, Phu Bai, or Danang.

It had started to rain, but only hard enough to be irritating, not enough to comment on the situation. Feeling guilty — indisputably, the emotion with which she was most at home — about having acted disagreeable, Rebecca decided to lighten the atmosphere.

"A-bee-dee-da-dum, ba-dee-ba-dum," she sang, just loudly enough to be heard.

"No scat," Major Doyle said instantly.

Right. Rebecca laughed, and stopped singing. Before her life had gone to hell in a handbasket, she *had* sort of had a tendency to walk around singing. Badly. But with *great* enthusiasm.

They kept walking.

"Was that going to be 'Night in Tunisia'?" Major Doyle asked.

Rebecca nodded.

"Oh." Major Doyle thought about that. "I rather *like* 'Night in Tunisia.' "

Rebecca shrugged. Too late now.

"And — it was aptly chosen," Major Doyle said.

Rebecca nodded.

"My tough luck," Major Doyle said.

Rebecca nodded, and they both grinned. Good. Now they were definitely back to being — stilted — if well-meaning — friends again.

They separated at the nurses' hootches — the one for high-ranking officers wasn't much nicer, but she had heard that the rooms were bigger.

Major Doyle put out one final cigarette, shredding the butt and using the heel of her mud-encrusted boot to bury the pieces. "See you in the morning, Rebecca," she said.

Rebecca nodded. "In the trenches."

Major Doyle nodded wryly, pointed a "*watch* it" finger at her, and climbed up the flimsy wooden stairs to her hootch.

Long night. Ba-bee-dee-da-dum, da-dee-da-da.

Slowly, she walked into her own hootch. It was very dark and she tripped, but quickly recovered herself, not wanting to wake anyone else up. In her room, she took the alarm clock out of her jacket pocket, then let the wet jacket and boonie hat fall to the floor, not remembering the flashlight in the other pocket until she heard it bang against the plywood.

So much for being quiet.

She sat down on the edge of her bed, feeling cold, and wet, and tired. Not that Michael, and every other grunt in this war, wasn't feeling even worse right now.

Speaking of whom. She *really* owed him a letter. Although it would probably be nice if she read the end of *his*, first. And also check how he signed it, so she could respond accordingly.

She flipped through the stack by the side of her bed, extricating the letter she had most recently started reading — when? Yesterday? Her mind was a near-total blank. Quickly, though, she skimmed the parts she could remember, before getting to the paragraph where she had left off.

My knee is still pretty bad.

He *had* been limping when she saw him — apparently, he had hurt it jumping out of a helicopter back in November, but never really told anyone.

Mostly, I'm used to it, but today it really hurts. But I know they need every guy they can get out here, so . . . guess I'll just take a couple of aspirin — and wish like hell I could call you in the morning.

> Love(!),
> Mike

Love(!). Hmmm. Well, she would cross that bridge when she came to it. She pulled over a notebook, and took a damp pen from her hip pocket, frowning down at the empty page.

Dear Michael.

She was being felled by a sudden attack of writer's block.

I'm sorry I haven't written sooner — things have been a little crazy here.

And then some.

Now though, it seems to be calming down, and I really hope things are quiet where you are.

She hoped that more than a little. And doubted it even more than that.

Please be careful. And if your knee gets worse, get Doc —

Who was the medic she had met in the jungle — a young, testy, and competent kid corpsman.

— to have you sent, at least, to see your battalion surgeon. I really think you have a cartilage problem there.

End of lecture.

Anyway. Say hi to Snoopy and Sgt. Hanson —

Sergeant Hanson, being his very serious, very attractive squad leader. Sidney Poitier only *wished* he looked like Michael's sergeant.

— and the rest of the guys, and please take care of yourselves.

Time to cross the bridge.

The way I hear it, Vietnam rhymes with ''beet-jam.''
— Rebecca

When in doubt, avoid the issue entirely. Something she did very well.

It was almost three in the morning and, if she was lucky, she would be able to get about two hours sleep. Too tired to take the time to address an envelope, she just let the notebook fall onto the floor, and turned off her light.

She lay there for a few minutes, trying to fall asleep, then turned the light back on.

P.S., she wrote at the bottom of the page. *I miss you. (!)*

Okay. *Now*, maybe, she could sleep.

Chapter Five

By the end of the month, things had slowed down enough so that they were only working sixteen or seventeen hours a day. At one point, Rebecca had actually been scheduled for a day off, but so many people were sick — with exhaustion and otherwise — that the rest of them had to cover extra shifts, and her day off turned into two hours sitting on the rainy beach, talking to a series of persistent and flirtatious guys. Among the nurses she knew, only the very boldest had the nerve to walk down the cliff road wearing their bathing suits. She, for one, would never do so unless there was a group of them going together, and she had some protective coloring — and probably a fatigue shirt and cut-offs for good measure.

Michael was still writing, and writing, and she had to admit that his letters were becoming the highlight of her day. *Her* letter-writing skills were barely a step above thank-you notes, but — for a seemingly inarticulate guy — Michael's tended towards lively ruminations. Things he was doing, things he had done, things he *wanted* to do — almost as if she were a treasured diary. The brief, vague jottings he received in turn must be disappointing, but they seemed to be the best she could manage.

She read his letters on breaks, during meals — and then again before she went to sleep. The fact that she was pretty much keeping to herself didn't draw much attention, since a hell of a lot of other people were, too. Tet had just been — too goddamn much, for too goddamn long, and regenerative hibernation seemed to be the general mode of behavior.

The only *good* thing about Tet was that it had pretty much taken over her sleeping and waking thoughts. But even when she closed her eyes, she would get little specific flashes, beyond the numbing stream of casualties. Like Rosario's expression — and immediate regurgitative reaction — when he saw his first maggot-infested wound. They had decided not to tell him — yet — that often, they left the maggots *in*, to "clean up" any decaying flesh.

Not a piece of information one shared in letters home.

If she let her mind wander at all, the flashes would take over. A black-haired kid, his face startlingly handsome, the rest of him burned beyond species-recognition after his tank had exploded, screaming for her not to let him die during the endless minutes it took him to do so. Since there was nothing else left that she could really touch, she'd held his face in both hands, doing her best to ease him on his shrieking, terrified way. Movie images to the contrary, not too many of these guys went gently, or quietly.

A little pale kid with a thatch of blond hair, his mind lost somewhere deep in a firefight, going completely berserk in the front of the ER and letting loose with a full clip from his M-16 before anyone could wrestle him to the floor. The spray of bullets killed one already-wounded boy, and hit two others, a corpsman, and the census officer. Another kid, both legs gone above the knee, dove off his litter when he heard the gunfire, adding a broken arm and a concussion to his troubles. The kid who had caused all of the damage just lay on the floor, yelling, "Kill! Kill! Kill!", while four or five people tried to hold him down, and one of the doctors pumped him full of Thorazine.

There really wasn't anyone she could talk to — everyone was carrying their own little platter of hell around, and didn't need to add *hers* to their loads — but she was beginning to wish that she could write some of it to Michael. Keeping everything bottled up was exhausting.

It was — as far as she knew — early March, and she sat in the officers' mess with her ankle propped up on an empty chair, sipping coffee and reading his latest. She had to think to remember if she was going *on* shift, or coming off, but it was dark out and she was on days this week, so she must be coming off.

She checked her watch. Past ten. People were coming in and out to get coffee, or take away sandwiches, but for the most part, the place was quiet.

Milt, the bulky and blustering mess sergeant, came out with a tray.

"Want to see you *eat* this, missy," he grumbled, setting it down in front of her.

Food. She stared at the tray stupidly, trying to remember if she had requested it. Surely not — she wouldn't have bothered any of the mess staff this late at night. "Um, thank you," she said, "but I didn't mean for you to — "

"You finish it," he said, "*hear* me?"

The way his voice carried, they could probably hear him down in the Delta.

"I will," she said. "Thank you."

He sat down to watch her, the folding chair sagging under his weight.

Great. Like she wasn't already self-conscious enough. On top of which, her hands always shook now, and she didn't want him to see that.

"Your tour about up?" she asked.

He nodded, frowning at her untouched plate.

She picked up her fork — and her damned hand shook. "Good-bye, Green Machine?"

He nodded. "Near to got my twenty."

She nodded, too, and tasted her dinner. Tomatoey, sweetish, very thick spaghetti. Salad that appeared to have had as long a day as she had had. "It's good," she said, and took another mouthful.

"You want seconds, you tell me," he said, lumbering to his feet and away.

Once he was gone, she put her fork down and picked Michael's letter back up, finding her place.

Got another picture of Otis today.

Otis was his *much*-beloved dog, and his brother Dennis sent him monthly, elaborately-posed, pictures.

Has a paper heart around his neck that says, ''Will you be mine?'' and a straw hat with roses on it. Dennis is pretty damn funny. He looks good (Otis, I mean).

During their last conversation, lying on her rain-soaked bed, he had mentioned — grimly — that his old girlfriend, Elizabeth, had *not* liked Otis. Something about the way he said it though, made her wonder if Elizabeth was really out of the picture.

Not that she was jealous — they barely knew each other.

Right?

The thing is, like I told you, this is the only time I've ever left him, and I really want him to be okay. He'd even come in the car when we went to church, you know? Carrie —

Who was his little sister.

— would put dumb ribbons on him, but even if they were purple or something, he'd still look pretty okay.

Church. What religion was he? His last name was Jennings, so he *could* be Catholic, or — probably Protestant. Catholics were usually easy to peg. All that guilt, and sanctimony.

I miss him a lot. Lately, we're not seeing so many in the villages. I don't know if they got scared off by all the fighting, or if people are eating them.

Don't think I want to know.

She didn't want to know, either. A scraggly brown mongrel that lived up at the motor pool had had a litter of puppies — most of whom mysteriously disappeared after the hootch maids left one day.

Finnegan's really losing it, and I'm pretty worried.

Who she couldn't quite place, but was one of the guys in his squad. Snoopy, and the incredibly gorgeous sergeant, Hanson, were the only two she *really* remembered. And, of course, cranky, impatient Doc. Finnegan must be the one with the leprechaun face. There had also been a gawky kid carrying the squad radio — some kind of ethnic name; Polish, maybe? — and a tall, silent one with an M-60. Viper. That's right, the quiet kid had been named Viper. The only other guy who had been there — Thumper? — had already gone back to the World — the lucky recipient of a badly broken leg while they were playing football during their stand down. *Multi*million dollar wound, as the saying went.

It had been kind of funny, actually — they'd all come to the hospital with him, loud and filthy and sweaty, but she had a feeling it was more to check *her* out than to keep Thumper company. When they'd seen her in the jungle, she hadn't exactly looked her best. Anyway, they'd all come noisily into the surgical ward where she was working, Snoopy shouting, "Hey, she's *cute!*" While they gathered around, shaking hands with her and insisting on posing for Instamatic pictures and so forth, Michael just stood there, arms folded — his arms were pretty much *always* folded — a Cheshire cat grin on his face. The only thing he said, the entire time, leaning over so that his mouth grazed her ear warmly, was, "Guys just *love* a woman in uniform." When she'd answered, "Combat boots are a girl's best friend," he gave her such an intense and intimate look that, even several feet away, she felt the heat, and promptly blushed and tripped over her cast.

Anyway.

LT keeps saying he's put in transfer papers, but it's been a hell of a long time already. I swear I'm just going to have to shoot the guy, get him sent out of here. All the new guys think he's crazy, the way he's charging bunkers, and all. I don't know, maybe he is. Shit, maybe we all are.

Charging bunkers would seem to indicate that things were pretty bad out there. Damn.

Someone sat down across from her, and she looked up to see Major Doyle.

"Don't tell me," she said, holding a steaming cup of coffee, and a thick sheaf of official stationery. "That bad-tempered private?"

Michael always referred to *her* as "that foxy major." It was kind of a touchy subject, since officers and enlisted men were absolutely *not* allowed to fraternize. When people did, and got caught, things like transfers and Article 15s were the usual results. "Actually, he's a bad-tempered Spec. 4 now," Rebecca said. Due to a very recent, and unexpected, promotion.

"Of all things," Major Doyle said, enigmatically, and lit a cigarette.

"We're, um, we're just friends," Rebecca said. Maybe.

Major Doyle shrugged. "I didn't ask."

Rebecca looked at her uneasily. "Are you *going* to? I mean — "

"When you're all off-duty," Major Doyle said, "I don't consider it any of my business what you're doing, or with whom you're doing it. That is, as long as it doesn't come into the hospital."

Rebecca had to laugh. The 63rd Evac. was a *sea* of broken, and flowering, relationships.

Major Doyle lifted an eyebrow at her. "What?"

"Well — " she had to know already, right? — "I mean, it's Peyton Place around here," Rebecca said.

Major Doyle shrugged, apparently entirely unconcerned. "As long as it doesn't interfere with the work. Frankly, I'd be worried if there *weren't* romances flourishing."

Which opened the door partway, and Rebecca was tempted to jump through. Explore the subject that inspired the most virulent speculation, as far as the Major was concerned. Especially considering that at least half the doctors on staff followed her around with their tongues hanging out. Christ, *Michael* lusted after her. Said she made Rita Hayworth look homely.

Major Doyle indicated her almost untouched plate. "Are you going to eat that, Lieutenant?"

Rebecca shook her head, and Major Doyle helped herself, obviously ravenous, using the side of the bent fork to cut the spaghetti into manageable pieces.

"So, um — " go for it — "who are *you* seeing, ma'am?" Rebecca asked.

Major Doyle looked up from her tepid meal. "Are you that sure that I am?"

Rebecca shook her head. She wasn't sure about much of anything when it came to the Major.

Major Doyle nodded, and resumed eating. At the rate she was going, the plate would be empty in the next few seconds.

"So — you aren't?" Rebecca asked.

Major Doyle frowned at her, the fork halfway to her mouth. "I am extremely disinclined to share that information with you, Lieutenant."

But it was okay for *her* to ask about Michael. Rebecca shrugged, more than a little annoyed. "Fine, ma'am," she said. "Enjoy my dinner."

"Well, *someone* should," Major Doyle said, and attacked the limp salad.

Fine. Whatever. Rebecca picked up her letter to finish, turning away in her chair.

"I'm sorry," Major Doyle said, after a minute. "I get peevish when I'm hungry."

Rebecca glanced at the now-empty plate. "I bet you're even *more* fun with indigestion."

Major Doyle grinned, then motioned Milt — who was glowering up by the front counter — over. "Sergeant, I seem to have polished off the

Lieutenant's supper," she said. "Is there anything else left back there?"

Milt looked greatly displeased. "Made that up for her *special*, ma'am," he said.

Major Doyle nodded. "I see. Well, would you mind if I went into the kitchen and threw together some sandwiches?"

He sighed elaborately, and went up front to do it himself.

Major Doyle watched him go, then lit a cigarette. "What do they call me behind my back?"

It was always hard to avoid direct questions. "Um, who?" Rebecca asked uneasily.

"Anyone." Major Doyle shrugged. "Everyone."

Oh. "Um, Joan of Arc," Rebecca said.

Major Doyle considered that, and shrugged again.

"Her Majesty, Her Highness," Rebecca said. "Miss Perfect."

"Okay, okay." Major Doyle held up a hand to stop her. "I'm following the general trend." She paused. "Are there any others?"

Well — yeah. Plenty. "Um — " Rebecca avoided her eyes — "Betty Bitch."

Major Doyle frowned at her. "What?"

"You *asked*," Rebecca said defensively.

Major Doyle continued the frown, then her face relaxed. "No," she said. "I am not presently seeing anyone with anything resembling regularity."

Ever cryptic. "I didn't tell you just to be mean," Rebecca said.

"No," Major Doyle agreed. "I'm sure the thought didn't even flit across your mind."

Well, okay. It flitted, and it floated — and out it

flew. Although Rodgers and Hammerstein put it better. "You're a little hard for me to figure out, ma'am," Rebecca said. "I'm not sure when you're being the Chief Nurse, and when you're not."

Major Doyle nodded. "That's fair." She looked around, then knocked her ashes into the now-empty salad dish. "It's your misfortune that you remind me of someone."

Hmmm. Somehow, Rebecca just *knew* that edification was not forthcoming. "Long story," she said, "right?"

Major Doyle nodded, her expression quite blank.

Naturally. Rebecca glanced towards the kitchen, hoping to see Milt coming out with their food. Despite not being hungry.

"I had a brief, and ill-considered, fling with Captain McNulty," Major Doyle said.

Whoa. A totally unknown — and red hot — piece of news. Captain McNulty was one of their surgeons — and one of the ones she actually liked. Not as experienced as some of the others — he had barely completed his residency when the Army grabbed him — but a good, quick worker, and rarely arrogant. "What do you mean, ill-considered?" Rebecca said. "He's *nice.*"

Major Doyle helped herself to a fresh cigarette, snapping her Zippo open to light it. "I am disinclined to dissect the situation, Rebecca."

She wasn't Betty Bitch — she was Clara Clipped. Rebecca shook her head, more amused than she was probably supposed to be. All those cocky married jerks chasing her around, and she went for the bashful, single one with glasses. How about that.

"I assume this information will go no further," Major Doyle said, with a tiny flicker of what might be alarm in her eyes.

"I don't know," Rebecca said. "Are you going to be nice to me?"

Major Doyle exhaled some smoke. "Sporadically."

"Well, then." Rebecca leaned back in her chair, almost knocking it over by accident. "Good luck to you and the Boston Red Sox." A very common remark where she came from, used to refer to the most unlikely of events.

Major Doyle looked slightly bemused, and slightly uneasy.

Milt carried out a well-laden tray, putting it down with a gruff "Eat *every* bit, missy" to her, and then returning to the kitchen.

Two peanut-butter-and-jelly sandwiches, each with a pile of mostly broken potato chips, and a couple of mushy pickles. There were also two glasses of milk, and some nondescript cookies. Brown cookies, of some sort. Ginger, or over-cooked sugar, or — oatmeal, maybe.

"À ta santé," Major Doyle said, and dug in.

Was there anything more irritating than model-slim women who ate like linebackers? Not that Rebecca was exactly obese herself — but she still found it aggravating. She picked up a sandwich half, the grape jelly already leaking through the bread.

"Ruth tells me you and Jessup went at it again today," Major Doyle remarked.

Ruth. She absolutely never thought of Captain Stockman as — Ruth. Then again, she *never* thought of Major Doyle as — Maggie. "Is this mealtime small talk?" Rebecca asked.

Major Doyle nodded, dispatching with the pickle and getting to work on her potato chips.

It had actually been an uglier scene than usual, during which Jessup had used her *least* favorite obscenity referring to women. "We had — " the fact that the word "gook" had started popping, unbidden, into her mind on a regular basis didn't mean that she had to use it — "an indigenous child in with severe blast trauma — " read: an arm and a leg gone — "and he couldn't even spare *five* seconds for her," Rebecca said. "She's screaming, and he just goes over to pick splinters out of some supply clerk's hand."

Major Doyle sighed. "Well, at least his tour is up soon."

The sooner, the better.

"So, try to keep an even keel," Major Doyle said.

Rebecca nodded, popping an antacid — she had started carrying them around loose in her pockets — and then taking a bite of her sandwich. Time to redirect the small talk. "What's that?" she asked, indicating the sheaf of official stationery spilling out of its OD folder and across the table.

"Oh." Major Doyle looked a little surprised. "Well, I write to their families."

"*All* of them?" Rebecca asked. A daunting task, indeed.

Major Doyle nodded. "The KIAs, and the most serious WIAs. And, of course," she bit into a cookie, "anyone I know."

As *she* knew. "So my parents tell me," Rebecca said.

Major Doyle shrugged. "I wanted to offset that damned telegram."

If such a thing were possible. Rebecca nodded. "It made them feel better."

"Well," Major Doyle pushed the stationery neatly back into the folder, "I took some liberties with the truth."

She *must* have. "Told them I was fine," Rebecca said.

Major Doyle nodded. "It seemed the humane thing to do."

Yeah. She, personally, had written letters to Wolf's and Spike's parents that were — very lovely fiction. Both of their mothers had sent back poignant, and generous, letters in return.

"My God," Major Doyle said. "Are you going to hog *everything*?"

Rebecca looked down at her plate, surprised to find it almost empty. There were some potato chip crumbs, and two cookies left — and it seemed clear that the Chief Nurse wanted at least *one* of them. Rebecca, carefully, took a small bite out of each. Undercooked molasses.

"Apparently, you want them both," Major Doyle said.

Rebecca nodded, taking two more small bites.

"Very well." Major Doyle opened her folder, squinted, and pulled a pair of reading glasses from her shirt pocket. "I look forward to your next efficiency report."

The Army's version of report cards. About which she could care less. Rebecca ate the cookies in as lengthy and enjoyable a way as possible, making her milk last until they were gone. Then, she frowned.

"Did you just trick me into eating a good-sized meal?" she asked.

Major Doyle nodded, writing away.

Oh.

Chapter Six

It was later, and she had just gotten into bed, wrapped up in her mosquito net, and turned out the light, when she heard a familiar high whistle. Then, an explosion, maybe somewhere out on the flightline. Oh-three hundred — the VC's *favorite* time for rocket attacks. The alert siren started blaring, and a stentorian male voice came over the outside speakers, announcing that the base was under attack, and they should immediately take cover.

Like maybe none of them had *noticed*?

Although actually, one of the nurses in her hootch, Pat, almost always slept through rockets and mortars. The rest of them found this impressive — and unnerving.

Very few of them bothered going to the bunkers anymore. Too many snakes and rats. Besides, they were always *tired*. So, they were supposed to keep a flak jacket and helmet at the bottom of their beds, put them on, and then roll *under* the bed for protection. Rebecca usually just stuck on her helmet, and left it at that. Let God make the call.

More rockets were coming in — the idea was, if you heard the whistle, you were okay; the one you *didn't* hear would be the one that nailed you — but none of them seemed to be landing anywhere nearby, and she didn't hear any secondary explosions, either. The first night they got hit during Tet, an ammo dump had gone up, and the explosions had lasted for about a day and a half. Tonight, it sounded like the rockets were all shooting harmlessly out into the ocean.

A few of the other nurses were yelling comments to one another — mostly speculating on whether Pat was, in fact, awake — and after a long pause, Pat shouted back that she was *now*, sounding aggrieved. Wilma Sinclair, a relentlessly cheerful sort, was trying to get everyone to join in in a round of "Row, Row, Row Your Boat" — to the raucous amusement of the nurses in the cubbys adjoining hers. The atmosphere wasn't quite as much like a surreal slumber party as it had been when her friend Gail was still in-country, eating popcorn and drinking beer, with her helmet jammed over her curlers — but it was close.

"Becky!" someone — Lieutenant Mosby? — yelled, sounding more serious. "You under your bed?"

Oh, for anonymity. "Yeah!" Rebecca yelled back — and got under her bed, propping her flak jacket up against the outside wall. Her face and upper body always seemed safer that way, and besides, there wasn't much *room*. Flak jackets hadn't been designed with women's chests in mind, and wearing the damn thing was just too bulky and uncomfortable.

More rockets were whistling and crashing outside, and she should probably be terrified, but she wasn't. Survival during rocket and mortar attacks was purely due to random luck, and since she figured she was on borrowed time *anyway*, she had decided to stop worrying about the possibilities. She usually kept a flashlight and a book under the bed, so she would have something to do during the attacks, but tonight she was too tired for that.

So what else was new.

Whistle, brief silence, boom! Jesus, was it going to go on *forever*? Had it been five minutes? An hour? Christ, she was tired of *war*.

One night during Tet, they heard — falsely, it turned out — that the perimeter had been overrun, and the hospital security had been breached. This was right after a mortar attack, and she had been down on one of the wards, helping the corpsman on duty protect the nonambulatory patients with mattresses. As she limped swiftly through the walkway to go back to the ER, she came upon Lieutenant Oliver, who was clutching an M-16, guarding Wards 2 and 3. Even for a nurse, Lieutenant Oliver was a noticeably kind and compassionate person, and out of all of them, always looked the most ill at ease in her fatigues. Clearly a woman who was only comfortable in pearls, white gloves, and pillbox hats.

On that night, however, her eyes were so eerily cold and furious that Rebecca took the precaution of saying, "Nadine, it's me," before coming any closer. Lieutenant Oliver stared, then motioned her past with a jerk of the gun, and if Rebecca had had any genuine interest in self-preservation, she probably would have stayed right where she was. She still wasn't sure what had bothered her the most — the almost inaudible stream of obscenities Lieutenant Oliver was mouthing about what she would do if any of *them* came in after her patients, or the sight of those blank killer eyes. Eyes that were mad in more ways than one.

The next time she saw Lieutenant Oliver, when the red alert had lifted and they were both in triage again, those eyes looked utterly lost and miserable — and familiar. Visual residue of what was left when a person first *really* made the malevolent acquaintance of War, and all of the evil and horror therein. Looked at it, and saw that incubus smiling right back. There wasn't anything more terrifying than that dark feeling of War, suddenly wild and alive, someplace deep inside, thrashing around where nothing of the sort had ever existed before. Or maybe it had *always* been there, silent and still, just waiting for the right ugly chain of events to come bursting out.

Now she wondered, ceaselessly, if once that darkness was awakened, it would ever *leave*. She had never been one to stand around in front of mirrors beaming at herself, but now she couldn't look in at *all* because she was afraid of what she would see lurking in her eyes. And if she could recognize it in other people, they must be able to see it in *her*, too.

Michael had seen it. In a way, that made her feel self-conscious about the idea of being around him, but in *another* way, it made her feel safe, because she didn't have to pretend to be something she wasn't. Like unselfish, and good, and an ideal representative of her profession. He had said that she could tell him *anything*, and he would understand, and although she hadn't taken him up on the offer, she had believed him. He might think less of her — but he would understand.

It had been a while since she had heard a whistle, and the rocket attack was apparently over for the night. She could hear Lieutenant Mosby on their field telephone, talking to the hospital, making sure that everything was okay down there, and none of them were needed.

"We're cool," Lieutenant Mosby said, loudly enough for all of them to hear. "See you in the morning, guys."

Good. They would be able to get some *sleep*. Rebecca was too tired to crawl out right away, and decided to close her eyes for a few minutes to work up the energy. Naturally, she fell asleep, and the next thing she knew, her alarm was going off and she had spent the entire night on the hard, damp floor.

She dragged herself out, managing to hit her head on the metal frame on the way. She could hear wind and torrential rain outside, and had to fight the urge to go right back underneath her bed again.

Time to start another wonderful day in the Republic of South Vietnam.

Work. Try to eat. Try *not* to think. Pop Darvon. Try to sleep. Work again. And, it went without saying, that if she had the night off, she would drink too much. People threw parties for the most trivial reasons imaginable, and being loud, and unruly, and teetering at the edge of sanity were considered *normal* things to do.

A new OR nurse had arrived, looking very young and nervous, and been given Gail's long-vacated room, but the extent of their conversation so far had been the nurse introducing herself, and Rebecca saying, ''Oh, yeah, hi,'' before going into her own cubby to sleep.

She was so tired all the time that she had to struggle not to snap at people, especially when forced to deal with any form of ineptitude. Captain Stockman took her aside, on several occasions, to yell at her, finally telling her to lose the surgeon's ego, and do it *fast*. She'd nodded, and apologized — and found herself on the brink of snarling at someone twenty minutes later.

As good a reason as any to get plastered that night. And the next night — and the night after that.

Which did nothing to change the fact that the ER was constantly filled with scared, torn-apart kids. The fighting and dying were as bad as ever, and there was a constant little buzz of rumors about the way the situation was deteriorating out in the field, mostly stories about village incidents, some of which were so bad that she assumed they couldn't possibly be true. Although they *were* getting more and more civilian casualties. On the other hand, they were the victims of VC and NVA fire at *least* half of the time.

They were also starting to get more alcohol poisonings and drug overdoses. White guys hurting black guys, and vice versa. A sudden, frightening rash of officers being attacked by their own men. *Killed* more often than not. Jesus. It was as though everyone in the country was going crazy simultaneously.

As she led the parade.

One late afternoon, just as she finished prepping an abdominal case and sent him down to the OR, Bart, one of the newer corpsmen, came over to get her.

"Hey, Lieutenant, there's some guy asking for you," he said.

She stiffened. "What? I mean — what unit?"

Bart shrugged, gesturing towards the front of the room. "They just brought him in."

Oh, God. She pushed past him, hurrying towards the litter, seeing a skinny, dark-haired guy who — oh, thank God — wasn't Michael. She stopped for a second, so relieved that she felt dizzy. Okay, okay. It wasn't Michael. Okay. It was just a guy who must remember her from having come through the ER some other time — which happened a lot. *Too* often.

She took a deep breath, and walked the rest of the way over, giving him a quick visual scan. GSW to the thigh. Compound fracture of the femur, significant blood loss. She checked his tourniquet, then glanced at the wire to make sure he had already been hooked up with an IV and some blood.

"Hi," she said, smiling at him and brushing his hair back from his face with her free hand, while she scanned his medevac tag and started taking his vitals with the other. "Don't worry, you're going to be okay."

The kid, whose face was damp with a combination of perspiration and tears, grabbed her arm so hard that she fell against the side of the litter.

"Ma'am? Do you remember me, ma'am?" he asked, out of breath.

No. So many guys came through, day after day, that it was hard to remember *any* of them. "Of course I do," she said. "Hi. Relax, you're going to be fine."

He clung to her arm, and she saw that he had started crying.

"They killed them, ma'am," he said weakly. "They killed *everyone*. Janny, Doc — they — they — "

"I know. I'm sorry," she said, still stroking his hair back as she took his pulse.

The kid was breathing hard, and on the verge of hysterics. "He — he made me *promise*, he — don't you *know* me, ma'am?"

"Of course I remember you," she said, wrapping a blood pressure cuff around his left arm. "Don't worry, everything's going to be okay."

"I *promised*," he said, trying to get into one of his fatigue shirt pockets, tearing frantically at the button. "Meat, he — "

Meat. She couldn't move for a second, and then she stared down at the kid's face, trying to see past the mud and tears.

"I'm *Finnegan*, ma'am," he said. "Don't you remember me?"

Oh, Jesus. Now she did. The tense Irish kid Michael always worried about. "Is he all right?" she asked, clenching her hand around the side of the litter. "Michael, I mean?"

"He *saved* me, ma'am, he — " Finnegan yanked some paper out of his pocket and shoved it at her. "I'm s'pposed to make sure you get this."

Rebecca took the note, recognizing Michael's handwriting, and stuck it in her pocket, despite a desperate urge to rip it open immediately. But Captain Stockman had come over to the other side of the litter and gotten briskly to work, cutting off Finnegan's fatigues.

"Anything wrong, Lieutenant Phillips?" she asked, the question more of a sharp reprimand than anything else.

"No, ma'am." She pulled out her own scissors. "Everything's under control, ma'am."

Captain Stockman nodded, and moved on.

Rebecca quickly drew four tubes of blood, handing them to Rosario to take down to the lab, and then cut off the rest of Finnegan's uniform. Christ, the poor kid was *emaciated*.

"So, Michael's okay?" she asked, hearing her voice quaver.

Finnegan nodded, then motioned towards his leg. "He did it, ma'am. He *saved* me."

She stopped cutting off his boot, realizing what he meant. That something had finally snapped, and Michael had decided it was time to get his friend out of the war. She didn't know what to say, so she just picked up his hand, giving it a squeeze.

"They got Janny, ma'am," he said, tears spilling over again.

Janny. Jankowski. She instantly pictured the polite, gawky guy with the PRC-25 radio. "I'm sorry," she said, and *really* meant it.

Finnegan gulped. "They got Doc, too. And LT."

Oh, no. Oh, *hell*. "You mean the kid?" she asked.

He nodded, crying.

Damn it to hell. She felt tears in her own eyes and had to close them for a few seconds. That kid *might* have been eighteen — but probably only seventeen. Damn it, damn it, damn it.

"I shouldn't've left 'em," Finnegan said. "They're gonna *need* me."

Considering that he had a leg wound that might well be permanently crippling, he didn't have a whole lot of choice in the matter. "They'll be fine," she said, doing her best to sound soothing. "You just worry about getting better, okay?"

He looked up at her, tears rolling down his cheeks. "Will I have to go back out there?"

Not bloody likely — but only the doctors were allowed to tell patients things like that. "I, uh — the doctor will be talking to you about your rehabilitation," she said. "It's likely to take — months."

He stared up at her, his expression twisted in that familiar combination of relief and guilt she saw on so many of them. Overjoyed to be out of the bush, but unable to bear the idea of leaving their friends out there.

"Meat said," he struggled to stop crying, "if they try to make me come back, to just hurt it again."

If Michael had been standing next to her, she would have hugged him — and then smacked him.

A shattered femur was serious stuff. "Don't worry," she said, squeezing his hand. "You're going to be fine."

He nodded, then started crying all over again. "Shit, ma'am," he said. "*Janny.*"

She hugged him for a minute — he was covered with mud and blood — and leeches — and then started cleaning him up so that he could go down as soon as the OR was ready for him. When Gomer and Bart appeared to take him down, she went along most of the way, promising that he was going to be *just fine*, and that she would see him after.

When she came back, the ER was empty, except for one boy whose minor scalp wound was being sutured by Annie and Captain Jessup, while everyone else cleaned and restocked. Her first instinct was to snatch Michael's note from her pocket and read it, but instead, she pitched in, her hands shaking with worried anticipation. Once the place was back in decent order, she took out the battered note, leaning up against the supply shelves as she tore it open.

His handwriting was much sloppier than usual. Frantic, really. The paper was dirty, and slightly bloodstained, and just looking at it made her shiver.

Rebecca —
Things are really bad out here. I know I shouldn't tell you that, but you're the only one I feel like I can tell.

I wish I had always known you. I wish I always would know *you. I wish — Jesus, I'm scared. I'm really glad you're* not *here, but I wish you were.*

Take care of my buddy, okay?

Love,
Mike

If it were possible to grab an M-16 and get on the next chopper out there — she would.

She read the note a couple of times, before folding the paper gently and putting it in her pocket. Then, she sank back against the shelves, closing her eyes.

"Are you all right, Lieutenant?" Captain Stockman asked, sounding rather more kind than she had before.

Rebecca opened her eyes. "Yes, ma'am." She looked around for something else to do. "No problem, ma'am."

Captain Stockman frowned at her suspiciously, and Rebecca sighed.

"I hate the war, ma'am," she said.

"On that, Lieutenant, we are in total agreement," Captain Stockman said, and sent her in the direction of the nearest mop.

When she got off shift, she washed her face and hands, and put on a clean scrub shirt before heading down to the surgical wards to find Finnegan. He turned out to be on Ward 3, and she paused to talk to Lieutenant Oliver, who was giving pain meds.

"Hi," she said. "How's the kid with the femur doing?"

The night shift had barely started, but Lieutenant Oliver already looked very tired. "Which one?" she asked.

"Finnegan," Rebecca said, gesturing down the ward.

"Still a little groggy," Lieutenant Oliver said, "but no complications. He'll evac. out in the morning."

Good. "Back to the World?" Rebecca asked.

Lieutenant Oliver nodded. "Japan, first."

Well, okay. A guy she knew was finally going to make it home *alive*. As she walked down the ward, more than one boy remembered her from triage, and she paused to talk briefly to each of them. Finnegan was awake, and waiting for her, by the time she got to his bed.

"Thank you, ma'am," he said. "For coming to see me."

These kids were always so polite, and so unbelievably grateful for the smallest things. "Rebecca," she said. "Not 'ma'am.' "

He was still somewhat out of it, and she picked up his chart, skimming the notations. The surgeons had had to do a fair amount of reconstruction, stabilized by external fixation, but the damage wasn't as bad as it could have been. Length and circumferential integrity had been pretty well maintained, although he would need further surgery once the danger of infection had passed. He would probably always limp, but he would be able to walk. The femoral artery was in decent shape, and so far, his circulation was fine. Fluid balance, drainage, vitals — all good.

"How do you feel?" she asked, pulling over a chair.

"Fine, ma'am," he said.

Ma'am. She checked his chart again to find out

his first name. "Do they call you Edward?" she asked.

He shook his head. "Eddie."

She smiled. "Call me Rebecca, okay, Eddie?"

He looked shy, but nodded. He was Irish-handsome — black hair, very blue eyes, puckish mouth — but his face was so drawn and haggard that it made her sad to look at him. One of those kids who came over here bright and happy, and went back elderly.

"How's the pain?" she asked.

He shrugged wanly, which meant that it was pretty bad.

"Well, I'll stick around until your next shot," she said. Since it was going to get worse before it got better, and talking would help distract him.

"Am I, uh," he swallowed, looking down at his cast, which ran from his chest to his toes on his bad leg, and almost as far on the other leg, "going to be crippled?"

"No," she said. "It's called a spica cast. The femur is a pretty major bone, so they need to keep the rest of your body immobilized to help it heal. Plus, they'll be taking you to Japan tomorrow, and it makes it safer for you to travel."

His eyes filled up. "I'm really going home?"

Well — "Did the doctor come by and talk to you?" she asked.

He nodded. "He said I get to go. That after Japan, they'll send me to a hospital near my house."

"Where you from?" she asked.

"Massachusetts, uh, R-Rebecca," he said, stumbling over her name.

"Really?" She perked up immediately. "Where?"

"Brighton," he said.

Which was part of Boston. It was always exciting to talk to someone from New England — forget Massachusetts. "I'm from Marblehead," she said.

He nodded. "Meat told me."

"Oh, yeah?" She grinned. "What *else* did he tell you?"

"Nothing, ma'am," he said quickly.

She reached out to pat his hand. "I'm kidding." When he didn't move it away, she knew he wanted her to take it, so she did. "I wonder if they'll send you to the VA out past Northeastern."

His eyes got brighter — in a positive way, this time. "You mean, right out on South Huntington?"

"Yeah," she said. "I'm not exactly sure how they assign people, so don't get your hopes up, but that'd be pretty damn convenient, wouldn't it?"

He nodded, his eyes practically shining.

Despite the many things she was avoiding at home, the thought of being in a plane, hearing that they were on their final approach into Logan Airport, would probably make *her* eyes look like that, too.

They sat quietly for a long time, Finnegan telling her about his family, *exactly* where they lived, and how much he *loved* the Red Sox, digging out a baseball from the personal effects bag next to his bed to show her. A baseball that, it developed, his father had caught at Fenway Park — hit by Ted Williams, no less — and he had brought with him in-country for luck. Anyway, they talked about the Red Sox — who she also loved — until he got sleepy, and started drifting off a little.

"Um, about Meat," he said suddenly.

She had been so sure that he had fallen asleep that she had to jerk herself to attention. Wake herself up, actually. "What?" she asked, feeling her body tense.

He looked at her, his eyes very worried. "I know he comes off all mean, but, you know, he's *not*."

She nodded.

"I know it's like, none of my business, but — " He stopped. "Even if you didn't, you know, feel much, you wouldn't go and send him a bad letter, would you? While he's out there?"

"No," she said. "I would never do that."

He nodded, looking relieved.

"I'm, um, not doing too well with letters," she said, "but — " But what? She could try honesty, maybe. "I'm not doing too well with the *war*, Eddie, and — well, I guess he writes me a lot more than I write him."

Finnegan nodded.

"Well." She let out her breath. "I would never *intentionally* do anything to hurt him, Eddie — I can promise you that." For what little it was worth.

Finnegan nodded.

Lieutenant Oliver was at the next bed, and Rebecca stood up, taking Finnegan's vitals and checking his IVs and catheter and such to save her some time.

"Is she going to give me something?" he asked.

"Yeah," Rebecca said. "It should help you sleep, too."

He nodded, although he looked like he wasn't going to *need* much help.

She waited another twenty minutes, until he had

finally dropped off, then bent to give him a light kiss on the forehead before leaving.

"Ma'am?" the boy in the next bed said, his voice barely above a whisper. His lower body was a mass of bloody, bulky dressings, and his left arm was gone below the elbow.

She stopped, and moved to the side of his bed. "Everything okay?" she asked, careful not to wake anyone else up. "You need anything?"

"Would you give me a kiss, too?" he asked. "Ma'am?"

She bent down, kissing him very gently. "You sleep well," she said. "Okay?"

"Yes, ma'am." He managed a little smile back. "Thank you, ma'am."

She kissed him again, waited for him to close his eyes, and then straightened up to go.

Over, and over, and over, these kids broke her heart.

Chapter Seven

She was going to go straight to her hootch, but she took the long way, past the administrative offices, on the off-chance that — indeed, the Chief Nurse's light was on, and yes, she was in there, doing paperwork.

Major Doyle looked up, then took off her reading glasses, blinking to focus. "Hi, Rebecca."

This was stupid. She should have just gone straight to her room. "Is it okay if I — " she shifted her weight — "sit down for a minute?"

Major Doyle motioned her into the office, and Rebecca sat in the metal folding chair across from her desk.

"So," Major Doyle said. "What's up?"

Rebecca shook her head. "I didn't come in here to interrupt you, ma'am. I just — thought I might sit here."

Major Doyle leaned back in her chair, folding her hands across her stomach.

"Really," Rebecca said. "Please don't let me disturb you."

Major Doyle looked at her for a long minute. "Feeling sadder than usual tonight?" she asked.

That just about hit the nail on the head. Rebecca nodded.

"Hmmm." Major Doyle reached inside one of her desk drawers, coming out with a cookie tin. "Want one? My sister-in-law keeps me well supplied."

"No, thank you," Rebecca said. "But they look good."

Major Doyle shrugged, took three, and left the tin sitting at the edge of the desk.

"So, um, you have a brother?" Rebecca said.

Major Doyle nodded, crunching. "I have two." She glanced over. "How about you?"

"One," Rebecca said. "Brother, I mean."

Major Doyle nodded, and they sat there, Rebecca focusing on the scuffed metal front of the desk. She could hear distant hospital sounds — and artillery, of course — but for the most part, it was very quiet.

"Um, what are they like?" she asked. "I mean, are you close?"

"We were very close," Major Doyle said. "That is, we *are* close, we — " She stopped, her expression increasingly remote. Then, she let out her breath. "My family can be hard for me to talk about."

Which made them members of the same club. Rebecca nodded, slouching down in her chair, absentmindedly rubbing her left upper arm, feeling the dent from the scar and the tissue loss. It didn't hurt much anymore — not the way her ankle did — but the surface area was still pretty numb, and a couple of her fingers had yet to regain full responsiveness. Then, feeling Major Doyle's eyes on her, she quickly dropped her hand into her lap, avoiding her gaze.

"I'm sure this will come as a surprise to you," Major Doyle said, after a pause, "but I was a shy, and reserved, child."

Oh, yeah. Rebecca had to smile. *Big* surprise.

"We moved around so much that your family really becomes your whole world," Major Doyle said, her voice noticeably slower than usual. Cautious. "And even though I was the oldest, I — we'd go to a new posting, and *Patrick* would immediately have a big gang of friends, but I could never seem to — " Her grin was barely there. "I guess I spent a lot of time riding my bike."

Rebecca nodded, finding that pretty easy to picture. When she wasn't trailing around after Doug and Billy, she'd spent a fair amount of her *own* childhood that way.

"Officers' quarters are pretty much the same all over, so — " Major Doyle stopped again, and reached for a pack of Winstons, lighting one. "So we'd get there, and Caitlin and I would set up our room, and Buddy and Patrick would do theirs, and by the time we were finished, my mother would have the rest of the place sparkling." She rested the cigarette on the edge of an already-full ashtray, Rebecca surprised to see her hand shake a little. "Dad was always off — fighting wars, or on TDY, or some such." TDY, being temporary duty.

Rebecca nodded. With *her* father, it was always the hospital.

"And, you know, the service is so much a part of your life that you forget sometimes, what it is that soldiers really *do*," Major Doyle said. "You forget that it isn't just a *job*."

Rebecca nodded, already knowing the direction that this story was taking.

"They let us stay on post when he went to Korea because he was the battalion CO, and — anyway, there we are, at Fort Benning, and — " Major Doyle smiled stiffly — "I was out riding my bike."

Rebecca nodded, her arms tight across her chest, listening.

"I knew," Major Doyle said, "as soon as I saw the cars. Because, you see it happen to other families, and — you just know. So, I went inside, and Patrick is sitting on the couch, crying." She shook her head. "Actually still has his baseball glove on. And General Trevor's wife is telling me to sit down, that I have to be very strong, and I'm saying, I know, I know — and I didn't know at all."

Suddenly, Rebecca *did* know, and she sucked in her breath. Gasped, really.

"They drove off-post," Major Doyle said, her face entirely empty, "because there was this ice-cream shop that Caitlin and Buddy really liked." She frowned. "That is, I *assume* that's where they were going — Buddy can't remember." She shook her head again, and looked up at the ceiling.

"Your mother?" Rebecca said hesitantly.

Major Doyle nodded. "And Caity."

Oh, hell. "I'm sorry," Rebecca said. It wasn't much — but there wasn't much *to* say.

Major Doyle just nodded. "Neither of them even made it to the hospital. And Buddy was critical." Her hands tightened visibly on her desk. "Both

legs, his pelvis, and — see, he was pinned, and — ''
She swallowed, also visibly. ''They pulled Dad back
from the front, and — well, it was a pretty rough
time.''

The room was so quiet that Rebecca didn't even
want to *breathe*.

''You, um, you would have been the one who
took care of Buddy,'' she said.

Major Doyle nodded. ''I certainly *tried*.''

And stayed with nursing, and taking care of people — and the Army — because that's what she
knew. Where she felt safe. Rebecca shook her head,
looking down at the floor.

''Well,'' Major Doyle said, and took a sip from
what must have been an ice-cold cup of coffee.

She was on shaky, shaky ground here, but —
''What were they like?'' she asked.

Major Doyle studied a small photograph on her
desk, Rebecca only able to see the back of the frame
from where she was sitting, although it was presumably a picture of her family.

''My mother was *everything* to us,'' she said finally. ''Of course, we loved my father, but — our
lives revolved around *her*. She and I were — I was
always so shy, and she made me feel — she always — '' She stopped, but then went on, just as
abruptly. ''And Caitlin was — '' She smiled. ''Well,
everyone loved Caity. Always had this — '' she motioned with both hands — ''grin on. Spent most
of her time getting into trouble, but then she'd give
you that little grin, and — even my father could
never really yell at her.'' She smiled, her eyes very
faraway. ''I was so unsure of myself, but she would

follow me around like I was just the most *wonderful* person in the world. And — well, anyone who picked on *her*, definitely had to answer to *me*.''

Something unexpectedly clicked inside Rebecca's head, and she sat up much straighter.

''Yes,'' Major Doyle said quietly. ''You do. From the very first day I met you.''

Now she *really* couldn't think of anything to say, and so she just looked down at her hands, both embarrassed and immensely flattered.

''I, um, I kind of follow you around sometimes, don't I,'' she said.

Major Doyle grinned. ''Yeah.''

Oh. Rebecca ducked her head, feeling herself flush.

''I always wonder what she would have been like. How she would have grown up,'' Major Doyle said. ''And — the first time you gave me that little 'What are you going to do, send me to *Vietnam*?' look, I thought, oh, boy, *this* one's going to be able to push me all over the base.''

Rebecca flushed more. ''I was just kidding.''

''You were exactly what we needed.'' Major Doyle shook her head. ''All that joy and energy.''

It had only been six months since she'd gotten in-country, but it was hard to remember *ever* being like that.

''Which may explain,'' Major Doyle said, looking right at her, ''why it is so *particularly* hard for me to sit around and watch you disintegrate.''

Rebecca shrugged, her eyes on her hands. ''Everyone's having a rough time.''

''*Everyone* is not tearing themselves apart right in front of me,'' Major Doyle said.

No. Everyone also wasn't sitting in her office, clearly in desperate need of help.

"What *really* happened out there, Rebecca?" Major Doyle asked.

A direct question. And — maybe it was time. Time to try, anyway. Rebecca looked at her. "I ran into a boy. Maybe in his late teens."

Major Doyle nodded, leaning forward to listen, folded arms resting on her desk.

"I, uh — " She could hear some noise down the walkway, and turned to listen, but whoever it was was going in a different direction. Away from them. "I think Spike was already dead when we crashed, but Wolf — had time to be scared." Had time to die in her arms. "And, uh — " She shook her head. *Damn.* She wasn't going to be able to do this.

"Close the door," Major Doyle said.

Good idea. Rebecca closed the door.

"Why did you leave the helicopter?" Major Doyle asked.

Well — why else? "They were coming," Rebecca said. "I could hear them. So, I grabbed Spike's gun, and took off."

Major Doyle nodded.

There was no way to describe what it was like to run for a couple of hours on a broken ankle — so she wasn't going to try. "I, um, I was going to rest for a while," she said, "but suddenly, there's this *kid* there, and — he has a gun, and *I* have a gun, and — there we are." Stand-off.

"VC?" Major Doyle asked when she didn't go on.

Vietnamese, was the only thing she knew for sure. "I don't know," Rebecca said. "I guess so." Weeks of fighting to knock that jungle clearing out of her mind, and now here it was, right back again. Steaming heat, bugs everywhere, her head dizzy with pain and grief. Fear and fury.

Major Doyle was watching her, her chin resting on folded hands now.

"He didn't seem to want to shoot any more than *I* did, so even though I knew he couldn't understand, I kept talking," Rebecca said. And talking, and talking, and *talking*. And — it had almost worked.

"And," Major Doyle said.

Rebecca looked up. "I slipped." It was muddy, her leg was asleep, she tried to stand on her bad ankle, and she just plain *slipped*. Christ, the whole thing was so *stupid*. "I, uh, I was trying to put the gun down, but my ankle gave out, and — " she automatically touched the dent in her arm — "he fired, and — " she was *not* going to be able to handle having this woman think less of her — "I fired back," she said, almost whispering. She had never fired a gun in her life, and she was so scared that she fired the entire clip. Right into him.

Major Doyle nodded a few times, maybe to herself.

"So, anyway," Rebecca said, and couldn't repress a hard shiver.

"What happened then?" Major Doyle asked.

Rebecca frowned at her. "What do we *do*, Maggie?" she said. "We try to help, and then we just hold their hands, and keep them company."

Major Doyle's eyes widened ever so slightly. "You *stayed* with him?"

Well — yeah. Rebecca nodded. It had been rainy, and dark, and the hand the poor kid was clutching belonged to his murderer. "I tried to kill myself, the next morning — " actually had the gun *in* her mouth — "but — " Damn. She sighed. "I didn't have the guts."

"Maybe you had the guts *not* to," Major Doyle said.

Rebecca shook her head, so utterly ashamed that she couldn't bring herself to look up. And she was ashamed of not being even *more* ashamed of herself. The truth was, she just hadn't wanted to die.

"It's considered a normal thing," Major Doyle said, "the will to live. Even an *admirable* thing."

Rebecca just shook her head. As far as she was concerned, self-preservation instincts *sucked*.

"What would you tell one of these kids — " Major Doyle gestured to indicate the hospital as a whole — "if he told you the same story?"

Trick question. "I would give him very good, and ultimately very meaningless, advice," Rebecca said. Like that it didn't matter. That he had done what he had to do. That it was a war, and these things unfortunately happened.

That he was still a good person.

In her case, it was utter folly.

"You did your best, Rebecca," Major Doyle said. "I can't imagine a God who could expect more than that."

Rebecca wasn't sure if she could imagine a God, period. "You want to know the worst part?" she asked.

Major Doyle nodded.

"I was *so happy*," Rebecca said. "Before I realized what had happened, and I just knew that I was still alive, I was — *euphoric*."

It was quiet for a minute.

"I think that makes you a human being," Major Doyle said.

A sorry excuse for one. "What would *you* have done?" she asked.

Major Doyle shrugged. "I imagine I wouldn't even have been brave enough to run away from that helicopter on my broken ankle."

Which was glib and, therefore, irritating under these circumstances. "That isn't a question you can trivialize, ma'am," Rebecca said, stiffly.

Major Doyle nodded, looking very tired, one hand moving up to rub her eyes.

"The whole thing's obscene," Rebecca said. "I eat, and I sleep, and life goes on, and because nobody knows, it's like it never happened. And you're all *extra*-nice to me, as though I *deserve* — " All right, talking about it obviously wasn't going to help. The more she went over it, the deeper in she went. On top of which, she was starting to feel pretty damn tired herself. Dazed. Disoriented. *Embarrassed*.

Exhausted.

They sat there, not looking at each other — or much of anything else.

"Jesus," Major Doyle said, without much energy.

Rebecca nodded. Her sentiments, exactly. "Come out, come out, wherever you are," she said, and they both laughed weakly.

The hospital was still very quiet. There were

probably crises here and there, but the silence indicated that they were small ones. Major Doyle leaned forward, pressed the metal cover onto the cookie tin, and then stuck it back in her drawer.

"Lost your appetite?" Rebecca asked.

Major Doyle nodded, her arms not so much folded as wrapped around herself. Looking down, Rebecca saw that she was sitting the exact same way.

There was a knock on the door, and then it opened, Dr. McNulty sticking his head in. His scrub shirt was bloodstained, and he had obviously just gotten out of surgery.

"Hi," he said. "I know it's late, but I thought you might want to — " He stopped, seeing Rebecca, and ran his hand back through matted-down, thinning, blondish hair. "Hi. That is, excuse me."

"I appreciate the offer, Captain," Major Doyle said. "But not just now, thank you."

He nodded about four times too many. "Right," he said. "Right. Okay. Right." He nodded at Rebecca. "See you later, Becky."

As he left, softly closing the door behind him, Rebecca sneaked a glance at Major Doyle, who was, in an extremely dignified way, blushing. She didn't — quite — have the nerve to say anything.

"Well," Major Doyle said, and straightened her collar with tremendous precision.

Rebecca couldn't resist grinning at her.

Major Doyle looked sheepish. "Just be quiet."

She *was* being quiet. She was just — grinning. In spite of it all.

"On-again, off-again, and slightly on-again," Major Doyle said. Blushing.

"Dating below rank," Rebecca said. "I'm *shocked*."

"Likewise," Major Doyle said dryly.

Well — yeah.

"Go get some sleep," Major Doyle said.

It was more of a suggestion than an order, but Rebecca nodded, and they both stood up, very slowly.

"Um, I — " It was hard to know where to start. "I, uh — "

To her complete surprise, Major Doyle came over and hugged her. She was a little shy about hugging back, but she did, and then found herself not wanting to let go. They both got self-conscious at about the same time, and moved away from each other.

"You know where to find me," Major Doyle said.

Rebecca nodded. "Thank you."

Major Doyle looked at her, then also nodded. "It's going to be okay, Rebecca," she said.

Maybe. "Either way, thanks," Rebecca said, and opened the door.

This time, she went *straight* to her hootch, and sat on the bed, turning on her little mechanic's light. Sleep seemed unlikely, and a letter to Michael was an obvious top priority, so she took a piece of her best stationery from the box her mother had sent her. He had lost some very close friends today.

Dear Michael,

I don't know what to say, except how sorry I am. I wish I could do more *than that. I know how much you loved them, and — I'm sorry, Mike. I really am.*

Eddie's going to be fine. I was down on the ward with him until he fell asleep. They're sending him out to Japan tomorrow, and from there, home. I can't imagine how hard it must have been, but you did the right thing. Saved his life.

This wasn't the time to tell him that shooting him in the foot would have been a lot better than the femur.

I know I'm not writing you enough. I'm sorry. I think about you, and worry about you, all the time. I wish I was out there, in your squad, just a couple of steps away if you needed me.

Please take care of yourselves, and be safe — and let me know if there's anything — anything — I can do.

Love,
Rebecca

Shades of her mother's controlled hysteria.

She sealed the envelope and addressed it, writing his name as neatly as possible. God only knew what was happening to him at this very *second* out there. She both wanted to know, and couldn't stand the thought of knowing.

She could hear the Box Tops playing somewhere down the hall, a couple of low voices, and — soft crying. The plywood walls were very thin, and she could tell that the crying was coming from next door, where the new nurse was. Her last name was Fleming, or something like that.

Maybe when someone helped you, the best way

to pay them back was to go and try to help someone else.

She went out to the hall, and knocked lightly on the doorjamb.

"Who is it?" a shaky voice asked.

"Rebecca," Rebecca said. "From next door." When she didn't get an answer, she took a chance, and went in anyway.

The room was dark, except for some squat candles, and the new nurse was sitting up on her bed, pretending — unconvincingly — that nothing was wrong. She had light brown hair, tied in small, loose ponytails, and looked much too frail and young to be anywhere near a combat zone. And her name was — Karen? Carol? Sharon? No, Karen. She was ninety-five percent sure it was Karen.

"So," Rebecca said. "Aren't you glad you came?"

The new nurse managed a smile, whisking a bright red kerchief across her eyes.

"You're — Karen, right?" Rebecca said, to be sure.

The new nurse nodded, twisting the kerchief in her hands.

It was late. She felt intrusive. Sleep beckoned.

"I hope I wasn't disturbing you," Karen said.

Rebecca looked up. "What? I mean, no. I just thought I'd, uh, say hi." Yeah, right.

Karen wasn't buying that one, either.

"You get used to it," Rebecca said. "It doesn't necessarily get *better*, but it gets — familiar."

Karen nodded, unhappily.

Did she have the courage, and strength, to make

another friend who — one way or another, somewhere down the line — she was going to lose? And even if she didn't, did she have a *choice*?

She took a deep breath, and sat down at the bottom of the bed.

"So," she said. "Where you from?"

Chapter Eight

She went back to the hospital early enough to say good-bye to Finnegan before her shift. Wish him luck, tell him to say hello to Fenway Park for her. She was kind of dreading running into Major Doyle, but when she came through the ER around midmorning, she was in her Chief Nurse mode, and just said, "Good morning, Rebecca." Rebecca said, "Good morning, ma'am," and that was that.

Over the next couple of days, she got letters from Michael that he had sent before his friends were killed, and it was awful to read little anecdotes about Doc getting ready to go on R & R, and Jankowski stirring up about the most *disgusting* C-rat meal Michael had ever eaten, and the fact that Finnegan seemed more cheerful, and maybe things were going to be okay. Christ.

A couple of weeks after her friend Billy had died, back in '66, letters from him were *still* showing up at her parents' house. Each time, he sounded so alive, and so much like himself, that she and Doug hadn't been able to bring themselves to open all of them. Even now, there were sealed envelopes tucked away in her jewelry box at home.

The idea of possibly having to go through that *twice* was one she couldn't even let into her mind.

Because, yeah, Billy had been more than a friend.

She had been put back on nights, and when she woke up on Friday afternoon, she found several new letters — Michael and her mother, mostly — in a neat pile by her door. It was over a hundred degrees outside, but the sun was shining for once, and she sat out on the splintery wooden steps to read them.

Her mother's letter was the now-routine newsy tension — speculation about LBJ's "shall not seek, and will not accept, the nomination of my party" speech, and the bombing halt he'd imposed; alternating with was she *sure* she was all right, and was she taking care of herself comments. She also got very nice "Hope all is well, looking forward to seeing you when you get home" cards from Billy's mother, and her aunt Kate.

She saved Michael's letter for last. It was written on the back of a piece of notebook paper, which had an illegible letter from his brother Dennis on the front. Michael's writing was very small, and sqeezed into the margins.

Dear Rebecca,

Sorry about this paper — it's all I have. We heard Finnegan went to the 63rd, so I hope you saw him. If you did, you already know what happened. If you didn't — well, let's just say it was a real goddamn bad day.

We're in this village, getting the usual "No VC, No VC" crap, and as soon as we move out through this rice paddy, we get hit from the tree-line. They sent us right into a damn ambush. LT and his RTO get hit right off, but LT isn't too bad, and he just yells, RTO up! So Janny runs and just as I'm thinking, be careful, he goes down. LT tries to help him, and he gets one in the head. So Hanson's yelling where he wants us to concentrate our fire, but Doc doesn't wait, just goes crawling right out there and — like I said, a real damn bad scene. I mean, I'm still chewing half a piece of gum Janny gave me, and we're zipping him into a bag. I know you didn't really know him, but he was a great guy. Hell, they all were. Christ, Doc wasn't even eighteen yet.

Everyone was in bad shape — we hadn't lost anyone for a pretty long time, and suddenly, we lose a bunch of guys at once — but we have to pull out and hump another couple of hours for no damn reason that I could see. Finnegan's totally out of it, all pale and shaky and not talking to anyone, and so when we're digging in, I just thought, hell with it, went over, and did it. I thought I might not hurt him as much if I used my 9.mm, so I did. He is okay, right? He's lying there, all surprised and bleeding, and I'm yelling like my gun went off by accident, but everyone knew it didn't. After the medevac left, about ten guys shook my hand. Hanson just gives me a look, but then, all he said was for me and Snoopy to dig in extra-deep, and that was it. Our squad's in pretty sorry shape, with just me and Snoopy and Viper, and a couple of new guys. Bozo's still down at Cam Ranh Bay with malaria, and we heard they might be giving him a job in the rear, so he probably won't be back at all. We're supposed to be

*getting some more new guys, but — I'm just sick of it.
Sick of everything.*

Wish I could think of something not *bad to tell you,
but I can't. I hope you're okay.*

> *Love,
> Mike*

Well, the antithesis of uplifting. Rebecca lowered
the paper, but then, out of curiosity, turned it over.
She didn't approve of reading someone else's mail,
but he wouldn't have sent it to her if there was
anything personal in there, right?

Hey, Mike, the letter started out. Dennis's handwriting just might be the worst she had ever seen.
Including her own.

Here's another ugly pose of your fat friend.

A picture of Michael's dog, no doubt.

*Miss March, he ain't. (Speaking of which, how's
that nurse? Mom says she sounds really smart, but what
I say is, if she likes you, how damn smart can she be?
Or maybe she's really ugly? Glasses? Buck teeth? But,
what the hell — go for it, bro.)*

Hmmm.

*Made baseball, but yeah, I already got kicked off.
Popped out, and didn't run — and wouldn't you
know, the guy drops it. Old Bailey was screaming at
me, and I told him to shove it, and — well, Dad's got
free help down at the station again. (went over to the
factory to see if I could pick up something there, but I
guess they think I'll go and drink up all the profits.)*

Oh, right. Michael lived somewhere near the Coors brewery — half the town worked there, apparently.

He didn't say much, but I know he was pissed. Mom just looked at me all sad. One good thing though — got an A– in geometry, and they about had a heart attack. Carrie, of course, got every damn A in the world.
Don't do anything I wouldn't do —

— D.
P.S. So, what's she look *like, man? Like Elizabeth, or what? No way a guy gets that* lucky *twice.*

Double hmmm. Served her right though, for reading someone else's mail.

It was getting late, and she had just enough time before her next shift to take a shower, slug down a Coke, and eat a couple of brownies from the batch her mother had sent her.

She had only been there for about an hour, when the word came in that Martin Luther King, Jr., had been shot, everyone in the ER reacting with stunned silence. All AFVN radio said was that he had been leaving a motel room in Memphis — and someone killed him. No one was sure if it was a lone assassin, or a conspiracy — or maybe even a cop. The only thing they *did* know, was that the guy had been white.

The news had barely had time to sink in, when Captain Stockman called all of them together, quietly explaining that they were expecting trouble on the base, and so *everyone* was on call. Until further notice.

The air had a kind of nervous, simmering tension to it, but nothing out of the ordinary happened. They were busy on and off, but *every* night was like that. Captain Stockman hung around until almost midnight, and Major Doyle and the hospital CO, Colonel Cartwright, were through a couple of times, but nothing about the emergencies seemed worse than usual. Some guys were brought in who had been hurt in a fight at an EM club that *could* have been racial, but that was a nightly event, too.

Everywhere she went for the next few days, the radio was on. There was rioting in over a hundred cities across the United States, curfews were being set — like it was a *police* state — and in more than one place, the National Guard had been called out. There was looting, and arson, and general insanity. Thousands of people had been arrested, and the last she'd heard, about thirty people had been killed. In what was supposed to be the greatest country on earth.

Tensions on the base continued to run high, but mostly, people were being careful with one another. There was more nerve-wracking silence than outright hostility and, as often as not, she noticed people being a lot more polite than would ordinarily be the case. "Excuse me" and "no, please, you first" weren't phrases that got used much in Vietnam.

And yet — they got in a black sergeant, who'd had both legs blown off when someone rolled a grenade under his hootch. A white PFC who'd gotten shot, up near the motor pool. A *bunch* of guys, black and white and every shade in between, who'd had a chair-smashing brawl in one of the mess tents, resulting in plenty of concussions and broken bones.

At about 2230 one especially busy night, the ER was still crowded with casualties, and every staff member who could be spared for triage duty. As one of the emergency room nurses with the most seniority — when the hell had *that* happened? — Rebecca was serving as a supervisory floater, moving from litter to litter, pitching in or giving instructions, as seemed indicated.

One of the outside doors slammed open, and as a male voice yelled, "grenade!" and threw something inside the room, she heard a small, metal object rolling across the floor. She had just about enough time to think oh, *hell*, before she jumped in the direction of the sound, trying to land on top of it, crashing into more than one other person on the way. She felt something spurting up — shrapnel! — and forced herself down into the spray, closing her eyes as tightly as she could so that she at least wouldn't have to see it coming. Someone else was tangled up with her, and they both lay very still, waiting for it to be over.

Several long seconds passed, and although she hadn't heard the explosion, she was dimly aware that her face and shirt front were soaked. The shrapnel must have — she must be — she looked at whoever had jumped with her, and was surprised to see Captain Jessup looking back at her with identical dazed confusion.

"Jesus, it's goddamn *beer*," someone above her said, and she saw that Rosario was one of the other bodies in the jumbled pile.

Captain Stockman was the other one and they all stared down at the now-empty can of Pabst Blue Ribbon. There was a small, jagged hole punched in the side, and some jerks must have thought it would be funny to shake the can up, and then throw it through the doors.

Yeah. It was hilarious.

All around the room, people were lifting themselves up from wherever they had ducked, or thrown themselves across patients. Rosario was on his feet, and swearing, while Captain Stockman got up more slowly, her face taut with pain. Captain Jessup held up the dented can to show everyone else the "grenade," and while there was a nervous ripple of laughter, almost as many people looked angry, or just plain scared.

"From now on," Major Doyle said, her voice very wry, as she patted a trembling, bleeding kid's arm to calm him down, "I think I'll appoint a designated hero for every shift. That way, we won't lose half the *staff* at one fell swoop." There were a few more laughs, and she snapped her fingers to indicate for the people around her to get back to work, before she came over to inspect the damage.

Rebecca extricated her legs from Captain Jessup's, and they looked at each other. Christ, if she'd had to get blown to bits with someone, he certainly wouldn't have been anywhere on her list.

He didn't look too thrilled, either, but then he smiled at her. "Guess the old reflexes are as sharp as the tongue, huh, Lieutenant?"

Someday, someone somewhere was going to give her a compliment that *wasn't* left-handed.

"Just looking for an excuse to be close to you, sir," she said, but smiled back at him.

"You all right?" Major Doyle was saying to Rosario, who was now shaking uncontrollably. "Sit down and take it easy for a few minutes, okay?" She looked at Captain Stockman, whose face was white. "Your back?"

Captain Stockman nodded, but gestured for a corpsman, Rosario stumbling back to his feet. "Let's get this mopped up!" she ordered. "Before someone falls and gets hurt."

Work. They had to get back to work. The place was still *filled* with casualties. Captain Jessup was holding a hand out, and she let him pull her to her feet, hoping to hell that she wasn't going to burst into reaction tears. Jessup was wincing and trying to flex his other hand.

"You okay, Malcolm?" Major Doyle asked.

He nodded, and walked unsteadily over to one of the litter cases that needed help. Rebecca started to follow him, noticing that she'd given her ankle a *hell* of a bad wrench, but Major Doyle stopped her.

"Look at me," she said.

Rebecca looked at her, confused.

"You still with us?" Major Doyle asked.

Rebecca nodded.

"Okay. What's your favorite book?" Major Doyle asked, eyes peering intently into hers.

Rebecca blinked. "Uh — *The Prime of Miss Jean Brodie*."

"Really. Well — okay," Major Doyle said, and then pushed her towards an AE and AK amp — above the elbow and above the knee amputations — who was thrashing and groaning on his litter.

Rebecca gave her head a hard shake to force it back into auto pilot, and limped over there.

Reaction tears were going to have to wait.

It turned out that Captain Jessup had broken his wrist, and since everyone else was already down in the ORs, Rebecca ended up putting the cast on him, which they both found somewhat amusing, although they didn't discuss the situation.

"Check back with me in four to six weeks," Rebecca said when she was finished.

He — sort of — smiled.

By quarter to three, most of the surgery had wound down, and Rebecca was — as was often the case late at night — sitting alone at the ER desk, bringing all of the paperwork up to date. She still felt trembly and sick, and her ankle was killing her, but that didn't make tonight different from any *other* night.

The Pre-Op doors opened, and Major Doyle came in, wearing bloodstained scrubs and a surgical cap. She lowered herself into the chair beside the desk, massaging the back of her neck in obvious discomfort, but nevertheless, looking at her steadily. Angrily.

"Any major injuries I should know about?" she asked, her voice clipped.

Rebecca shook her head. A few bruises, and general vexation.

Major Doyle nodded, but kept looking at her. It was not a friendly look.

Christ. She was too tired to get into this. "It

doesn't count as suicide if you don't care one way or the other," she said defensively.

Major Doyle frowned at her. "The hell it doesn't."

Fine. Whatever. Rebecca shrugged. "If it'd been real, you'd be damn glad that the patients were saved."

"If it had been *real*," Major Doyle said, through her teeth, "we'd still be mopping you off the walls."

Rebecca shrugged without much interest. She'd cleaned a few walls here herself. "You've got three other people you can go yell at."

"I don't suspect *them* of sentience," Major Doyle said.

Jesus. Even at Radcliffe, she hadn't known anyone who spoke like that. "Gee, ma'am," Rebecca said. "What's *your* favorite book?"

Major Doyle scowled at her. "Could you at least pretend to be intimidated by me?"

Yeah, right. Never happen.

"*Wuthering Heights*," Major Doyle said.

Okay. Why not. Rebecca grinned.

"To return to the matter at hand," Major Doyle said, and looked at her without even the smallest trace of a smile.

The matter at hand was really none of her damn business. Rebecca picked up her pen and examined her paperwork.

"Remind yourself that I'm still your commanding officer," Major Doyle said stiffly.

Rebecca pushed the papers away so hard that she almost knocked her cup of coffee over. "Maybe you're some genius who can think that fast," she said, "but all *I* did was hear the damn thing roll by and go jump on it." The kind of instinctive reaction for which people were often given *medals*.

Something flashed in Major Doyle's eyes, so her temper must be pretty close to the surface, too. "It landed right by Ruth and the kid corpsman," she said. "*You* had to cross half the room and knock people out of the way to get there."

Yeah. So? Rebecca shrugged.

"Indicating," Major Doyle said, "that you are either an egoist of epic proportions, *or* that you have deemed yourself utterly expendable." She moved her jaw. "My instinct inclines towards the latter."

It might be nicer to have a Chief Nurse who just yelled at her for her hair touching her collar, and not blousing her pants, and that sort of thing. "I was the float. I'm supposed to — " Rebecca winked at her — "pitch in, wherever necessary."

If the Chief Nurse was amused, she was keeping it to herself.

"Besides," Rebecca picked up her pen, "Captain Stockman's been lecturing me about my ego from day one."

Major Doyle looked annoyed. "Your insubordination towards doctors is another matter entirely."

And one, no doubt, she was about to pursue. "Sorry to be such an endless source of difficulty for you, ma'am," Rebecca said, and started filling in a casualty report.

"Your latitude with me is *not* limitless, Rebecca," Major Doyle said. "Understood?"

Maybe, but it was kind of late in the game for

that. "What are you going to do," Rebecca paused long enough for her to *hear* the "send me to Vietnam?" without her having to say it, "put everyone else in for Bronze Stars, and give me a Section Eight?" Better known as the psycho discharge.

Major Doyle didn't answer right away, her jaw rigid. "I haven't ruled it out," she said finally.

Swell. Rebecca went back to the casualty reports.

Now, Major Doyle sighed. "I'm just trying to decide how worried I should be."

"Yeah," Rebecca said, writing. "By taking advantage of the fact that I recently trusted you with some very ugly, and private, information."

Major Doyle started to respond to that, but then stopped.

"*Trusted* you," Rebecca said. "And it'll be a long cold day in — " "hell" wasn't strong enough — "Vietnam — before I do it again."

The words hung so heavily in the air that she didn't have the nerve to look over, focusing on her paperwork instead.

After what seemed like a long time, Major Doyle sighed again. "You think we're *ever* going to have an easy conversation, Rebecca?"

Didn't seem likely. "You mean, banter, and pleasantries, and cutting each other's bangs?" Rebecca asked.

Major Doyle nodded. "Trading nail polish, giggling over boys."

Before she could answer, Captains McNulty and Gilchrist came out from Pre-Op in their scrubs. The timing was so perfect that she and Major Doyle both broke up. Dr. Gilchrist was unfazed by this, but McNulty looked uneasy.

"So, Becky. Guess nobody's ever going to try to get between *you* and a drink," Dr. Gilchrist said cheerfully, dropping his hand on her shoulder on his way out.

Rebecca smiled, but felt herself blushing.

"The Colonel's looking for you," Captain McNulty said to Major Doyle, who nodded and stood up.

"I look forward to exploring these issues with you further, Lieutenant," she said. Archly.

Rebecca shrugged. "As long as you bring the Jiffy Pop."

Major Doyle didn't — quite — laugh. As she walked swiftly away, Captain McNulty watched her go, and Rebecca watched him watching, looking away just in time for him not to catch her.

"Uh, have a good night, Becky," he said, started to leave, but then came back, shoving his hands into his pockets. "You're, uh, pretty good friends?"

One of the issues they were exploring, actually. "I think so," Rebecca said. Hoped so.

He nodded a few times, his hands deep in his pockets, and she couldn't help thinking that, nice as he was — or maybe *because* he was so nice — he was completely out of his league.

"I'll take a really *smart* person, over an easy person, anytime," she said.

He nodded, and then sighed.

"So — I figure it's worth hanging in," she said.

He nodded, looking in the direction of Pre-Op. "She's short, you know."

What? Rebecca looked over there too, alarmed. "What do you mean?"

"End of June," he said.

Oh. Okay. In Vietnam, two and a half months was a *long* time.

"Well," he said, and turned to leave.

Poor guy. He didn't stand a chance.

Chapter Nine

The war went on. The peace talks, except that maybe there weren't going to be any peace talks, were going to be held in Geneva, or Paris, or Phnom Penh, or Vientiane — or, wait, maybe not at all. Unless they were held in Djkarta, New Delhi, or Warsaw.

Her personal suggestions were Anaheim, Poughkeepsie, or Providence. And — Omaha was always nice, this time of year.

On the subject of locations, Michael's battalion had gotten shipped up north to Camp Evans, to support the First Air Cavalry. It was a little bit of a relief, since she would now be able to hustle right over to casualties without having to worry about what unit they were from, but on the other hand, if something — God forbid — happened to him up there, she might never find out. The letters would just stop coming. It was also a constant effort not to think about the fact that her friend Billy had been killed somewhere north of Phu Bai, and — well, she didn't like Michael being up there.

Reading between the lines, he seemed to be involved in some heavy fighting, but his letters were fairly cheerful. Chatty, even. When she was working nights, she would sit outside in the hot sun in the afternoon, read his latest, and write back. When she was on days, she would read them in the mess hall after her shift, only half-participating in whatever conversation was going on at her table.

"You two must be pretty serious," Karen said one night, as the two of them sat with Annie, drinking coffee and waiting for the night's late movie — John Wayne; hardly a novelty — to start in the main dining area.

"Are they *serious*?" Annie said, with great drama. "I have seen her turning down admirers, far and wide."

Oh, yeah. All those admirers.

Karen looked curious. "Is he a platoon leader?"

Annie laughed, which made her curls bounce.

"No," Rebecca said. "He's, uh — "

"*Enlisted*," Annie said.

Karen's eyes got big — despite having gone to nursing school in New York City, she was easily shocked — and she looked at the table where Major Doyle, Captain Stockman, and Captain Higgins, who was the OR head nurse, were eating, and talking at length. Captain Stockman only had a couple of weeks left in-country, so they were constantly conferring. "Do they know?" she asked.

Yes. "No regulations against getting letters from someone," Rebecca said.

"So — " Karen lowered her voice — "he's a grunt?"

And how. Rebecca nodded.

"He's cute," Annie said. "He looks like this *total* thug, but — he's cute."

A thug whose emotional *raison d'être* revolved around a small, brown shepherd mix back in Colorado.

Karen frowned. "I can't see you with a thug, Becky. I'd put you with a PhD candidate."

So would her father. "He's not a thug," Rebecca said. "He's just — a grouch."

Annie sat back in her chair, folding her arms, tilting her head, jutting her jaw, and cocking an eyebrow.

A decent imitation, actually. "A *big* grouch," Rebecca said, and looked at her letter.

"You should see him," Annie said to Karen, sitting up normally. "This wavy hair, smouldering eyes — he's *hot*."

Rebecca grinned. Yeah. He was hot.

Annie and Karen were now off in a conversation about some pilot they thought was very, *very* hot, so she concentrated on her letter, picking up where she'd left off.

Anyway, yesterday Viper's orders came through, resupply shows up, and he's on his way back to the World. Snoopy and I were shooting flares off after him and all. He's the first guy — the whole time I've been here — who went back in one piece. Kind of gives you some hope. I'm going to miss him like hell, but I was damn glad to see him go. Finally found out his name too. Archibald. Go figure. No question, "Viper" is way cooler. He and Hanson were really tight, so the guy's been looking pretty lost today. Sat and ate dinner with us, even.

So, we're trying to cheer him up, right? (me chomping on some chicken and noodles with Tabasco — just delicious). Everyone's talking guy talk, and someone says, okay, Meat, you got the Lieutenant (yeah, that's you), the Playmate of the Year, and Raquel Welch, and they're all *standing here, smiling at you — which one do you pick? So, of course, I said you. And, you know what, I* meant *it.*

Because — I don't know if anyone's ever told you — but, you are really built, *Rebecca.*

Love(!),
Mike

She laughed. What a jerk. A thug, even.

P.S. Are you laughing, or sitting there all pissed off?

Laughing. Especially because — no one had ever told her — and the thought was not one that crossed her mind with regularity.

"What?" Annie asked, and tried to get the letter from her. "Let's see."

"No way," Rebecca said, and grabbed it back to finish.

P.P.S. Meant that with nothing but respect, ma'am.

Oh — she hoped not.

Any chance you might send me a picture with no clothes on? Promise I'd only show it to the twenty or thirty guys I know best.

Jerk.

I can't get an R & R slot for another couple of months, but — well? Seems to me you have a buddy in high places, and — you, me, Tokyo? Taipei? Bangkok? Write back and let me know?

Love(again!),
Mike

There were probably a million rules against their going on R & R together, but — yeah — she had a friend in a position to pull a string or two. And Rebecca would damn well talk her into doing so.

"So?" Annie asked, clearly *dying* of curiosity, Karen also leaning forward on both arms to hear the dirt.

Rebecca just grinned, carefully buttoning the letter into her shirt pocket.

Built.

She could live with that.

Right around the time the peace talks were set to begin in Paris, the fighting picked up even more, and they worked another series of nightmarish, around-the-clock days. Already, the new offensive was being called "Mini-Tet."

In the middle of the chaos, Captain Stockman's orders came through, and since her hands were full of a kid's intestines at the time, she just kept right on with what she was doing. During a momentary lull, Major Doyle told her to go finish packing and, after a fatigue-dulled pause, Captain Stockman left for her hootch, moving in the stiff-legged hunch that was the residue of her back injury.

When she returned, they had just finished with

two more loads of patients, and were hurrying to get ready for the next. Captain Stockman was walking around, saying quick, numb good-byes, and it was so different from the usual big send-off people got that Rebecca concentrated on hanging fresh IV bottles, unable to watch.

"Lieutenant Phillips," Captain Stockman said, behind her.

Rebecca turned, suddenly feeling tearful.

Captain Stockman reached out to shake her hand. "It was a privilege serving with you, Lieutenant."

"You, too, ma'am," Rebecca said. This stern, demanding nurse was the same person whose gentle hand she had clung to while waiting to go down to the OR for her *own* operation. "Thank you for everything, ma'am."

If she hadn't known better, she might have thought there were tears in Captain Stockman's eyes, too.

"Lieutenant," she said, very serious, "you are one of the finest medical talents it has ever been my pleasure to work with."

An actual *right*-handed compliment. Rebecca looked at her doubtfully. "Really?"

Captain Stockman nodded. "You have a great gift." Then, she frowned. "Don't screw it up."

Well, good. *That* was more like it. Rebecca grinned. "As long as they don't get in my way," she said, gesturing towards the nearest doctors.

Captain Stockman cracked a smile, shook her hand again, and went over to Major Doyle, the two of them walking to the doors and outside — conferring all the way. When Major Doyle came back in, wearing the blank rigid expression Rebecca now recognized as her form of grief, it was very quiet in the room for a few seconds. Captain Stockman *was* the ER, and without her, it was going to be — but then, helicopters and ambulances started showing up with more casualties — and in an amazingly short period of time, the ER was just the ER, and they were working the way they always did.

It was a hell of a way to leave a war.

When the new ER head nurse, a Captain Turner, showed up a few days later, she gave every indication of being as strict and irascible as Captain Stockman — and only half as good. Rebecca had been, with Major Doyle's blessing, the acting head nurse, and the first thing she heard Captain Turner say was, "What's that little butter-bar think she's doing over there?" Without taking the time to think first, Rebecca just lowered her clipboard, said, "Running the show, ma'am," and went back to work.

Not an ideal introduction to each other.

Shortly thereafter, Captain Turner, who was tall and broad-shouldered, with very severe blond hair, gathered the ER nursing staff together for a mandatory meeting — just as they were all getting their first break in hours. Major Doyle was leaning up against the admissions desk about ten feet away, and it was *possible* that she was just going over papers, but Rebecca's guess was that she was standing there as a visual reminder that they should keep their tempers in check.

Captain Turner *started off* by saying that they gave the appearance of a slack and sloppily-attired group, and that they would be mustered into shape, or *she* would know the reason why. Annie was shifting her weight, and looking so mutinous that Lieutenant McCormack actually stamped on her boot once to prevent her from saying anything. Rebecca, well aware of a certain major's eyes burning into her back, just stood there with her arms folded, looking at the floor. The floor that needed *mopping*. Badly.

As Captain Turner told them that the wearing of soft covers — hats — was to be required at all times, that jewelry was not to be permitted on duty, and that their hair was either to be tied back appropriately or cut, Rebecca did her best to tune her out, rocking slightly on her heels, noticing that her ankle hurt like hell.

"Why is it, Lieutenant," Captain Turner said, glaring at her, "that they all keep looking at you?"

Jesus, were they looking at her? "Thanks a lot, guys," Rebecca said.

Captain Turner's eyes narrowed. Squinty, washed-out hazel eyes. "Answer the question, Lieutenant."

They were *probably* looking at her, because they knew she was the most likely to make a flippant remark. No reason to disappoint them. "Because I'm so strac, ma'am," Rebecca said. Strac, being slang for the epitome of Army decorum. "They feel they can learn from me."

Over by the desk, Major Doyle cleared her throat.

Okay, okay, okay. "I also have eight months incountry," Rebecca said, "and I've been the acting head nurse since Captain Stockman left."

"*And*," Captain Turner said through little, narrow teeth, "you have a serious problem with insolence that I will not *stand* for."

Rebecca had to bite her lip to keep from saying, "So then — sit down." "A lot of us have been on duty for the last forty-eight hours, ma'am," she said, trying to sound — if not pleasant — civil. "So, this really isn't the most opportune time to address our shortcomings." Diction the Major would enjoy.

"Damn straight," Annie muttered, and there was a general rumble of agreement.

Upon which, Major Doyle detached herself from the desk, and came wandering over.

"Captain, let's sit down and figure out the duty roster for tonight," she said. "If you all hold on for a minute, we'll see how many of you we can start dismissing for dinner."

Captain Turner's eyes got squinty, but she didn't say anything, following Major Doyle over to the desk.

"Jesus, I thought *Stockman* was a lifer," Lieutenant Averill said, and the rest of them nodded.

"She'll have to ease up," Lieutenant Thorpe said, "right?"

If not — things were going to get ugly.

Ugli*er*.

After a few minutes, Captain Turner came back. "All right," she said, sounding as though she were having trouble speaking around the very large lemon wedge in her mouth. "Everyone but Averill and Phillips can go, although you're all on call. Thorpe, McCormack, you'll relieve them in an hour for a dinner break. Carella, you're to return at oh seven hundred. Any questions?''

There were no questions.

"Then, you're dismissed," Captain Turner said, gave them a short nod, and strode back over to the desk.

Rebecca let out her breath. Christ. Another eight hours of work. It would be a miracle if she didn't pass out.

"I want to see this floor presentable, ladies," Captain Turner said from the desk.

Rebecca and Lieutenant Averill looked at each other.

"Are you a lady?" Lieutenant Averill asked.

Rebecca shook her head.

"Neither am I," Lieutenant Averill said.

Rebecca was grimly mopping away when she felt someone come up behind her.

"Do me a favor," Major Doyle said, "and don't swat me across the face with that thing."

Rebecca made a little feint in her direction, then resumed mopping.

"I *am* aware that I'm taking advantage of you here," Major Doyle said.

Good. Rebecca mopped.

"You two going to be able to make it through okay?" Major Doyle asked. "I thought you could help each other stay awake."

"We can pass the weary hours polishing our boots, and shining our brass," Rebecca said.

Major Doyle smiled. "Give her a chance. It's tough taking over a new command."

Rebecca looked up from her mopping, "I despise denigration."

"Yes," Major Doyle said. "I know that about you."

Rebecca nodded, and mopped.

"For God's sake, *don't* give Annie Carella any more encouragement," Major Doyle said. "Insurrection can be very contagious."

Hmmm. "Did you say 'insurrection' because *I* said 'denigration'?" Rebecca asked.

Major Doyle grinned at her. "Well, I can't have some crummy little butter-bar thinking she's the only one around here who's ever picked up a book."

Betty Bitch, indeed. "That's right," Rebecca said. "You read *Wuthering Heights*, didn't you."

"Twice," Major Doyle said, and gave her a friendly little push before walking away.

She and Captain Turner came to an unspoken truce, essentially just staying out of each other's way as much as possible. But it probably wasn't a coincidence that she had been put back on nights again. By herself.

Her mother's letters were still coming almost every day — there had been no word from Doug; wherever the hell he *was*, presumably, of course, Canada — and her father had taken to jotting stiff postscripts at the bottom, often Red-Sox-related. Like that the team was badly weakened without Conigliaro, but that Ray Culp seemed to have been a good pickup. She actually got box scores in *Stars and Stripes*, and was pretty much up-to-date — but there was no point in telling him that. He probably meant well.

Michael's unit had been moved back to their old

AO, in the Que Son Mountains, so she was, once again, a nervous wreck every time a medevac touched down. Their R & R was looking tenuous, because now he wasn't going to be able to get a slot until August, and by then, the new Chief Nurse would have long since been in place. Until he had a firm date, she couldn't put in for it *anyway*, so, for the time being, she had decided not to worry about it one way or the other.

The concept of being alone with him for five days, in some foreign city, in a *hotel*, away from the war, was both tantalizing — and daunting. How well did she actually know him? Sometimes, she worried that they might be figments of each other's despairing imaginations. In fact, it had occurred to her, a number of times, that he might just be fixated on her because he was in the middle of a war, and she was the only American woman he had *seen*. The way he had looked at her made it seem as though she were the only woman he *wanted* to see, but — she wondered. Worried.

None of which changed the fact that she lurked around the mailboxes on a near-constant basis.

It was a Thursday, and when Captain Turner told her she was free to leave at 0900, she decided that she was too exhausted to check on any of the previous night's casualties, and was just going to go get something to eat, and fall into bed.

Breakfast was thick, salty, disgusting chipped beef on toast, but she forced it down, along with two glasses of reconstituted orange juice, and some overly-peppered grits. She had fallen into a "food is fuel" mentality, and the notion of having an *appetite* seemed very quaint.

When she got back to her room, Truong, their hootch maid, was sweeping the hall, raising clouds of fine, sandy dust. Before the crash, she had always tried to greet Truong in Vietnamese and be guiltily respectful, but these days — she mostly just said hi. Avoided her. Truong appeared to be in her forties, which meant that she probably had children Rebecca's age. Sons, maybe. If she *did* have a son, he was almost certainly a soldier, and as likely to be VC as ARVN. Maybe even more likely. After all, the day Tet started, Truong and most of the other civilian workers hadn't shown up at all. Suggesting that they concealed even more than she might have suspected behind those empty smiles.

But, every time she started thinking about anyone Vietnamese, she would end up thinking about the boy. See his young, terrified face, and that wide-eyed trust. Hear his bubbling gasps, smell the indescribable warm, rich stickiness of the blood. Her own *and* his.

Truong was smiling and saying something to her, and Rebecca managed a polite nod back.

"*Chào bà,*" she said stiffly. Hello. "Uh, *xin lỗi.*" Excuse me. She had hoped, out in the jungle, that "*xin lỗi*" meant "I'm sorry," since that's what she desperately *wanted* to tell him — but she'd even gotten *that* wrong.

Truong was nodding and saying something in return, but, feeling disgusted by herself, Rebecca just smiled nervously and ducked into her room. The *last* thing she wanted was to get everything all churned up again.

So — sleep. She should sleep. The dregs of a fifth of scotch was on the floor — she and Annie and

Karen had been sitting around with Nadine Oliver, listening to Hendrix a couple of nights earlier — and she unscrewed the cap, finishing it off in a couple of gulps. She thought about throwing up, but then just took off her fatigue pants, and curled up on her bed, trying to sleep.

It was hot — stifling — and noisy, and the room was much too bright. She dozed fitfully, the cacophony of helicopters, and trucks, and jeeps, and radios, and shouting voices, and everything *else* pounding into her head, even with her pillow jammed around her ears. She felt sick and awful and jumpy, and when she heard someone saying her name, she couldn't tell if it was a dream or not. But she forced her eyes open, blinking away a layer of grit. Her head must have twisted free from the mosquito netting while she was asleep because her face and hair were *covered* with sand.

"Rebecca," the person said, again, standing just inside the door.

Major Doyle. Major Doyle? Oh, *Christ*, she had slept through her shift. Oh, *hell*. "I'm sorry, I — " Her eyes were stinging, and she tried to rub the sand away. "I didn't mean to, I — " Where was her damn clock? Hadn't she set it? But if the *Chief Nurse* had come to roust her out of bed, she was in big — she scrambled off the cot, glancing down to see what she was wearing. A rumpled T-shirt and underwear. Okay, uniform. She needed a uniform, and —

"Rebecca," Major Doyle said, sounding more resigned than urgent. "Take it easy, okay? Just sit down for a minute."

"I really didn't mean to do this," Rebecca said,

yanking on the nearest pair of pants. "I guess I forgot to set my alarm, I — it won't happen again, I — "

"Becky." Major Doyle came all the way into the room. "Sit down, okay? I need to talk to you."

Becky. The Major had never, not even once, called her Becky. Her mind was clearing just enough for that to penetrate, and she froze, holding a boot in each hand. Her parents. Something must have happened to her — Michael. She felt her breath come out in one scared rush, and stood there, staring into Major Doyle's sad, tired eyes. Oh, Jesus, it *was* Michael.

"It's not life-threatening," Major Doyle said quickly, "but they brought him in a little while ago."

It must be bad. It was obviously bad. She waited, clutching her boots.

"AK amp," Major Doyle said. Above the knee. "MFWs, compound clavicle."

She took a couple of seconds to absorb that, then pulled her boots on, feeling very dizzy and hot, and as though a large swarm of bees had begun buzzing inside her ears.

"Where is he?" she asked, lurching to the door. "Still in triage?"

Major Doyle shook her head. "Finishing up in the OR. I scrubbed in for the worst of it."

Rebecca paused long enough to stare at her. "And you didn't *call* me?"

Major Doyle shook her head again. "We were moving too quickly, and I — " She stopped. "I wanted you to be told in person, not — "

"And you couldn't *send* someone?" Rebecca said.

Major Doyle sighed, reaching out to touch her face for a second. "Rebecca, we both know I couldn't have let you anywhere near that OR. So I thought — " She stopped again. "I just couldn't do that to you."

Rebecca stared at her.

"He *begged* me not to," Major Doyle said. "The only reason anyone knew who he was, was because he kept saying he didn't want you to see him like that, and when he said I would understand, they called me."

Rebecca just stared at her.

"I promise I would have gotten you if he'd been dying," Major Doyle said. "I *promise*."

It was an eminently rational decision. Too goddamn rational.

"Take a few deep breaths, wash your face, and we can get over there before he goes to Post-Op," Major Doyle said.

Deep breaths could damn well *wait*. She started to leave, but Major Doyle pulled her back.

"Come on, give yourself a minute," she said. "It'll make the next few hours easier."

Since she clearly wasn't going to take no for an answer, Rebecca shook her hand off and sat on the edge of her bed, swiftly tying her boots, aware that she was close to hysterics. Major Doyle opened the canteen on her steamer trunk, spilled some water onto a small OD towel, and then handed it to her.

Rebecca held the towel against her face, taking several deep breaths. Okay. Okay. If she lost it, she wasn't going to be any help to *anyone*. She pressed the wet cloth against her still-sandy eyes, and then let it fall.

"All right," Major Doyle said, putting her hand out. "Let's go."

Rebecca ignored the hand, standing up on her own. She let Major Doyle hold the hootch door open and followed her numbly down the hill to the hospital.

"He's going to be okay," Major Doyle said. "I promise."

Yeah.

What was left of him.

Chapter Ten

It wasn't until Major Doyle was opening the ER doors for her that she remembered a question she should have already asked.

"Did he, um — " she took another deep breath — "come in alone?"

Major Doyle shook her head. "There was another kid."

Damn. "Did you, um, get a name?" Rebecca asked.

"No. I'm sorry," Major Doyle said, and paused, her eyebrows coming together as she tried to remember. "I think he might have been black."

Damn. Snoopy. Rebecca swallowed. "About his size, and really thin?"

Major Doyle shook her head. "Big kid. Over six feet."

Damn it. *Hanson.* Rebecca pulled in another deep breath. "Was he — okay?"

"Uh — " Major Doyle avoided her eyes. "I think he took the brunt of it. He was — very critical."

Damn it. "A mine?" Rebecca asked, sort of

stunned that her voice could still sound so normal when everything inside her was blowing apart.

Major Doyle nodded. "Looked that way, yeah."

And the point guys always got it first. First, and worst. She stopped, and took a deep breath. "Um, about Michael," she said.

Major Doyle stopped, too, and waited.

"Was there — " she didn't want to know the answer, but it would be better to be prepared — "genital involvement?"

Major Doyle shook her head. "Just slight scrotal perforation."

Who did this supposed friend think she was, jerking her around like this? Releasing information at her own discretion. "What do you mean, *slight*?" she asked.

"I mean *slight*," Major Doyle said. "A couple of slivers. Some minor vascular damage, but there won't be any impairment."

Jesus. It was lunacy that in Vietnam, that *was* slight. "Anything else you're keeping from me?" Rebecca asked stiffly.

Major Doyle shook her head, looking very tired.

Good. Rebecca nodded, barely, and headed towards Post-Op, hoping to leave her behind. Jane Mosby, who lived in her hootch, was on duty, and Rebecca intercepted her.

"Mike Jennings?" she asked, again amazed by the routine calm in her voice.

Lieutenant Mosby nodded. "Just came in a few minutes ago. He's still out, but good strong vitals." She paused, "I'm really sorry, Becky."

Following the direction of her hand, Rebecca veered over to the bed, but when she saw him, her heart — and entire body — felt as though it had been shocked into utter inaction.

He looked — small. Very small. Swathed with dressings, his face chalky underneath his tan, his hair stiff with dried mud and blood. His right shoulder was thickly bandaged, with his arm strapped across his chest, and his left leg was — gone, about eight inches below the hip. He looked gaunt, and frail, hooked up to an IV, a blood-line, a catheter, and more than one drain. Tubes, and needles, and various liquids flowing in and out.

It was too hard to look at him, so — reflexively — she picked up his chart, reading the long list of what was wrong with him. Starting with traumatic amputation, above the knee, and going on from there. The shrapnel had torn up parts of his right leg pretty badly, but no vital structures had been compromised, and there was almost no chance he would lose it. The damage to the scrotum was, indeed, a couple of superficial slivers. Extensive lacerations to the left buttock, a few small frag wounds in his left side and left arm, the afore-mentioned compound clavicle. His chest and abdomen were fine, so he must have been wearing his flak jacket. He was very malnourished, almost certainly suffering from some sort of intestinal parasites, and — Christ, she couldn't look anymore.

She hung the chart at the end of his bed, not sure *where* to look. The only thing to do, was to treat him like any other patient — and that meant checking, and re-checking. So, she started with his vital signs.

"You're sprung from the ER tonight," Major

Doyle said quietly, standing by the bottom of the bed. "But try to help out where you can."

Rebecca nodded. "Who did the work?" she asked, wrapping a blood pressure cuff around his left upper arm.

"Walker," Major Doyle said. "Gilchrist assisted."

Walker was good, but — "Why not Vreeland?" she asked. Who was easily the best surgeon they had.

Major Doyle sighed. "The other kid needed him more."

Rational. *Toujours* rational. Rebecca looked up from what she was doing. "How *is* the other kid?"

Major Doyle indicated the ORs. "I think they're still running the bowel. He'll lose at least one eye."

Jesus. Rebecca nodded, taking Michael's pulse. Okay. His vitals *were* good.

"Let me know if you need anything," Major Doyle said.

Rebecca nodded, checking his tubes and drains and dressings. Other than continually monitoring him, the only thing she could really do now, was wait for him to wake up.

About an hour later, Sergeant Hanson was brought into recovery, and since Michael was still unconscious, she went right over to meet him.

"How's he doing?" she asked Karen, who was accompanying the gurney, her scrubs disturbingly bloody and stained.

"He's tough," Karen said. "We almost lost him a couple of times, but he kept coming back."

From what she knew of Sergeant Hanson, that sounded characteristic — even under anesthesia. "How bad is he?" she asked.

Karen let out her breath. "Nephrectomy — " which was the removal of a kidney — "stomach resection, patched up the small bowel and left iliac — "

She shook her head. "The usual mess."

Rebecca nodded, scanning his chart. He'd lost his left eye; the right cornea had been scratched by a frag, but he would probably regain at least partial vision. Fractured cheekbone, ruptured eardrum. And, of course, sundry frag wounds to the arms and legs. Christ almighty.

"How's, um, your friend doing?" Karen asked tentatively.

Rebecca just shook her head — and went back to him.

When he finally started stirring a little, she was right by the bed, holding his good hand, and smoothing back the hair she'd tried to wipe clean.

"It's okay," she said. "I'm right here. You're in the hospital, you're safe."

It took a while, as he drifted in and out, but then his eyes seemed to focus on her. First, bewilderment, then, fear — then, pain.

"It's okay, Michael," she said. "I'm right here."

He tried to say something, but then just groaned.

"I'm sorry," she said. "I know it hurts."

He was still coming out of it, and either didn't recognize her, or wasn't sure what she was doing there. He tried to move, and groaned some more, falling back. There was no panic in the sound, so he must not have realized yet — or remembered — that he'd lost his leg.

"Michael, it's Rebecca," she said. There weren't too many places she could touch without hurting him, so she just kept stroking his hair back away from his forehead. "You're here at the Evac., you're going to be okay." None of which seemed to be getting through, so she sponged his face off, trying to make him feel comfortable, and safe. Among friends.

She ran through the standard post-operative checklist, talking softly the whole time in what was probably just a vague hum of words in his ears. BP, temperature, respiration — all fine. Urinary output, adequate; color and nailbeds still pale. She was checking the patency of his IV and blood-lines, still talking, when he suddenly gasped, staring up at her as if she were Marley's ghost. She felt more like crying than anything else, but she smiled at him.

"Hi, Mike," she said. "I'm right here. We're in the Recovery Room at the Evac. It's — " when was it? — "Thursday afternoon." When in doubt, reorient.

He tried to say something, but then choked a little, Rebecca instantly ready with an emesis basin, just in case. The hardest part of nursing was trying to figure out what people needed before *they* even knew what they needed. Since he was pretty badly dehydrated, his mouth was probably very dry, and she moistened the corner of a small cloth, so he would be able to suck on it as soon as he was ready.

He looked down before she expected him to, and his whole body went rigid, as he looked back at her with huge eyes.

Oh, hell. "I'm *really* sorry, Mike," she said. "But, you're going to be okay."

His eyes were very bright, and his pulse and respiration had picked up considerably. "T-They didn't fix it?" he asked weakly.

With an ordinary patient, she could handle this, but right now, her mind was blanking out. "I — you're going to be okay," she said. Help. "You're safe."

He might not know that he was crying, but he was, and she automatically wiped off his face. He was trying to twist his head away from her, mumbling something about not looking at him, and she gulped, starting to cry a little herself. But — *this was not the time*. She had to —

Lieutenant Mosby came over to the other side of the bed. "How's he doing?" Her eyes moved in a quick visual assessment. "You're at an American hospital, Mike. We're going to take good care of you." She glanced at Rebecca. "Get a TPR on the kid behind you, okay? His name's Enrique."

Rebecca was going to argue, but then just turned to the next bed, her vision so blurred by tears that she couldn't read her watch-face as she tried to take the kid's pulse. She shook her head, pulled her sleeve harshly across her eyes, and took the boy's vitals. Checked his tubes, drains, and dressings; spoke his name several times, telling him where he was, and that everything was okay, making quick TPR and observational notations on his chart. Finished, she turned back to Michael.

Lieutenant Mosby nodded. "Right now, he needs a nurse a lot more than he needs a girl-friend," she said mildly as she walked past on her way to check another patient.

Rebecca nodded, absolutely *determined* not to cry again. Ever, if possible.

"I didn't mean to upset you," Michael said, sounding weak and shaky.

"Ever" was a very short period of time. She rubbed her hand across her eyes, and then smiled at him. "It's okay," she said. "Everything's okay. Do you know where you are?"

"I'm *sorry*, Becky," he said. "I really — " He had to stop, coughing and groaning at the same time. "It hurts. My leg *really* hurts."

After an amputation, patients felt phantom pains in the missing limb — sometimes for years. She caught Lieutenant Mosby's eye, mouthed "Mor-phine?" at her, and Lieutenant Mosby nodded. In the ER, she knew exactly what she was doing, and when the hell to do it, but she had less experience in Post-Op work, and — better safe than sorry.

"I know the pain's bad. This is going to help," she said, preparing the shot, even though he was already half out of it again. "Everything's okay, Mike. Everything's going to be fine."

His eyes were tightly closed, a few tears still slid-ing down his cheeks — and "fine" and "okay" were about as far from the truth as it was possible to be.

The rest of his time in Post-Op was a long haul. The work was more grueling and methodical than the swift ER decisions and dramatic interventions she was used to — and falling into the rhythm took some adjustment. He was still asleep for the most part, but he knew his name, and where he was, and all of the other signs they looked for — satisfactory urinary output and the like — were in order, so a couple of corpsmen showed up to help transfer him to one of the surgical wards.

Rebecca stayed by the side of the gurney, holding onto his limp hand, and helping the corpsmen lift him onto his new bed. There were several other recent admissions on the ward and, between watching and sitting by Michael, she forced herself to pitch in. More than once, she heard helicopters, and felt guilty about not being in the ER, about not being more help in the ward, about not being able to stay by him every single second. She knew he was more awake than he was pretending to be, but — well, she didn't really know what to say, either.

Captain Walker showed up on early evening rounds, checking on all of his admissions. When he picked up Michael's chart, she was already on her feet, waiting for his reactions.

"He's doing well, Lieutenant," Captain Walker said. "You can let some color come back into your face."

Rebecca nodded, tightly gripping the bed rail so he wouldn't be able to tell how dizzy she was.

"All right." He hung the chart up. "No changes. Just keep up with the fluids, and doing what you're doing. If he continues to progress like this, I'll have him scheduled for the afternoon flight tomorrow."

In an evacuation hospital, the idea was to move patients out, and on to a more comprehensive facility as swiftly as possible, but — "That *soon*?" Rebecca said.

Captain Walker gave her a tired smile, and she noticed that his hair was much greyer than she remembered it being when he got in-country. "We need the bed. And I don't foresee any complications here, so it's better to get him on his way home."

Right. Rebecca nodded, and sat back down on the small metal stool, taking Michael's hand again.

By this time tomorrow, he'd be in Japan.

It was almost midnight, and the ward was peaceful. They'd had a kid arrest at about 2230, and the patch on his vena cava must have ruptured, because he was gone before they could do much of anything. The ward got very quiet after that — seeing, and *hearing*, another boy die didn't do much for patient morale — and Rebecca helped the night nurse, Lieutenant Cristofaro, soothe and calm everyone. Lieutenant Cristofaro only had about three weeks in-country, and Rebecca barely knew her, but she seemed reasonably sure of herself, and quite efficient. Also sort of chirpy, with bright red barrettes in her hair.

Michael mostly slept, opening his eyes when the pain was unbearable, but she could only give him a shot every four hours, and if he woke up early, she would just hang onto his hand and talk about nothing in particular until he either fell back asleep, or she could legimately give him more morphine. When she talked, he didn't really respond, or even *look* at anything other than the ceiling. She would keep rattling on, nervously, feeling her hand trembling almost as much as his was in hers. A couple of times, he asked about Hanson, and she answered him with false platitudes.

Around 0100, while most of the rest of the ward slept, his eyes opened again, looking pain-exhausted, but — for the first time — completely lucid.

"Hi," she whispered.

He nodded, his hand tightening around hers.

"How's the pain?" she asked.

He shook his head, closing his eyes briefly.

He was due for more morphine, but — not yet. "I'm sorry," she said. "I can give you a shot soon."

"Jesus." His mouth moved into something like a smile. "What's a guy got to do to get special treatment around here?"

"You have to know people," she said. "Important people."

He smiled a little, then looked worried. "Is Hanson okay? Can I see him?"

She'd called the ICU at 2200 to get an update, and found out that he had started producing a little urine, and might be upgraded from critical to serious. "He's doing fine," she said. "He's down on another ward."

She could tell he didn't really believe her, but he nodded.

"Jesus, Mike," she said. "I'm *so* sorry about all of this."

He nodded, not looking at her.

She should probably just shut up. "Mike, I — "

" 'Least it was my bad knee," he said bitterly.

She heard a sound come out of her throat that was either a laugh, or a sob. Both, maybe.

"I didn't see it," he said, "but he did. Tried to stop me."

She wanted to say something comforting, but it was better just to nod, in case he wanted to go on.

"Jesus." Michael's eyes were very bright. "He was *short*. And I'm bopping around like some goddamn cherry."

Rebecca nodded.

"And we left *Snoopy* out there," he said. "Alone. He's the only one left."

Christ, he was right. In just a few months, two of the eight guys in the squad had been killed, four seriously hurt, one — Viper — made it home, and now, Snoopy was on his own.

"I'm sorry," she said. "He'll be okay. They'll probably transfer him to the rear." Probably *not*. That would be too humane.

Michael shook his head, staring up at the flimsy wooden support beams and corrugated tin roof. "It's not bad enough, I blow *myself* up," he said. "I have to go and take another guy with me."

Guilt. Responsibility. Mistakes. Vietnam, in a nutshell. "It's not your fault, Mike," she said. "It's just the goddamn *war*."

He shook his head, turning away from her.

"Michael," she started, after a couple of silent minutes. "I — "

He turned barely enough to look at her. "Just — don't, okay? *Don't*."

Okay. She nodded, able to feel from the tension in his hand that he didn't want her hanging onto him, either. She let her grip slacken a little, and he slid his hand free, covering his eyes with his arm. So, she folded her hands tightly together in her lap, noticing, for the first time, that her shoulders and neck were so bunched up that they hurt. She could hear a boy a few beds away whimpering with a nightmare, and was going to get up, but saw Lieutenant Cristofaro already on her way over.

After a while, Michael lowered his arm, but kept his fist clenched — a clear indication that he didn't want her holding hands with him again. So, she just hunched on her stool.

"I can't feel anything," he said suddenly, looking down at the sheet with specific urgency. "Am I okay?"

Okay, in the male sense. She nodded. "You have a catheter. That's why you don't feel anything."

"There's bandages," he said, sounding scared. "I can feel bandages."

"You're *fine*." She touched his fist for a second. "A couple of tiny splinters. That's all."

His eyes got even bigger.

"I promise you're fine," she said.

He stared at her accusingly. "Did you look at me?"

God, no. What kind of person did he think she was? She shook her head.

"I don't want you seeing me," he said. "It's not right."

She nodded. She'd had to check his catheter for patency, and his dressing for staining, repeatedly, but she'd gone out of her way *not* to look at him. Despite their being on her bed during their all-too-brief kissing session the night before Tet, she'd gotten called in to the hospital before they got very far. Before they even really *touched* each other.

"Michael, I would never do that," she said, since

he was still scowling at her. "I mean — Jesus. It's *private*."

He nodded, and now she was very aware of, and embarrassed by, how exposed he was under that thin cotton sheet. While she sat, fully clothed, completely unmaimed, probably hurting him more than she was helping.

"Michael," she started.

"I don't want to talk," he said. "*Okay?*"

She nodded, and hunched. "Let me know when the pain gets too bad."

"Yeah," he said, and closed his eyes.

Chapter Eleven

Michael was still asleep, or faking, when Major Doyle came into the ward about twenty minutes later, stopping to talk to Lieutenant Cristofaro before walking over to where she was sitting. Rebecca nodded at her, but didn't stand up.

"Take a break," Major Doyle said, wearing scrubs, looking almost as tired as Rebecca felt. There were *a lot* of new admissions; it must have been a bad night out there. "I'll watch him."

Christ, she *needed* a break. Rebecca hesitated.

"Come on," Major Doyle said, resting her hand on her shoulder. "A shower, something to eat, even grab some sleep if you can."

Yeah, right. This was the *perfect* time for a nap. She got up slowly, her legs numb and stiff, her ankle so sore that she had trouble putting weight on it. "I'll only be gone a minute."

Major Doyle looked up from Michael's chart. "An hour. Minimum."

Ten minutes. *Tops*. She shrugged, limping, very

slowly, out of the ward. She stopped at the latrine first, then went to the nurses' changing room to wash off her face and upper body, putting on a clean scrub shirt, and throwing her crumpled, sandy T-shirt into an overstuffed laundry bag.

From there, she went to the workroom to get a cup of coffee, gulping the hot liquid down in seconds. Then, she refilled the cup, adding extra sugar, and headed for the ICU, where she fell into step with Marge, a beefy and jolly captain who was the night head nurse.

"I came to see Hanson?" she said, hoping to God that she wouldn't hear the dreaded "Too late" answer.

Marge pointed with her chin, since her hands were full of bags of blood. "Three down from the station. He's hanging in — but, only a minute, okay?"

Rebecca nodded, stepping cautiously over to the bed. The closer a patient was to the nurses' station, the more serious his condition was. According to his chart, his remaining kidney was producing darkish urine, and the arteries were holding. So far, so good. Looking at the thick bandages wrapped around his eyes, and the left side of his face, she thought about how handsome he had been. Tall, muscular, and dripping heroism from every pore. A walking recruitment poster.

She must have made some kind of sound because he moved his head, even though he couldn't see.

"I'm sorry, Sergeant," she said softly, resting her hand on his. "I didn't mean to wake you up. Is there anything I can do for you?"

He shook his head, falling back against the pillow, the tendons in his neck flexed with pain.

"I'm really *very* sorry, Sergeant Hanson," she said. "I — I'm not sure if you remember me, I — "

"Miss Nightingale," he said, his voice faint and raspy.

If only. "Yeah." Rebecca squeezed his hand. "One and the same."

"H-H — " He tried to say something, stopping in frustration. He was obviously having trouble swallowing, and although she couldn't give him anything to drink with the internal injuries, she moistened his lips with the damp washcloth on the table by the bed. "How is he?" he asked.

Back in the World, they were calling these guys baby-killers, but as far as she was concerned, they were the most unselfish and generous people she had ever known. "Worried about *you*," she said.

Sergeant Hanson shook his head weakly, and she could tell that whatever energy he'd had, had already been taxed.

"He's fine." She kissed his right cheek as gently as she could. "Try to rest now, and I'll be back to see you later."

As she started to leave, he hung onto her hand.

"Tell him — " He stopped to pull in a shuddering breath. "Tell him it's okay."

"I will." She brushed a kiss across the back of his hand, then set it carefully on the sheet by his side.

He fell asleep right away, and she watched to make sure that it *was* just sleep, relieved to find his respiration light, but normal. His pulse and BP were fine, too.

She retrieved her coffee from the nurses' desk, offering some to Marge before limping back to the surgical ward. Her rarely-dormant Darvon temptation was violently rearing its head, but she stopped off in Ward 2 and took some aspirin, instead. Too many, probably, but if her ankle got much worse, she was going to be reduced to public tears. Right now, the throbbing was the harsh kind that made her feel feverish and sick to her stomach. Familiar feelings, of late.

On the other hand, the damn thing was still *attached* to her, so she really shouldn't complain.

When she walked into Michael's ward, she saw that Major Doyle was holding his hand, and that they were deep in conversation, Michael barely seeming to pause for breath as he talked, Major Doyle nodding and listening. Rebecca stopped short, her first reaction an almost physically painful jolt of jealousy at the sight of him being so animated and intense — with someone else. Someone so much more attractive, and — all right. All right. If he wanted to talk, he *should* talk, and she should — stay out of the way. Leave before they saw her.

She pivoted in place, going right back out to the walkway, and sat down near the ward doors, covering her head with her arms as she rested against upraised knees. She stayed like that, taking deep breaths, and keeping her mind blank. A couple of people went by, but she didn't look up and, after the briefest of pauses, they would keep going. She sat until her "hour, minimum" was over, and then walked into the quiet ward, nodding at Lieutenant Cristofaro, who was mixing penicillin.

Michael appeared to be asleep, and Major Doyle

was holding his hand with her left hand, her right hand touching his hair. The roiling, furious jealousy came right back, and Rebecca stopped to try and collect herself. To repress the urge to go over and *hit* her.

Seeing her, Major Doyle eased her hand from his and came over, Rebecca feeling so murderously angry that she couldn't look at her. She must have been giving off some very dangerous vibrations, because Major Doyle actually took a step backwards.

"Need some more time?" she asked, too careful.

Rebecca shook her head. Once.

"Okay, then," Major Doyle said, and took a sort of sidestep past her.

"You two have a nice cha*t*?" Rebecca asked, hitting the "t" extra-hard.

Major Doyle sighed. "He's a very proud young man who's feeling completely emasculated right now."

"I don't need you," Rebecca said, "to, uh, explain him to me. Okay?"

"Right," Major Doyle said, her eyes going so remote and wintry that Rebecca could feel the chill three feet away.

They looked at each other — damn near *circled* each other — then, Rebecca went over to the bed, sitting down on the stool, and Major Doyle walked out of the ward. Quickly.

She was hanging a fresh IV bottle when Michael opened his eyes, and although she searched them for disappointment — that she was there, and not the Major — she didn't see much of anything in them at all. Pain. Weariness. Pain.

"You okay?" she asked.

He nodded dully.

"Anything I can do?" she asked, hearing her voice shake.

He shook his head, watched her work for a minute, and then closed his eyes again.

Christ. She swallowed, but continued taking his blood pressure, willing the wet blur in her eyes to go away.

Doing her — limited — best to be a good nurse.

She gave him his next pain shot right before a corpsman and a GMO showed up to take him down for D & I — debridement and irrigation. There was so much filth in war wounds — dirt, metal, bits of charred uniform, and the like — that they had to let them heal from within, and so, the gaping holes were left open. Therefore, patients had to be taken, usually a couple of times a day, to have the debris and dead tissue cleaned out, and fresh sterile gauze packed in. Not a painless procedure.

He'd made it clear that he didn't want her to come — because she would *see* him, presumably — so she stayed behind in the ward, putting fresh sheets on his bed, and then helping the morning shift with meds, hygiene, and whatever else the patients needed. The wardmaster suggested, strongly, that she take a break, but she pretended not to hear him, helping a boy — splenectomy/colostomy — write a letter home to his fiancée.

When Michael was wheeled back, he looked awful, and even when she covered him with a blanket, he couldn't stop shivering.

"Do you want another?" she asked.

He shook his head, shivering.

"Do you want *anything*?" she asked.

He shook his head. Shivered.

She stood next to the bed ineffectually, not sure if she should leave him alone, or — the ward doors swung open, an officious one-star general in full dress uniform coming in, trailed by an aide, and the chaplain, Father Gallagher. Who she wasn't crazy about because the only thing he ever looked at head-on was his watch.

"Who's that?" Michael asked.

The regular bizarre charade of medal presentations to the wounded. "Purple Hearts," she said. Which was fine, but they handed out other medals, based on the severity of the injury. Usually, the general's aide was a tall, slim second lieutenant, but today's helper was a not-so-slim Red Cross worker. They were known as Donut Dollies, and had a reputation for being very promiscuous with field-grade officers, who, rumor also had it, considered them to be their personal property. On the other hand, Army nurses had the exact same reputation, so Rebecca found the notion highly suspect, at best. This particular Red Cross worker was wearing her light blue uniform, a nervous, toothy smile, and a brown beehive that was frizzy with humidity.

"I don't want one," Michael said grimly.

"If you just smile and nod, they'll leave right away," Rebecca said.

Michael scowled.

It took them a while to work their way down,

the general giving each kid a hearty handshake —
if he still had a hand — and pinning the medal on
his hospital pajamas if he didn't.

"How come she's taking pictures?" Michael
asked, as there was a flash at each bed. "Keeping
a damn *scrapbook*?"

Sometimes, the boys smiled, but most of the
time, they just looked dazed and drugged. "So you
can send it home, and your family can see that
you're okay," she said.

He stared at her. "Is that a joke?"

Would that it were. She shook her head.

"Great," he said. Grimly. "It'll make Mom's
day."

The general stopped with great efficiency at the
bottom of his bed. "Specialist, Fourth Class Michael R. Jennings? How are you doing today, son?"
he asked, then went on without waiting for a response. "On behalf of the United States Army, I
hereby present to you this Purple Heart, for wounds
received in action, in the defense of the Republic
of South Vietnam."

"With the thanks of a grateful nation," Michael
said to Rebecca. Sneered, really.

She nodded, resting her hand on his arm.

"Also, Specialist Jennings, I bestow upon
you — " the general reached his hand out, snapping his fingers, and Father Gallagher gave him
another small medal box — "this Bronze Star, in
recognition of your distinguished service with the
Americal Division. Your country thanks you." He
paused to smile. "Would you like me to pin them
on you, son?"

Michael's smile back was very bitter. "I'm getting a medal, for falling over a fucking *tripwire*?"

The general didn't miss a beat, moving forward with the small black cases. "Please step aside, nurse."

Rebecca hesitated, then backed away.

Michael tried to grab her arm, but missed, wincing. "I don't *want* her to step aside."

The general ignored that. "I would also," he said, pinning the two medals to Michael's pillowcase after studying the bandages strapping his arm across his chest, "like to inform you that you are, at this time, hereby promoted to the rank of E–5."

Not much consolation for losing a leg.

"Now." The general smiled again. "How about a picture for your folks back home, Sergeant?"

"No," Michael said. "I don't — "

The Red Cross worker snapped a Polaroid, catching him in midsentence. Then, they all instinctively stayed still, waiting for it to develop.

"Could you," Michael said through his teeth, "maybe take *another*, so the nurse here could be in it?"

The Red Cross girl smiled nervously. "They, um, cost a dollar."

"Oh, yeah?" Michael said, smiling back, his eyes furious. "Well — don't worry, honey, I'm good for it. You can see I've got" — he indicated his stump — "a real promising financial future here."

Rebecca knew the Red Cross worker vaguely — her name was Bonnie, or Donna, or something like that — and she quickly took ten MPC dollars out of her pocket. "Here," she said. "Will this cover the other kids on the ward, too?"

Bonnie, or whoever she was, nodded, and took the money. "I-I don't make the rules," she said, "I — " She gave them an embarrassed smile, and handed Rebecca the picture.

"You send that to your folks right away, Sergeant. Put their minds at ease," the general said, and then saluted him before moving on.

Now, it was Father Gallagher's turn. "What religion are you, son?" he asked, leaning on the bed-rail.

"Mormon," Michael said.

Rebecca smiled. Yeah, *right*.

"Well, the Mormons are good people, son," Father Gallagher said gravely. "Would you like — "

"Wait." Michael looked over at Rebecca. "Did I say Mormon? I meant, *Muslim*."

Father Gallagher's head snapped around. "I'll thank you not to mock me, Lieutenant."

What? "I wasn't, Captain," Rebecca said. "But, I think it might be better if you — "

Father Gallagher cut her off. "Just let me do my job, nurse. I don't need interference from *you*."

"Hey!" Michael said, sounding very much like his old self. "You show her some *respect*, bud. Hear me?"

The whole ward had heard him.

Father Gallagher looked from one of them to the other. "I'll just come back later, son," he said, glared at Rebecca, and went over to the next bed.

Rebecca shook her head, and ripped the protective covering off the Polaroid, holding it so he could see the results once it had fully developed.

"Oh, yeah," Michael said, his teeth gritted.

"That'll put their minds at ease." He pushed her hand away. "Get rid of it."

She glanced at the photograph herself. Yeah, it was a winner, all right. But, even so. "They still might feel better if they can — "

He motioned towards the Bronze Star. "Get that fucking thing out of here, too," he said. "You know who deserves it."

She sighed. "Michael — "

"Just *do* it," he said. "Jesus, are you some kind of goddamn lifer, too?"

She shook her head, slipping the picture into her pocket, and unpinning the Bronze Star, placing it back in its case.

"*Thank* you," he said, his fist tight by his side.

"I saw him before," she said quietly. "He said to tell you not to worry, that everything was okay."

Michael laughed the jarringly bitter laugh.

"He doesn't think it was your fault," she said, "so you shouldn't either. I mean — " Seeing his expression, she stopped. "I'll just, uh, run a quick check here, okay?" She put on her stethoscope, and reached for a blood pressure cuff.

TPR, BP — all good. The dressing on his stump was staining, and she gently reinforced it with extra gauze, then checked his catheter. She was leaning across him to look at his IV bottle, when she realized that her chest was right in his face, and she straightened up, blushing. "I'm sorry, I — excuse me." She walked around to the other side of the bed, Michael's expressionless eyes following her.

When she was finished, she put her hands uncomfortably in her pockets. "Is there anything I can — ?"

He shook his head.

"Let me fix your pillow," she said, and — even though it was the most elementary of nursing skills — she turned it very clumsily. "Do you want to write a letter home, maybe, or — "

He shook his head.

"You didn't eat," she said. "How about — ?"

He shook his head.

If he were a normal patient, she would be talking to him about encouraging things, so — she should do that. "It's not going to be as bad as you think it is," she said. "Once they fit you with your prosthesis, you're still going to be able to drive, and walk, and — " This wasn't a normal patient; this was *Michael*. The Colorado jock. "You're still going to be able to ski."

"Yeah," he said. "I can be the mountain freak. Maybe they'll even charge admission."

When the other guys said things like that, she always had a cheery response ready. "I know it seems that way now," she said, "but — "

He looked right past her, his eyes in what was known as the "thousand-yard stare." Maybe even *ten* thousand. "I just want to sleep, okay?"

She nodded and, not sure what else to do, sat down next to the bed to wait for him to open his eyes again.

Chapter Twelve

She must have dozed off, because when Lieutenant Oliver touched her back, she jerked upright, not sure where she was.

"I'm sorry, Becky," she said. "But Walker was by before, and they're going to want to take him soon."

Take him. Oh — the afternoon evacuation flight. She nodded, rubbing her hands across her eyes, trying to wake up.

"I've already filled out his medevac tag," Lieutenant Oliver said.

Jesus. He was really going. "Thanks, Nadine," Rebecca said, and stood up, her ankle so weak that she had to grab the bedrail. And, to make matters worse, Michael was awake, and watching her.

"You all right?" he asked, his voice sounding flat.

She nodded vigorously, fumbling for her stethoscope. "I'm sorry. Was I asleep long?"

He shrugged.

"Did you see the doctor when he was down

here?'' she asked, after she'd taken his vital signs.

Michael nodded.

"So, you know what's happening," she said.

He nodded.

"Okay." Her mind was even more of a blur than her eyes. "Do you — have any questions?"

"Did they throw away my stuff?" he asked.

She shook her head, indicating the cloth bag — known as a ditty bag — hanging from the bed-frame. "Anything you had with you should be in there."

He nodded. "Can I have it?"

She opened the drawstring, seeing a thick wad of filthy, water-stained letters — most of them from her — and holding the bag so he could reach it. He dug around inside, pulled a photograph out, and folded his hand around it. Almost certainly a picture of his dog.

She hung the bag back up. "Otis?"

He nodded, but didn't look at it, or her.

There didn't seem to be much to say, and she concentrated on the busywork of getting a patient ready for air-evacuation, her hands trembling.

"Do I get to see Hanson before I go?" he asked.

Depending on what kind of shape he was in. "I'll find out," she said.

The idea was not greeted with enthusiasm, but when she suggested that they run it by the Chief Nurse, the answer came back yes. And, shortly thereafter, the Chief Nurse herself appeared. Rebecca stood up and moved out of the way, not quite able to look her in the eye after their last encounter. She could tell that Major Doyle was equally ill at ease, and that this might be an opportune moment to have something terribly important to look at down by the nurses' station.

When she saw Major Doyle shaking his good hand, she walked back over.

"Good luck to you, Michael," Major Doyle said, and winked at him. "You're going to be okay."

Rebecca met eyes with her for a second, catching an alarming little glitter in there, and quickly looked away. Obviously, the last thing either of them wanted was for Michael to pick up on the situation — but, he wasn't stupid. He watched Major Doyle leave without comment, and then looked at her — without comment.

The silence was extremely awkward, and Rebecca shifted her weight.

"So," she said. "You call *her* honey, too?"

Michael smiled slightly. "I don't call any woman who might hit me 'honey.' "

Wise policy. "You've never called me honey," she said.

He shrugged his good shoulder. "There you go."

There, indeed. She smiled back, slightly, and went to get a fresh IV bottle.

Time was getting short, and it was obvious that they weren't going to talk about any of the things she would have expected. That they weren't — he wasn't — going to get personal, or even acknowledge that such a thing might be a nice idea. So, she just kept doing what she had been doing, trying not to let him know that she was on the verge of tears. Again.

Still.

Once his hospital discharge had been fully processed, a couple of corpsmen came to transfer him to a gurney, from which he would be put on a truck-ambulance, and then driven up to the airstrip for his flight out. It seemed clear that she would be saying good-bye to him at the ambulance, rather than going all the way up to the airstrip.

The corpsmen didn't seem too thrilled about taking a detour to the ICU, but they weren't about to countermand the Chief Nurse, so they did it, Rebecca explaining to him what sort of condition Hanson was in, and how it looked worse than it was. Not a white lie, a *grey* one. The news that he was definitely blind in one eye, and might be in the other, didn't go over well.

Michael gasped when he saw him, and Rebecca realized that yeah, maybe it *did* look even worse than it was. But — he was conscious, and that was progress.

She wasn't sure if she should stay close and be supportive, or move back and give them some privacy, so she played it halfway.

"Hey, Sarge," Michael said, his voice barely under control. "How you doing?"

"I'm okay," Sergeant Hanson said, his voice also thick.

There was a long silence, and Rebecca could feel her own throat tightening up with emotion.

"Sarge, I — " Michael stopped. "I don't — "

There was another silence.

"Meat, it's *okay*," Sergeant Hanson said. "Okay?"

Michael gulped. "I'm really sorry, man, I — Jesus, I'm *sorry*."

"Well — no one ever said it was much of a war,"

Sergeant Hanson said, and they both laughed weakly.

One of the corpsmen made a "speed it up" motion with his hand at Rebecca, who pretended not to notice.

"I gotta go now, man," Michael said.

Sergeant Hanson nodded. "You take care of yourself, Meat."

Michael lifted himself enough to touch his leg for a second. "Yeah," he said, sounding tear-choked. "You too, Sarge."

Then, they both slumped back, and Rebecca nodded at the corpsmen to get moving.

Outside, it was sunny, and breathlessly hot, a light wind whipping sand around as the corpsmen lifted stretchers into the ambulance.

Jesus, they only had about two seconds left here, she had to say something. *Do* something. Michael was still crying a little, and resolutely not looking at her. In fact, she'd seen that look before. His body might still be in Vietnam, but he was already gone, his eyes shifting from one thing to another, averting from hers if they happened to meet.

Realizing that this was *it*, that she might never see him again, she felt her breath come bursting out, and tried to pull it back in when he glanced sharply at her.

The corpsmen only had a couple more people left to load.

"Michael." She took a deep breath. "My tour is — "

For the first time in hours, he held her eyes with his. "Please don't."

She blinked. "But — "

He shook his head, very hard, and looked away again.

Oh, Jesus. She rubbed her sleeve slowly across her eyes.

"Uh, Lieutenant," one of the corpsmen said. "We really have to — "

Right. She nodded, feeling dizzy with loss, and stepped away from the gurney. "Please, um — " Crying and fainting were distinct probabilities. "Please take care of yourself, Michael. Please — be okay."

He nodded, and then, as they lifted his stretcher inside the truck, shoved something into her hand.

"I'm sorry," he said, looking right into her eyes, and then he looked away — for good.

Jesus Christ. She really *wasn't* ever going to see him again. She was too stunned to say anything back, and the truck doors were closed now. One of the corpsmen gave the side panel a slap, and the truck pulled away, covering all of them with a spray of sand.

At first, Rebecca couldn't move, but then she looked down at her hand, seeing the picture. Otis. What he loved most on earth.

It seemed very likely that she was going to die, right here, right now.

She went to her hootch and slept without moving, dreaming, and — possibly — breathing. Her alarm rang about ten hours before she was ready to hear it, but she got up, showered, mechanically ate a can of cold spaghetti and meatballs from the emergency store of C-rations in her room, slugged down a Coke, and made it to the ER ten minutes early for her shift.

There were four bleeding, groaning casualties lying on litters, surrounded by doctors, nurses, and corpsmen, yelling instructions to one another. Rebecca pushed up her sleeves — and joined in.

Once things were quiet, Captain Turner briefed and instructed her, and then left her to count narcotics with Zeke, the night corpsman on duty.

Major Doyle came through, surveyed the room for a long minute, and they exchanged terse nods before she continued on her way.

"Thought you and the honcho were big buddies," Zeke said.

Rebecca frowned at him. "Don't make me lose track."

Zeke shrugged, and they resumed their counting.

Over the next few days, she spent almost all of her non-sleeping spare time keeping an eye on Hanson. Sometimes they talked, and sometimes he just floated along in his morphine or Demerol-induced haze. His improvement was slow, but steady, and he had been moved out of the ICU.

What she found out, during those hours, was that he was a very nice man — twenty-one was a man, right? Was twenty-one a *woman*? Anyway, he was a man she was proud to know.

The day of his evacuation flight, she sat with him most of the morning.

"I'm pretty scared," he said, sounding, as he always seemed to sound, very calm and serious.

"I think you just have to take it a day at a time,"

she said. "The same way we get through here."

He nodded, his hand both firm, and relaxed, in hers. The way she'd wanted Michael's hand to feel.

They sat together quietly. Calling each other by rank was stupid, but he wasn't doing very well with "Rebecca," and she couldn't seem to manage "Bubba," his nickname. "Walter" seemed strange, too.

"I guess I mean my wife," he said. "Do you think she — I mean, if I can't — " He didn't finish the sentence, but she knew that the word he had left off was "see."

"I think any woman lucky enough to have you would hang on as tightly as she could," she said.

He smiled, and shook his head.

"You're *special*," Rebecca said. "If she doesn't already know that — which I'm sure she does — she's a lunatic."

"I hope so," he said, almost inaudible.

"I *know* so," Rebecca said, and squeezed his hand.

They sat, quietly.

"I'm still getting letters from him," she said. "From the bush." Only one of which she'd read. A happy letter, telling her that his R & R had come through for July 18th, and could she see what she could do.

Sergeant Hanson didn't answer right away. "I've never known a more stubborn son-of-a-bitch in my life," he said finally.

Likewise. "I don't think I'm ever going to hear from him," Rebecca said. Actually, she *knew* she wasn't.

Again, it took him a while to answer. "Never

saw anyone fall that hard, either," he said. "One minute, he'd be his normal pig-headed, surly self, and then resupply would come, and he'd be sitting in his hole with a dumb grin on his face."

Before Tet, she'd *seen* that dumb, cocky grin.

"I don't know, Rebecca," he said. "I think he's just the kind of guy who is what he is, and I don't think any of us — you, me, the U.S. Army — were ever going to be able to change that."

No. Probably not. "So — what do I do?" Rebecca asked.

Sergeant Hanson shrugged, painfully. "Go home. Find yourself that Harvard guy he was always worried about."

Harvard guys had never done a damn thing for her. Milquetoast men. She sighed. "I don't know why we ever came here, Walter." Personally, collectively, whatever.

"You got me," he said.

When they came to take him, she — once again — followed the gurney out to the ambulance, and they exchanged good-byes and good lucks, as they waited. Right before the corpsmen loaded him aboard, she leaned down to give him a kiss and, to her surprise, he lunged up to meet her, his arms firm across her back, the kiss turning into something very long, and real, and intense. When they pulled apart, she was almost *more* startled, automatically checking his dressings for staining, aware that the flush in her cheeks had very little to do with embarrassment. Regardless of whether any of the corpsmen had been watching.

"I'm sorry," he said, out of breath. "I guess I just wanted to do that once."

"I guess I did, too," she said. An *understatement*, it would seem.

They gripped hands tightly, and then the corpsmen came over and loaded him onto the ambulance, closing the doors. Rebecca watched it drive away, her arms wrapped across her chest, wishing him nothing if not Godspeed.

She had a very stressful night shift. First of all, she and Major Doyle barely managed to *nod* at each other, and then, later, she got in trouble for saving someone's life.

She had been alone in the ER, except for a corpsman, when a kid came in badly wounded, and in hypovolemic shock from the blood loss. He had a very faint, thready pulse, his veins were collapsed so that it was impossible to get an IV started, and she didn't have time to screw around — or wait for a doctor — so she just yelled for a cutdown set, and got to work. Nurses were *absolutely not* allowed to do cutdowns — which involved making an incision, going in to find a vein directly, and inserting an intracath so that fluids could be infused *quickly* — but, Christ, the ER was called *Emergency/Receiving* for a reason. Seconds later, she was able to get another line running into the subclavian, up by his neck, and then turn her attention to the severed artery near his groin — too high for a proper tourniquet — which was one of the main reasons he was bleeding out in the first place.

The damage was so bad that she had to keep her

hand in there to try and control the bleeding until a damn doctor finally got there — at which point she had been about ready to throw in some swift sutures herself — and then keep it there all the way down to the OR. When the doctors took over, she was fairly brusquely shoved aside, and okay, they were surgeons and she wasn't, but it was still kind of like being yanked out of the game while in the *middle* of an inside-the-park home run.

So she ended up standing alone in the ER, drenched with blood, half-crazed with adrenaline, her hand — no, actually, her whole *arm* — cramped and shaking from the long minutes of pressure against what was left of the artery. The pressure of fighting to keep a dying kid alive by sheer force of will had, as ever, taken its toll, too.

Later, when three separate doctors took turns upbraiding her for exceeding her authority, she suggested — forcefully — that she might not have had to *take* such drastic measures, if they had just *shown up*, for once. A remark which, unfortunately, only escalated the situation.

Jim McNulty was one of the three doctors, and although he had contributed his share of invective, when he was leaving, he muttered, "Nice work, incidentally."

Her response was both childish and vitriolic.

She was in no mood for Captain Turner when she came in a couple of hours later, but gave her a complete, and honest, report of the night's events, and then left at the first possible opportunity. After, of course, receiving further castigation.

Despite the fact that the boy had come through

the operation, and had already had his condition upgraded from critical to satisfactory.

She went over to the mess hall, and sat in her blood-stiffened uniform, mildly appalling herself by alternating spoonfuls of cold, thick, lumpy oatmeal, and lumpier cold grits. Recently, she and Karen and Annie had even greatly enjoyed a late night snack of sliced, straight-out-of-the-can Spam on very dry crackers. Her palate had definitely gone downhill.

Some of the other nurses and corpsmen coming off the night shift dragged her to a morning party — complete with a black light bulb, the Doors, and debauchery — and she went for a couple of hours, reeling over to her hootch, much the worse for wear, just before noon.

There were four new letters on her pillow — two from her mother, one from a cousin she only saw at funerals, and yet another from Michael. Since her judgment had been blunted by alcohol, she decided to read it.

He had written *Wednesday(?) night* in the top right corner, and they'd brought him in on Thursday morning, so she hoped — prayed — that this was the last one. But — either way — another drink might be in order.

Her balance was so unwieldy that she managed to bang into Truong, who was just coming out of Pat's cubby with an armload of crumpled sheets. Predictably, Truong did a lot of apologetic bowing and scraping — which kind of bugged her.

"No, it's *my* fault," she said. "*I'm* the ugly American here, not you."

Some of the sheets had spilled onto the floor, and she picked them up, almost toppling over in the process, Truong still jabbering on and bobbing her head, and — this woman was her mother's age, why didn't she just yell at her for not looking where she was going? Christ, she had really *had* it with Vietnam. She pushed the sheets into Truong's arms, mumbling *"xin lỗi"* about five times, and continued on her way to the common room, grabbing a Budweiser out of the refrigerator.

She had to slug down half of it before she could get beyond *Dear Rebecca*.

Hot as hell today, and I'm out of bug juice. Managed to slide about fifteen feet into this lousy gully — rocks all over — and my knee looks like someone should be dribbling it around a gym. Fun.

One of the new guys flipped out this morning, and the new LT starts yelling at him, until Hanson had the doc from Three Squad come over and take his temperature, and it turned out the kid was half fried.

Another swell day in the Republic of.

So, Tokyo. Sydney would be better, but . . . I don't want you thinking I'm pressuring you or anything. We can do whatever you want to do, right? I can't stop thinking about it, though.(well, okay — yeah.) But then, I keep thinking about sitting in a restaurant, and you're there, and it's just like we're on a date or something. Like normal *people. Or I picture us, at a movie. And me opening the car door for you, and all that normal, ordinary stuff. Sometimes, especially late at night, pulling guard, I get this weird feeling I might have made you up or something. You know? Or I try to figure out what you're doing, if you're working or whatever, and if you're okay, and if you would even have talked to me, back in the World.*

Is it just me, or am I being kind of a mopey son-of-a-bitch here? I should probably just rip this up, and start over, but Snoopy gave it to me, and it was his last piece. Besides, I try to write true stuff to you, even if it seems stupid when I look at it. Like — this seems stupid.

So, I hope you're okay, and that your new head nurse is being less of a jerk lately. (Did you try slapping her? Might work. Or get the foxy major to do it for you — tell her I said so.)

He'd probably told her himself.

Got a new picture of Otis today. Little paper crown, daisies on his collar, pink towel over his back. Apparently, he's supposed to be "King of the May Parade." What the hell. I have to say, he looks pretty cool.

Love(!),
Mike

A normal person would cry.

Chapter Thirteen

She got about half as much sleep as she needed, but luckily, it was a slow night. A couple of flurries of activity, a few routine accidents, some dysentery, fevers of unknown origin, and malaria. By midnight, she was at the desk, sipping a Coke and doing paperwork, while Haystack, her farmboy corpsman, took a quick nap on one of the gurneys.

The doors from Pre-Op quietly opened, and when she looked up, she saw — big surprise — the Chief Nurse.

Gee. Maybe they were going to circle each other some more.

Major Doyle paused on her way across the room to run her finger along a couple of the shelves, examining it carefully for dust each time, and then brushing it off on her pantsleg. Which was annoying, but also amusing. Then, she sat down in the chair next to the desk, her back perfectly straight.

The very model of a modern major.

"So," Rebecca said.

"So," Major Doyle said.

They looked at each other.

"Still steamed?" Rebecca asked.

Major Doyle nodded.

"Me, too," Rebecca said, and reached into one of her envelope pockets, taking out a Hershey's bar and setting it on the desk between them. The real stuff — not the Army tropical kind — that her mother had sent her, and she always kept in the hootch refrigerator, so they didn't melt. Much.

"Is that supposed to appease me?" Major Doyle asked.

Okay. Rebecca took out a second candy bar, placing it next to the first one, carefully lining up the corners.

Major Doyle looked at the candy. "Well," she said, and picked one up. "You're on the right track."

"Tastes better if you unwrap it first," Rebecca said.

Major Doyle took a large bite out of the bar, foil and all.

Rebecca shook her head. "You've been in the army too long."

Major Doyle nodded, picking little bits of paper and tin foil out of her mouth, and they looked at each other. There was still a tangible charge of tension in the air, but it had definitely eased.

"Rough week?" Major Doyle asked.

She nodded. Right up there with Christmas.

"I really *was* trying to do my best," Major Doyle said.

Yeah.

They sat without speaking.

"You push me around a lot, Maggie," Rebecca said finally.

Major Doyle shrugged. "And you push *back*."

Yeah. But, still. She took a deep breath, then let it out. "I hate it that he talked to *you*, and not to me."

Major Doyle nodded.

"So — I got mad," Rebecca said.

Major Doyle grinned wryly. "That part, I figured out."

It would have been pretty hard to miss. She reached for the other candy bar, eluding the instant swipe Major Doyle made at her hand. A casual acquaintance might assume that she was kidding — but Rebecca suspected that such was not, in fact, the case.

They ate their candy bars, Rebecca breaking hers into small neat pieces, Major Doyle indiscriminately gobbling. The ER was still, except for Haystack's sporadic snores, and the loud hums of the refrigerator and the nearest outside generator.

"The OR business didn't help matters any," Major Doyle said, crumpling her empty wrapper.

Well — no. Right decision, or not. Losing interest in eating, Rebecca pushed what was left of the candy over to her, crunching an antacid and taking a sip of Coke instead.

The refrigerator — already on its last legs — was making noisy shudders and ominous clankings now, and Major Doyle leaned over, giving it a solid thump with her boot, the machine kicking back into its normal hum. Sometimes, when people were upset or frustrated, they went over and pounded the thing even when it *wasn't* acting up.

"I wasn't mad," Rebecca said, "so much as, um — jealous." Insanely so.

Major Doyle shrugged, eating the small, neat pieces. Two at a time. "Sure. He was having a hard time talking to you."

Well, that was *part* of it. And she might as well spit the rest of it out. "Because you're so much prettier than I am," she said. "And he really — " lusts after — "likes you."

Major Doyle stared at her. "Are you serious?"

Oh, yeah, like she didn't know. "He's crazy about you," Rebecca said. "And I'm just — " Second-best. "I'm not — " A woman anyone would look at twice, unless he was in Vietnam — and desperate. She shook her head, and pulled the right desk drawer open, helping herself to a couple of aspirin.

"Do me a favor, Rebecca," Major Doyle said, "and look in a mirror sometime, okay? Just — give it a try."

Yeah, funny. Rebecca swallowed the aspirin, chasing them with another antacid.

"The ankle, or your head?" Major Doyle asked.

Both.

The refrigerator hummed, and shuddered, and hummed again.

"Am I going to hear from him?" Rebecca asked.

Major Doyle sighed. "He was still in shock — I don't think he knew what he was doing."

That didn't sound too good. "Did he tell you stuff in confidence?" Rebecca asked.

Major Doyle looked uncomfortable.

Great.

"Give him some time," Major Doyle said. "His whole life was blown apart — it'll take a while to adjust."

She just wished she could be there to help him through it. "Do you — " she hesitated — "think bad things can happen to other people because of something terrible *you* did?"

"No," Major Doyle said gently. "I don't think that at all."

The thought of other people getting punished, for *her* transgressions, was sickening, but too many of the people she cared about the most weren't exactly getting through life intact. "If my friend Billy had made it home, I would have married him," she said.

Major Doyle looked at her thoughtfully. "I don't think you've ever talked about Billy."

She'd never discussed Billy with *anyone* — even Doug. "He was my brother's best friend," Rebecca said. "And so, naturally, I fell in love with him when I was about thirteen." She always tried to remember his freckles and the constant grin, and not the fact that a mortar round had torn all of that apart. "He was in the Fourth Marines, and — well, it destroyed my family almost as much as it did his. I mean, we haven't heard from *Doug* in — " Could she tell a person whose entire life had revolved around the military about her brother? Without being hated? "He, um — I guess they don't have mailboxes up there in Canada," she said finally.

Major Doyle blinked, but she didn't react otherwise.

"And so, what do *I* do," Rebecca said, "but give

my mother the real knock-down blow, by signing up."

"First big, terrible sin?" Major Doyle asked.

Rebecca nodded.

"People die in wars," Major Doyle said. "And people get maimed — and it has nothing to do with being a good, or a bad person, or any shade in between."

War, the perpetual cruel joke. "So, Billy, and *Wolf*, and Spike, and *Michael* — they're all just aberrations?" She shook her head. As far as she was concerned, God should have the guts to punish *her*, personally, and lay the hell off everyone else she knew.

"It would be nice if it could be clear," Major Doyle said. Mused, really. "A life for a life, and so forth." She glanced over. "If it had been a *grenade*, instead of Pabst."

Much too astute for her own good.

"You know." Major Doyle opened the refrigerator, reaching behind the bags of blood for a Coke. "There's an ugly rumor going around that you overstepped your bounds last night and — among other invasive and ambitious procedures — did a cutdown."

So she *had* heard about that. Rebecca avoided her eyes.

"The interesting codicil to the story," Major Doyle said, "is that a boy from Scranton is alive today, because he was fortunate enough to come across someone with the ability, if not the medical authority, to save his life."

Codicil. Rebecca shrugged self-consciously.

"According to Jim," Major Doyle said, "they were all so damn impressed that they almost forgot to yell at you."

The operative word being — almost.

Major Doyle studied her over the Coke can as she tipped it up to her mouth. "There seems to be little doubt that you'd be happier being a doctor, than you are as a nurse."

Yeah. So? Rebecca frowned at her. "Who says I have the right to be happy?"

Major Doyle frowned back. "Who made *you* the All-Powerful Supreme Being who decides these things?"

This conversation was going to drive them straight back into not speaking. She had taken a life, thereby forfeiting her future chances for good fortune. Simple as that.

"Do you remember the Richard Speck case?" Major Doyle asked suddenly.

Rebecca nodded. It was a hard one to forget. A guy who had broken into an apartment building in Chicago a couple of years before, and killed eight nursing students. Only one of the nurses there that night had been able to escape, after hiding under a bed.

"I've always wondered," Major Doyle said, "how he managed it. One man, one knife — eight women. Obviously, they were very afraid, but —" She stopped, shaking her head. "I guess I wonder if I would *also* go quietly, and cooperatively, to my death."

Rebecca frowned, not sure where this was going.

Major Doyle was frowning even harder. "If someone came in here," she gestured around the room, "and held one of you hostage, and we couldn't talk him down — even if it meant sacrificing the one person, in order to save the rest of you — *that* would be the decision I'd have to make."

Kind of like triage. Cold, dispassionate — and very, very rational. "Oh, come on," Rebecca said, sarcastically. "You mean, you wouldn't exchange *yourself* for the hostage?"

Major Doyle looked at her. A rather withering look. "I think we both know that *you* would beat me to it."

Yes, she was the proud owner of an extremely tarnished hero complex. "I'd save you," Rebecca said, aware that she was probably only half-kidding. "I'd save *all* of you."

"Die trying, more likely," Major Doyle said wryly.

Much more likely.

Pabst.

"If the two of us were out in the jungle," Major Doyle said, "and that young soldier was going to kill me, and you had that gun — would you hesitate?"

No. Rebecca shook her head — without hesitating.

"And, if it were Michael?" Major Doyle asked. "Or Annie, or your family, or any one of a number of people?"

"I would shoot him," Rebecca said quietly.

Major Doyle nodded.

If she hadn't just taken two aspirin, she'd swallow a couple more. Instead, she pressed her somewhat cool soda can against her forehead for a few seconds, the headache strongest right above her eyes.

"You *fought back*," Major Doyle said. "You saved yourself. And that boy from Scranton isn't the only person who's alive today because you did."

Time to throw her own words back at her. "I thought you said it doesn't work that way," Rebecca said.

"No," Major Doyle agreed. "Because, with the number of lives you save on a regular basis, you would have *long* since tipped the scales."

During Tet alone, they'd all saved a hell of a lot of lives. None of which had taken her off the hook.

Major Doyle looked at her seriously. "I've seen you at your very worst, Rebecca. So, what does it say that I still absolutely treasure, and value, you as a human being?"

Rebecca grinned at her. "Says you're pretty hard up."

Major Doyle didn't smile back. In fact, she looked furious. "I'm not kidding, Rebecca. Tossing that off belittles *my* value to *you*."

Conversations with true intellectual equals were exhausting. Rebecca rubbed the sides of her head, gradually massaging her way in to the bridge of her nose, spending extra time above her eyes.

"I suggest you give that some thought," Major Doyle said. Not smiling.

The lights in the ER were too bright, so she rested her head on her arms briefly. Then, she looked up.

"How short are you?" she asked.

Now, Major Doyle looked tense. "Nineteen days."

Jesus. "Am I going to hear from *you* again?" she asked.

Major Doyle hesitated. "I don't know very much about staying in touch with people. It's — not something I've ever really done."

Great. "So," Rebecca said, "*twenty* days from now, it'll be like I never knew you?"

Major Doyle hesitated some more. "I don't know."

Terrific. Yet another person in her life exiting permanently.

"I'm going to try," Major Doyle said. "And normally, I don't even *try*."

Not terribly comforting.

Major Doyle sighed. "I'm facing my immediate future with a great deal of trepidation, Rebecca, and — I don't know *what* the hell I'm going to end up doing."

"Get out of the Army," Rebecca said, "presumably."

Major Doyle patted the pocket where she kept her cigarettes. "I don't know," she said, sounding almost — skittish. "I'm not sure I can find a place for myself, as a civilian."

"I don't think you have a monopoly on that one, Maggie," Rebecca said. She couldn't imagine having to go back to the World *herself*.

Major Doyle nodded, drinking the last of her Coke, and then flipping the can towards the nearest wastebasket. It went in — of *course* — with a loud clang, the noise waking up Haystack, who looked guilty, and jumped off the gurney, grabbing a mop.

Major Doyle just shook her head, then looked

back at Rebecca. "So. Do you have any additional snack foods?"

Rebecca shook her head.

"How devastating," Major Doyle said, and stood up to go.

The news about Bobby Kennedy being assassinated came in a couple of days later, and although Rebecca had thought that nothing could shock her anymore, *that* did. Jesus. With Dr. King, and the riots, and now *this* — America was as insane as everyone over here. The thought of going back there in the near future was rapidly becoming as terrifying as the idea of having to stay in Vietnam forever.

Her own personal conundrum.

The night before Major Doyle left, they had a big party for her at the O Club, but no one was surprised when the guest of honor barely made an appearance. Rebecca drank her share — and Jim McNulty never left the bar, silently getting plastered. Without question, the morose victim of a very recent breakup. Turning down the predictable, enthusiastic offers of accompaniment from a couple of drunk pilots, she decided to take a walk on up to the chapel, stuffing cans of beer into various pockets. Unless she missed her guess, the guest of honor was going to be easy to find.

And indeed, as soon as she walked around to the darkest side of the building, she saw the bright glow of a cigarette. She sat down next to her, cracking open one of her many beers.

"He's in total despair," she said.

Major Doyle shrugged, staring straight ahead at

the hootches below them, and there was just enough light for Rebecca to be able to make out the tearstains on her cheeks. "What was I supposed to do, make matters worse by giving him false hopes?"

Rebecca took a few gulps of Schlitz. "I'm just telling you."

"Well — thanks," Major Doyle said, her voice slurring, and Rebecca saw that she was working on a fifth of Johnny Walker Black. Making plenty of progress, too.

"Will we all still drink like this?" she asked. "When we get home?"

Major Doyle shrugged, drinking. "My father's been drunk since 1952."

Oh.

It was hot, but there were lots of mosquitoes, so Rebecca rolled her sleeves down, and turned her collar up, to avoid as many bugs as possible.

"I've looked into extending for a few months," Major Doyle said, "but they've got so many officers waiting to get their tickets punched that they want to push us in and out of our commands as quickly as possible." She shook her head. "Ridiculous way to run a war."

Granted, but — "Why would you want to *stay*?" Rebecca asked.

"Oh, I don't know." Major Doyle fumbled her cigarette into the sand, swore, and lit another. "Keep my eye on a deeply depressed lieutenant, maybe."

Yeah, right. "I think I can manage to take care of myself," Rebecca said.

Major Doyle looked over, seeming to be having

some trouble getting her eyes to focus. "So — you won't do anything stupid?"

Rebecca shook her head. Nothing stupider than usual.

"Good." Major Doyle slugged away at her bottle. "You'll all like Gwen Coggeshall. We served together at Fort Sam, and she's — unflappable."

The new Chief Nurse, who — so far — Rebecca had only seen from a distance. She was large. "Is she going to like *me*?" Rebecca asked.

Major Doyle grinned around the mouth of the bottle. "She'll think you're a pistol."

Well — okay. Sounded more promising than Captain Turner. She finished her beer, and opened another. They might as well *both* get ripped.

"I am — " Major Doyle took a deep breath — "unlikely to be able to say a satisfactory good-bye."

Really? Rebecca laughed.

"I don't know where I'm going to be, but — " Major Doyle reached into her shirt pocket — missing twice — and pulled out a folded file card. "You can reach me through my father."

Rebecca took the card, sticking it in her own pocket. "Why would I go and do that? I like just cutting people off."

Major Doyle was obviously drunk enough not to be sure if she was kidding. "Well — " she frowned — "please do me the courtesy of at least letting me know that you have, once again, set foot on American soil."

Jesus. What a stiff. "Can I send it C.O.D.?" Rebecca asked.

"Sure," Major Doyle said, expansively. "Two-star generals love that sort of humor."

No doubt. She couldn't think of anything else to say, so she listened to the usual Vietnam sounds of outgoing artillery, air traffic, crickets, young male voices, and twangy country music.

"I'll miss our merry chats," Major Doyle said.

Rebecca laughed. "I'll think of you, whenever I enjoy snack foods."

Major Doyle smiled, but then looked worried again. "You *are* going to make it out of here, right?"

Rebecca nodded. It was, in fact, a top priority. "Count on it," she said.

Chapter Fourteen

Lieutenant Colonel Coggeshall — good old New England name — turned out to be cheerful and hearty, with the booming voice of a girls' gym teacher. Wry asides and soft-spoken suggestions were — instantly — a thing of the past.

As promised, Major Doyle's official farewell consisted of an abrupt hug, and swift striding away. Rebecca didn't watch the helicopter take off, because — well, she just didn't. There was plenty of work to do, and as ever, that's what she did.

With the change at the top, the atmosphere at the hospital changed dramatically. More easygoing, somewhat *less* efficient. On the other hand, their casualty load had gone down a little since the May offensive, and that might be part of it, too.

Whenever her mail came, she quickly fanned out the envelopes, searching for Michael's neat, sharp handwriting, but it was never there. The only person she heard from regularly was her mother, and the only news of note was that Doug had called from some unknown, faraway pay phone for a three-minute hello. He was doing okay, working in a restaurant — and very upset when he found out that his little sister was in Vietnam. So, they didn't know *where* he was okay, but they knew *that* he was okay.

She got a very short note from a certain cerebral major, with a new address at Walter Reed Army Medical Center in Washington, D.C., and "I know, I know, *don't* say it" written underneath.

Time seemed to drag, and disappear, at the same time. The highlight of each day was when she got to cross off another box on her calendar. Marking it with a thick, black, and very satisfying X.

Annie was one of the only ones left who remembered that she had — had a bad Christmas — and it was a relief to no longer be a subject of sympathy and concern. Actually, since she had been in-country longer than almost anyone else at the hospital, she had now become a source of counsel and advice for half the nurses on staff. The terribly nearsighted and amblyopic leading the blind.

Lieutenant Colonel Coggeshall would lumber into the ER as the day shift started, and boom, "Good morning, Lieutenant! How are you today?!" "Good morning, ma'am! Fine, ma'am!" Rebecca would yell back, never sure if the new Chief Nurse simply didn't mind being tweaked — or thought everyone bellowed their way through life.

She was going over some requisition forms with Captain Turner one morning when Lieutenant Colonel Coggeshall appeared to confront her, clutching her 201 file.

"Lieutenant!" she said.

"Hi!" Rebecca said, and Captain Turner looked displeased.

"It has come to my attention," Lieutenant Colonel Coggeshall waved the file, "that you have neglected to take your R & R."

The other shoe had finally fallen, after lo these many months. "You're mistaken, ma'am," Rebecca said. "I went to Taipei. It was *swell*."

Lieutenant Colonel Coggeshall peered at her suspiciously over her half-glasses.

"Five days and nights of unremitting fun," Rebecca said.

Lieutenant Colonel Coggeshall peered at the file now. "It's not in your records."

"Well — " Rebecca looked sad — "I hate to be the one to say it, but that Major we had before was a slacker."

"Oh, shut up, Lieutenant," Captain Turner said, taking her clipboard away from her and going over the supply lists alone.

Rebecca looked down at her empty hands, then up at Lieutenant Colonel Coggeshall. "It's, it's like being — defrocked, ma'am," she said, making herself sound frail.

"Shut up, Lieutenant," Lieutenant Colonel Coggeshall said cheerfully. "And be advised that you're leaving in the next available slot."

No way. Rebecca took two running — and then, two limping — steps to catch her. "Ma'am," she said, no longer boisterous. "If I put part of one foot out of this country for *part* of one second — I am *never* coming back."

Lieutenant Colonel Coggeshall frowned. "Are you continuing to play with me here?"

"*No*," Rebecca said.

Lieutenant Colonel Coggeshall looked her over, then slapped the file shut. "Humph," she said, and walked away.

The next thing Rebecca knew, she and Annie were both given three-day passes for an *in-*country R & R at China Beach. Annie, who had gone to Bangkok on her R & R a month before and had nothing but fun, thought this extra-added trip was a very terrific idea, and they spent most of the three days either sleeping on the beach, or sleeping in a very small and sandy transient officers' barracks. Wherever they went, men insisted upon buying them steaks, and drinks, and being otherwise charming, and — finding herself caught up in Annie's bubbly enthusiasm — Rebecca had a much better time than she would have expected.

The best part was getting to sleep for ten hours straight three days in a row.

They got back to the hospital just in time to help with a mass-cal of twelve critical cases and fifteen walking wounded, and within ten minutes, it was like never having been away at all.

She had a lot of mail piled up — none of it from Michael, *damn* — but, surprisingly, there *was* a letter from her father. Just holding the envelope made her nervous, and she couldn't bring herself to open it until she was alone in the ER late that night, with Haystack helping out down in the workroom.

Had she gotten a letter from her father all year? No. Notes on some of her mother's letters, and occasional boxes full of hard-to-find medical supplies. In the boxes, he would enclose a page with a few concise sentences, specifically related to the supplies within. She always thought of them as being textbook-tender.

She looked at the envelope, tapping it against her left hand with her right. Most of the doctors she knew took a strange pride in their illegibility, but her father had the handwriting of a poet. And — unlike most doctors — he didn't use abbreviations and acronyms in all possible situations.

For what it was worth, he didn't golf, either.

Dear Rebecca:

A colon, for Christ's sake.

I hope this finds you well, and safe.

It sounded almost as if they had — met on a bus once.

I've just been sitting here in the den, thinking about you. (They lost again — blew a 6–0 lead in the late innings. How a team can fall so far, so fast is beyond me.) I sit, night after night, watching the news, and try to imagine you over there in the middle of all that carnage. I look at the pictures you've sent your mother, and it still doesn't seem possible. I realize, also, that I don't even know how you feel about the war. It disturbs me that I've not the vaguest notion — about that, and so many other things — and disturbs me all the more that this percolates in my brain when you're half a world away, as opposed to across the breakfast table.

After Doug left, their breakfasts — her mother pretty much stopped getting up for them — had tended towards suppressed anger, masked by lovely table manners, and occasional pleasantries.

Your mother's silences fill the house these days, and I wonder, often, if I will ever be able to get any of you to forgive me. I recognize my culpability, without knowing how to rectify the situation.

Scary to think that her *entire* family spoke that way.

I can only hope that you're not still as angry as you were when you left.

Well, he was out of luck *there*.

I know you won't believe it, but I'm really very sorry about everything. Clearly, I'm not a demonstrative man —

Oh, *really*? Then again, in many ways, much as she wanted to be, she was not a demonstrative woman.

— but I don't think I've ever really understood what you wanted from me. Simple respect, perhaps. It's hard for me to believe I can have failed so utterly with both *of my children, but the evidence is indisputable. Over this past year, I have spent time wondering if I've destroyed so many vital structures that I'll never be able to repair the damage.*

The lapse into surgical imagery was inevitable.

At this stage, you may not even want me to do so. I'm not sure I'd know where to start, but I am sorry. I do love you. I have never not loved you.

Not a bad start, as starts went.

I don't know what else to say, but you'll be home in a very few weeks now, and I thought I should try to say something. I just wish I could do a less clumsy job of it.

Please keep yourself safe, Beckalou — your mother and I never stop worrying.

> *Love, from your father*

Her father was the only person in the world who had ever called her Beckalou — and *he* probably hadn't done so for about ten years.

She read the letter through again, trying to make sense of it. Had her mother dictated it, maybe? If she were a better person, her anger would probably just nicely, sweetly, dissipate, but — she was her father's child. Plain and simple. They both walked around, full of arrogance and acrimony, characteristics covered by the barest veneer of deceptive charm. They were good on asperity and acerbity, too. Why her mother put up with *either* of them was beyond her.

She read through the letter a third time. She didn't have a whole lot to say, but she might as well try writing back. Address it to him at his office so she could be sure that her mother wouldn't read it. Although she'd have to hold off on *total* honesty, since he might show it to her later.

Dear Dad,

I don't really know what to say. It's been quiet for a couple of hours, but we had two kids in here tonight who are going to wake up tomorrow morning without genitals. Another two, paralyzed. A kid with his face and arms blown off, who we hoped was dead, but he wasn't. So many burn cases that even though the place has been mopped and cleaned twice, it still reeks of it. Maybe it's just in my uniform — I can't tell anymore. I'm sitting here with a cup of coffee that tastes like Lysol, and I'm so far gone, I wish it was a drink. I wish it was about ten *drinks.*

I also wish I knew what to say. I don't. I know I've never been able to live up to any of your expectations, but — I'm not even really sure what your expectations are. Married, and living on Ocean Avenue? A secretary in some G.P.'s office? I'd like to be someone you could respect. I'd like to be someone I could respect. I feel kind of like that damn village they destroyed, in order to save it. So, I know I'm not supposed to be angry, but I'm never *not angry anymore. Sometimes, I think I should just stay here, and* never *come back. Never let anyone see what I've become. In fact —*

She was beginning to get the feeling that this was a letter she was never going to send.

After carrying the thing around for two days, unfinished, she finally tossed it into a barrel where a corpsman was burning some infectious waste, and sent her father a "thank you for your letter, I hope we can make things better, too, see you soon" note. It was the coward's way out, and she didn't admire herself for it, but what else was new?

The main thing was that she was short. Very short. For over eleven months, she had been dourly fatalistic, but now, she was so jittery that something as simple as someone popping open a can of soda nearby sent her diving to the floor. She only had twenty-five days left, and she began to worry that she was never going to make it.

Then, it was twenty.

Fifteen.

Twelve.

She was in her workroom after her night shift, setting up instrument trays when Rosario came in to get her.

"Some guy's looking for you, LT," he said.

Everyone she knew was *gone*, so it had to be a former patient. Sometimes, they came back to say hi, either to show everyone how happy they were to be okay, or because they were *worried* about being okay, and being sent back out to the field.

She followed Rosario out to the ER, and he pointed up at the main doors, where a very thin black kid in fatigues and a boonie hat was leaning. A stranger. She was tired, and not feeling terribly chatty, but she put on a smile and headed over there.

Captain Turner, who was busy nit-picking and overseeing, stopped her on the way. "Did you finish the setups?"

"I will in a minute," Rebecca said, and kept going. As short as she was, not even Captain Turner was likely to give her any grief. "Uh, hi," she said, when she was a couple of feet away from the kid. "They said you were looking for me?"

He looked up, and despite his face being cadaverously gaunt and sad, she recognized him right away. *Snoopy.*

"Do you remember me, Lieutenant?" he asked.

"My God, *of course,*" she said. "Are you okay? What are you doing here?"

He looked at her unhappily. "I'm going home."

Thank God for *that.* "Oh, I'm so glad, Snoopy," she said. "When?"

He touched his right shirt pocket, and she heard paper crackle inside. His orders.

"*Good.*" She wasn't sure if he would mind, but she hugged him, anyway. "I'm really glad."

He nodded, not really hugging back, and she released him, feeling a little embarrassed.

"Is he okay?" Snoopy asked, with true anguish in his eyes. "Did he make it home?"

Oh, that son of a bitch. It was bad enough that he had dropped *her,* but Snoopy was supposed to be his best friend. "I think so," she said, and suddenly felt sick, wondering if something awful and unforeseen *could* have happened to him. Respiratory arrest, uncontrolled infection, *suicide* — "He was stable when he left here," she said, too loudly. "They transferred him to Japan."

"You mean —" Snoopy looked sort of stunned — "he hasn't written to *you?*"

Rebecca shook her head.

Snoopy frowned. "I thought it was just me. Like, he got back to the World, and up and remembered he was Whitey."

Up and remembered that Elizabeth was the most

wonderful, and beautiful, girl on earth. "I don't know," Rebecca said. "I wish I did."

Snoopy nodded, his hands stuffed deep in his pockets. Then, he looked around. "I know you're busy as can be, ma'am," he said. "I didn't mean to come by bothering you, I just thought — "

Rebecca held up her hand for him to wait, then took a couple of steps in Captain Turner's direction. "You mind if I leave?" she asked.

Captain Turner shrugged without much interest. "Your shift ended over three hours ago."

Rebecca nodded, then looked at Snoopy. "You have time for some coffee, or — ?"

"Yes, ma'am," he said quickly. "Sure do."

She nodded, motioning for him to follow her outside.

It was too early for lunch, so the mess wasn't crowded, and they took their coffee over to a table by the screened side of the room, where it — might — be a little cooler. She put in her usual scant teaspoon of sugar, while he shoveled four in, and two of powdered cream. It was wonderful to see a kid from the field going home *whole*, and she couldn't stop smiling at him.

"I'm really glad you're leaving," she said.

He took a small, polite sip of his coffee. "How short are you, ma'am?"

"I'm so short I need an elevator to get out of bed," she said, and for the first time, saw a flicker of the sweet smile she remembered.

"That's good, ma'am," he said. "That makes me real happy."

She nodded, and they looked at each other.

"I loved him a lot, ma'am," Snoopy said. "If, you know, a guy can love a guy."

Rebecca nodded. A guy could definitely love a guy.

"Our LT heard the Sarge made it okay?" Snoopy said, looking at her for confirmation.

"Yeah, he was okay. He was badly hurt, but —" she found herself grinning — "he seemed to be getting his second wind."

"So, you saw him?" Snoopy said.

Rebecca nodded, and grinned. What Sinatra was to singing, Walter Hanson was to kissing.

"It got real bad out there," Snoopy said, both hands gripping his chipped mug, "after we lost him, and the Sarge. I mean, it's kind of hard to explain, but they were like the *enforcers*. When they were there, everyone *acted* right, you know? In the villages and all."

Rebecca nodded.

"Except," he said uncertainly, "you being so nice and good and all, you maybe *don't* know."

She sighed. "I know all too well, Snoopy."

He looked at her, deep pain in his eyes. "Things got *real* bad, ma'am. I mean, mostly it wasn't fighting anymore, it was *hurting* people. You know? Breaking the rules."

She nodded. There had been so many rumors about atrocities since Tet that she had always known that some — maybe even *more* than some — of them had to be true.

Snoopy was hunched in his chair, not looking at her. "I wasn't *doing* it, but — Meat and the Sarge, they would have *stopped* it, and — guys would've listened up. I just — I didn't have any buddies left, and — there was this one guy, Mojo, and we'd just go away, you know? Sit down in the road or something, like we didn't know them.''

Rebecca nodded. Judging from the stories boys had told her, the scared onlookers generally felt much more responsible than the actual participants.

"I just — wanted it to be over,'' he said unhappily.

Sounded familiar. She reached over to push his boonie hat into a tilt. "What matters is that you're okay, and you're going home, and you're *out* of the damn war.'' Which sounded more like the cerebral major's philosophy, than her own. "Just go home, and do your best. Do all the things you've always wanted to do. And — be happy, Snoopy. You deserve it.''

Snoopy nodded, looking very *un*happy.

"He *loved* you,'' Rebecca said. "He couldn't stand it that they left you alone out there. Whatever his problem is now, it doesn't have anything to do with you.''

Snoopy didn't seem convinced, but he nodded.

She should, in no way, lay her insecurities on this poor sad kid. Even though he was the only one who might really know the answer. "Do you think he, um, cared about *me* a little?'' she asked.

Snoopy's grin flashed. "You were only 'bout *all* he talked about. He'd be all smiley, which is surely *not* like the Meat *I* knew. He was just real nervous, on account of you're smart as can be, and it seemed like he should study up.''

Her intelligence was regularly overrated.

"He always — " Snoopy stopped. "Is it okay if he let me read with him, since lots of times, I didn't get any mail, and I could pretend-like I did?"

Michael was a total son-of-a-bitch for not letting this sweet kid know he was okay. "Of course," she said. "I wrote hi to you in most of them, anyway."

He nodded, smiling at her. "I know I don't know you, but it made me feel like I did."

She didn't know him very well, either, but that didn't change the fact that she felt a very strong connection. Friendship, and love. "If I gave you my address," she said, "and you heard from him, would you let me know that he's okay?"

He nodded, taking the pen she handed him, and scribbling on a napkin. "Would you let me know, too? Ma'am?"

"*Rebecca*," she said, and reached for another napkin.

Chapter Fifteen

Ten days left.

Nine.

Eight.

Seven.

Six.

Only, now that she thought about it, maybe she wasn't ready to go home yet. If she stayed here longer, she wouldn't have to finish up her two-year hitch stateside, and being here, bad as it was, probably made more sense than feeling hopeless and alone in the middle of the Land of Plenty. The World.

After a year, *Vietnam* had become her world.

So, as soon as she got off shift, she went down to the chief nurse's office, tapping on the door, even though it was already open.

Lieutenant Colonel Coggeshall looked up from a mound of files and papers. "Lieutenant!" she said, sounding tickled to see her. "Come in!"

Rebecca nodded, and sat in the metal folding chair. Being in this room made her miss Maggie profoundly, but then again, this wasn't a conversation they could have had.

"So!" Lieutenent Colonel Coggeshall slapped the top folder shut. "What can I do for you, Lieutenant?"

"Well — " She should just spit it out before she lost her nerve. "I, uh, wanted to see you about extending, ma'am."

"Extending," Lieutenant Colonel Coggeshall said.

Rebecca nodded, her hands folded in her lap.

Lieutenant Colonel Coggeshall didn't say anything, leaning back and cracking her knuckles. A sound that Rebecca had always hated, and drove her father, the surgeon, to instant, virulent nausea.

"Yes, ma'am," she said. "For six months."

Lieutenant Colonel Coggeshall cracked her knuckles again, then smacked her hands flat against the desk, Rebecca flinching. "She *said* you'd pull this."

Well, they hadn't called her Miss Perfect for nothing. "I know there's a lot of paperwork," Rebecca said, "and I thought I should — "

Lieutenant Colonel Coggeshall shook her head. "Not a single chance in hell."

The Army was supposed to *like* it when people re-upped. "I just need the forms, ma'am," Rebecca said. "So I can fill them out, and — "

Lieutenant Colonel Coggeshall shook her head firmly.

Ten thousand miles away — and the woman was still trying to run her life. "*You're* the chief nurse, ma'am," Rebecca said. "So, it's really your — "

Lieutenant Colonel Coggeshall cut her off. "She told me that if I allowed you to stay here even one minute after your tour was up, that she would hunt me down and hurt me."

Oh, big deal. Rebecca shrugged. "That sounds like hyperbole, ma'am."

"Maybe," Lieutenant Colonel Coggeshall agreed cheerfully, "but the Doyle temper is *legendary*." She opened the top folder in the big pile. "Get out of here."

Being pushed around in a jolly way was *still* being pushed around. "What's my next step, ma'am?" Rebecca asked. "Should I —"

"You should *pack*," Lieutenant Colonel Coggeshall said.

Rebecca frowned. "So, you're saying I have no recourse, ma'am? Even if —"

"Is that a little fly buzzing in my office?" Lieutenant Colonel Coggeshall asked her coffee cup.

No. It was an extremely irked second lieutenant. "You can use every good ER nurse you can get," Rebecca said. "And I have a solid year of —"

Lieutenant Colonel Coggeshall peered at her over her glasses. "Lieutenant, you're so short I can't see you, *or* hear you."

Rebecca waited a few more seconds, realized she wasn't going to get anywhere, and stood up with her arms tight across her chest.

"*Legendary*," Lieutenant Colonel Coggeshall said, gaily, and waved her away.

Five days.
Four.
Three.

Right after she got into bed — after the second party in her honor in as many days, to celebrate her twenty-second birthday, not that she *cared* — mortars started coming in, and the alert siren went off. They were landing closer than usual, maybe even right up here on the hill, in the compound, and she was so scared that she couldn't move.

"You have your flak jacket on?" Karen yelled from the next room.

She was too scared to move as far as the bottom of the bed.

"Becky, you there?" Karen yelled.

She closed her eyes, gulping down a scream with each exploding crash, feeling the ground beneath the hootch vibrating up through the legs of her cot.

"You idiot!" Karen was in her room, forcing her into her flak jacket and helmet, as her own hung askew. "You want to get killed your last *week?* Get under the bed!"

If the hootch took a direct hit, they would all be trapped under jagged sheets of metal, and wooden beams. They would all be dead. *Pieces* of them would be — what if she was the only one who didn't die, and the rest of them were all —

Karen yanked at her arm, pulling her onto the floor. "Get under the damn bed!"

It was too small. She'd be *trapped.*

Karen swore again, dragging the mattress off the bed, and on top of her.

"You come under, too," Rebecca said shakily.

"*I'm* not short," Karen said, but got under the mattress.

The rounds kept coming — crashing, smashing, slamming — metal tearing, and wood splintering somewhere nearby — and Rebecca pressed her teeth into the thick edge of her flak jacket so she wouldn't scream. Her borrowed time had run out. She was *sure* of it. Barely twenty-two was *young*. Way *too* young. She wasn't ready to — the all-clear signal was coming through the loudspeakers now, but she stayed down, her arms covering her head.

"Becky," Karen said, either shouting, or calm — she couldn't tell. "They were landing all over, a lot of people are going to be hurt. We have to get down to triage."

The phone in the hall started ringing, and she could hear bare feet jumping into boots, and the screen door banging open and shut.

"Come *on*," Karen said.

Rebecca nodded, getting up and staggering outside after her.

They worked through the night, and into the next day. First, on countless casualties from around the base, and then, on the usual morning rush. It was a routine she could do in her sleep, and by lunchtime, she pretty much was. When she finally got off work, at about 2200, she was too tired to do anything but go straight to bed, barely waking up in time for her last shift.

Her last shift. Jesus.

It was pretty clear that she was going to be worthless, and after an early flurry of kids who had been waiting, bleeding, out at some firebase all night for a medevac to come in and get them, Captain Turner shunted her off to scut-work. Inventory, and cleaning, and restocking.

She was in the middle of counting narcotics with Annie when someone jabbed her in the shoulder.

"Lieutenant!" Lieutenant Colonel Coggeshall said, and handed her some neatly folded paper. "You are confirmed on the fourteen hundred to Cam Ranh Bay."

Rebecca took it, confused. Her orders. "What do you mean?"

"I mean, *good-bye*," Lieutenant Colonel Coggeshall said.

"But — " Rebecca blinked. Jesus. "I'm not supposed to leave until tomorrow."

"Fourteen hundred," Lieutenant Colonel Coggeshall said. "Don't be late."

Less than three hours. Jesus. She looked at Annie. "I'm not ready."

Annie shrugged. "You're packed, you passed your Golden Flow — " the urine tests they had to take to make sure they were drug-free; apparently, the Army didn't care about blood that was one hundred proof — "what the hell," she finished.

Yeah, but — "I'm not *ready*," Rebecca said.

Now, Captain Turner came over. "Consider yourself relieved, Lieutenant."

She *at least* needed one more day. If not another six months — or even another whole tour. Everyone she knew was here. Everything she knew how to *do* was here. She was used to being the *recipient* of the dazed hugs, and nervous promises. The one who got left behind.

"Go take a shower and get changed, so you'll have time to come back and say good-bye," Annie said.

Jesus. Say *good-bye?* Go *home?* Slowly, she handed over her clipboard, and headed for the doors.

It was hot as hell, and by the time she walked back to her room after her shower, she was already perspiring again. Her dress uniform smelled mildewed and musty, and when she put it on — the last time had been some dumb general's party she had been *ordered* to attend, months before — the damn thing hung on her even more than it always had. She must look like some moronic child playing dress-up.

Playing soldier.

The room was almost empty — she had either given everything away, or shipped it home. That way, she would only have to carry her duffel bag, and the cheesy black Army issue handbag. She stuffed her boots and fatigues into the duffel bag, along with her toothbrush and a few last-minute things. She had already bequeathed her spare tampons, and other such luxuries, to Karen and Annie.

Okay. She was packed. The room was bare. She sat down on the thin, battered mattress, her dress hat perched on her head, holding her little white gloves in one hand. She would expect to be crying, or nervous, or excited, but she didn't feel much of anything. Tired, maybe.

Her sheet-door slid to one side, and Truong came in, then stopped, looking surprised.

"Chào bà," Rebecca said. As far as she knew, hello and good-bye were the same in Vietnamese.

Truong rattled something at her, and since she motioned towards the duffel bag, Rebecca nodded.

"I'm going home," she said. "To America."

More rattling, the only part of which she recognized was "*chào cô.*" Good-bye, to an unmarried female.

"*Cám ơn,*" Rebecca said, which she was pretty sure was "thank you." If she knew how to say "good luck," she would have.

Truong bowed, and left the room, still talking.

Rebecca took most of the MPC she had, and went after her. "*Xin lỗi?*" she said, remembering at the last second that it was insulting to give someone Vietnamese a gift unless you held it out with *both* hands. Using just one was considered demeaning. "Um, *cám ơn. Chào bà.*"

Truong nodded, and smiled, showing betel-nut-stained teeth, tucking the money away in her blouse. Rebecca nodded and smiled too, feeling uncomfortable, then went back to her room.

She should probably go say good-bye now. She looked around one last time to make sure she had everything, and then again, just to look around. The room was *small*. Ugly.

The duffel bag was heavier than she'd expected, and she didn't argue when one of the MPs outside the compound offered to carry it down to the hospital for her. So many people yelled "good luck!" to her, a number of whom she didn't think she knew, that she figured they just saw the duffel bag and the dress uniform, and were glad to see someone getting *out*.

To her surprise, she even found it hard to say good-bye to Captain Turner, although Karen and Annie were obviously the worst. Karen was in the middle of surgery, her eyes looking stricken above her mask when she glanced up and saw Rebecca standing there in her dress uniform. She had five months left; Annie had about forty days. Since she was scrubbed in, and it was busy, they couldn't hug or anything, and were only able to exchange a few words. In the end, Rebecca found herself giving her a little salute, seeing Karen's eyes fill up in response.

Things in the ER were picking up, too, and most of the good-byes she got were on the run. Everyone seemed to be getting along just fine without her, and she felt very strange and detached, standing there watching. As soon as Annie was free, she hurried over, but then, neither of them knew what to say.

"We had a *really* good party planned for to-night," Annie said finally.

"Well — I'll be there in spirit," Rebecca said.

Annie nodded, looking down at her boots.

"You're next," Rebecca said.

Annie nodded. "Thirty-seven and counting."

Another stretcher case came in, and they both looked over as other staff members jumped to help the kid.

"Go," Rebecca said.

Annie nodded, but paused for one last second. "You done good, sport — no matter *what* you think."

She had *tried*, anyway. "You helped me get through," Rebecca said. "Thank you for that."

Annie nodded. "Take it easy on yourself, okay?"

Never happen. "Always," Rebecca said.

They clasped hands, and then Annie darted away to help as two more litters were rushed in.

She couldn't just *watch*, and since she no longer

worked here — Jesus — she lugged her duffel bag over to the door, feeling very small and lost, returning the waves she was given.

Outside, it was glaringly sunny. Hot. Familiar, and foreign.

The guy who was going to drive her up to the airstrip was waiting by a jeep, his OD cap tilted over his eyes. When he saw her, he straightened up, dropping his cigarette.

"You ready to go, ma'am?" he asked.

No. She nodded, pulling on her gloves and slinging her pocketbook over her shoulder as he lifted her duffel bag into the back. Her shoes had very sensible low heels, but she still felt clunky in them.

"Ma'am?" he asked, waiting.

She looked around. Another medevac coming in. Other helicopters landing and taking off, jets thundering, jeeps careening. Men — boys — *soldiers* — everywhere. The business of the hospital, and the war, continuing on without her, not even pausing. Guns. Artillery. *Heat.*

"We, uh — " The guy looked at his watch. "Ma'am, we *really* have to — "

She nodded, trying, and failing, to be graceful as she got into the jeep.

Home.

Jesus.

Lines, lines, and more lines. Papers, and forms, and vouchers, and snafus. Throughout which, it was very, very *hot.*

Finally, late the next day, after not nearly enough personal hygiene — and even less sleep — a bunch of them were herded onto two buses and driven to a sort of holding pen near the runway at Cam Ranh Bay, surrounded by chain-link fencing, through which they could see a shiny silver commercial airliner waiting. The Freedom Bird.

Possibly the prettiest thing she had ever seen.

"We ain't gonna make it," some kid behind her kept saying. "Somethin's gonna happen, and we ain't gettin' out. Don't *nobody* get out of the Nam."

Not a very perky thought on such a bright sunny afternoon.

The plane had brought a full load of young, wide-eyed soldiers in-country, who filed past them, silent and overwhelmed. There was a fair amount of jeering from her group, of the "Fresh meat!" and "you're gonna get wasted!" variety, and knowing that a lot of those nice healthy kids *would* end up on operating tables in the near future, she couldn't look at them. It was all such a goddam *waste*.

When the orders finally came for them to board, some of the guys broke out of line and went running across the tarmac; some walked with slow, reluctant looks over their shoulders; the rest — including her — took deep breaths, and put one foot after the other.

She was near the front of the line, which meant that she ended up sitting near the *back* of the plane. It was crammed full, and the only other women she saw were the stewardesses, who looked strained — already.

It wasn't too late. Something bad *could* still happen. They could get shot out of the sky, the engine could fail, they could run into a terrible and freakish storm.

The two guys sharing her row — a lanky, somewhat feral grunt, and a corpulent corporal — told her to take the window seat, and she didn't argue, strapping herself in, and folding her hands neatly. Squeezing them together as hard as she could.

"You okay, ma'am?" the kid grunt asked.

"Um, nervous flier," she said. Yeah, right.

"We *made* it, ma'am," he said. "Smile."

She smiled, hoping it wasn't obvious that her teeth were clenched.

When the plane started taxiing, she gripped the arm of her seat with her left hand, swallowing over and over. They were picking up speed, and the takeoff was very sudden, and steep. A couple of people cheered as they lifted off, but most of the plane was quiet.

Rumors had always swirled around that the VC and NVA wanted, more than anything, to shoot down a Freedom Bird, because of what that would do to American morale. Even now, they might be within seconds of — the plane was levelling off, and she found enough nerve to look out the window at what they were leaving behind. Green land, long white beaches, beautiful jade-blue ocean. All of which made the signs of war look even uglier — if such a thing were possible.

They flew on, and she kept clutching her seat arm, so tightly that her fingers hurt. Jesus Christ, she was on a *plane*, going to the *United States*. If they made it.

An intercom clicked, and a deep Texas twang came on, with the old "This is your captain speaking.'' But what he was announcing was that they had just left Vietnam's airspace.

Now, almost everyone cheered, and Rebecca let her hand loosen. There was a mood of general celebratory joy and she could hear drinks from PX-purchased bottles being poured all over the place.

Her seatmates turned out to be pleasant, and not very talkative, which was ideal. The kid grunt was Buck, who was from West Virginia and had spent his whole tour humping the Central Highlands. He'd gotten hit during Dak To — showed her some of his scars — and then, been sent right back out to the field. The other guy, Jeff, had spent his tour in the rear in Qui Nhon, doing something with radio relays. He was from Michigan, and was worried that his girlfriend hadn't waited for him, which he said while looking worried and touching his rounded stomach.

The only time she got up was when she *had* to use the bathroom. As she walked down the aisle, wishing that the female dress uniform wasn't quite so conspicuous, some jerk — no Combat Infantryman's Badge, she noticed — pulled her onto his lap and kissed her sloppily, most of the guys nearby laughing. She didn't like it, but — she was outnumbered.

She asked one of the stewardesses to watch the door for her — make sure no one threw it open or something, trying to be funny — but the woman didn't seem to want to, so she asked a tired-looking first lieutenant, instead. His response was immediate and gallant, and she felt pitifully grateful. She was too shy to ask him to escort her back down the aisle, and when she passed that same group of guys, some of them grabbed at her, much emboldened by drink. Crying, or really having *any* sort of reaction at all, would only make things worse, so she just said, "Come on, guys, give me a break," and extricated the hands, and herself.

They stopped twice for refueling — in Japan, and then, Guam — and while many of her fellow passengers headed straight for the nearest bar, she didn't do much more than go to the ladies' room — she had no interest in repeating that trip down the aisle — and buy a few trinkets.

Mostly, they were just on the plane, eating tepid, tasteless food, and droning endlessly forward. Buck told her, at length, about the nurse — *his* nurse — who had taken care of him after Dak To, saying with heart-wrenching disbelief that she had been *very kind*, and came in day and night, on duty or off, just to be sure he and the other guys were okay. How he would never, ever, *ever* forget that.

She had served with, and admired, more than a few of those quiet heroes herself.

The last hour of the flight was almost silent. The enormity of going home, of *surviving*, of the impending pressure of trying to fit back into their old lives, was nothing if not daunting.

"I'm fat," Jeff said dully. "I went away to war, and I got *fat*."

Pretty much everyone Rebecca knew had gone one way or the other, weight-wise.

The stewardesses were making preparations for landing, and the pilot instructed them to look out to the left, where the coastline would soon appear.

Rebecca looked so hard that she practically went cross-eyed, straining to see through clouds and darkness, worrying that something bad still might happen, that they might not — wait, she saw lights. A bright scattering of beautiful lights spread across the ground below. America. Civilization.

The World.

Part II

THE WORLD

Chapter Sixteen

California was *cold* — and it was *damp*. She started shivering as soon as she stepped outside the plane at Travis Air Force Base, even as other people around her were grinning, and slapping palms with each other, and bending down to kiss the cement and such.

"You gonna kiss the ground?" Buck asked.

She shook her head. "I think I'll pass."

He nodded, and they wished each other and Jeff good luck before going their separate ways to various lines inside, to get their baggage, go through customs, and be assigned to buses going to Oakland Army Terminal. She couldn't stop shivering, and she dug through her duffel bag until she found her flight jacket, bundling into it.

She fell asleep almost as soon as she sat down on the shuttle bus, waking up just in time to hear the end of a lecture a grouchy master sergeant gave them, with specific orders *not* to shame their uniforms by responding to provocation by yellow-bellied in-dee-vi-jwals of the hippie persuasion.

The E−5 in the next seat — one of the many guys who had already changed into civilian clothes, although their haircuts were dead giveaways — told her that she had slept through the egg barrage by a motley little crew just outside the gates of the base.

Somehow, she wasn't sorry she'd missed it.

There was a big AMERICA THANKS YOU banner hanging up at the Army Terminal, but there seemed to be something halfhearted about it. Maybe because it was almost midnight, and the place was pretty much deserted. Since she wasn't lucky enough to be separating from the service — she still had several months left to complete on her two-year hitch, her out-processing was — comparatively — minimal and after waiting in yet another series of inefficient lines, she was officially on her thirty-day leave before having to report to her next duty station.

Unfortunately, they were a good distance away from the airport in San Francisco, and the place was neither crawling with taxicabs — nor good-hearted souls who might want to give her a ride. So, for lack of a better idea, she set her duffel bag down against a wall, using it as a backrest. Over the past year, she had learned to grab sleep whenever, and wherever, she could. Regardless of whether she was *comfortable*.

When a beanpole of a PFC nudged her shoulder a few hours later, she was completely disoriented, but after splashing some water on her face from a drinking fountain, she managed to stumble outside and find a group of guys who had called a cab and didn't mind having her tag along to the airport with them. The kid whose lap she ended up sitting on seemed especially cheerful about the situation.

When they got there, they were greeted by a few waving signs, and some "Hell, no, we won't go!" business, but it was early, and the group's energy level seemed sluggish. She ignored the taunts as she walked inside, although she happened to meet eyes with one particularly grungy-looking man with hair past his shoulders, who promptly scowled and flipped her off.

Yes. It was *so* nice to be home.

One of the guys from her cab, who was still in jungle fatigues — he had pretty much gone straight from combat to his plane ride home — assumed that the gesture was meant for him, and the situation rapidly deteriorated into shoving. She, personally, just kept walking.

The airport was big, and clean, and busy, and everyone else seemed to know exactly what they were doing, and where they were going. Seeing so many civilians — of all ages, and both sexes, dressed like normal Americans — was intimidating, and she retreated to the most out-of-the-way wall she could find, clutching her duffel bag, trying not to panic.

It was too clean. Too modern. Too *crowded*.

She took a few deep breaths, reminding herself that falling apart, while still three thousand miles away from home, wasn't such a great idea. What she needed, was a flight to Boston. A simple enough task.

So, okay. She walked with her head down to the nearest ticket counter, getting at the end of the line. There were plenty of GIs around, a lot of them waiting in lines, or hurrying to catch flights, while others were slouching on top of their duffel bags with blank expressions, or lying next to them, asleep. Although she could feel a certain amount of hostility from people going by, the main response to her being in uniform seemed to be absolute and complete disinterest. Coming from, going to, big deal. *What* war?

When it was finally her turn, the woman behind the counter — who was about twenty-five — wouldn't make eye contact with her.

"Hi," Rebecca said, opening the shoddy clasp of her pocketbook. "I'd like a ticket on your next flight to Boston, please."

"Don't have any," the woman said abruptly.

Oh. The perk was *supposed* to be that as long as they were in full uniform, they were allowed to fly on the standby rate. "I see," she said, and gritted her teeth. "Would you have a ticket if I paid full fare?"

The woman shook her head, looking somewhere off to her right.

Great. She closed her pocketbook. "Do you have any suggestions?"

The woman shrugged. "Try another airline."

Right. "Thank you," Rebecca said. "You've been so kind."

The upshot of the deal was that she waited on another slow line, at a different counter, and was finally issued a standby ticket on the 2:17 to Boston.

A good four hours away.

After checking her bag, she put the plane ticket carefully inside her purse — she was carrying a lot of cash and, the way things were going, someone would probably rob her — and looked around at the bustling terminal. So many people were wearing bright, summery colors that it kind of made her dizzy. Her life for the past year had been utterly monochromatic.

Okay. Time to call home, let them know when she'd be getting in. They had a general idea of what day it would be, although, to be on the safe side, she had told them that it would probably be a few days later than they expected. At the moment, the only thing she knew for sure was that it was morning.

She had to wait in line again at the bank of telephones, and since her fellow Americans weren't exactly tripping over themselves to be helpful, she was too embarrassed to ask anyone if she could borrow a dime once she realized she didn't have any change. Instead, she went over to the nearest newsstand, bought a pack of gum, took the change, and got back in line.

When she lifted the receiver from the hook, she blanked out on her phone number for a few seconds, but by the time the operator came on, and she told her she was placing a collect call, she remembered it.

Her mother answered in the middle of the second ring, and said that *yes*, she would accept charges before the operator even finished asking.

"Is that you, Rebecca?" she asked. "Are you all right?"

Oh, boy, it was *good* to hear her voice. "Yeah," Rebecca said, and leaned her head against the side of the booth. "Hi."

The connection wasn't all that great, but she didn't have any trouble hearing her mother burst into tears.

"I'm fine, Mom," Rebecca said, although she knew perfectly well why she was crying — and felt like joining in. "I'm at the airport — "

Her mother gasped. *"Already?"*

Oh, hell. "The airport in San Francisco," Rebecca said. Damn, maybe she should have waited and called from Logan. "I've got a flight out of here in a few hours, and I'll be in Boston at about ten o'clock your time."

"Okay, let me get this down," her mother said, crying, and Rebecca read off the airline, flight number, and actual ETA. "You're really all right?" her mother asked, when she was finished.

"Yeah." She was swell. "I'm kind of tired, but — I'm fine."

Even though people in line were looking impatient, she stayed on a little longer, as her mother — atypically inarticulate — just kept asking over and over if she were *really* okay, and thanking God that she was home.

When she hung up, she had to brush one of her white gloves across her eyes before emerging from the booth. Then, she stood uncertainly in the crush of people, not sure what to do next. Find her gate, maybe, and sack out again.

She checked the departure board, then studied signs that seemed confusing until she found the right direction to go. On the way, she saw a small, dimly lit bar, and veered inside. At least a *bar* seemed familiar.

She climbed up on a stool, smoothing her skirt

down over her knees. She was the only one there — probably because it was midmorning — but the bartender, after a brief glance up from his newspaper, didn't come over.

"Um, excuse me," she said, after a minute or two. "Could I get a drink?"

His sigh was very loud as he dropped his newspaper and ambled down her way, big arms across his chest, looking her over with a sour expression on his face. "Got any ID?" he asked.

ID. "It's okay," she said, "I just turned twenty-two." This very week.

He looked at her, without blinking.

Her driver's license certainly wasn't handy, and she didn't feel like digging around for her military ID, so she just sighed. "All right,' she said, "How about a Coke?"

He frowned, then grudgingly drew one for her, setting the glass down hard enough for some of the soda to slop over.

She looked at it — no ice, no napkin, the sides of the glass sticky — then shook her head, pushing it away.

"A *nice* girl doesn't come into a bar alone," he said, with great disgust.

No. She probably didn't. "Well," she said, "*Chuck.* I'm not a nice girl." She considered throwing the glass at him, but then she just knocked it over, and walked out, hearing him growl a few short obscenities after her.

And — she'd really *wanted* that drink.

No one else bothered her, although a hippie girl with long black hair and a leather thong tied around her head, who was sitting on the floor with her whacked-out boyfriend, hissed something that didn't sound like "Peace" as she walked by them. In fact, for the most part, no one even *looked* at her, forget smile, or say hello. Whenever she passed a soldier, they would give each other tired nods, but keep going.

She killed some time in a gift shop, buying postcards, Life Savers, a couple of magazines, and a pair of sunglasses — which made her think of Michael, who, except when he was brought in, never seemed to take his *off*. She put her new pair on, hoping that he was alive, and well, and that there would be a letter waiting for her at her parents' house.

She bought a Coke and a cheeseburger at a snack bar, sitting quietly in a corner to eat, and watch people walk by in their cheerful clothes, and blithe ignorance of what was happening — at this very moment — an ocean away.

When she was finished, she took out a pen and one of the postcards of the Golden Gate Bridge, wrote *Does California count as America?* across the back, scribbled her address in Marblehead at the bottom, and dug out Maggie's note so she would know where to send it. Looking for a stamp machine wasted another fifteen minutes, and once the card had been safely mailed, she decided to go to her gate. Get her seat assignment, doze a little.

For a while, it didn't look as if she would be able to get on the flight at all, since it was overbooked; then, at the last minute, the guy behind the counter frowned and gave her one of the remaining seats.

The gate area was crowded, but nobody came near her during the entire time that she waited.

When the flight was finally called and she was able to board, she ignored the stewardesses' plastic smiles and found her seat on her own, keeping her sunglasses on. The plane was just about full when her seatmate, a businessman in his thirties, showed up. He practically recoiled when he saw her, and glanced around the cabin, apparently in search of another place to sit. When he didn't find one, his lips tightened, and he stuffed his garment bag into the overhead compartment and sat down, arranging himself as though she weren't even there.

"I'm happy to sit on the aisle, if you'd rather not, sir," she said.

He gave her the barest shake of his head, already deep in a magazine.

Whatever. She stared out the window, wishing they would just take off already. A stewardess was moving down the aisle, closing compartments and checking seat belts, and Rebecca resolutely looked out the window, not wanting to see her exchange pained glances with her seatmate about his having to sit next to a veteran.

Shortly after they took off and "reached cruising altitude," the same stewardess appeared back at their row.

"Excuse me," she said. "Miss?"

Rebecca looked up, putting on a thin smile, so as not to dishonor the dignity of her uniform.

The stewardess — her age, or a little older, with blonde hair sprayed stiffly into what could only be described as a *coif* — made a "follow me" gesture with her hand. She was actually very pretty, in an open-faced, Midwestern sort of way. "We have another seat for you," she said.

A *segregated* seat, no doubt. The guy must have requested that she be moved, while she was concentrating on staring out the window.

"This one is fine," Rebecca said, "thank you."

"Please come with me," the stewardess said. "Will you let her through, sir?"

Rebecca was too tired to make a scene, so she slowly gathered her things together, the man damn near *leaping* from his seat to let her by. Her *new* seat was probably going to be out on the wing, or inside the turbine, or someplace. The baggage compartment, maybe.

"This way, please," the stewardess said.

Rebecca nodded, following her up the aisle.

The stewardess stopped in the first-class section, indicating two wide empty seats by the window. "I thought you might be more comfortable here," she said.

Wait a minute, someone was doing something *nice?* Rebecca hesitated. "Thank you, but I only paid standby, I — "

The stewardess was already folding her flight jacket, putting it away in the overhead compartment, and spreading her magazines across the aisle seat. Then, she smiled. "I'm sure you're very tired. You'll have room to stretch out here."

Rebecca hung back another second, but then returned the smile shyly and sat down, finding the seat much bigger and softer than the one back in coach.

The stewardess bustled away, coming back with

a blanket and pillow, which she placed neatly on the aisle seat. ''Would you like a drink?'' she asked. ''Or something to eat?''

Actually, *sleep* sounded pretty good. Rebecca shook her head. ''No, thank you.''

''Well, my name's Laurie. Anything you want, you just let me know.'' The stewardess gave her a big smile. ''It's on us.'' Then, she winked, ''Just wait. I'm going to go spill coffee on his lap.''

Rebecca laughed — for the first time in hours — and Laurie went off.

A little while later, she was back with a soda and some peanuts, which Rebecca was grateful to accept. Then, she perched, precariously, on the arm of the aisle seat.

''Are you a nurse?'' she asked.

Rebecca nodded.

''Are you just on leave, or coming home?'' Laurie asked.

''Coming home,'' Rebecca said. Such as it was.

''Well, thank God for *that*,'' Laurie said. ''I'm sure it was very terrible for you.''

Yep. But Rebecca just smiled, and shrugged, sipping some Coke.

Laurie folded her arms, still perching. ''My brother's over there, and we're sure worried about him.''

Not all that surprising, somehow. ''Where is he?'' Rebecca asked.

''A place called Long Binh,'' Laurie said, pronouncing the name carefully. ''Is it awfully dangerous there?''

Probably less so than New York City. Rebecca shook her head. ''No. It's considered very secure.''

Laurie looked worried. "They were attacked during the Tet."

Just hearing the word "Tet" made her tired. "It's still not a bad place," Rebecca said. "Really. What does he do?"

Laurie frowned. "Something with supplies."

Which meant the guy spent most of his time lugging boxes, and checking off lists. The biggest risks he was probably facing were VD and alcoholism. "He should be fine," Rebecca said. "*Really.*"

"I hope so." Laurie shuddered. "We're all worried sick." She shuddered again, then recovered herself. "Will your family be able to meet you?"

Rebecca nodded. "My parents."

Laurie smiled. "I'll bet they're counting the seconds."

A very safe bet.

Laurie checked on her regularly throughout the flight, fetching and carrying and being so genuinely enchanting that Rebecca found herself, against all odds, starting to relax. She dozed on and off, and it was very nice to walk down the aisle to the ladies' room without being assaulted.

Laurie came back, right before the plane started its final approach, to see if she needed anything.

Which she did. "Could I have some scotch, or whiskey?" Rebecca asked. "Right after we land?"

Laurie nodded. "Of course. Ice? Soda? Anything special?"

Rebecca shook her head. "Just straight up, please."

Laurie nodded, and then her face softened. "It's

going to be *fine*, you know. They're going to be really happy to see you.''

One of them was, anyway.

Laurie brought her a glass of expensive single malt scotch as soon as they touched down, and Rebecca held onto it with both hands, as the plane taxied to the gate. When it started to slow into its final turn, she tossed the drink down in two gulps, then closed her eyes and unbuckled her seat belt. She checked her pocketbook to make sure she had everything, then took down her flight jacket, draping it over her arm.

Okay. Time to deal with something that scared her more than the Viet Cong.

She let a few people who seemed very impatient go by first, before moving out into the aisle herself. Laurie was standing by the door, smiling and saying good-bye to everyone, and Rebecca stopped next to her.

''Thank you,'' she said. ''For everything.''

''Thank *you*,'' Laurie said.

They smiled at each other, and then Rebecca took a deep breath, and stepped off the plane.

Chapter Seventeen

It was very crowded inside, and her parents didn't seem to be there. She looked around again, trying not to panic, gripping her pocketbook tightly. What if they hadn't come, or —

"*Rebecca*," someone said, and she was being hugged by her mother before she even realized who it was. She hugged back tentatively, feeling sort of confused and otherworldly. She heard her father saying her name, and then, he was hugging her, too.

"All right, let me look at you," her mother said, holding her away a few inches.

"I'm *much* taller," Rebecca said.

Her mother smiled, but the tears in her eyes weren't just tears of joy. She looked as though she hadn't smiled — for a year. Her father stood next to her, tensely happy. He had gained weight, which looked funny on him, and her mother had lost a lot. They both seemed greyer, and somehow less authoritative than she remembered. They also looked frankly shocked by her appearance, and it had been so long since she had seen a mirror, that she wondered a little herself.

"All I have to do now," she said, to break the uneasy silence, "is *stay* thin, and *get* rich."

They both smiled, but not much.

Okay, so she was going to have to keep making jokes. Be the person — long since lost — they remembered. Her mother was hugging her again, so her father did, too, but she could tell that he was uncomfortable. That made two of them.

"I'm *so* glad you're here," her mother said, choking back tears.

Rebecca nodded, not sure what to say. She should probably be crying too, but she just felt — strange. Like she had walked into a concrete *wall* of fatigue. "We, um — I had to check my bag through," she said, "so, um — " She took a step, hoping they would follow. Something about being in the middle of this crowd — people seemed to be looking at them, and *not* with empathetic smiles — was making her feel like screaming.

But now, her parents were walking with her, her mother's arm hooked possessively through hers.

"How's the ankle?" her father asked instantly.

She was *much* too tired not to limp. "It's okay," Rebecca said. "I'm used to it."

"Well, I'd like to have Conyers and Morgan take a look," he said.

Top orthopedic people. Christ, he was going to *flip* when he saw her arm. "It's really fine," she said, although she could see from one quick glance down that it was, in fact, badly swollen. At least the pain wasn't psychosomatic.

It was very odd to be walking along with her mother being *clingy*. Her family was never clingy. But she smiled at her, and the tears in her mother's eyes spilled over again. Not sure what to do, Rebecca *stopped* smiling, but her mother kept crying.

"It's really okay, Mom," she said. "I'm *home*. It's fine."

Her mother nodded, crying.

"It wasn't that bad," Rebecca said. Just — beyond hellish. "And I'm *okay*." Yeah, good luck to her and the boys at Fenway Park. Speaking of whom. She glanced at her father. "Did they win tonight?"

He gave her mother a "See? I told you" look, and Rebecca knew that he must have had the radio on in the car, and her mother had been angry about it.

"They had gone into extra innings," he said.

Ah. "Ah," she said, since her mind was a blank.

They were passing a closed gift shop, and she snuck a look at her reflection in the window, surprised to see that she was taller, and even thinner, than she would have thought. She also looked quite well-turned-out, considering how long she had been travelling, and — what she looked like, was a *soldier*. Sort of brisk, and distant, and self-assured. Like an *adult*.

Realizing that she had slowed them down, she picked up the pace, embarrassed.

"I, uh — it," she indicated her uniform, "held up okay, didn't it? I assumed I looked a lot worse."

"You look *wonderful*," her mother said, and hugged her again.

Her father hesitated, and then patted her arm. Jesus.

When they got to the baggage claim, none of the luggage was there yet, and her mother went fluttering off to find out what was taking so long. Left alone with her father, Rebecca folded her arms, staring up at the baggage conveyor belt as though it weren't empty. Her father was looking at her — her face, actually — and it took her a few seconds to figure out what his problem was. Her nose.

"I broke it," she said. Would it have been that hard for him to *ask?*

He looked worried. "How did that happen?"

She shrugged, peering up the conveyor belt. "In the crash. I slammed it on the chopper floor."

This time, he frowned. "I'm not sure I — that is, I thought you — "

She might as well come out swinging. "Oh, come on, Dad," she said. "You didn't actually *buy* that business about the jeep accident, did you?"

He stiffened.

"I got shot down," she said impatiently. "I was MIA for a day and a half."

He looked startled — and alarmed.

"Don't tell Mom," she added before he could say anything, catching sight of her mother heading back over.

As her mother explained that they had assured her that the luggage was supposed to start coming out *any* second, her father just stood where he was, looking absolutely stunned. She felt a little guilty, but gave him a sharp frown to make sure he wouldn't say anything to her mother. At least, not right at this moment. She had no control over later.

"What does your bag look like?" her mother asked.

Well — *a lot* like she was in the Army. "It's a duffel bag," Rebecca said, "Anything else, I shipped."

Her mother nodded, staring intently up the empty conveyor belt.

Rebecca glanced at her father, who was looking even more uptight than usual. It had, just perhaps, been immature of her to hit him *that* hard, right off the bat, even though it had been a preemptive blow.

"Relax, Dad," she said quietly. "I still seem to be in one piece."

He nodded, patted her arm, and looked awkward.

Amazing to think the man had a reputation for a superb bedside manner. Maybe he did better with people he didn't know very well. It had been a long time since he had let her follow him around on rounds. Right around the time she started skipping grades, and overachieving in her science and math classes. Falling asleep in home economics.

Luggage started spilling down the conveyor belt, her mother now jittery and hyper-alert. And — therefore — unfamiliar. When her duffel bag rolled down, out of place among all of the conservative suitcases, Rebecca quickly moved forward to grab it. Before she got there, she saw a guy about her age frown at the bag, about — just possibly — to do something very unpleasant, like spit on it.

A real Ivy League type, unfashionably neatly dressed. Her probable, unfortunate future.

"Don't even *think* that thought," she said in a low voice, right behind him. Her most dangerous voice.

He looked surprised, and then repulsed, running his eyes up and down her uniform, spending just that second too long on her ribbons, and her chest.

"It's a very heavy bag," she said, "and I would appreciate it — " he looked like every guy she'd known when she was at Radcliffe, so she took a specific shot — "Mr. Eliot House, if you would lift it down for me."

He scowled at her — a future banker, lawyer, or senator, in his navy-blue crew neck sweater, white oxford shirt, and grey flannel slacks. His loafers were scuffed, so that must be his hippie statement. "Lowell House," he said.

Either way, the reek of Harvard was unmistakable. "Nevertheless," she said, trying to hit Katherine Hepburn's inflections from *The African Queen*.

A joke *Michael* probably would have gotten, and this guy didn't, scowling at her instead.

Her father came over, elbowing politely through the crowd, his eyebrows up. "Rebecca?"

"This nice young man was just helping me with my bag," she said, nodding at him.

"Oh." Her father looked pleased — he *liked* Ivy League types — but lifted the bag himself. "It's all right, I've got it."

Her father always enjoyed having something to do, so she didn't argue as he carried it away. In the meantime, the guy was taking two very expensive dark leather suitcases off the carousel. He saw her looking, and curled his lip.

"You know things are bad," he said, "when a girl like you goes over to the enemy."

Last she'd heard, *North Vietnam* was supposed to be the enemy. She glanced down at his bags — too long, the way he'd studied her chest. Goddam bourgeois bags. "*Catcher In the Rye* go to your head?" she asked, and walked away.

When she got over to her parents, her father nodded in the guy's general direction.

"Nice to see a boy your age act like a gentleman," he said.

She *couldn't* let one go by, when it came right down the middle, all nice and fat like that. "Dad, right before you showed up, he was about to spit on my bag," she said. And then, who knew, maybe on *her*. As a smugly self-authorized booster of the heroic People's Army.

Her father's posture straightened and this time, the look he sent in the guy's direction was a black stare.

Her mother put her arm around her shoulders, and it felt so comforting that Rebecca leaned against her a little. "Martin, let's go," her mother said. "Okay?"

The sooner, the better.

When they were finally outside, her father hustled off to get the car, Rebecca waiting with her mother. It was unbelievably cold, and she zipped up her flight jacket. She was going to comment on the unseasonable weather, but then noticed that her mother was only wearing a light cardigan, and it wasn't even buttoned. So, she just shrugged a few times, trying not to shiver.

"It's okay," her mother said. "We'll be home soon."

She had hoped that her trembling wasn't that obvious. "Is it — cold, or am I just used to a hundred degrees?"

"I think it's about fifty-five." Her mother looked worried. "Would you like my sweater?"

"I'm fine." Time for a new subject. She shook a deep breath. "Did I, um, get any mail?"

"Well, bank statements," her mother said. "Some tax papers. That sort of thing."

Damn. Rebecca closed her eyes, so disappointed that it actually made her stomach hurt. "There aren't any letters?"

Her mother shook her head, reaching over to rub her shoulder. "No. I'm sorry."

Probably hadn't been any letters in Newark, waiting for Snoopy, either. "Well," Rebecca said, and folded her arms, attempting not to slump over them. The perfect lousy end to a perfectly lousy year.

"Rebecca — " her mother started.

"I *really* just want to get home," Rebecca said.

Her mother nodded, and rubbed her shoulder.

When she saw her father's big old Buick, it was such a relief that she wanted to kiss it. Finally, for the first time in months, she would be *out* of public. Could do some falling apart.

Which would certainly be a delight and thrill for her parents.

Opening the back door, she was met by a panting, wiggling dervish of black fur. Their dog, Jack.

"Hey!" she said, and hugged him tightly. They

had had him for almost ten years, and if he *hadn't* been happy to see her, it would have been pretty upsetting. Normally, Jack only rode in her mother's ancient Studebaker wagon, and she grinned at her father as he put her duffel bag in the trunk. "He's getting fur just *everywhere,* Dad."

He smiled at her, and closed the trunk without comment.

Shoving eighty pounds of dog out of the way so she could get in took some effort, but then she hugged him again. It was *nice* to see a dog that no one was going to cook up for lunch.

"All right, sit," she said.

Jack panted, and wagged his tail, and tried to lick her face again.

"Okay, don't sit," she said, and pulled out the bobby pins holding her hat in place, letting it fall off onto her lap. What would it be like *not* to be exhausted.

Marblehead was only about fifteen miles away, straight up Route 1A to the North Shore, but it was going to be hard to stay awake. On the other hand, her father was zipping along — Jesus, they were going *fast* — and she sat up uneasily.

"We're, um, going kind of fast, aren't we?" she asked.

Her father glanced at the dashboard, then at her mother, and Rebecca leaned forward to check the speedometer. Only forty.

"I'm sorry," she said, slouching back. "It just feels fast."

Her father slowed down and, okay, it felt really *slow.* She had gotten used to balky jeeps, and chugging trucks, on bumpy, clogged roads, and — cars were a lot faster. So, of course, were American highways.

"It's okay, Dad," she said. "I'm just screwed up, I — " Was there any need to elaborate? They had *eyes*, they could figure it out.

Her mother started talking about the supper she had waiting for them at home, unless Rebecca was too tired to eat, in which case, she could just get into a hot tub, and go to bed, and have a tray; or, really, anything she wanted — all she had to do was ask. The whole line of conversation was very soothing, and Rebecca nodded, or said yes or no where it seemed indicated, and watched landmarks go by. Suffolk Downs, the racetrack, although concerts — like the Beatles, a couple of years before — were sometimes held there, too. Fuel tanks, car lots, factories. Revere Beach, the Lynnway. There was a beach on the North Shore called Phillips Beach, and she and Doug had always told people that it was named for their family, although there was, in truth, no relation whatsoever. Her mother was the one from Massachusetts, not her father.

When they turned off 1A onto 129, she began to get both nervous and excited. In a way, it was good that it was dark, because it was somehow less overwhelming. And, at this time of night, they weren't going to run into anyone walking around her neighborhood, either. She wouldn't have to answer any questions. Or smile.

Marblehead. They were in Marblehead. On Atlantic Avenue.

"Do they still live there?" Rebecca asked, as they

passed a house on the corner of Beach Street. Her Brownie troop leader — of whom she had not thought in years.

Her mother shook her head. "No. I think Calvin got transferred to Chicago."

Ah. Rebecca nodded. Not that it really mattered, so she wasn't sure why she had felt such urgency about asking.

Her father signalled right, turning onto Ocean Avenue. Billy's family lived just off Ocean, on Wallace Road, and he had always come pedalling over to the Neck on his bike to see her and Doug.

They were on the little causeway now, and she sucked in her breath as she got her first sight of the harbor. Marblehead considered itself the sailing — no, *yachting* — capital of the world, and she had always sat out on the rocks up by the lighthouse, watching the boats come in at sunset. She didn't much care to be *on* the boats — although Doug had done some crewing, and had summer jobs at most of the yacht clubs — but she found *watching* the boats very pleasant, indeed.

Except for outside lights, most of the houses in the neighborhood were dark, but when they turned onto her street, she could see that *her* house had a light on in almost every window. Oh, hell, they hadn't planned a *party*, had they?

"There isn't anyone else here, is there?" she asked, trying to sound calm.

Her mother shook her head. "I knew you'd be exhausted."

Thank God. Rebecca nodded, sinking back. Her father hadn't even turned into the driveway yet, and Jack was already trying to get out. Crawling all over *her*.

Her house. Big and comfortable, white with black shutters. Quintessentially Puritan. Picket fence, mammoth trees, basketball hoop over the garage. They were on one of the inside streets, instead of being right on the water, but she and Doug had always been glad, since that meant they had a bigger yard and, when they had been children, they had always worried that a sudden and catastrophic tidal wave might come whipping in off the ocean — and they had decided that they would rather not see it coming.

Her father was out of the car now, getting her bag, and Jack was running around the backyard, barking.

"Okay?" her mother asked.

Right. She should maybe try something bold — like opening the door and going inside. "I was thinking about the tidal wave," she said.

Her mother smiled. "You two were a lot of fun during storms."

No doubt. Either shrieking with laughter, or just plain shrieking. Hurricane Carol had been quite a scene.

"I really *missed* you, Rebecca," her mother said.

"Me, too," Rebecca said. "I mean — you."

They looked at each other, nodded, and then slowly got out of the car. Grass. It was great to walk across actual green *grass*. A lawn. There was a big, handmade WELCOME HOME! sign hanging up above the front door, and she smiled. Her father held the door open for them, balancing the duffel bag under his arm, and once they were inside, her mother headed straight for the kitchen.

"Let me go get everything ready," she said.

Which left her standing alone in the front hall with her father. There was a HAPPY BIRTHDAY! sign hanging up, several dozen fresh flowers in three separate vases, and the bannister was festooned with streamers.

"Nice," Rebecca said.

Her father nodded, and they smiled nervously at each other, looked away, then quickly looked back and smiled again.

For them, a profound exchange.

"Would you like me to take your things upstairs?" he asked.

She shrugged, pulling off her flight jacket. "Sure. I mean, thanks."

It had been so long that it was hard to remember what she *normally* would have been doing. Standing in the front hall like a shy guest was unlikely, though.

Maybe what she needed was a little privacy. Some decompression, however brief. So, she went back outside to the yard, closing the door softly behind her.

It was dark, and quiet, and *cold*. No flares, no artillery, no overtaxed generators. No air too thick to breath, no horrible smells of fuel, and sewage, and death. There weren't even any *mosquitoes*.

Jesus, it was great to be home. A peaceful, safe neighborhood, the air sweet with the smell of the ocean. Just-raked leaves. Thick grass. Fresh brownies.

She walked down to the garage, pulling in lungfuls of the cool air. The sky was full of stars, and a bright moon. No helicopters. No jets.

No noise.

No death.

In the light from the moon, she could see the faded red lines of the half-court Doug and Billy had painted on the driveway. A very long time ago. They had measured, and argued, and measured some more — and the lines had still come out a little wavery and crooked. Close enough.

More often than not, they would play until after dark, out of breath and banging into each other. Fierce, endless games, with two or three of their other friends from school. Doug had said that if she was going to play too, he didn't want to see any dumb two-handed set shots. *Girl* shots. In fact, he would make her practice one-handed push shots and jump shots when no one else was around, just to be *sure* she wouldn't embarrass him. The fact that she had turned into a ferociously aggressive player — all elbows and audacity — had embarrassed him even more. She threw so many bold and ambitious passes that Billy and the other guys took to calling her "Cousy."

Which she knew had pleased Doug more than he ever admitted.

She stood in the driveway, looking up at the rusty hoop and weathered net. Maybe one — just one — for luck. She went into the garage, rummaging around until she found the ball wedged in among some folded lawn chairs.

She carried it outside, bouncing it twice. A little flat, but not terrible. Which a guy — a junior, on the track team — who had taken her to a dance in tenth grade had actually said to her, while his hand roamed around during one of the slow ones. She had known better than to remind him that even though she was a sophomore, she was barely thirteen. She had been pretty upset though, and *hadn't* known enough not to tell Doug, who got in a big pushing match with the guy in the parking lot later. Nobody — not no one, not no how — insulted his little sister. *He* was the only one who could do *that*.

This would be a very different homecoming if he and Billy were here. Then again, if they were still here, she never would have *gone*.

She looked up at the hoop. In younger, more confident times, she would have stood at the red foul line — or maybe even at the top of the key. But, at this stage of the game, she could really *use* some luck, so there was no point in taking chances.

She moved up until she was only about four feet away, standing just to the right of the hoop. Where she had always stood when she was boxing out. "Cousy, you nut!" Billy would yell, as she went plunging in after rebounds, taking on half of Marblehead's football team.

Damn. She *missed* them.

Damn.

She looked up at the hoop. One, for luck. All the marbles. At the buzzer. For the championship. She dribbled twice, then arched the ball up — one hand to push, the other to guide.

Swish.

Chapter Eighteen

Walking back to the house, she saw her mother standing in the doorway.

"Everything okay?" she asked, looking worried.

Rebecca nodded.

"Okay," her mother said, and smiled. A worried smile. "Are you hungry?"

Was she? "I think so," Rebecca said. She was *definitely* thirsty. Even though her body had gotten pretty acclimated to dehydration.

"Good," her mother said, and Rebecca followed her into the kitchen, picking up Fred, one of their cats, on the way. When she'd left for Vietnam, they only had two cats, but her mother had gotten two more since then — neither of whom she'd seen yet. Fred was a fat black-and-white cat, while Adam was grey — and even fatter.

The kitchen. Her family always spent a lot of time in the kitchen. Not so much because they never stopped eating, but because the table was where they all liked to sit. Reading the paper, talking on the phone, doing little projects — there was always *someone* at that table.

So, she sat down, on the side where she always sat. Doug's chair, she noticed, had a stack of magazines and newspapers on it. Her mother gave her a glass of iced tea, which she gulped agreeably. No point in starting *off* with a beer.

The kitchen was very clean, and felt very safe, the stove covered with pans that were bubbling away with what smelled like at least *three* different meals. There was a ham cooling on one of the counters, next to several fresh loaves of bread, and a pan of brownies.

"Smells good," Rebecca said.

Her mother nodded, jumping up to check two of the pots. "I wasn't sure what you'd want, so I fixed a lot of your favorites."

She was too tired to make any decisions. "We can eat in a while, maybe?" Rebecca said.

Her mother nodded, lowering the heat under the pans. Then, she sat down for a few seconds, but popped right up again to look inside the oven. Her mother had always been energetic, but this was ridiculous.

"Relax, Mom," Rebecca said. "Everything smells great."

Her mother nodded, and sat back down. "I just — want everything to be perfect."

Her mother's fatal flaw. Rebecca grinned. "If you burned it, and dropped it on the floor a couple of times, I'd *still* eat it." Too true to be funny.

A small tiger cat jumped onto the table, investigating the plate of brownies.

Rebecca patted her. "Which one is this?"

"Eloise," her mother said.

"Cute." Rebecca patted her some more, but Eloise seemed far more interested in the brownies, the pitcher full of flowers, and a pencil. Once again, it was nice to see animals who weren't going to end up augmenting someone's stew.

Her father came in, looked around, and then stood near the wall, putting his hands in his pockets.

"Martin," her mother said, indicating the unclaimed glass of iced tea.

He took it, and they all looked at one another, holding tea.

"So," Rebecca said. "Where, in the litany of horrors, should I start?"

Her parents looked uneasily receptive.

"Just kidding." She finished off her tea, and opened the refrigerator to see what else she could have.

Orange juice. Swell. She poured some into her glass, and tasted it. Fresh, and sweet, and delicious. Nothing reconstituted in *this* glass. She was going to pour herself some more, when she saw a jug of cider. She *loved* cider. So, she gulped the orange juice, and filled her glass with cider, instead.

Watching all of this seemed to make her parents nervous. She'd have to be sure *not* to chug a boilermaker in front of them. She flirted with pouring some milk in the cider, just to alarm them, but was able to control the impulse. On the other hand, there was some Narragansett beer on the second shelf, and she found Narragansett beer *hilarious*, so she took one.

"Um," she glanced at her mother, "I drink a lot now." Emphasis on *a lot*.

Her mother nodded, hands folded around her tea glass.

"Alcohol, I mean." Rebecca sat down. "I should be straightforward about that."

Her parents nodded.

Better to tell them, than *show* them. She looked at her father, who was still leaning against the wall, over by the floor register. When she was little — and, okay, *not* so little — she had always liked standing on that register in her nightgown, letting the heat from the furnace come up and make it billow out. Scarlett, on her way to the barbecue. Doug had been fiendishly jealous, since all his pajama bottoms would do was flap. Slightly.

"Sit down, Dad," she said. "Stay a while."

He stiffened, then nodded and sat across from her.

"Is anyone hungry?" her mother asked, up again.

Rebecca and her father both shook their heads, and she sat back down. Adam came yawning in, heading straight for the cat food dishes without giving any of them a second look. He was trailed by a blotchy looking calico kitten.

"Gretchen?" Rebecca asked, and her mother nodded, scooping the kitten up and holding her on her lap.

So, okay. Here they all were. Finally. And no one seemed to have anything to say. Her mother was unrecognizably jumpy, and her father looked — well, guilty, actually. Sad eyes. Tight shoulders. Almost — furtive.

Unfamiliar.

There was a sudden crash in the pantry, some-thing metal rolling onto the floor, and she almost dove off her chair, cringing and covering her head with her arms before she could stop herself.

"It's all right, it's all right," her mother said quickly. "It's just Fred."

Fred. Cat food. When he got particularly hungry and querulous, he always knocked cans off the shelf.

She sat up, acutely embarrassed. Then again, it could be worse. She might have tried to *smother* the damn thing with her body. Feeling shakier than seemed indicated, she closed her eyes for a minute.

"Feed them, will you?" her mother said in a low voice, and her father got up.

Cat food. Christ. Out of nowhere, she was close to tears — if she started, she might never stop — and she opened her beer, tossing down about half of it in a couple of long pulls. Ripping off a stream of obscenities wasn't going to go over well, so she swallowed *them* too, along with the beer.

Her mother came over to hug her, and Rebecca found herself clutching at her.

"I-I think I want to just go take a bath," she whispered.

"Okay," her mother said. "Let's go upstairs, and I'll run one for you."

Rebecca nodded, getting up slowly, wishing she were small enough for her father to carry her, and both parents to tuck her in.

"Come on," her mother said, taking her arm.

She hung back, looking at the stove. "You went to a lot of trouble, I — "

"It'll keep," her mother said.

So, Rebecca followed her upstairs without arguing. She stopped in the doorway of her bedroom to look inside, finding it beautifully clean, and warm, and inviting. The opposite of her sweltering, sandy cubby. Everything looked exactly the way she had left it, but — more vivid, somehow.

"Is something different?" she asked.

Her mother nodded. "I didn't want to change anything, but I wanted it to look nice."

"So — " Rebecca frowned, a little confused — "you redid it all, but *exactly* the same way?"

Her mother nodded sheepishly.

Oh. "Well — it looks good," Rebecca said. Coming back and finding it different would, definitely, have been upsetting. "It really does. Thank you."

"I used a darker shade on the baseboards," her mother said — in her own defense, apparently.

Rebecca grinned at her.

Her mother's smile back was hesitant. "I wanted to be sure you know how much it means to me to have you here."

Jesus. Look what she and Doug had done. Turned their parents into basket cases. "I'm really *sorry*, Mom," she said. "I never meant to — " Just because an action was inadvertent didn't mean that it didn't have consequences. "I'm sorry."

Her mother started to say something, then shook her head. "Rebecca, the only thing that matters to me is that you're here, and you're all right, and — you're *here*."

For tonight, maybe that *was* enough. Rebecca nodded, slouching back against the doorjamb.

Her mother touched her hair gently. "I'll start your tub," she said, and went down the hall.

Almost too tired to remember how, Rebecca started unbuttoning her green cord coat. She was tempted to throw it across the room, but — people had *died* for that uniform, and she owed them her respect. So, she undressed very carefully, draping each piece over her desk chair. The desk itself seemed extra shiny — newly varnished, maybe?

It occurred to her that her father might make his awkward way upstairs — and be disconcerted to find her undressing. She went over to close the door, then opened her closet, where her bathrobe was hanging on the inside hook. Right where she had left it.

Jesus. Had she *always* had so many clothes? So many bright colors? Flouncy-looking skirts, at least twenty dresses, a rather obscene number of cashmere sweaters. Plain wool crew necks and skirts, several cardigans, even a kilt or two. Capri pants galore. Sneakers, loafers, flats, pumps.

And, of course, a set of pristine, perfectly pressed white nurses' uniforms — that she had an intense desire to crumple and destroy.

She kicked her shoes off, and struggled out of her stockings, leaving *them* in a heap. She had about five pairs of slippers — none of which she really liked — and so, she stepped into a pair of beach-faded blue Keds. There was a clean flannel nightgown already spread out on her bed, and she unzipped her duffel bag to get out some underwear. Except — she didn't have to do that. She was home now. She opened her top dresser drawer, amazed by how much underwear she had. Christ, for the last year, she and Annie and everyone had bitched and moaned as they wasted precious free time hand-washing — the hootch maids were inclined to manhandle lingerie, so they always did it themselves — increasingly frayed and dingy bras and panties. Lieutenant Mosby had had all these racy red and black bras — which had impressed the hell out of the rest of them, although they had masked this by scoffing at her.

And here she was, with her abundance of riches, while so many of her friends were still *back* there, wading through mud and blood.

There was a knock on the door.

"Be right there," she said, in case it was her father, and quickly belted her robe.

A book. It would be nice to take a book into the bathtub with her. There was a stack of novels on the table next to her bed, and she picked up the top one.

The Senator. Fine. She liked political novels. On the other hand, *Rosemary's Baby* was underneath it, and she had been *dying* to read that for months. So, she stuck that under her arm instead, and opened the door.

"It's all ready," her mother said. "Is there anything you want me to bring you?"

A *drink*. "Could I have a Coke?" Rebecca asked. "And some ice water?"

Her mother nodded, already halfway down the stairs.

The door to her parents' bedroom was ajar, and she saw her father sitting stiffly in the rocking chair by the fireplace, a magazine rolled up in one hand.

She went in there and, once again, they exchanged nervous smiles. Then, she glanced at the clock on his side of the bed. Almost one.

"Do you — " She stopped, trying to think. "What day is it?"

"Monday." He looked at the clock. "That is, Tuesday."

Okay. Whatever. "Do you have surgery tomorrow?" she asked.

He shook his head.

"Figured you might be off your game a little," she said.

He nodded.

Not surprising. Her father liked to be prudent. "It's still late though," she said, "and I plan to take the longest bath in history, so don't feel like you have to wait up or anything."

He looked uneasy. "Well, I — "

"Dad, you have *rounds*," she said. "I know the importance of rounds." Might be nice if she could stop snapping at him. "So, please get some sleep. I'm not going anywhere."

He nodded, and they pretended to look at each other, although they really weren't. At least, she wasn't.

"Where else were you injured?" he asked.

Well, okay. He certainly deserved that much. "My arm," she said.

He nodded. "May I see it?"

The sight wasn't going to make his day, but she put down her book and pushed up her sleeve.

Her father motioned her over to the lamp, so he could examine it more closely, and then let out his breath. "Good God."

"It's not that bad," she said. "There was just — a lot of debridement. And — some residual epidermal scarring from the Sulfamylon."

"No brachial damage?" he asked. "Or fracture?"

She shook her head. "Just the cephalic."

He nodded. "How about nerve impairment?"

"It pretty much came around, the last few months," she said.

He nodded, turning her arm to scrutinize the entire area, and when he looked up, she looked back at him pleadingly, praying that he wasn't going to ask the obvious question. *How.*

"It — looks like you had a fine surgeon," he said.

She nodded, so grateful that he had actually understood that a couple of tears came spilling over, and he reached his hand up to brush them away.

"I hope you'll be able to tell us about it, Beckalou," he said quietly.

Which only made her cry more. "There were maggots, Dad," she said. "I had *maggots* in me."

He nodded, his hand resting on her shoulder now.

"I was still alive," she said, "and when they opened up the bandage, there were *maggots* in me."

He nodded, pushing her sleeve down over the scar, and then pulling her into a careful hug.

"Please don't tell Mom, okay?" she asked. "I don't want her to know about stuff like that." If he wasn't a doctor, she wouldn't have told *him.*

"Okay," he said.

She was going to ask him to promise, but one thing about her father, he always kept his word.

He said he wasn't going to help Doug; he didn't. He said he didn't approve of her going to medical school — he had used words like "inappropriate" and "impractical," when he *meant* unfeminine — and that he wouldn't support her in *any* way, which he didn't. Presumably, he'd also thought that she wasn't smart, or tough, enough, either.

Old news.

She edged away from him, quickly rubbing away any tears that might be left, and put on a smile.

"Well, um, anyway," she said, and retrieved her book.

He nodded.

"I guess I'll — " she took a few steps back towards the door — "see you in the morning."

He nodded, straightening his glasses. "We're very happy to have you home, Rebecca."

Oh, yeah. So far it was going swimmingly. But, she nodded back, put on another smile, and then went out to the hall.

Her mother was in the bathroom, her sleeves rolled up as she readjusted the temperature of the tub, the Coke and ice water ready and waiting on the edge. Seeing Rebecca, she straightened up quickly, some water splashing across the front of her skirt. A nice grey wool one she had had for years, and Rebecca had always liked. Had *borrowed* on more than one occasion.

"Anything else you need?" her mother asked. *"Anything?"*

Rebecca shook her head.

"Well, would you like me to — " Her mother stopped, and looked at her. "Maybe you should just call me if you need me."

Rebecca nodded.

"Okay, then," her mother said, and smiled, hesitantly. "I'll just be in the other room."

Rebecca nodded.

Once she was alone, she took off her robe, hanging it up. Then, she slipped off her sneakers and, careful not to spill the two glasses, got into the tub. At first, the water felt so hot that she winced, but then the heat felt good, and she sank down into it. Jesus. She hadn't had a bath for a whole *year*.

It felt *great*.

She lay there for a while without moving, then began alternating sips of her Coke and ice water. Having a book within arm's reach seemed like more luxury than she could handle yet, so she left it on the bathmat, lying down until the water reached her chin. Maybe, just maybe, she would be able to get *clean*. Stop literally reeking of blood and guts.

She stayed in the tub for a couple of hours, her drinks long gone, reading about a hundred pages into the book. When the water temperature cooled slightly, she would drain some out, and then turn on the hot water faucet full blast to refill it. Water in Vietnam was strictly rationed, and it was *fun* to waste it.

She soaped, and resoaped herself, and did an extremely precise and skillful job of shaving her legs. Using a safety razor was much nicer than a straight blade. Her muscles were more defined than she thought of them as being, and it seemed funny that she'd gotten both thinner, *and* stronger. Strange little ropy muscles. Not terribly attractive.

The simple truth was that she looked like a — female — grunt.

When she finally got out — automatically sprinkling Comet in the tub and scrubbing it down — she saw a brand-new toothbrush, still in its box, on the sink, and helped herself. It was fun to waste *toothpaste*, too.

Looking in the mirror, her face seemed different, but she wasn't quite sure how. Older. Sad. And — neither pretty, nor ugly. Just sort of — normal. *Had* her eyes changed? They didn't look scary, or menacing, or — just different. Somehow not the way she remembered them.

There was one small light on in her parents' room, at her mother's side of the bed, and Rebecca stuck her head in.

"Um, good night," she said.

Her mother, who was reading, lowered her book and sat up. "Would you like something to eat?"

Yeah, actually, but — Rebecca looked at the clock. "It's four in the morning."

Her mother shrugged, getting out of bed.

"It's okay," Rebecca said, "I can — "

"Why don't we throw your uniform in the wash while we're at it?" her mother suggested. "And anything else you have."

Well — because it was four in the morning. Then again, her family, except for her father when he was working crazy hours, tended to be night people. Preferred winter to summer, fall to spring. Cold to hot. Sometimes even *rain* to sunshine. Just your average cantankerous New Englanders.

Her mother followed her into her room, watching as she removed her second lieutenant's bars and other insignia from the uniform jacket. After she put them down on top of the dresser, her mother reached forward and touched the ribbons on their little ribbon holder.

"So many medals," she said, almost to herself.

None of which she deserved. Rebecca shrugged, rebuttoning the jacket.

"What do they all mean?" her mother asked.

That she was the object of favoritism. "Mostly just that I showed up," Rebecca said.

Her mother nodded, her shoulders hunching a little in her nightgown as she looked at them.

Okay. Rebecca pointed at the gold-bordered one, yellowish-gold ribbon, with three red vertical stripes. "This one's important. It's a Presidential Unit Citation. We got it because of Tet, mostly." If the Chief Nurse still had career ambitions, it was the sort of thing that looked *great* on a Commanding Officer's record.

Hell, if she had Army ambitions *herself*, she had been over-decorated in a way that would bode well for her promotional future.

"What's this?" her mother asked, pointing to a red ribbon, with a blue vertical stripe bordered by slim white ones.

Damn. "It's, um, a Bronze Star," Rebecca said. "It wasn't a big deal or anything — I mean, they didn't have a ceremony, I just — " She sighed. "The stupid Chief Nurse made me take it." Would brook no argument at all, in fact.

Her mother stared. "You got a *Bronze Star*?"

"She *made* me," Rebecca said. "It was more — procedure — than anything else."

Her mother frowned, but pointed to the ribbon next to it. "What's this one?"

Should she lie? She *hated* lying. "Purple Heart," Rebecca said, trying to sound offhand. "Because of my dumb accident."

Her mother sucked in her breath, staring at the ribbon — deep purple, with a white stripe at either end.

"It's over," Rebecca said briskly, and pushed all of the various insignia into a jumbled pile. "It's been over for a long time." Since she wasn't going to need them again for another month, when she had to report to Fort Dix, she swept the pile into the top drawer, closing it sharply.

Her mother started to speak, but then just picked up her uniform from the chair. "What else do you have?"

Enough already. Rebecca shrugged. "Just an Army Commendation Medal." That her *second* Chief Nurse had forced upon her, *in particular recognition of an incident involving a gravely wounded —* "It was no big deal," she said.

Her mother nodded, and shifted her weight. "I, uh, meant laundry, actually."

Oh. Rebecca grinned. "You mean, you don't want to hear about my medal?"

"No, I — of course I do, I — " Her mother saw her grinning and relaxed. "Get your laundry, Rebecca."

"But, I want to *tell* you," Rebecca said. "I want to tell you *everything*."

"Get your laundry," her mother said.

Rebecca grinned, and opened her duffel bag.

Chapter Nineteen

She ate ham, and scalloped potatoes, and two pieces of meat loaf, and some carrots, apples, and onions sauteed together. Her mother sliced up a bright red native tomato, and some of the just-baked bread — and she ate that, too. During which, her mother sipped tea, and nibbled toast, and watched her uneasily.

"Didn't they *feed* you over there?" she asked.

Rebecca shrugged, helping herself to more of the carrot mixture. "I usually wasn't hungry." And the food was pretty lousy.

Her mother nodded, and watched her eat. Rebecca had very little interest in talking, and was quite content to sit there and get caught up on various relatives and neighbors as she ate. Who was married, who was pregnant, who was happy, who wasn't. Life. No death.

"So," she said, when she was finally sated, and just drinking coffee. "You only got that one call?" Doug.

Her mother nodded.

"But — he sounded okay?" Rebecca asked.

"Worried about *you*," her mother said, "but yes."

Being here, at their kitchen table again, made it even harder to accept the notion of her brother off in *permanent exile*. The war was wasting so many more lives than the goddamn casualty lists ever reported.

"Did he do the right thing?" her mother asked.

That was a stupid question. Rebecca frowned at her. "Ask Mrs. McDonough."

"I almost *was* Mrs. McDonough," her mother said. Snapped, really.

Well, okay. Fair enough. Her coffee needed some — perking up — and she walked over to the cupboard where her parents kept the liquor, hoping for Jack Daniel's, but settling for Dewar's. She carried the bottle back to the table, pouring a shot into her mug.

"I'm sorry," her mother said. "That was a terrible thing to say."

Rebecca shrugged. "On the money, though."

Her mother looked unhappy, her shoulders hunching up again. Then, she started clearing off the table, putting away leftovers and stacking dishes in the sink. Rebecca got up to help, but her mother shook her head, so she sat down and methodically drank her coffee, after — improving — it again.

"To answer your question," she said, once her mother had finished, "I don't think I saw a single person over there who *really* survived, so — *yeah*, I think he did the right thing."

Her mother leaned against the sink, wiping her hands with a dish cloth.

"You don't have to stay up. I mean — " Rebecca glanced at the clock on the wall. Almost six. Jesus. "It's really late."

Her mother nodded, folding the dish towel and hanging it on a hook to dry. "Would you rather I went upstairs?" she asked.

No. Not even remotely. Rebecca shook her head, adding just the tiniest bit more scotch to her coffee.

Tentatively, her mother sat down, and neither of them spoke for a couple of minutes.

"I don't want to do anything wrong, Rebecca," her mother said finally.

"Neither do I," Rebecca said, beginning to feel the scotch enough to grin at her. "Think either of us has a shot in hell?"

Her mother's smile back had almost nothing behind it.

It was too hard to try to be someone she couldn't remember *ever* being. "Is it okay if we just sit here for a while?" she asked. "Just — be here, in the kitchen?"

Her mother nodded, and they sat there.

Very quietly.

They were still sitting there, although Rebecca had switched back to plain coffee, when her father came downstairs to let Jack out. He stood in the doorway, already dressed for work, obviously surprised to see them.

"You two are up early," he said.

Rebecca and her mother looked at each other.

"Up late," Rebecca said.

Her father checked his watch, frowned, but then opened the back door, Jack tearing outside into the morning fog.

Her mother stood up, looking so tired that Rebecca felt guilty.

"Is anyone hungry?" she asked, opening the refrigerator. "I can — "

"Go on up to bed, Nan," her father said. "You're exhausted." Then, he glanced at Rebecca. "That is, if you two — "

Rebecca pushed away from the table. "I'm going to go to sleep, too." She looked at her mother. "I'm sorry, I guess my time clock's all — " this wasn't Vietnam; she shouldn't swear — "screwed up."

"Are you sure you don't want something else to eat first?" her mother asked.

Very. "No, thank you," Rebecca said, but took a Coke from the refrigerator so it would be next to her bed when she woke up. A bottle, not a can. She didn't know if it was true or not, but in Vietnam, everyone said that the goddamn — indigenous population — opened all the bottles and resealed them after putting ground glass inside, so Americans who drank them would die. Cans were supposed to be safe.

They all said good night — good morning — whatever it was — and then Rebecca went upstairs, suddenly so tired that each step seemed more impossible than the one before.

When she climbed into her bed — a *real* bed, with a good mattress — the sheets felt cool, and so crisp that her mother must have ironed them. The blankets were warm, but she pulled up the quilt from the bottom of the bed anyway. A nice, thick quilt, that her Aunt Shirley had given her for Christmas when she was about thirteen.

The breeze coming in through the open window felt cold, but it smelled so clean that she decided she would rather be cold. It was strange to be in a place where nothing smelled awful — including herself — and it was especially nice to be between sheets that weren't slippery with mildew, and rank with that indescribable rice paddy stench from being ineptly laundered.

Was there a new nurse in her hootch yet? Probably. Homesick, and overwhelmed, and wondering how the hell she had gotten herself into this mess. And her new next-door neighbor, Karen, was just short enough to feel conflicted about making friends with her.

Maybe they were all in the middle of a masscal, or getting mortared, or — there was no point in thinking about it, because there was nothing she could do, one way or the other.

As she lay here in this soft, warm, *comfortable* bed.

Maybe Michael was happy and thriving, somewhere in Colorado, and maybe Walter Hanson had perfect vision in his remaining eye. Maybe they were *both* languishing in VA hospitals. Maybe —

Maybe she shouldn't think at all.

When she woke up, it was dark, and she didn't know where she was. There was something heavy draped across her stomach and chest, and when she felt fur, she almost screamed, afraid that it was a rat. But — rats didn't purr.

A cat. A cat she didn't *know*. The new kitten, Gretchen. Okay. She patted her, squinting around the room in the dim light from the hallway. *Her* room. Okay.

She reached for the Coke, remembered that she didn't have an opener, and knocked the cap off using the edge of her night table. One of the many bar tricks she had picked up, although it probably hadn't done the table any good. She gulped about half of the Coke down, only spilling some, wondering what time it was. What *day* it was.

The kitten didn't want to move, and Rebecca wasn't too crazy about the idea herself, but she slid out from underneath the covers, feeling the floor with her feet for her boots.

No boots. Just Keds. Okay. And no reason to turn them upside down and shake them in case a scorpion or a lizard or something had crawled inside. She turned on the lamp next to her bed, blinking and shading her eyes. According to the clock, it was almost seven, and it was dark out, which meant she had slept either twelve hours — or thirty-six. Sixty. Eighty-four.

She stood uncertainly, in her Keds and nightgown, and tried to decide what to do next. The kitten was rolling happily around on the blankets, playing some private game, and she watched her while she finished the Coke.

Maybe she should get dressed, and go downstairs. Yes. A sensible plan. She put on a pair of jeans from her bottom drawer, which felt too baggy, and an old light blue Oxford shirt of Doug's. Her Red Sox cap was hanging on one of the bedposts, and she put it on, too, because — she felt like it. At least she could *look* the way she had always looked.

When she got downstairs, she found her mother sitting alone at the kitchen table, with a drink. Vodka, or gin. Her mother, who rarely even had wine with dinner.

"Uh, hi," she said.

Her mother, who was staring down at *The Boston Globe* without turning pages, looked startled. "You're up."

More or less. Rebecca nodded, taking another Coke out of the refrigerator — and an opener from the silverware drawer. No pointing in banging up the kitchen table, too.

"How do you feel?" her mother asked, on her feet, and starting to fidget around.

Tired. "Fine, thanks." Rebecca drank half of the Coke in two swallows. "Is Dad here?"

Her mother motioned with her chin. "In the den."

Never a good sign, when her parents chose to sit in different rooms. But Rebecca just nodded, leaning over to glance at the newspaper headlines. On the other hand — did she want to read *anything* even *related* to Vietnam? So, she pulled the sports section out, only to see that they had lost in fourteen innings, after blowing a 4–0 lead. Yastrzemski had *not* come through in the clutch, and — well, she was *already* depressed, so she dropped the paper on the table, and drank her Coke.

"Are you ready for dinner?" her mother asked, taking a salad that was a true work of art out of the refrigerator.

Rebecca waited a second too long to answer, and

her mother put the salad back. "I didn't mean for you to — " Rebecca started. Too late. "I'm sorry, I'm just — "

"Not sure what time zone you're in," her mother said.

Or even what *country* she was in. Rebecca nodded.

"Well, it'll keep," her mother said. "Why don't you go tell your father he can help himself, if he wants."

Rebecca found him sitting on the couch in the den, reading *The New York Times*, with a couple of issues of *The New England Journal of Medicine* spread out next to him. The radio was on, tuned to the Red Sox pre-game show.

"Uh," she stayed in the doorway, "Mom says dinner's ready, if you're hungry."

He nodded, folding the newspaper. "How are you feeling?"

"I'm not sick," she said defensively.

He nodded, avoiding her eyes as he got up.

What had possessed her to tell him about the damned maggots? "Um — who's pitching?" she asked.

"Lonborg," he said.

Who, lousy season or not, was *still* their ace. "Oh," she said. "I mean, good."

He nodded, and they both shifted their weight.

"I'm — going to eat later," she said.

He nodded, and touched her shoulder lightly before leaving.

Judging from the position of the magazines, he didn't want anyone else sitting on the couch with him, so she chose an easy chair, looking over at the blank television screen. He might mind if she turned it on, but then again, it was the only one in the house, and there *were* other radios, so — the program listings were on the right corner of the coffee table, and she scanned the page. Season premieres, mostly. A new crime drama on ABC, that sort of thing.

She was *extremely* partial to crime dramas.

Her father came back in with a full plate. Baked chicken in mushroom sauce, rice, salad, carrots again. Carrots, being one of her very favorites. After Vietnam though, she could kind of do *without* rice.

"Is it okay — " she indicated the television — "if I watch something? We can keep checking the score?"

He shrugged. "Sure."

Her mother came in now, with a less full plate. "Do you want to try some of this, or — ?"

What the hell. "Okay," Rebecca said, and then thought better of the idea. "Unless it's yours."

Her mother shook her head. "Mine's still out there."

An unlikely story, but Rebecca accepted the plate, while her mother went out to the kitchen and got another. Her parents hated the notion of eating in front of the television — but here they all were.

The show was called *The Mod Squad*, and it was *swell*. Young, hippie cops, torn between duty and beach volleyball. Honor, and hedonism. There was some brooding, and some earnestness, and some overacting. Add a California backdrop, and lots of blondes — and it was a thing of beauty. Made her — almost — proud to be an American.

Her parents seemed less taken with the show than she was, although they made no comments, her father simply turning up the radio during the commercial breaks. Naturally, the team was losing, rather than welcoming her home with a bold and inspiring victory.

"Well," her mother said, when the show was over. "They are certainly very — mod."

Yes. Terribly hip and cool. Rebecca grinned. "That's what *I'm* going to do," she said. "When I get out of the Army."

Her parents both looked horrified.

Jesus, had they gone and lost *their* senses of humor, too? "I'm going to be blonde," Rebecca said, "also."

Her mother smiled; her father's expression faded from horror into mere unease.

"Because, you know, blondes have a *whole* lot more fun," she said.

Now her father smiled — and turned up the radio.

They watched television straight through until eleven o'clock, hearing the Red Sox get pounded 10–2 along the way, despite Carl Yastrzemski's home run. She ate her share of dinner, going back for second helpings, and putting away a couple of beers, too. When the news came on, she didn't want to hear anything about the war — or Richard Nixon, or Hubert Humphrey — so, she jumped out of her chair.

"I'll go do the dishes, okay, Mom?" she said, and left before she could hear anything more about a Republican campaign promise to make troop reductions. How about a promise to *stop* the damn war?

She had washed half of the dishes by hand before she remembered that they had a dishwasher. When she was finished, it was almost eleven-thirty, and the most ambitious plan she could come up with was having another drink. Taking a bath. Reading a book. Going to bed.

No one would ever accuse *her* of being dull.

She spent the next week pretty much the same way. Her parents had a late birthday celebration for her, with a cake and lots of nice presents, while she returned the favor by giving them some of the souvenirs she had picked up in Vietnam and Japan. A beautiful tapestry, a delicate porcelain bowl, and some odd wooden candlesticks for her mother; a couple of primitive medical implements she had picked up in a village on one of the MEDCAPs — an Army program to foster civilian aid — and a baseball cap with a dragon on it for her father. They gave *her* books, and clothes, and a little note inside an envelope with the promise of picking out a new car with her. She felt funny about that, since she had plenty of money saved up, but they compromised by agreeing that she would get something decent, but secondhand, and they would pay for it.

They made phone calls to most of her relatives, and she made a big effort to be hearty, and cheerful, and unchanged. Her Aunt Shirley sounded so strained when she told her that two of her cousins "weren't home," that Rebecca figured they were actively anti-war, and just didn't want to speak to a fascist warmonger like her.

Other than that, she read, and slept. Had nightmares. Drank beer. Shot a few baskets. Her mother was full of ideas about places they could go, and things they could do, but she couldn't work up much enthusiasm about even leaving the backyard. Most of the time, she didn't even leave her *room*.

She was outside shooting baskets, when her mother came out, carrying a blue sweater.

"Are you warm enough?" she asked.

Rebecca nodded, and took a shot. Swish.

Her mother caught the rebound, clumsily, and tossed the ball to her underhand. "Do you want to go for a walk? Down to the lighthouse, maybe?"

The lighthouse really was one of her favorite places. "I don't know." Rebecca shot. Clang. "Maybe later."

"Okay." Her mother put her hands in her pockets. "Want to come down to the store with me?"

Where she would run into God-only-knew-who from her past. "No, thank you," she said, and shot.

Clang.

Damn. She retrieved the ball, and shot again. Swish. *Good.*

"You should call some of your friends," her mother said. "Let them know you're home."

Her friends were scattered across the country in unknown places, still in Vietnam — or dead. "I don't know." Rebecca shot. Swish. "Before I leave, I guess."

"I know Irene's waiting to hear from you," her mother said. "And Nora, and — "

Rebecca lowered the ball instead of shooting. "What do I have to say to them, Mom?" Then, she shot. "I mean, I don't — " clang — "have much of anything to say to *anyone*."

"I know it'll be hard at first," her mother said, after a pause, "but once you start — "

Rebecca cut her off. "Maybe in a few days, okay?"

Her mother nodded, then sighed, looking out at the quiet street.

"It's not going to be any great loss for them," Rebecca said, "*believe* me."

"Well." Her mother sighed again. "I know everyone *missed* you."

Maybe, but high school had been over for a long time, and — they were in very different worlds now. Or, more accurately, she *wasn't* married, and *didn't* have children. Didn't have any prospects in that direction, either. Anymore.

Damn it to hell. She dribbled a couple of times, her ankle weak and unsteady beneath her, and sent up a shot. Clang.

"Mary McDonough called again, before you were up," her mother said. "Wanting to know how you were."

It was Rebecca's turn to sigh. "I guess I have to go over and see her." Tell her lies.

Her mother nodded.

Mrs. McDonough being someone who would *need* to see her. Someone who had also gone out of her way to send her letters, and be thoughtful, and supportive. "Okay," Rebecca said. After Billy had died, she had forced herself to go over and visit Mrs. McDonough as regularly as she could, since she always had, and it didn't seem right to stop — but it had never gotten any easier. She let out her breath. "I'll do it tomorrow."

"You want me to come with you?" her mother asked.

Rebecca nodded. Very much.

"Okay," her mother said. "I'll go call her now."

Rebecca nodded, and shot the ball.

Clang.

Chapter Twenty

She couldn't face church, since if she went, she was supposed to wear her dress uniform, so she stayed in bed. Her mother finally came in around twelve-thirty, and she dragged herself up, and into the tub. Ate half a piece of toast, drank some coffee, and took her weekly malaria pill, since she had a few weeks to run on the eight-week cycle and even though she was back in the World, her system still might succumb to it. The pills always gave her nice flu-symptoms like nausea and diarrhea — but the notion of malaria in Marblehead was rather more than she could face.

She put on a skirt and sweater, partially because it was Sunday, and partially because it seemed like the right thing to do if they were going visiting. Even though Mrs. McDonough had seen her in *countless* casual, often ill-fitting, outfits over the years.

They drove over in the Studebaker, Rebecca clutching the little Japanese fan she had bought when the plane had stopped for refueling. Somehow, it didn't seem right to give a woman whose son had been killed in the war a *Vietnamese* souvenir.

Garth and Diane were in the yard, raking leaves, and they stopped when they saw her. Garth looked like he'd grown about four inches, and Diane had made that crucial jump from sixth grade to the big, bad world of junior high.

"Hey!" Garth said, dropping his rake. "When you get back?"

"A few days ago," Rebecca said. When she'd heard, in a letter from Irene, that the Army doctors had found a slight heart murmur, and he had therefore been classified 4-F, it had come as welcome news, indeed. "How are you guys?"

"Fine," Garth said, and Diane nodded shyly.

"Well — that's good," Rebecca said. She had only been here for a few seconds, and she was already out of things to say.

"You — doing all right?" Garth asked.

"Oh, yeah. Although it's good to be home," she said, and they nodded, and smiled, and nodded.

Okay. Now what?

The back door opened, and Mrs. McDonough came out, with a bright yellow apron on over the dress she had probably worn to church. Seeing them, she smiled.

"Well, look at you," she said, and came over to hug her.

"Hi." Rebecca hugged back. "It's good to see you." Good. Everything was *good*.

Mr. McDonough appeared with Billy's youngest brother, Ryan, and their two dogs, and Rebecca received hugs, and handshakes — and licks on the face — until they all moved in a big clump into the house, where they ate cake, drank coffee and soda, and brought Rebecca up to date on their lives. Garth's freshman year at B.C., Diane's flute-playing, Mr. McDonough's travails with his boat. The McDonoughs had always been pretty noisy, and spent a lot of time interrupting one another. Even the *dogs* barked constantly.

But, after a while, they all went noisily away to finish raking leaves, and scraping the hull of the boat, and Rebecca and her mother were left alone with Mrs. McDonough in the living room.

"Um, here," Rebecca said, and handed her the thin, tissue-wrapped package. "I hope you like it."

Mrs. McDonough looked teary even *before* she opened it. "Thank you," she said. "It's beautiful, Rebecca."

"I got it for you in Japan," Rebecca said — so she'd know, and wouldn't have to avoid looking at it.

"Well, it's beautiful." Mrs. McDonough got up, gave her a little squeeze, and then placed the spread-out fan gently on the mantelpiece.

Right near the studio shot of Billy, in his uniform. Probably the only picture she'd ever seen where he wasn't smiling, although she could tell from his eyes that he wasn't going to be able to maintain the solemn expression much longer. For years, until Billy joined up, the McDonoughs had had a picture of President Kennedy up there.

Everywhere she looked, she saw something she didn't want to see. Billy's ribbons and medals, some of them posthumous, perfectly mounted and framed. A picture of him in his baseball uniform.

In his altar boy robes. A picture of the three of them — Billy and Doug on either side of her — all grinning and wearing their caps and gowns at graduation.

She swallowed, and looked over at her mother, who had been very quiet so far. Withdrawn, really. Her hair had always been brown, with strands of grey, and Rebecca still had to look twice every time she noticed that it had gone *completely* grey. There were lines at the corners of her eyes and mouth that were new, too.

Mrs. McDonough also looked a lot older. Much heavier. Settled. Her hair was crisply grey, as opposed to her mother's softer waves, and Rebecca watched them gather and stack the cake plates, remembering the way their families, along with the Hennesseys and the Darrows, would have cookouts in the summer. There had been something rather dashing and devil-may-care in the way her mother would hold a beer, and a cigarette, and work the grill. Her father, when he was in the right mood, could be screamingly funny, and she would hear the other fathers laughing as they stood around with him. All of the men would call her over, and try to stump her with baseball trivia, and when they failed, her father would look pleased — and disconcerted.

It occurred to her that she should be helping them clean up, and she stood just as Mrs. McDonough came back in with a fresh pot of coffee.

"No, sit down," she said. "Would you like some more?"

Rebecca glanced at her mother uncertainly, but then nodded. "Thank you."

After Mrs. McDonough finished pouring, the silence seemed oppressive.

"Diane's certainly looking pretty these days," her mother remarked.

"She's growing so fast I can hardly keep up," Mrs. McDonough said, and they both nodded, and smiled.

She wasn't sure if her mother and Mrs. McDonough had much in common, beyond their children. Irishness, although her mother was lace-curtain, and the McDonoughs veered more towards shanty. They had both been active in the schools, but most of her mother's friends were in Boston, and Newton, and Winchester, as opposed to the McDonoughs, who were from Revere, and Winthrop.

Okay, one of the big differences was that her parents were kind of — rich. Not that it mattered, but — it probably did. Or, at least, created a certain awkwardness.

"It's so good to see you home," Mrs. McDonough said.

Rebecca smiled, holding her coffee cup. "Yeah."

"What are you going to be doing now?" Mrs. McDonough asked.

The $64,000 question. "I have to report to Fort Dix in three weeks," Rebecca said. "And I should be getting out of the service in May."

Mrs. McDonough nodded. "Then, will you come back to one of the hospitals around here?"

The $128,000 question. Rebecca didn't look at her mother. "I'm — going to take things slowly, I think."

Which was pretty cryptic, but Mrs. McDonough

nodded. She snuck a glance at her mother, who was sitting so straight that she suddenly realized that she *hadn't* come along for moral support, but in the hope of hearing answers to some of the questions she hadn't yet been able to bring herself to ask.

Rebecca took a deep breath, and looked at Mrs. McDonough. "I guess you're — wondering what it was like?"

Mrs. McDonough nodded, leaning forward.

Jesus. Where to start. How much to *tell*. "It's very hot," Rebecca said. "I mean, you keep thinking you're going to get used to it, but it's just *hot*." This would be easier if her mother weren't here, but — she could almost hear Maggie pointing out that she was not the All-Powerful Supreme Being who decided what, in life, was going to be easy, and what wasn't. "It rains a lot, too. And it smells — " how was she going to finesse this one? " — like you're in an utterly foreign place. A — primitive place." Sewage Central.

Mrs. McDonough, and her mother, nodded.

She was never going to be hired to do travelogue. "I flew up there on my day off," she looked at Billy's picture, "about a month after I got in-country. Phu Bai, I mean. Just to look around the base, and — it's *huge*. Dust and sand, tents, Quonset huts, concertina wire, helicopters and jeeps all over the place. And these massive green mountains, off in the distance." Chu Lai, Phu Bai — same difference. Same war.

Her mother was listening so intently that she was tempted to remind her to breathe.

"I stopped by the surgical hospital, and — it was

a lot like my hospital. A little smaller, but — " she looked at Mrs. McDonough — "they took *really* good care of people. Took care of *everyone.*"

Mrs. McDonough didn't say anything, her eyes filling with tears.

"If you were an American, you were never alone," Rebecca said. "Even if you were surrounded by total strangers, they would treat you like the best friend they'd ever had." Which made her picture Michael's squad, all of them alive and unmaimed, worrying and trying to help her, even though they'd never seen her before in their lives.

"Do you think — " Mrs. McDonough started, and then her voice faded off.

"Billy would have been *especially* loved," Rebecca said. "By anyone who met him. When you saw someone smiling, you wanted to be with them all the time, because it made the things around you seem less — awful. And — you got all those letters, Mrs. McDonough." From guys in his company. Which she knew, because she had been shown them. "People over there cherished him. And, I know from my hospital, that we cared about every single boy who came in. Made sure they knew — " if their brains were still functioning enough to be cognizant — "that they were loved, and they weren't alone. It was *always* like that, no matter what."

Mrs. McDonough was crying, and when Rebecca looked at her mother, she saw that her eyes were brimming with tears, too.

"I, um — " Rebecca released a breath that hurt coming out, since she was probably holding back some tears of her own. "I know I never told you how much I loved Billy, but I — '' Help. "He was — I never — '' That was about as much as she was going to be able to get out — and the most she had ever managed.

Mrs. McDonough reached over and touched her hand. "You didn't have to tell me, Rebecca," she said. "You *showed* me, every time you came over here to see how I was, and to try and make me feel better."

Well, she'd tried, anyway, in her own inept and undemonstrative way. She smiled weakly, and poured herself a little more coffee. It was starting to get dark outside, and she could hear the dogs barking.

"Have you — '' Mrs. McDonough sounded very hesitant — "met anyone else?"

Not a question she could answer, with Billy looking at her from all over the room. She quickly shook her head, stirring some sugar into her coffee.

"Our losing Billy," Mrs. McDonough said kindly, "doesn't mean that you're supposed to give up *your* life, too."

No. The reasons behind her giving up her life were much more complicated than that. "I, um — '' Jesus, this woman would have been her *mother-in-law*. Her family. Rebecca let out her breath. "I — met someone by accident," she said. "I wasn't *looking* to, but — '' this living room was not the appropriate place to discuss Michael — "it, uh, didn't work out."

"I'm sorry," Mrs. McDonough said. "I hope the next person will."

An extremely selfless response. "I hope all of *you* are okay," Rebecca said. "That's what I hope."

"I know you do," Mrs. McDonough said, and smiled at her.

It was a relief when, a few minutes later, Ryan came running in with the dogs, wanting to know when dinner was. There was an exchange of noisy good-byes, Rebecca promising to stop by again, although the only thing she *really* wanted to do was go out to the car. Go home. Go to bed.

Finally, she was sitting in the front seat as her mother, who still wasn't saying much, turned on the ignition.

"I'll ride up to the lighthouse?" she suggested.

Why not, since it was dark. Rebecca shrugged. "Okay."

The lighthouse was only a few blocks from their house, and usually, she would have walked up there, more nights than not. Her mother pulled into the deserted parking lot, and they looked across the small grassy park at the rocks and ocean beyond.

"I guess you came along, hoping I was going to talk," Rebecca said.

Her mother nodded.

Right. Rebecca opened the door, getting out of the car. It was windy, but the air smelled good. Salty. Her mother followed her across the grass to the rocks, where they sat down, the water rolling up below them in small splashes.

"There's so much I want to ask," her mother said.

And so much she was never going to tell. "There's not much point," Rebecca said. "I'm only going to give you half-truths, anyway."

Her mother's sigh was so soft that Rebecca almost didn't hear it over the waves. "Well, that's been true for a long time, hasn't it," she said.

Yes. Rebecca folded her arms around her knees, looking out at the dark ocean.

Her mother sighed again. "You used to have so much energy, your father wanted me to ration your Cokes."

He had also, once in high school, when he found her in her room singing about everything being up-to-date in Kansas City, and dancing with one of the cats, accused her of getting into diet pills. "No, Dad," she'd said. "I'm just *like* this." He'd left, rather nettled.

"Well," her mother said, "I miss you. That's all."

A situation about which Rebecca could do very little. She had gone *over* there in relatively lousy shape — and come back in no shape at all. It walked, It talked, but It didn't actually exist.

They sat on the cold rocks, in the wind.

"I've never really grieved for him," Rebecca said. For any of them. By now, she had so many different sources of grief jumbled up inside that she wouldn't even know where to *start*.

"No," her mother agreed. "I don't think you have."

A fishing boat slowly chugged by them, with lights at the bow and stern, but only visible as a silhouette in the night.

"I think it helped Doug that he *could*," her mother said.

No doubt. Might also have helped that he had just loved him, as opposed to being *in* love with him.

"Were you talking about your friend Wolf before?" her mother asked.

It was hard to remember what she had, and hadn't, put in letters. Maybe she should just assume that except for the weather, and lies about her health, she hadn't put in much of *anything*. "No," she said. "Someone else."

Her mother nodded, her shoulders seeming to crumple in on themselves.

Damn it. Her ankle was throbbing, and she automatically rubbed it. "I, uh — " what a liar — "never mentioned Michael?"

Her mother shook her head.

Oh. Because she had met him in the jungle, and she'd never mentioned the jungle. "He, um — " Now the question was, had her father told her about her being shot down, or not? "I met him when his squad found me, after I was hurt," she said.

Her mother nodded, tightly. "The — jeep — accident."

Great, so she probably knew about the maggots, too. *Damn* him. "The helicopter crash," Rebecca said.

Her mother seemed to be holding her breath.

"I *couldn't* tell you," Rebecca said defensively. "You were worried enough, as it was."

"That's why all the medals," her mother said, almost inaudible.

Rebecca shrugged. "Mostly, that was the stupid Chief Nurse overreacting." Giving the murderer a special plum. She gritted her teeth. "Anyway, Michael started writing to me, and — " This was the part where she always got lost. "I guess I — fell in love with him." One-sided love, apparently. Leaving her not only sad, but *humiliated*.

Her mother was waiting for her to go on.

"He was badly hurt a few months ago," Rebecca said. "By a mine. And I guess he — " went back to Elizabeth — "didn't want to write to me anymore."

"Maybe you should write to *him*," her mother said.

And be further humiliated, when he didn't write back? Rebecca shook her head. "I'm not even sure where he is. Just — someplace in Colorado." Wherever it was that they made Coors.

"Well," her mother frowned, "maybe — "

"I'm pretty sure he has a girlfriend," Rebecca said. By now, probably a *wife*. "And I'm really just going to forget about it."

Her mother nodded, shivering in the wind. Actually, now that she thought about it, she was shivering, too.

"Should we go home?" she asked.

Her mother shook her head.

Yes, they were *such* stalwart Yankees, that they didn't mind being cold.

Climatically speaking, of course.

"What's the ocean like over there?" her mother asked.

The same. Different. "Very pretty," Rebecca said. "Greener." Clear. Tranquil. Ominous.

"The pictures were beautiful," her mother said.

Rebecca nodded. "I like it better here. When it gets sort of grey, and stark, and choppy." Whitecaps. She loved whitecaps. She looked over. "You and Dad should travel more."

"To *Vietnam*?" her mother said.

Well — no. "I just meant — " What *did* she mean? She wasn't exactly the Travel Queen herself. "You should — have more fun."

Her mother sighed. "He's really trying, Rebecca. You must be able to see that."

He should try keeping his word. "I know," Rebecca said. "I am, too." Not that she couldn't do better.

Her mother nodded.

"The truth is — " would, perhaps, lightning strike? " — it doesn't have all that much to do with him, anymore." She should stick with half-truths. "I'm mostly just disappointed in *myself*." To put it mildly.

"Now you sound like Doug," her mother said.

Really? She frowned. As far as she could tell, her brother rarely seemed to think twice. Sometimes, not even *once*. She looked at her mother, unnerved all over again by seeing her so subdued, and defeated.

"Ever wonder how you got in the middle of all this?" she asked.

Her mother smiled a little.

"At least the rest of us screwed things up for *ourselves*," Rebecca said.

"And what was I, asleep?" her mother asked. "I think I'm probably entitled to my share of blame."

Oh, these bleak conversations, under the protective cover of nightfall. Rebecca shook her head. "I think you would have liked my Chief Nurse."

"I thought you said she was stupid," her mother said.

Rebecca grinned. Miss Perfect was *really* Miss Perspicacity. "I guess she was my best friend over there. I mean, just about everyone I met was great, but — I really felt like she was my *sister*." *Still* felt that way.

"She sent me a letter, after you were hurt," her mother said, and paused thoughtfully. "It was very well written."

Which, coming from her mother, the constant reader, was somewhat akin to being blessed by the Pope.

"It sounded a lot like what you were telling Mary McDonough." Her mother looked over, still shivering, in the fall wind. "Was any of it true?"

"It was *all* true," Rebecca said. Although she hadn't actually read it. "She just left out the ugly parts."

"Which I should always assume you're doing?" her mother asked.

When in doubt. Rebecca sighed. "Yeah," she said.

Chapter Twenty-one

It was almost a week before she could get up the nerve to go out in public again and this time, she only went as far as the grocery store. She was jittery enough to consider staying in the car, but then followed her mother inside, trailing the grocery cart up and down the aisles, and occasionally fetching things. They ran into her fourth-grade teacher in front of the Campbell's soups, and Mrs. Vilmer's reaction to seeing her was, to her relief, more routine than excessive. But, she was probably a little out of touch, since she asked how Doug was, and her mother said, Fine, without going into detail.

They also ran into the minister's wife — near the paper towels — who welcomed her home enthusiastically, asking if they could expect to see her at services on Sunday? Rebecca nodded noncommittally, in lieu of saying, "Yeah, *right*."

When they were alone again, her mother selecting napkins and Kleenex, Rebecca sighed. Deeply.

"You're an adult, Rebecca," her mother said. "If

you don't want to go to church, you don't have to go to church.''

Yeah, right. It wasn't as though it wouldn't get all over *town*.

"Please go get some cat food," her mother said.

Yeah, yeah, yeah. Rebecca went off to get cat food.

The checkout line was longer than usual — at least, as she remembered it — and her mother was doing a much better job of pretending not to be impatient than she was.

"Want me to go down and get the stuff at the drugstore?" she asked. "Save time?"

Her mother shrugged. "Sure. If you want."

She wanted.

She had just started down the sidewalk, when she saw someone familiar coming towards her. Someone very familiar. Her friend Irene, pushing a stroller with Robert, who would be almost two, in it, and Kevin, Jr., who was four, walking happily next to her. All in all, idyllically suburban.

Oh, *hell*. Rebecca stopped, about to go the other way, but it was already too late.

Irene stopped too, staring at her. *"Becky?"*

Rebecca managed to smile. "Hi."

"My God, I can't believe you're — " Irene shook her head, and took off her sunglasses. Big, funky white ones. "When did you get home?"

"A few days ago," Rebecca said. Sort of.

"Oh," Irene said, and digested that, some of the welcoming pleasure sliding out of her expression, hurt feelings replacing it. "Well, uh, it's good to see you. How are you?"

"Fine," Rebecca said quickly. "I mean, a little tired, maybe, but — how are *you*?"

Irene nodded. "Fine. We're all fine."

They both lapsed into stilted silence, and Rebecca noticed Kevin staring at her with extreme, and perplexed, concentration.

"*I* know *you*," he said.

"Yeah." Rebecca crouched down to be at his level, and smiled at him. "Hi." She smiled at Robert, who certainly wouldn't recognize her, but was glad to see her, anyway. "Hi," she said, and batted her hand against his a couple of times, which he seemed to find hilarious. Then, since their mother was uncharacteristically evincing no pride in their general cuteness and charm, she stood up. "They've, uh, really grown a lot."

Irene nodded, pushing her pocketbook strap back up to her shoulder as it slipped down. She was wearing pedal pushers — old pink ones Rebecca remembered from high school, although they were tighter now — a slightly rumpled white blouse with a Peter Pan collar, and penny loafers, her hair tied back in a thick ponytail.

"Irene," Rebecca started, "I — "

"I guess I'm lucky I happened to run into you," Irene said, putting just the slightest bit of stress on the word "happened."

Yeah, that was fair. "My mother *made* me leave the house," Rebecca said. "Since I got back, I — I haven't even really been leaving my *room*."

Now, Irene actually looked at her. "Are you all right?"

No. "It was — kind of a long year," Rebecca said.

Irene nodded, her eyes worried.

"As soon as I got the — " What? Rebecca let out her breath. "The first person I called was going to be you."

Kevin and Robert were starting to get bored — and a little petulant, Rebecca and Irene both glancing down at them.

"I thought you'd be home by now," Irene said, "but I just — assumed you'd call me."

Rebecca didn't know what to say, so she shrugged.

"Well, maybe we could — Boys!" Irene said sharply, and then went on in the same calm tone — "get together this weekend. You could come over for lunch, I could invite some of the old gang — does that sound okay?"

Except for the "gang" part. "Sure," Rebecca said, and put on a smile. "What should I bring?"

She brought brownies. It was the first time she had driven in a year, and even though it wasn't far, she was nervous being behind the wheel. Overcautious.

There were three cars parked in front of the house, none of which she recognized. A couple of old Chevys, and a Plymouth Belvedere wagon. Irene's station wagon was in the driveway, along with Kevin's battered red pickup truck. It had been old when they were still in *school*.

She had hoped that she was going to be early, but the combination of dread, and twenty-miles-per-hour, had made her a good ten or fifteen minutes late. With luck, though, the gang wasn't going to get any bigger than the three cars already here. Unless some of them had carpooled.

When she rang the bell, Irene's husband, Kevin, answered the door. He had been a year ahead of them in high school, and the center on the football team.

"Hi!" he said, in his big, deep voice and gave her such a healthy hug that he almost lifted her off the ground.

She managed to hug back, and keep the brownies from falling — once a waitress, always a waitress — at the same time. "Hey, P.B.," she said, which was short for Polar Bear — both because of his size, and his being notorious for swimming in the ocean every day, year-round. Sun, rain — or snow.

"Looks good," he said, helping himself to a couple of brownies. "How you doing, anyway? C'mon, they're in the living room."

She followed him through the house, tripping over a small yellow truck, but once again, able to hold the brownies aloft.

Irene stuck her head out of the kitchen. "Hi, Becky. I'll be right there."

Rebecca nodded back, hearing a fair amount of noise coming from the living room. Children. Lots of children. She didn't really want to go in, but P.B. was boisterously ushering her along, sneaking another two brownies. From the door, she saw Nora Anderson — a very quiet girl from her class, who was considerably more clever than she gave herself credit for being — and Susan Tabor, who had gone into nursing, and — oh, great — Faith

Quinton, sitting on the couch, holding a little girl who looked to be about ten months old.

"Hi, Becky," Nora said. At first glance, she was very plain, but when she smiled, she was always entirely transformed.

"Hi," Rebecca said, and gave P.B. the brownies, since he seemed to be enjoying them so much.

Susan's hello was a little shy, but cheery; Faith's less so. On both counts.

Oh, Christ, they were all wearing *dresses*. She had figured that Saturday Lunch was a near certainty for slacks. Apparently such was not the case, among the young-married set. But, hell — even Laura Petrie wore slacks sometimes. And Donna Reed probably *owned* some.

Irene came in with a tray of three iced drinks, handing them out, then smiling at Rebecca. "What would you like?"

To go home. "Is that tea?" Rebecca asked. "Looks good. Need help?"

Irene shook her head, going back into the kitchen.

Okay. She looked around, then sat in an old padded chair she remembered from Irene's mother's house.

"How are you?" Susan asked. She was round, and amiable, and placid. Rebecca liked her well enough, but they had never really been close, because — even back in junior high — Susan had always seemed to find her a little intimidating.

Rebecca nodded. "Fine. How are you?" Then, she noticed the — large — diamond engagement ring perched on her finger. "Hey, congratulations."

Susan looked pleased, and shy.

"When's the big day?" Rebecca asked.

"Next June," Susan said.

Rebecca nodded, resisting the urge to stick her unadorned left hand in her pocket. Her *jeans* pocket. "Your baby's very cute," she said to Faith. "What's her name?"

The baby didn't seem happy about being on the couch, but Faith kept her tucked close. "Millie," she said.

Ah. How effusive. Then again, she and Faith had pretty much *always* disliked each other. Hard to figure out why Irene had *invited* her. "You didn't bring your kids?" she asked Nora.

"No," Nora said, and broke into her sudden smile. "*He's* handling them today."

Her husband Carl. Yet another Prom date who ended up being the real thing.

"The phone will begin to ring any second," Nora said, and catching another glimpse of the dazzling smile, Rebecca smiled, too.

Irene returned with the tea, and they all sat there, rather formally.

"You must be glad to be back," Nora said.

Hmmm. Rebecca shrugged. Faith's baby had clambered off the couch and was tottering around now, so she reached out automatically to pick her up, stopping when she saw Faith wince.

"It's okay," Rebecca said, and grinned. "I'm a nurse — we wash our hands a lot." Faith's expression didn't change, and she glanced at Susan. "Back me up on this one, Susan."

"Millie," Faith said sternly. She waved a thick, round rattle and Millie wandered back over.

The silence in the room — broken only by Kevin, Jr., chattering as he played with some blocks in the corner — seemed very loud.

"Okay," Rebecca said, against her better judgment. "Humor me. Tell me *which* delusion it is that you've gotten into your head."

Faith didn't look at her, lifting Millie onto her lap. "I don't know what you came back with."

Nightmares, and a short temper. "Jet lag?" Rebecca said.

Irene shook her head at her.

Okay, fine. She would drop it. She turned to Susan. "What did you end up specializing in?"

"Pediatrics," Susan said shyly.

Rebecca nodded. Not something to be self-conscious about. "That's hard work." Having to watch a child die was the very worst.

"W-What did you do?" Susan asked.

The tea was good, but a beer would be better. Several beers. "Triage, mostly," Rebecca said. "I was in Emergency/Receiving."

Susan gasped slightly. "That must have been awful."

Yep. "Well," Rebecca said, and shrugged.

It was quiet again.

"Maybe *you* think pediatrics isn't good enough," Faith said, rocking Millie in her arms, "but Susie did the right thing. She helps *children*."

Faith was the kind of person who had such a sweet face that she never really got proper credit for being such an unbelievable bitch. "Who's a child?" Rebecca asked, actually able to *feel* the color rising in her cheeks. "What's a seventeen-year-old kid who doesn't shave yet, who's lying there in pieces, and trying not to cry because all he wants is chocolate ice cream? But before you can even turn around to ask a corpsman to go find some, he's already dead, and — " She shook her head. "The ER was *filled* with kids, every day."

There was another silence.

"It must have been terrible," Nora said.

Rebecca kept frowning at Faith. "What *else* are you wondering about?" she asked. "My no-doubt prodigious promiscuity?"

Faith shrugged, not looking at her as she gave Millie a plain cracker from the hors d'oeuvres tray on the coffee table.

"Mondays, Wednesdays, and Fridays, we all serviced platoons of men," Rebecca said, "and the rest of the week, we embraced lesbianism."

"I wouldn't be surprised," Faith said, primly.

Jesus. "The problem with guys over there," Rebecca said, both calm and furious, "is that they kept dying, or getting maimed, on you. So, we had to — make do."

"Please don't do this," Irene said in a very quiet voice. "Okay?"

Yeah, fine. Whatever. Rebecca nodded, pressing her teeth together — but then saw that Irene was looking at Faith, not her.

"What," Faith said, "we're all suddenly going to pretend to be *for* the war, just because *she's* here?"

"How about because we're in *my* house, and I want things to be nice?" Irene suggested.

Even though the barn door was already swinging open, with the horse galloping wildly down the road.

Rebecca decided to find a new conversation topic. "What's your fiancé like?" she asked Susan. "Do I know him?"

Susan looked pleased, and ducked her head. "He's one of the attendings at the hospital. He's — he's just *wonderful*."

So, they all talked about The Doctor, and Susan's already well-developed and complex wedding plans, and everyone's children, and how cute they were, and how much work it all was — and a bunch of other things that made Rebecca feel like Belle Watling, had she unexpectedly found herself in Aunt Pittypat's parlour.

Lunch seemed to be delicious, and recipes were exchanged, but Rebecca's stomach hurt, and if she had been at home, she would have pushed her plate aside and opted for a stiff drink, instead.

"Are you dating anyone?" Susan asked, over the tetrazzini.

Rebecca shook her head, and reached for the pepper.

"Oh," Susan said, and looked embarrassed.

Just for a little devilment, Rebecca glanced at Faith. "Maybe you know someone? You could fix me up?"

"Mmmm," Faith said, and came close to smiling.

It would be tactless to remind everyone that she had once, back when they were juniors, gone to a movie with the guy — a senior — who was now Faith's husband — and found him deadly dull.

"Carl might know someone," Nora said thoughtfully.

"No, it's okay," Rebecca said. "I — I'm really not looking to meet anyone."

Susan pursed her lips, also thinking. "There are *lots* of nice doctors at the hospital."

Especially not a doctor. "Thank you, but I'm not going to be here that much longer, anyway," Rebecca said.

Faith's head snapped up, away from the high chair Irene had set out for Millie. "Are you going *back*?"

An idea not without merit. "My next duty station is Fort Dix," Rebecca said, disturbed to hear herself sounding like — a lifer.

Faith nodded. "Making sure they're in tip top shape, so they can go right over and get killed?"

What did *she* know about it? "No," Rebecca said, toying with her roll. "Taking care of the ones who've already been, I would imagine."

Once again, silence reigned.

"When do you get out?" Irene asked.

Rebecca shrugged. "I haven't decided yet," she said. Which, increasingly, seemed to be true.

After Irene had served coffee, their group dwindled — Susan, off to go meet her Doctor, while Faith felt that Millie's nap was long overdue. And, perhaps, that her oxygen was being contaminated by being in the same room as a Vietnam veteran. So Rebecca sat in the living room with Irene and Nora, while Kevin and Robert — and P.B. — appeared at regular intervals, full of requests and problems, big and small.

"I'm sorry," Irene said. "She kind of invited herself."

Rebecca shrugged, eating one of her own brownies. Not as good as her mother's, but okay.

"Nobody blames *you* for what's happening over there," Nora said.

Maybe. Although if they knew that she had played a much bigger role in the ugliness than they realized, they would be condemning her more than Faith had. "It's more complicated than it seems," she said. Dismissively.

"Well, what was it like?" Irene asked. "*Really.*"

They had all been friends for a long time — eaten lunch together in the school cafeteria every day, gone over to the Warwick to see all the movies that came to town, hung out at the beach, sat in the splintery stands at Marblehead football, basketball, and baseball games. But, that was a long time *ago.*

Irene shifted her position, crossing her right leg over her left, then going back to the way she had been sitting before. "I'm sorry. You probably don't want to talk about it."

That, too. Rebecca let out her breath. "You know how many guys came into the ER, built just like P.B.?"

Irene flushed. "It's not his fault he has a bad knee."

"I'm *glad* he has a bad knee," Rebecca said. "I wish they all did." Not that Michael's bad knee had kept *him* out of combat.

"So — " Nora paused uncertainly — "you're against the war?"

Stupid question. Who was going to be more antiwar than someone who had actually *seen* what it was like? Up close, and *very* personal. "*Ob*viously," Rebecca said. "I just — I'm not going to sit around trashing the guys who thought they were serving their country by going over. I mean — we're sitting here drinking coffee, while people are *dying*. People like Billy."

Irene and Nora nodded.

"Doesn't she even *remember* him?" Rebecca asked. "I can't be the *only* one who thought he was great."

"You're not," Irene said, and Nora nodded.

Well — good. Rebecca poured another cup of coffee, drinking half of it in one long swallow.

"Have you seen his mother yet?" Nora asked.

Rebecca nodded, as Robert came toddling in, swift and unwieldy, and crying over some unknown mishap. Irene bent down, giving him a kiss and a little tickle, and he smiled, climbing up to sit on her lap.

"I would have been *like* all of you," Rebecca said. "Married, and — " happy — "and — things would have been different."

Irene and Nora nodded.

Well. Anyway. Rebecca finished her coffee, and stood up. "Let me help you clear things away here."

"No, it's okay," Irene said. "I can — "

"No problem," Rebecca said, and collected plates and cups, carrying them to the kitchen.

As soon as everything was cleaned up — she could leave.

Chapter Twenty-two

While they were stacking and washing the dishes, Nora's husband called — for the third time — and she left, with a "Come over and see the kids, okay? Anytime." Rebecca nodded, and smiled, and squirted more Ivory liquid into the water.

After Irene saw her out, she came back into the kitchen, Robert bombing along behind her.

"You don't have to do that, Becky," she said.

Rebecca shrugged, washing dishes swiftly. "No problem."

Irene started to protest, but then just picked up a dish towel.

They worked without speaking, and as Rebecca scrubbed the tetrazzini baking pan, she felt a pair of small arms wrap around her jeans leg, just above her knee. She glanced down, and saw Robert beaming up at her.

"He seems to be confused," she said.

"He *likes* you," Irene said.

Oh. The happily trusting arms felt so good that

she *wanted* to bend down and scoop him into a big hug, but she hunched over the pan instead.

"I can really do this later," Irene said. "Why don't we just sit down for a minute?"

Was it her imagination, or was that the fat lady, starting to warm up? "Well — " Rebecca tried to think of a good excuse. "I should probably — "

"Please?" Irene said.

Rebecca let the Brillo pad fall into the water. Ten minutes, maybe, and then she could go. Say her parents were expecting her.

They sat at the kitchen table, arms resting on the red-checked oilcloth, looking down at fresh cups of coffee.

Irene sighed. "I'm sorry you didn't have a good time."

"It was great," Rebecca said quickly. "I mean — thank you. It was really nice."

Irene didn't say anything, pouring milk into her coffee.

Enough with the scales; time for the lady to waddle on out and sing the national anthem already. "Anyway," Rebecca got ready to stand up, "I know you went to a lot of trouble, and I really appreciate it."

"You stopped writing," Irene said.

Rebecca frowned at her. "I did not."

" 'I'm fine. How are you? It's hot,' " Irene said.

Like she needed this? "Perhaps you're familiar with the Tet Offensive?" Rebecca said.

Irene nodded, and Rebecca nodded too, shortly, bringing her still-full cup over to the sink.

"You always used to complain about your father being condescending," Irene said after her.

Rebecca turned on the water to wash the cup. "So?"

"So the fact that you're so smart doesn't mean that everyone *else* is stupid," Irene said. "Know what I mean?"

Rebecca shrugged. "I never said you were stupid."

"You didn't have to," Irene said grimly.

The little silence that fell was quite ugly, and the fact that Robert had come over and started playing around with her leg again seemed ill-timed, at best.

"The difference between you and your father *used* to be that you were never mean," Irene said.

"Well," Rebecca said, and left it at that.

Irene shook her head, looking down at her coffee. "I know that, compared to you, none of us has been anywhere, or done anything — "

"Well, you *did* create life," Rebecca said, Robert hanging on to her with what appeared to be rapture. "I hear God gives extra points for that."

Irene didn't smile.

Okay. "I'm sorry," Rebecca said. "I didn't mean to hurt your feelings, I just — " Couldn't seem to do anything right anymore. "I'm sorry." She bent down to disengage Robert's arms, then sent him over in his mother's direction.

Irene picked him up, but he climbed down again within seconds, toddling at top speed towards the family room.

"It's strange," Rebecca said, after a pause, "not to be funny anymore. I don't think I knew I *was* funny, until I wasn't."

Irene nodded.

"I *try* to make jokes, but — " She shook her

head. Was Embitterment one of the Seven Deadly Sins? The Sin people would probably be in touch soon, to see if she wanted to be this year's poster child.

"Is it mostly Vietnam," Irene asked, sounding hesitant, "or is Billy still a big part of it?"

Yes, and yes. Rebecca shrugged. "There's no way to separate them. I wouldn't even know where to — "

P.B. came in, with Robert riding up on his shoulders and Kevin, Jr., trailing along behind. "Hey, what's for dinner? You're going to stay, right, Becky?"

She and Irene both looked at him blankly, then looked at the clock on the wall.

Almost five. "I'm sorry, I didn't know it was so late," Rebecca said, and picked up her mother's freshly washed brownie plate from the counter.

"Why *don't* you stay, Becky," Irene said. "After, we could — "

Rebecca shook her head, edging towards the door. "Thanks, but — my parents are going to be wondering where I am." She gave P.B. and the boys a fast smile. "Good to see you. Thanks again, Irene."

Irene managed to catch up to her at the front door. "When do you leave?"

"Uh, pretty soon," Rebecca said. She could at least have the manners to be specific. "About two weeks."

Irene nodded, and they avoided each other's eyes.

"Will you call me?" Irene asked.

"Oh, yeah," Rebecca said, nodding vigorously. Irene wasn't fooled.

She took her time driving home, and then sat in the car, in the driveway. She couldn't quite face going inside and pretending that everything was fine yet, so she retrieved the basketball from the garage, and started taking shots in the dark. An appropriately futile activity.

After a while, she heard the back door open, and someone came outside with Jack, who went snuffling off through the leaves and bushes. She just kept shooting, missing many more than she made.

"Your mother and I were getting worried," her father said.

How prescient of them. She dribbled a couple of times, then shot, keeping most of her weight on her left leg. "I survived *Vietnam*, Dad — I think I can handle it here on the North Shore."

Her father nodded, and squinted up at the hoop. "Can you see what you're doing?"

Rebecca shook her head. "No." Clang. She grabbed the ball, and shot again. Missed again. Swallowed obscenities again.

He shifted his weight, looking uncomfortable. "Did you have a nice time?"

"Yeah." She missed another shot. "So I was out here celebrating."

He watched her shoot, and rebound, and shoot some more.

"Your brother called," he said.

She stared at him, her hands freezing on the ball. "*What?* When?"

"A couple of hours ago," he said.

Damn. She pressed tightly on the ball with both hands, trying to make it explode, so *she* wouldn't. "You hang up on him?" she asked.

Her father shook his head.

"Well." She held the ball against her body with one hand, giving it a punch with the other. "That's progress."

To his credit, he let that pass. "He wanted to be sure that you'd made it home, and were all right," he said.

It had been almost two years since she'd heard her brother's voice — and she'd *missed* it. She punched the ball again. Hurt her knuckles. "Is he going to call back?"

Her father sighed. "He's going to try."

She didn't say anything, hugging the ball against her chest, but then slammed it against the garage door as hard as she could. "God *damn* it!" The ball bounced back, and she threw it again, with all of her strength, fiercely pleased to hear one of the windows in the door shatter.

"Rebecca," her father started uneasily.

If he didn't watch it, the ball would slam through his *head* next. "I'm going for a walk," she said, pausing only to kick the front tire of the car, pain reverberating through her bad ankle. "Don't wait up," she said, and limped out into the street without looking back.

She went down to the lighthouse, and sat on the rocks in chilly fog, bent over folded arms, feeling as though every internal organ she had was taking sides in a vicious battle of frustration. Then again, maybe she was just pre-ulcerous.

Maybe she was *post*-ulcerous.

When she was pretty sure that she was under control — and couldn't stand the cold anymore — she got up, walking across the wet grassy park to the empty street. Sometimes she wondered if anyone in her neighborhood *ever* left their houses, off-season. Or stayed up later than nine.

Her house was quiet, too, but most of the lights were still on, and Jack started barking before she even set foot on the back steps.

So much for slipping in unnoticed.

Her mother was sitting at the kitchen table with a drink and a thick book, both of which she lowered.

"Uh, hi," Rebecca said.

Her mother looked at her without much expression. "Are you hungry?" she asked.

She had eaten very little lunch, so she actually was. Starving, even.

"I kept your dinner warm for you," her mother said.

Oh. She closed the refrigerator, then opened it again to get a couple of beers. Her place was already set, and she sat down as her mother took a foil-wrapped plate out of the oven and served it to her.

"Um, thank you," Rebecca said.

Her mother nodded, returning to her book and her drink.

Gin again. Jesus. "How is he?" Rebecca asked. "Is he okay?"

Her mother shrugged. "He says he is."

Which meant little or nothing. Rebecca opened a beer, her appetite rapidly fading. "Is he coming home?"

If possible, her mother looked even more unhappy. "No," she said.

She could have guessed that, so she shouldn't have asked. Her dinner looked and smelled delicious, but she ignored it, leaning her elbow on the table and slouching her head into her hand. "Do you think the FBI will show up again?"

"They always do." Then, her mother shrugged. "I've seen the cars around a lot lately."

Agents had had her house under surveillance periodically, and a couple of times — once when she was home, once when she was in Vietnam — they had come knocking on the door in the middle of the night, apparently trying to scare them into giving Doug up. The only thing they had gained was her parents', and her, permanent enmity.

"You mean, because I'm home, and they figure he might show up to see me?" Rebecca said.

Her mother nodded.

Bastards. They'd better hope *she* didn't catch them sneaking around.

Her father came in, and there was such an indecisive quality to the way he stood in the doorway — despite being a tall and broad-shouldered man — that it bugged her, and she concentrated on her beer. But he must have just come in to make sure she had gotten home in one piece, because after nodding at them, he withdrew, going back to wherever he had been.

"Martin," her mother said, but he was either already out of earshot — or just didn't feel like answering. She shook her head, and Rebecca saw the hand that wasn't holding her drink tighten until the knuckles were white.

Rebecca picked up her fork, wondering how long she should sit here before she could escape to her room. Very quietly, in the living room, she could hear the piano. Chopin.

They both listened, not looking at each other.

"A man who plays like that can't be all bad," her mother said, her voice so low that Rebecca had to lean closer to hear her.

"I never said he was all bad," she said.

Her mother looked at her for a few seconds, then looked down at her drink.

Jesus, there was a lot going on here. Clearly, she was *emotionally* too young for it, but it would be nice to be chronologically too young, too.

Off the hook.

"He's trying to apologize," her mother said.

Playing for them had always seemed to be the only way he knew how. "*I'm* the one who lost my temper," Rebecca said. "He just happened to be standing there."

Her mother nodded in a distant sort of way.

It occurred to her that things might *never* work out with her family, and the thought was terrifying. Maybe things had never been *perfect*, but they had always been — fine. Pleasant. Nice.

"He's thinking of giving up his practice," her mother said.

What? "Since when?" Rebecca asked.

"I don't know," her mother said, shrugging. "I guess he's afraid he's losing his nerve."

Surgeons needed lots of nerve, and *plenty* of ego. But the concept of her father quitting was right up there with the idea of the Vietnam War having a happy ending.

"He's cut down a lot," her mother said, "and — I don't know."

Yeah, right. Never happen. She must have rolled her eyes or something, because her mother frowned at her.

"He's *home* so much more, Rebecca," she said. "Haven't you noticed?"

Well, yeah, now that she mentioned it. "I guess I just thought he — " Rebecca stopped. Thought what? That he was hanging around to see *her*? "It would be dumb," she said, rather lamely. "His quitting."

Her mother shrugged, and drank some of her gin.

Going to Fort Dix was starting to seem enticing. Going up to her room, locking the door, and stuffing her head under a pillow also sounded good. Jack had come over, resting his muzzle on her knee, and she started to give him some of the meat on her plate, then glanced at her mother and put the meat back. Her mother didn't seem to notice, one way or the other.

They sat there for another minute, and then Rebecca got up, beer bottle in hand. "Excuse me," she said, and headed for the living room.

He didn't look up when she came in, but when he finished the passage he was playing, he lifted his hands from the keyboard.

"No, don't stop," she said, and sat on the couch, pulling her legs up.

He rubbed his right hand with his left. "I don't play as well as I used to, I — "

"Well, I have a tin ear," she said — which was equally untrue.

He hesitated, but then resumed playing. Quite beautifully.

"Mozart?" he asked, when he was finished.

She nodded, and listened. She and Doug had both taken lessons — for years — leaving her with rudimentary skills, at best. Doug had talent, but he had — in her father's regularly vocalized opinion — wasted it on garage rock thumping.

Partway through the concerto, her mother came in, and sat on the other end of the couch with her drink. Her father always liked having an audience, and when the piece was over, he glanced at her mother.

"Very nice, Martin," she said, which was what she always said, but she also always sounded as if she meant it.

Rebecca nodded. "Yeah, it was, Dad."

He looked pleased, slid his hands along the keyboard in a little glissando, then stopped. "Your brother says he's playing in a bar, a couple of nights a week," he said.

It really *was* progress if they were going to start dropping Doug's name in casual conversation. If the subject became less of a verbal minefield.

"Jazz?" Rebecca asked.

Her father shook his head. "Standards, mostly. Some ragtime."

She would really enjoy sitting in that unknown Canadian bar, watching Doug, with his long hair and beatnik shades — assuming he still had both — faking a wide smile as he plodded through "Moonglow." "I wish we could hear him," she said, and her parents nodded.

The room was quiet, except for Jack's tags jangling as he scratched over by the fireplace.

"So, um, do you know 'Greensleeves'?" Rebecca asked. "Or — 'Für Elise,' or any of that *real* piano stuff?"

Her father grinned, and started playing "Greensleeves."

Chapter Twenty-three

To make her parents happy, she went to church with them the next morning, feeling very conspicuous in her uniform. More people than she would have predicted came over to say hello to her, and that it was good to see her back, although there were a number of others who demonstrated rather more Yankee reserve than seemed indicated. But her mother stayed close to her side the whole time, and since she had always been very involved in the church, the odds were against anyone striding over and starting trouble with her newly returned veteran daughter.

As soon as they got home, she changed out of her uniform immediately, hanging it at the back of the closet. It had been decided that today was the day she and her father would go look for a car, and so they sat at the kitchen table, reading the classified ads in various local papers, and calling the phone numbers listed for the ones that sounded the best — Rebecca's priorities being not spending too much, and having a car that started more often than it didn't.

"Remember," her mother said after them, "don't buy the first thing you see."

Rebecca and her father left, nodding — and promptly ended up buying the first one they saw, a 1961 Dodge Dart that seemed pretty decent. Not that they were car experts, but the inside of the engine looked nice and clean, the radio worked, and they were able to bargain the owner down fifty dollars.

Rebecca drove it home, following her father, and then they waited in the driveway for her mother to come out and admire their purchase. When she didn't appear, her father leaned inside the Dart and beeped the horn a couple of times.

Her mother opened the back door, and sighed. "You bought the first one you saw."

"It seems like a *very* good car," Rebecca's father said.

Rebecca nodded. "And a bargain."

Her mother pulled on a sweater and then came outside, walking all the way around it, nudging at least two of the tires with her foot. After studying the car, she studied Rebecca. "You don't want something a little more — sporty?"

"It's *very* practical," her father said, and Rebecca nodded.

"That it is," her mother agreed, "but — wouldn't you have been happier with a convertible, maybe?"

Convertible? "Mom, I have to drive *far*," Rebecca said. New Jersey. "And it'll be winter soon."

Her father nodded. "Very impractical."

Her mother raised both arms, either washing her hands of the whole thing, or just giving up. "Okay," she said. "It's — very nice."

"Reliable," Rebecca's father said.

Rebecca nodded. "Dependable."

"Yes," her mother agreed. "It's — utilitarian." She paused on her way back inside. "And — you're *sure* about the color, Rebecca?"

The color. They hadn't really paid much attention to the color. On closer examination, in the fading light, it proved to be a flat, pale greyish-green. Kind of — utilitarian.

"It was owned by his mother-in-law," her father said, sounding a little defensive. "She rarely — "

"Drove it except to buy groceries and go to church," her mother finished.

Which was actually exactly what the guy had said. Hmmm. Rebecca and her father looked at each other.

"It's a *very* good car," Rebecca said.

Her father nodded. "Started right up."

Rebecca nodded, too. "First time we tried it."

"Well, good," her mother said, and opened the back door. "Happy birthday." She paused. "You aren't going to — name it — or anything, are you?"

How very banal. Rebecca shook her head.

"Good," her mother said, and went inside.

Rebecca and her father looked at each other.

"I don't think she likes it," he said.

Rebecca nodded. She didn't think so, either.

After dinner, she watched Ed Sullivan — liked Flip Wilson; despised Tiny Tim — and then, the

Smothers Brothers, not finding any of the comedy the slightest bit funny. An opinion her parents seemed to share. But they all stayed in the den, pursuing family togetherness — her parents reading books, while she half-watched television, and half-read the Sunday papers.

"Um, what do you think about the liver?" Rebecca asked her father during one of the commercials, indicating the Sunday *Globe*. Children's Hospital had performed a liver transplant on a little girl — only the fourth time the operation had ever been attempted on actual patients, the first three of whom had not survived.

Her father looked uneasy — she had always wanted to talk medical talk with him, although they rarely did — but then, he nodded. "I think the implications for the future are very promising," he said.

Well, yeah, but — couldn't he *elaborate*? Treat her like someone who was capable of holding informed opinions? She glanced at her mother, who was reading, but her shoulders were tense enough to indicate that she was listening, too. Waiting for friction.

Rebecca looked back at the television, where Nancy Sinatra had come out as a guest star. It was perverse of her to start this conversation when they had been sitting here so peacefully.

"We lost *so* many livers," she said.

Her father lowered his book, but she couldn't tell if he was really interested, or just humoring her.

"I saw some of our doctors perform real miracles," she said, "but when the casualties were out of control, we would have to triage out a lot of the livers. And the brain cases, of course.''

Her father nodded, but he was still holding the book, instead of putting it all the way down, so maybe she should drop it. Yank back her little trial balloon.

''I just — '' She was just wasting her time. ''Forget it,'' she said, and folded her arms, slouching over them.

Either the room was too quiet, or Nancy Sinatra was too *loud*. Her mother had stopped turning pages, and her father's jaw was set so tightly that it looked like his teeth hurt.

''I don't understand what you want, Rebecca,'' he said, sounding very stiff.

Yeah, well, Otis Redding had written a song about it. She looked around for her own book, so she could take it upstairs to her room.

''Let's please not start,'' her mother said quietly. ''Okay?''

All she had tried to *start* was a damn conversation. ''I'm really tired,'' Rebecca said, getting up, not looking at either of them. ''I'm going to bed.''

Her mother sighed. ''Come on, Rebecca, don't do this.''

Christ. Couldn't it be her *father's* fault for once? He was a renowned goddamned authority on medicine, and he could *teach* her things. Was that so much to ask?

Before her mother could say anything else, she turned to scowl at her father. ''Don't you get it at all, Dad?'' she said. ''They'd bring these poor guys in from the field, and sometimes it was me, writing them off.''

Her father frowned. "Surely, the onus of the final decision didn't fall on *you*."

If he went into the "you're *only* a nurse" speech now, her evening would, truly, be complete.

"Why don't you tell us about it," her mother said. "We'd be very interested."

Well — they'd put their books down, anyway. Every instinct she had was pulling her in the direction of her room, and a double scotch, but she forced herself to take a deep breath and sit back down. Hell, maybe he really *didn't* know what it was like, since he served on a hospital ship only briefly during World War II, and then, because the fighting was pretty much over, he'd been stationed at a couple of VA hospitals, stateside.

"Dad, I was *in charge* of the ER sometimes," she said. Many times. "During mass-cals, the doctors would all be operating, and — I was really *good* at triage, so — " Hell of a thing to be good at, triage.

"How much supervision did you have?" he asked, frowning.

"A lot," she said, "when it was busy, but none at night. They'd just put a corpsman on with me, and — the Chief Nurse would usually come by, and — " hang out — "check up, but — it wasn't like nursing here." Understatement of the millennium.

Her father nodded, but didn't seem thrilled by the idea.

Okay, enough for one night. Time to reestablish her personal paternal DMZ. "Anyway, I don't know," she said, and looked over at her mother, who was watching them with worried eyes. "I guess I just wish we'd been able to do better with the livers.''

"What sort of medical procedures did they permit you to *do*?'' her father asked, sitting back and folding his arms.

Oh, so now that he had a chance to *disapprove*, he was interested. "I don't know,'' she said. "Suturing and debriding, obviously. Severing non-viable extremities. Endotracheal tubes, chest tubes. Femoral and jugular sticks. Just about *anything* that only used a local.'' She checked his expression to see if he was medically offended yet. He looked — unsettled, mainly. "Lots of times, especially during Tet and Mini-Tet, they'd have you close in the OR, or — I did a few splenectomies, and that kind of thing, but I was almost always in the ER, because they liked me doing triage.'' They'd never really gotten used to her leaping in to do cutdowns and the like, but as long as the kid's life had been at stake in each given situation, they had finally given up on yelling at her.

Her father nodded slowly.

"Not too many bedpans and backrubs,'' she said.

"No,'' he said. "Doesn't sound that way.''

Okay. So far, so good. "It's, um,'' she carefully didn't look at her mother, "kind of dispassionate to say it, but the research possibilities over there are *incredible*. Conditions and complications you could never replicate in a lab.''

Her father nodded. Looked *interested*, even.

"I mean, if it were me,'' Rebecca went on, tentatively, "I'd probably want to concentrate on combatting infection, because — that was just overwhelming, or maybe ways to overcome shock lung, or respiratory distress in general, or — I don't know. You could spend your career just studying the *skin diseases* over there.'' Then, she waited for his reaction.

There was a long pause, the noise of the television droning in the background.

''I'm thinking of spending more time in research,'' her father said. ''And maybe teaching a full load at the medical school for a while.'' The medical school, meaning Harvard, of course, where he had been a highly valued — if somewhat non-participatory — member of their faculty for years.

''Is that what you want?'' Rebecca asked.

Her father took his time answering. ''I don't know,'' he said. ''For now, I think it might be.''

Okay. She nodded in a supportive sort of way, then tried to think of another conversational tack, but couldn't. Maybe she should quit before they got angry at each other again.

''What about you, Rebecca?'' her mother asked. ''What do *you* want?''

That was direct. ''Uh, well — '' In all honesty, what she wanted most was to hear from Michael, but she certainly couldn't say *that*. She let out her breath. ''I don't know. I — '' She shook her head. ''I really don't know.''

She had found that sleeping in little bursts — no more than an hour or two — was better than sleeping straight through, because she was less likely to have vociferous nightmares. Since she'd been home, her mother had had to come into her room, on a regular basis, and gently wake her up. In

Vietnam, plenty of people had shouted, or cried, or whatever, in their sleep, but here, it was considered weird. So, she now used a strategy of alternating napping, and reading, and if her mother went out, she immediately went upstairs and got into bed, surrounded by cats and glasses of — augmented — Coke.

She was lying down one afternoon, dozing over some of her father's cardiology journals, when her mother tapped on her door. It was an effort to open her eyes — a little more Coke, and a little *less* alcohol might be indicated — and she struggled to look alert.

"I'm sorry to disturb you, Rebecca," her mother said, opening the door partway, "but you got a letter."

She sat straight up in bed. "From where?"

Her mother squinted at the return address. "Washington."

Damn. The cerebral major. That is, it was *good* — but it wasn't Colorado. "Okay." She got up, stumbling over the rug. "I mean, thank you." She carried the envelope back to bed, pulling the quilts up around her.

"Do you want anything?" her mother asked.

Rebecca shook her head, already tearing the envelope open, and her mother withdrew.

Dear Rebecca,

Thank you for your card. Now, after the fact, I will confess to having worried a bit.

Only a bit. How — disciplined — of her.

*Rather jarring to be back, isn't it? I find myself fol-
lowing the news obsessively, hoping to see something,
or someone, familiar. To be sure it was all real. I did
get a note from Gwen Coggeshall, who says that things
proceed apace. I'm not sure if that's good, or bad, or
simply an indication that we each climb out of the water
after our year-long sojourn, without leaving a ripple.*

Well, she certainly wrote *exactly* the way she
spoke.

*Not a notion for either of us to dwell on, is it. I hope
that you're settling in nicely, and feeling at peace with
yourself, and being back in the World.*

Oh, yeah. One hundred and ten percent.

*And, if not — give it a try. I know that your leave
is up soon, and I hope you've been assigned someplace
sensible for your next duty station. (I assume you would
have mentioned it, if they'd given you Walter Reed?)
Anyway, let me know, in case I have friends wherever
it is, or have spent time there myself, and can pass on
any helpful information.*

*I still haven't decided what I'm doing with my own
future, although a most bizarre situation has developed
here. In a fit of apparent mental disarray, I decided,
one evening, to visit a local coffeehouse (deemed, as you
may imagine, quite off-limits to active military person-
nel).*

Coffeehouses were, of course, patronized almost
exclusively by anti-war types, although lately,
they'd been springing up near military bases, so

that off-duty soldiers could go and listen to people
with long hair make radical pronouncements about
the War and the fascist pig government. The idea,
was to foment dissension among the ranks, and
ultimately destroy the military-industrial complex
from within. Not surprisingly, the Army frowned
on this.

*So I went to this seedy little storefront, decorated like
my image of a civilian's basement rec room. I sat at a
card table, with my cup, and waited uneasily for the
strident tones of a frighteningly young true believer —
or, even worse,* folk music. *The coffee, as it happened,
was very good.*

*As I sat, what to my distressed eyes should appear,
but a strapping, bearded man, plucking the strings of
a guitar, just one table away. Naturally, he struck up
a conversation, although I admit that my responses were
terse.*

Hard to imagine, that.

*It developed that he was also thirty (we, neither of
us, had any business being there), and the son of a
master sergeant, U.S.M.C.(Ret.). Whereupon, the offer
was made to buy me the finest of steak dinners. I pleasantly demurred.*

What a surprise.

*However, as I prepared to take my leave, the offer
changed to a very large hot fudge sundae, and I made
the mistake of a fatal hesitation.*

Sweets. Always a sucker for sweets.

Off we went, and to my surprise, he turned out to be of an intellectual bent, and the time passed swiftly. Two months later, the time continues to pass. Swiftly. He thinks the service is fine; he thinks my not being in the service would be fine; he seems to think I'm fine, despite my tendency to be rather too reserved with people for whom I have strong feelings. I am, however, working on this.

So. That's the news from here. I'm not sure which direction I'm going in, but I seem to be going in one.

I would be very pleased to hear from you.

Affectionately,

Maggie

P.S. Made him shave the beard, but I guess you and I both already knew that I'm an unmerciful tyrant.

Indeed, they did.

But, that sounded good. Maggie definitely needed to take time and have fun being a *person*, not a cog in the Army machine.

She read the letter over again, kind of marvelling at the way it managed to be both formal, and intensely personal.

Affectionately.

Okay. Why not.

She moved over to her desk, which felt very small. As far as she knew, she hadn't really grown, but she *had* gotten used to having a full-sized desk. Dominating it, in fact.

Her mother had set out some stationery and postcards and stamps in a little basket — like she was a guest or something — and she chose a piece of stationery with their address embossed discreetly across the top.

Dear Maggie, she wrote, which felt weird in itself. Most of the communications she had written to the Chief Nurse had been on regulation forms, relating to hospital business. Sometimes, to be a jerk, she had scrawled *Eyes Only* across the top, but never *Maggie.*

It was good to hear from you. I'm home until the 23rd, when I have to report to Fort Dix. (No, it wasn't anywhere on my list of choices.)

Fort Devens, in Massachusetts — and two in Colorado had been.

I'm glad to hear about your new friend — good luck. He sounds nice. About that guitar, though . . .

I haven't heard from anyone else, but I guess Annie, at least, will be back in the World early next month. I hope they're all okay.

The thought of writing the way she was really feeling was tempting, but why lay it on her? Everyone had problems of their own.

I guess it will be strange to be back on a base, but at least it won't be hot. I may never wear a jacket again.

It really was good to get your letter. When I have my new address, I'll let you know.

> — *Rebecca*

She wasn't going to win any prizes for eloquence, but it was probably better to write a dull little note, than to send a long and alarming tome about her near-total despair.

She pulled on some jeans and the shirt she had worn the day before, and went downstairs, where she found her mother baking bread. Her parents had invited every relative within reasonable driving distance — and the neighbors and friends who were able to keep their various feelings about the war from clouding their personal relationships — to come over on Saturday, and she was already busy getting ready.

"Do you need help?" Rebecca asked, doing her best to sound enthusiastic.

Her mother probably wanted to say yes, but she shook her head.

"Well, I thought I'd, uh — " Rebecca waved her letter and car keys vaguely — "go out. Do you need me to bring anything back?"

Again, she had the feeling that the answer was yes, but her mother shook her head.

"Well, okay, then. I'll, uh — " She stopped. "I'm not sure when I'll be back. I mean, don't worry if I'm gone for a while. Or if I miss dinner."

More expressions flashed across her mother's face — worry, and curiosity, and things like that — but she just nodded. "Okay," she said. "Drive carefully."

Maybe. "Sure thing," Rebecca said.

The Dart started on her second try, but she was a little alarmed when it stalled at the light on Atlantic Avenue. Maybe she just hadn't let it warm up enough.

Maybe it was a lemon.

After mailing her letter, she drove around aimlessly, ending up at the lighthouse. It was almost dark, and the wind was really whipping in off the ocean, but she sat down on the rocks anyway, as close to the water as she could get.

A week from today, she would be in New Jersey, wearing a uniform, and having to snap to attention whenever she was given orders. She might not be having much fun at home, but it sure as hell beat the *Army*. And, Christ, she had almost another seven months left before her hitch was up. It was her own stupid fault — but, still.

She sat silently until she was so cold and tired that she was afraid she might fall asleep, and then she got up and headed for the car.

Time to go home and shoot some baskets.

Chapter Twenty-four

The family party was more of a going-away party than a welcome-home one, and even though it was a tremendous strain, she forced herself to be very cheerful and witty, so that no one would notice that she was in the middle of a long-term emotional breakdown. They all kept smiling, and saying that it was wonderful to see her still exactly the same — so it must have been working. Every so often, she caught her mother watching her with a strange sad expression, but she would just avoid her eyes and go bring her grandmother some more sherry or something.

Irene and Nora both stopped by during the afternoon, Nora with her twins, but it was clearly more of a family get-together than anything else, so neither of them stayed long. Most of her parents' friends and neighbors kept their appearances short, too.

It was hard to be around her cousins, several of whom tried to "get a dialogue" going with her, which turned so quickly into a lecture about how she betrayed her generation that she excused herself to go replenish the ice and mixers on the sideboard in the dining room — and maybe help herself to a quick shot while she was at it.

After everyone had finally gone, she and her mother spent some time cleaning up, and then sat in the kitchen, eating leftovers and, in Rebecca's case, having another drink.

"It was nice to see everyone," her mother said, her father off reading the papers, napping, or some combination of the two.

Rebecca nodded, working on a good-sized helping of potato salad.

"They all thought you looked great," her mother said.

Rebecca grinned. She expected to be hearing from the Academy any time now. The only question in her mind being whether they gave her Best Actress, or just Best Supporting. She would accept either. In the meantime, more potato salad and cole slaw would suffice.

"When are you going to have to leave?" her mother asked.

"I don't know." New Jersey was a long drive. "Early Wednesday, I guess." No point in leaving on Tuesday night, and missing *The Mod Squad*, unless she absolutely had to do so.

Her mother nodded. "Do you think they'll let you come back for Thanksgiving?"

Probably not. "I don't know," Rebecca said, and poured another inch of scotch into her glass. "But I might get a few days at Christmas." A holiday she had little interest in celebrating. All it was going to be this year — *every* year, from now on — was a bad anniversary.

Her mother nodded, only picking at her dinner. "Are you nervous about going?"

"You mean — the car?" Rebecca asked, not sure what she meant.

"The *Army*," her mother said.

Oh. That. Rebecca shrugged. "They're just going to yell at me a lot. Cut my hair, stand up straight, write more neatly." She shrugged again. "Kind of like junior high."

"You hated junior high," her mother said.

True. When it came right down to it, the Army was, in many ways, significantly less stressful. Rebecca nodded, taking a large gulp of her drink.

"Why don't you have some coffee," her mother said. Rather pointedly.

"No, thank you." Rebecca indicated her glass. Pointedly. "This is fine."

The silence that followed was long and tense.

"Well," her mother said, and poured *herself* more coffee. "Will they have someplace for you to live, or — ?"

Another confrontation deferred. Rebecca shrugged. "I don't know. I'm not sure if they'll let me go off-post or not. But I guess it'll be like Letterman." She'd served at Letterman Hospital in San Francisco during the couple of months while she was waiting for her orders to Vietnam to come through, and had had two roommates and an apartment within hours of arriving. At Fort Sam, where she had done basic, the Army had taken care of all that.

Her mother looked worried. "Your father and I would be happy to drive down with you, though. Make sure that you — "

"I'll be *fine*," Rebecca said. "Really."

Her mother nodded, and looked at her hands.

Christ. Rebecca reached for the pepper for the third time, a mess hall habit she had yet to shake. Somehow, even when food was beautifully prepared, she couldn't seem to taste things right.

"I, um — " Better to discuss it now, as opposed to during the holiday itself. She put down her fork. "Christmas is going to be hard for me. It's — kind of a bad anniversary."

Her mother nodded.

"Would it be okay — " This was selfish. "If I could be quiet, and not have to celebrate a lot?" And *that* was vague. "I mean, not have to go out and about and all? If possible?"

Her mother blinked a few times, clearly at a loss.

"I don't mean I won't try," Rebecca said. "It's just — " She shook her head. "I'm sorry. Forget it."

"Rebecca, don't worry about that now," her mother said. "Let's take things as they come. I promise it'll be all right."

She realized, now, why she had been able to tell Maggie Doyle. Even if she *had* received her utter disdain and disgust, it would have come from a person who, close as they felt to each other, she had only known for a few months, and would likely never see again after their tours were up. Her *mother's* disapprobation would be another matter entirely. Something she would never, ever be able to risk.

"Your letting me know that it's going to be difficult for you is a lot better than, two months down the road, pretending that you weren't able to get the leave time," her mother said.

Rebecca felt herself blushing, since that was an alternative that had crossed her mind. It wasn't easy, but she made herself nod. "I know. And I don't want to do that to you." Anymore.

Her mother reached over, her hand feeling very soft as she brushed some hair away from Rebecca's forehead. "I know you don't."

Rebecca glanced in the direction of the den. "*Either* of you."

Her mother smiled. "Well, that's good to hear."

It actually felt pretty good to *say*, too.

"The fact that we're even having this conversation means we've turned a corner," her mother said.

Rebecca nodded. She sure *hoped* so.

She was the only one home the next day, doing laundry, when the phone rang and she ran out to the kitchen to answer it.

"Hello," she said, balancing the receiver on one shoulder while she looked for a pen and piece of paper to take whatever message it was going to be for her mother.

"So, you made it back okay," her brother said.

She almost dropped the phone. "Doug! Are you all right? Where are you?"

He laughed a little bitterly. "A phone booth."

Oh. "Are you okay?" she asked. He sounded just the way he always had. Mingled teasing and intensity.

"Forget me," he said. "How are *you*?"

"Oh." She tried to think. "Well, you know — fine. I've been home about a month."

"Yeah, well, you don't sound too good." He let out his breath. "Why did you *go*? Was it because of me?"

Guilt made the world go 'round. "Because I'm a nurse," she said. "They needed nurses."

"Unh-hunh," he said, audibly skeptical.

Her brother was probably the only person in the world who never fell for even her mildest lies — and vice versa. Maybe because siblings knew each other in a different way than they knew anyone else. A deep and unspoken way. "I don't know," she said. "You, Dad, Billy, me being stupid — I just *went*."

"If *I* had gone, you wouldn't have," he said.

Well — no. Probably not. But, at this point, what the hell difference did it make? "I don't know," Rebecca said. "I was so damn mad about everything, I — " She shook her head. She'd had almost as many reasons for going as she now had for wishing that she *hadn't*. "It was just a stupid thing to do. If I'd known what it was *really* going to be like — " She probably *still* would have gone. "I don't know, Doug. I wish I did."

"Jesus." He let out a very hard breath. "How bad was it?"

"Very bad," she said.

"Yeah." His voice was unhappy. "Mom and Dad are freaked."

Yeah. "They're pretty different," Rebecca said. "They seem *old*."

He sighed. "They said you got hurt?"

"Yeah. Shot down," she said. Christ, it was nice to talk to someone without having to edit first. "It was a real mess. But — I mean, I'm okay now."

"Mom says you're all thin and jumpy," he said.

"Well," she said. She *was*. "I mean, you know."

He sighed again. "Jesus. You sound like hell."

She *missed* him. "Are you going to come home?" she asked. *"Please?"*

"I can't," he said. "You know there's no way."

Yeah, but — "Do you *want* to?" she asked.

Before he could answer, a disembodied operator's voice came on and her brother swore, dropping what sounded like several handfuls of change into the telephone.

"You still there?" he asked, after it all went through.

"Yeah," she said. "Can't you please come home, Doug? We could get you a *really* good lawyer and everything."

"Oh, yeah," he said. "Next stop, Walpole."

Which was the maximum security prison. "Yeah," she conceded, "but — would that really be so *bad*? At least it would be *determinate*, you know? Dad has a lot of people who owe him favors, and — "

Her brother laughed. *"Dad? He's* not about to help. He'll drag me down to the draft board, more likely."

Maybe. "I don't know," she said. "I think he's different now. Or — I think he *wants* to be."

"And what's Mom going to do?" Doug asked. "Bring me brownies on visiting day?"

"It would be better than *this*," she said. "We'd

know where you were, and when you'd be back, and — even if the worst happened, and you got sent over, I know a bunch of people now — '' like a major whose father was a two-star general —'' and I could make *sure* you'd be in the rear, some-where safe. But that wouldn't happen, because we'll get really good lawyers, and — can't we at least *try*?''

Her brother didn't answer for what seemed like a long time. ''Okay,'' he said finally. ''I'll think about it.''

Good.

They talked until Doug ran out of money, which was a lot sooner than she would have liked. But, in the end, he agreed that he would call again in a few months — Jesus — and see what they had found out from lawyers, and see if maybe, *maybe* — after hanging up, she felt better than she had in a long time. Felt the barest flickering of — hope.

Her mother's reaction was equally pleased, and uncertain as to their next step. After helping set the table and get dinner ready, Rebecca went out to shoot a few baskets, and she was standing at the faded foul line in the dark, when her father's car pulled into the driveway. She kept shooting as he got out of the car.

''Rebecca, this is turning into *Goodbye, Columbus*,'' he said, after watching her for a minute.

Humor. Apparently, he'd had a good day. ''Surgery go well?'' she asked.

He nodded. ''Looks that way, although I might take a ride back after supper.''

In a couple of days, she, too, would have patients

to check. She dribbled a few times. "Doug called."

Her father immediately threw his arm up in front of his face, pretending to duck.

"Funny," she said, and shot.

Instead of going inside, he stayed there as she went after the rebound.

She dribbled back up to the foul line. "I think he wants to come home." She stopped to look at him. "He needs our help. To find a lawyer, and negotiate a prison sentence, or whatever."

He nodded, almost without hesitating first.

Hmmm. "It will probably be ugly, and complicated, and take much longer than we expect," she said.

He nodded.

"And *expensive*," she said.

He nodded.

Okay, good. They were all on the same page. "And he *might* not ever call back," she said, "even though he said he would."

"Obviously, your mother and I will do whatever we can to help," her father said.

Obviously? Well, okay. She started dribbling, then paused. "Would you have, if we'd asked before?"

He took his glasses off and a hanky from his pocket, cleaning them. "I don't know," he said. "I guess I wouldn't have been happy about it."

Probably wasn't all that delighted about it now, either. But, at least, willing to put that aside, and try. They stood a few feet apart, looking at each other, and then her father extended his arms. In other families, that might mean that she should go over and receive a big hug, but in this case, it meant that he wanted the ball. So, she snapped him a crisp chest pass, which he caught, effortlessly.

"Play Pig?" she asked. Or Horse, or any variation thereof.

"Sure," he said, and moved back until he was about fifteen feet away from the hoop.

Oh, hell. He was deadly from the perimeter. "You'll never make it," she said.

He grinned, and sent his shot up.

Swish.

Early Wednesday morning, they packed up the Dart — which took a while, even though she wasn't bringing much, beyond her freshly laundered uniforms, some civilian clothes, and a lot of books.

"You're sure you know exactly where you're going," her father said, rifling through her pile of maps.

New Jersey. Beyond that — she'd figure it out. "Yeah," she said.

"And they're expecting you," he said.

Far as she knew. She nodded, indicating the envelope where she'd put her orders.

"Well." He stepped back, folding his arms. "Okay then."

Her mother came outside with what looked like enough lunch for a family of six. "Here." She set the bag on the passenger's side of the front seat. "In case you get hungry on the way."

Rebecca nodded. "Thank you."

There was an awkward little silence, and she had

to resist the temptation to look at her watch. If she didn't report in by 1700, there would be hell to pay.

"You'll call me as soon as you get there?" her mother asked.

"Well, I'll try," Rebecca said. "I'm not sure if they're going to put me right to work, or what. But I'll call the first chance I get."

As they hugged good-bye, her mother's eyes looked shiny, but this was certainly a lot better than the *last* time she'd left. After all, most people made it out of New Jersey in one piece. And, providing that she came back at Christmas, it would only be a couple of months before they saw her.

The Dart stalled out on her first attempt, and her parents looked nervous. But, it caught nicely the next time, and she got halfway to the street before stalling again.

Damn.

"I don't know about this," her mother said, nervously.

"It'll be fine," Rebecca said — and promptly flooded the engine, which meant that they had to stand around and look at one another some more, until she could try again. To kill time, she threw Jack a few sticks, none of which he brought back.

Finally, the car started, and she was seat-belted in, and ready to go.

"Don't brake unless you have to," her father advised.

"Martin!" her mother said. "Don't tell her things like that."

Since they tended to drive the same old cars forever, no one in her family had ever really had a reliable one. The neighbors, who leaned towards Cadillacs and Lincoln Continentals, did not approve.

"Don't worry," Rebecca said. "I'll see you soon." She put the car into Drive, and waved cheerily as she headed down Nanepashement Street.

Made it all the way to Ocean Avenue before she stalled out again.

Maybe the Dart didn't want to be in the Army any more than *she* did.

Chapter Twenty-five

Fort Dix was a waste of time. No, actually, Fort Dix was a *total* waste of time. After a couple of nights at the BOQ — Bachelor Officers' Quarters — she found a first lieutenant whose roommate had just shipped out to Germany, and now needed someone else to help her with the rent. The apartment was off-post in Wrightstown, and something of a flophouse, but as long as she had a bed, and a table upon which to pile books, Rebecca didn't really care.

When she called home to tell her parents about the apartment, she knew that her mother was picturing things like cheery flowered shelf paper and bright yellow curtains in the kitchen, and Rebecca decided not to disabuse her of this notion. Mattresses on the floor, pans in the sink, and a refrigerator heavy on beer and low on nutrition were closer to the truth.

Lieutenants were considered pathetic little beings — Walson Army Hospital was overloaded with majors and colonels — and she was assigned the graveyard shift, a large maxillofacial ward being her main responsibility. The ward for kids whose faces had been blown off. A ward rife with depression and suicidal impulses.

She fit right in.

Almost every morning, when she walked into the apartment after working all night, she would grab a six-pack out of the refrigerator, go into her room, and close the door. On her days off, she would drink significantly more. When she remembered to eat, she usually settled for Campbell's Vegetable Soup, and peanut butter or grilled cheese sandwiches. Which was boring, but kept her going.

Mostly, she just tried to maintain a low profile. The only time she got criticized was after morning report one day, when a passing lieutenant colonel got testy about the strands of hair trailing out from underneath her cap and, as soon as she got off duty, she went and got her hair cut very short. *So* short that she looked like she was auditioning for *Rosemary's Baby*, but she wasn't all that worried about her personal appearance, anyway. Male attention was nowhere near the top of her wish list these days.

Her ankle was bothering her so much that she finally broke down and made an appointment with Orthopedics, where two very cynical draftee captains told her that it was CFU — or, in layman's terms, Completely Fucked Up. They suggested that her options ranged from surgery to rehab to getting used to limping around in pain on a regular basis. For the time being, she decided to opt for the latter. Maybe, when she got out of the damned Army, she'd force herself to go see some of her father's cohorts and get *their* opinions. Right now, limping was easier.

After all her worrying about Christmas, the damn hospital didn't even give her the time off, and it wasn't until late January that she got five days leave — two of which she wasted driving back and forth to Marblehead. She spent most of the other three days sleeping, much to her parents' unvoiced, but obvious, dismay. They didn't like her haircut much, either.

Doug had finally called home, and now her father's lawyers were trying to earn their money. So far, the progress seemed to be one step forward, and three steps back. It turned out that he had recently spent a week in the hospital, diagnosed with a bleeding ulcer, although he'd insisted that he was fine now. Ironically, if he'd gotten it at home, the ulcer would have been enough to make him 4–F. He still might end up in jail, but the Army wasn't going to want him anymore. Not in combat.

Every so often, she got another letter from Maggie, which always gave her a lift, but it never lasted long. As a rule, the letters consisted of amusing anecdotes, often involving her friend — still in the picture — Richard, who was, it seemed, a man of energetic, impractical, and passing enthusiasms, the most recent being that the two of them would move to Vermont and grow vegetables together. The cerebral major had — big surprise — pleasantly demurred. Lately though, the letters were worried, because her little brother Buddy was in-country now, leading an infantry platoon in the Central Highlands with the Fourth Division. He had already been wounded once, and decorated twice. It seemed likely that Maggie was going through at least two packs a day.

When her enlistment was finally up in May, she passed her discharge physical, but the doctor in charge suggested that she think about eating more, drinking less, and taking a vacation someplace sunny. Unh-hunh, Rebecca said, with great indifference. She filled out forms, waited in lines, got her final pay voucher, ignored suggestions that she re-up, listened to information about the GI Bill, and accepted a Good Conduct medal, resisting the urge to laugh ironically and make bitter remarks. Then, with a good-bye and good luck to everyone in her ward, she drove to the main post gate — noticing, along with everyone else within half a mile, that her muffler was about to go — scraped her parking sticker off the rear bumper, flicked a final salute at one of the bored MPs, and — drove away.

Out of the Army. Next stop, Marblehead.

She spent most of her first week at home sleeping all day, and then, after her parents went to bed, sitting downstairs and drinking all night. During the last few months, she had decided that beer had too many calories, and made her feel bloated, so she had switched to Jack Daniel's. She had stocked up at the PX before leaving Fort Dix, and left the bottles — both empty and full — out in the trunk of her car, so her parents wouldn't know how much she was putting away, on a daily basis.

Which might, just possibly, indicate that she was turning into a drunk.

She thought about the boy in the jungle a lot —

too much — and hated herself for thinking about Michael even more. Too embarrassed to have her parents see, she would lock her door, and then sit and reread his old letters. Look at the terrible Polaroid that Red Cross worker had taken, and the worn picture of Otis, tolerant in his King of the May Parade getup. As a form of passive self-torture, it worked very well.

For the most part, her parents were leaving her alone, but she could feel the tension level in the house rising. She had been careful to stumble upstairs to bed before they came down in the mornings, so they hadn't actually *caught* her drunk yet, but — they weren't stupid.

So, when her mother suggested that they go out to dinner, making it sound like a command performance, Rebecca nodded agreeably, dragged herself up from the couch where she was watching the Red Sox lose, and put on a nice spring dress. Then, when her father ordered wine with dinner, she — just to be capricious — ordered a Coke for herself. Neither of her parents commented on this, one way or the other.

"You haven't said much about how the car is holding up," her father remarked, breaking off a piece of roll and buttering it.

Not much *to* say. "Well — I made a lot of new friends down at the motor pool," Rebecca said.

Her parents thought about that.

"Maybe you should bring it down to Kenny — " their regular mechanic — "and have him take a look," her mother said.

Rebecca nodded, being very, very agreeable. In fact, throughout the meal, she behaved like an enchanting and ideal daughter — whose hands seemed to shake uncontrollably for some reason.

"Your steak okay?" her father asked.

Rebecca looked down at her plate, seeing that she'd eaten much less than she'd thought. "Delicious," she said, and cut off a small piece. "Thank you."

There was a loud popping sound off to their left, and she ducked before remembering that she was in a restaurant, and it was probably just champagne. She glanced around quickly to make sure no one else had noticed, then checked the room until she located the table where the bottle was, seeing two parents, and what looked like grandparents, smiling at, and toasting, a bashfully grinning guy who was her age, or a little younger.

"Happy graduation," her mother said quietly.

Rebecca nodded — wishing she had something stronger than a Coke. She and Doug had been taken here to celebrate *their* graduation, too. She was heading off to Radcliffe, he was going to go to Tufts, and life was full of exciting possibilities.

Seemed like centuries ago.

After their meals had been cleared away, her father — who had ordered brandy, while she and her mother got coffee — leaned forward, clearing his throat.

"Now that you're out of the service," he said, "what are you going to do?"

So much for their nice, quiet meal. "Give me a break, Dad," Rebecca said, careful to sound calm. "I just got *home*."

"That's true," he agreed, "but you've given absolutely no indication that — " He glanced at her mother, then stopped and started again. "That is, your mother and I were wondering — "

"I'm going to play it by ear," Rebecca said, "okay? Just — give me a damn break. *Okay?*"

Her mother looked down at her coffee cup, while her father moved his jaw, and then picked up his brandy glass, not drinking any, the stem between his middle and ring fingers.

With her parents, she should err on the side of being polite, instead of belligerent. "I'm sure everything will work out fine," she said. Politely. "Please don't worry so much." And, if she was lucky, they would now drop it.

"Are you happy with nursing?" her father asked.

She frowned at him. "Happy?"

He nodded.

Happy?

"Do you *like* it," her mother said. "Does it make you happy?"

Happy. Whoa. Radical concept. "Well, I — " She should choose her words judiciously here. "I'm, uh, not sure that's a factor."

Not a response her parents liked.

"What do you mean?" her mother asked. "*Exactly.*"

Well — okay. What the hell. Lock and load. Rock and roll. "I guess I mean I don't even consider that," Rebecca said. "I mean — it doesn't come up for me."

Her parents were both staring at her.

"If you break that, Dad," she indicated the glass, "you're likely to sever at least one tendon."

He looked down, then instantly loosened his grip.

A surgeon had never lived, who would risk a tendon in his hand.

"I know it's been very hard for you," her mother said slowly, "coming back, but — "

Fire for effect. "The truth is," Rebecca said, "I wasn't all that thrilled with myself *before* I went, and now — " No. She should redirect. "The truth — " one truth, anyway — "is that I've kind of been wondering if I should maybe — go back."

Her father took his glasses off. "Back to *Vietnam*?"

Rebecca nodded. "I know I just got out, but — I don't think it's going to work, here, and — the hospitals in-country need every bit of help they can get, so — "

"Don't you dare," her mother said, sounding furious. "Don't do that to me."

She couldn't remember *ever* hearing her mother that angry, and instinctively eased her chair away a few inches.

"I can *not* do another year like that," her mother said, her voice trembling now. "I couldn't eat, I couldn't sleep, and after a while, I couldn't even really leave the house, because I was afraid I'd miss the telephone call, or the telegram, or the *goddamn Army car* pulling up in front of the house."

"Nan," Rebecca's father said, glancing around them to see if anyone was listening.

She ignored him, her eyes fixed on Rebecca, dark and unforgiving. "All of which, of course, *happened*."

Rebecca shifted guiltily in her chair. "That was a mistake — I was really all right, I — "

"You were *not* all right," her mother said. "You're not all right *now*."

No. She wasn't. Rebecca subsided.

"I don't know who, or what, you care about anymore," her mother said, "but — " She stopped, pushing away from the table. "Martin, pay the check. I'll be in the car." She strode out of the restaurant, Rebecca too unnerved to watch her go.

Her father also sat quite still, then took out his wallet. "You're *not* going to walk home," he said, "so don't bother suggesting it."

Right.

The silence in the car was so thick that she didn't even want to breathe. So she did as few times as possible, as softly as possible.

Once they were in the driveway, before her father had time to turn off the engine, her mother got out, slamming the door behind her and disappearing into the house.

Rebecca waited a few seconds, then reached out to open her own door.

"Don't," her father said without turning around. "Just sit here for a minute."

Rebecca withdrew her hand, then leaned her head back against the seat, tightly closing her eyes.

"Rebecca," he said, and then sighed. "The drinking has to stop."

Yeah, sure. Just like that. She felt both of her fists clenching. "*I'm* not the one I saw drinking tonight."

"Not *yet* tonight," he said grimly.

Fine. So they knew. So what. She slouched down, fists still clenched, folding her arms across her chest.

After what seemed like about a month and a half, her father let out his breath, loosening his hands on the steering wheel. "I don't know what kind of thinking human beings could stick a kid just out of nursing school in triage for a year."

Denigration. Her favorite. "I was *good* at it," Rebecca said. "They were happy to have me."

"I don't doubt that," her father said. "You've never done anything where you didn't test off the map."

Yeah, right. "Since when do *you* think that?" Rebecca asked. "You've only been disappointed in us our whole *lives*."

Her father sighed. Very heavily.

"I mean, is it *our* fault that *I* took after you, instead of him?" Rebecca asked. "You should've been *happy* I wanted to do what you do. It was a goddamn *compliment*."

Her father didn't say anything.

"Anyway." She opened her door to go inside. "I'm sorry to be such a disappointment."

"Rebecca," he said after her.

"Leave me the hell alone, Dad," she said, and slammed the door. As hard as she could.

She found her mother upstairs, just pulling her nightgown over her head. Rebecca waited until she was finished so that she could look her in the eye.

"I promise I won't," she said. "I won't even look into it."

Her mother seemed to catch her breath, then relaxed a little. "Absolutely *promise*?"

Rebecca nodded. "You have my word," she said, and headed for her room.

* * *

She was in trouble. Even *she* was smart enough to recognize that. And clearly the answer was not now, and might not *ever* be, in Marblehead, Massachusetts.

She sat on her bed, with the lights out, until she was sure her parents were asleep, and then started packing. With, okay, the help of a few good-sized drinks. She wasn't going to take off under the cover of darkness — the way Doug had had to — but maybe it was time to go away for a while. To be alone. To *escape*.

She was too tense to sleep, and at seven-thirty, when her parents came downstairs, she was in the kitchen waiting for them, drinking coffee to try and avoid her incipient hangover. They looked surprised to see her — and a little alarmed.

"You're up early," her mother said.

Well — sort of. "I already made the coffee," Rebecca said.

Her parents nodded, her father letting Jack out, while her mother opened the refrigerator to get breakfast ready. None of them spoke beyond the bare "Scrambled, or poached?" essentials, until they were all sitting at the table, not touching their breakfasts.

Okay. This was going to be a bad conversation, so she might as well just start. Get it over with. But, before she could open her mouth, her father beat her to it.

"Your mother and I have been talking," he said.

Oh, great. Time for the riot act.

"Are you still interested in medical school?" he asked.

She'd expected his fastball; he'd crossed her up with a looping curve. She put down her orange juice. "What do you mean?"

"You'd have some undergraduate work to make up," he said, "but, as I recall, you were well along in your studies, and your grades were right up where they should be."

4.0, to be exact.

"Anyway," her father said, "if you decide to go in that direction, I want you to know that you would have your mother's and my full support." He paused. "Financial, and otherwise."

Only five or six years too late. "Thanks, but — " She shook her head. No point in wasting her breath. She had long since written off the possibility of becoming a doctor.

"We were hoping to discuss it last night," her mother said.

Subtext: before she had ruined their pleasant meal with an ill-timed burst of honesty. Should she go for two meals in a row? She looked at her father. "How come you suddenly think it's okay? You don't figure I'll — embarrass your good name, or something?"

His eyes went a little cold behind his glasses, but he must have counted to ten, because when he spoke, he sounded more thoughtful than angry. "I *still* don't like the idea of your doing it. Medicine is difficult for anyone, but especially a young woman."

Right. Rebecca nodded stiffly. "We're frail. We're not — mentally tough, the way you are."

"You're *alone*, is what you are," he said. "Internship, residency, trying to establish a practice —

I don't know that she gets credit for it, but your mother is the main reason I was able to get through all of that. Going into medicine means giving up *a lot*, and — '' He sighed. ''In all honesty, I wouldn't wish it on you.''

She wondered, suddenly, apropos of nothing, if Billy would have wanted to be married to a doctor. He'd thought her being in nursing school was terrific, but — she would never know, so it didn't really matter. She wondered, though. Maybe he would have hated it. Wanted her to stay home and bear small Catholics. *Be* home all the time, to take care of them.

''Anyway,'' her father said, ''I just want you to know that if you decide that's what you want to do, we'll help you.''

Had he been thinking about this for a long time, or was it a whirlwind conversion? Pull the dipsomaniacal kid back from the brink. A decision of desperation. She turned to look at her mother, who was being her now-routine subdued self. ''What do *you* think?''

''I want whatever you want,'' her mother said. ''Whatever would make you happy.''

Great. Now they were back to happy. Too tired and, yeah, hungover to care what they thought, she slumped forward, resting her head on her arms. Did he have *any* idea what impact it would have had on her life if they'd had this conversation back when she was at Radcliffe? Christ, it was only the *last* thing she would have expected him to say at this point in time. After she was already irrevocably destroyed.

Her mother's hand — lighter, and more sure,

than her father's — came onto her back. "Rebecca, we'd do absolutely anything to help you," she said. "You *do* know that, don't you?"

Yeah. She knew that. She lifted her head, wanting either to collapse in her mother's arms and cry — or run out to her car as fast as she could. Or — both. "I, uh — " they weren't going to like this — "I think I need some time," she said.

Her mother nodded, still rubbing her back.

Well, okay. Not as hard as she'd expected. "I kind of — I'm going to do some driving around," she said.

Her parents' nods were enough on the perfunctory side for her to wonder if they understood what she meant.

"So, I, uh — " Had they maybe been *hoping* she would leave? "I don't want you to worry if you don't hear from me."

Okay. Now, they got it. Her father looked startled; her *mother* looked stricken.

"I packed last night," Rebecca said. "And I was waiting for you to come down so I could tell you."

Her mother's eyes were filling with tears, which made her feel even worse.

"This isn't like Doug," Rebecca said. "I just — I need to go somewhere and think for a while. Try and figure things out."

"What's a while?" her mother asked, her voice breaking a little.

Oh, hell. "I don't know," Rebecca said quietly.

Neither of her parents said anything, and as Jack scratched on the back door, her father got up mechanically and let him in.

No point in dragging this out. "I, um, I'm going

to go get my stuff," Rebecca said. "Okay? I'll be right back."

Her parents still didn't say anything.

Maybe leaving a note and sneaking out in the middle of the night wouldn't have been such a terrible idea, after all. Gutless, maybe, but in some ways, it would have been easier on them.

For a minute, up in her room, patting Gretchen — who had taken to sleeping with her, curled up in the curve of her right arm — she thought about just climbing into bed, underneath all of those warm quilts. But what would *that* accomplish, beyond a brief postponement of the inevitable? So she picked up her duffel bag, and a much smaller drawstring bag, and went back downstairs.

Her parents didn't seem to have moved, although she could tell that her mother had been crying while she was gone.

"Are you sure you've thought this out?" her father asked.

No. But Rebecca nodded.

"I'm very sorry about our disagreement last night," he said.

Maybe her mother wasn't the only one she was hurting here. "It's not that, Dad," she said. "I just need to go somewhere, and clear my head, you know?"

"What about the car?" he asked.

The *car* was the least of her problems. "It'll be okay," she said.

He nodded, glanced at her mother, and then got up awkwardly. "Would you like me to go warm it up for you?"

On the off-chance that it would actually start. And so she could have a minute alone with her mother. Rebecca nodded. "Thank you."

As he went outside, she and her mother looked at each other, and she could see her mother's upper lip trembling slightly.

"Mom, I just *have* to," she said. "Okay? Please don't be upset."

Her mother nodded. "Is there anything I can do?" she asked, her voice sounding choked.

"You can not *worry*," Rebecca said.

Her mother laughed weakly. "Oh. Okay." A few more tears came squeezing out, and she wiped them away with an impatient move of her hand. "I'm not sure I — " She took a deep breath. "Do you have enough money?"

The all-purpose parental question that meant so much more than the obvious. "Yeah," Rebecca said, and took a deep breath of her own. "I'll be fine."

Her mother nodded again. "Do you know where you're going?"

"No," Rebecca said, and sighed. "I have no idea."

Chapter Twenty-six

She started driving south. Past Boston, through Rhode Island and Connecticut, over the George Washington Bridge in New York, and into New Jersey. She stopped three times — once for gas, once for a sandwich and some coffee, and once to put water in her radiator. While she was at it, she threw in a quart of oil, too.

The afternoon seemed to go on forever, but then, suddenly, she was driving through Baltimore, and Washington, D.C., was only about an hour away. Once she was on the outskirts of the city, she stopped and asked for directions to Walter Reed Army Medical Center, and since Maggie's street turned out to run right along one side of the facility, she had no trouble finding it.

The hard part, was going to be getting up enough nerve to ring her doorbell.

She drove slowly, reading the numbers on the houses, and when she saw the right one, she looked for a parking place, pulling into a spot just up the block.

She wanted a drink. In fact, she had wanted a drink for *hours*.

She was tempted to forget the whole thing and drive away, but then she got out of the car — the door sticking — and walked back to the small, two-apartment house. The grass was cut perfectly, clay pots of geraniums were thriving on the porch, and a black-and-white cat with crooked ears was sitting on the front steps in the fading sunshine, washing its face.

Had she maybe driven to Norman Rockwell's house by mistake?

She bent down to pat the cat, then stepped over it, and knocked on the door marked 28A. She heard quick footsteps and the door opened.

"You're early," Major Doyle said, looking downright radiant in a bright blue dress, with her hair spreading out over her shoulders. Then, she stared, and took a step backwards.

"Uh, hi," Rebecca said, feeling like a complete jerk. Looking like one, too, no doubt.

Somehow, Major Doyle's smile seemed more forced than overjoyed. "Hello, Rebecca."

Yes, driving almost five hundred miles to Washington had been a truly brilliant idea.

They looked at each other, Rebecca wishing that a very large hole would open up, into which she could jump and hide.

"You have a date tonight, don't you," she said.

Major Doyle grinned wryly. "Well — I *did*."

Still did. "I'm really sorry," Rebecca said, retreating down the steps — to the cat's tremendous annoyance. "I was just, uh, passing through, and — " go directly to jail, do *not* pass Go — "I didn't mean to — maybe I can stop by tomorrow, or, I don't know, the next time I come to town.''

Major Doyle, who had nodded with noticeable irritation throughout this entire speech, frowned at her now. ''Are you finished?''

''Well — I'm still trying to come up with something that will make me seem like even *more* of a jerk,'' Rebecca said.

''Don't worry about that,'' Major Doyle said. ''You're doing just fine already.''

Right. Rebecca nodded, and started down the walk.

''Try not to *compound* the error,'' Major Doyle said.

Oh. Rebecca came back, sheepishly, and Major Doyle motioned her inside, giving her a rather hard thump on the back as she went past. Somehow, the fact that it hurt was more comforting than an engulfing hug would have been.

''Can the cat come in?'' Rebecca asked.

''The cat is allowed to do anything she wants,'' Major Doyle said.

Okay. Rebecca's kind of cat.

Major Doyle closed the door, looked at her watch, and walked over to a black telephone.

''Were you going to look even *more* smashing about half an hour from now?'' Rebecca asked.

''I was certainly going to *try*,'' Major Doyle said, pointed at the chair where she wanted her to sit, and then swiftly dialed.

Rebecca sat, cooperatively, in the chair, and looked around. The room was simple, but put together with undeniable domesticity. Warm braided rugs, solid wooden furniture, lots of books. There were nicely framed prints and family pictures on the wall, and the coffee table held a bowl of fresh flowers, a variety of magazines, and several neatly stacked issues of *The Washington Post*. The kitchen beyond the living room also looked spotless, and homey, and Frank Sinatra was playing on the stereo.

Date music.

She was a jerk of staggering proportions.

"All right, then I'll talk to you tomorrow," Major Doyle was saying. "Okay." Then, she laughed. "Me, too," she said, and hung up. With finality.

"Do you hate me right now?" Rebecca asked.

"Well — " Major Doyle went over to the record player, and turned it off. "Let's just say I'm not in good humor."

Seemed like a fair assessment.

Major Doyle sat down on the couch, reaching for a pack of cigarettes, and lighting one. "So," she said, and exhaled a short burst of smoke.

Her cue to explain herself — but she couldn't think of anything to say.

"It might have been nice if you'd called first," Major Doyle said.

Rebecca nodded, feeling too stupid to look up. "I, uh — I guess I was afraid you wouldn't want to see me."

Major Doyle's laugh was a little ironic.

Right.

"I assume you're not AWOL," Major Doyle said.

Rebecca shook her head.

Major Doyle nodded, and exhaled more smoke. "Good."

Then, they sat without speaking for a few minutes.

"I suppose it would be *possible* for you to look worse," Major Doyle said, "but I can't quite imagine how."

"I, uh, I guess I haven't been doing very well," Rebecca said.

Major Doyle laughed. With great irony. "How much are you drinking these days?" she asked.

Was she wearing a damn sign on her back or something? "What do you mean?" Rebecca asked.

Major Doyle looked at her without blinking.

Okay. Rebecca shrugged self-consciously. "I don't know. *Too* much, I guess."

"Well," Major Doyle said, and lit another cigarette. "If I may be brutally frank, drunks bore the hell out of me."

Rebecca shrugged, slouching down in her chair.

"Well," Major Doyle said, and sighed. "Have you eaten?"

Rebecca shook her head.

"Didn't think so," Major Doyle said, and got up.

Instead of their ordering out for pizza or something, which Rebecca would have expected, she found herself sitting in the terribly tidy kitchen, while the Chief Nurse cooked with cautious precision, chopping and sautéing between quick drags on a series of cigarettes.

"Do you cook a lot?" Rebecca said.

"It has been pointed out to me," Major Doyle said, chopping, "that my supply of snack foods would be unlimited, were I able to prepare them for myself."

Sounded like a qualified yes. Rebecca sipped the lemonade she'd been offered, since she had been far too embarrassed to ask for a beer. "I'm sorry I made you miss your date."

"Well," Major Doyle frowned at whatever was happening in her frying pan, and lowered the heat on the burner, "friendship has its unhappy burdens."

Hmmm. "Was your date with Richard?" Rebecca asked.

Major Doyle turned to look at her, her eyes as piercing as ever. "*All* of my dates are with Richard."

Okay. Feeling a little quelled, Rebecca nodded, and watched her as she washed lettuce, sliced tomatoes, and peeled carrots and cucumbers.

"I didn't mean to come here, Maggie," she said. "I just didn't know what else to do."

Major Doyle looked at her again. "I picked up on that, actually."

Fairly impossible to miss.

Major Doyle removed the onions and mushrooms from the pan, then formed hamburger patties, put them in, and scrubbed her hands. The third or fourth time she had done so. "How long have you been out?"

Of the service. "Week and a half," Rebecca said.

Major Doyle nodded, and used her spatula to lift one of the hamburgers and check it.

"Give them a chance to sear," Rebecca said.

Major Doyle frowned at her. "Forgive me, but — *whose* kitchen are you in?"

Right. "Your kitchen," Rebecca said.

Major Doyle nodded, and turned back to her pan. "Seen your parents?"

And how. "It wasn't very successful," Rebecca said.

Major Doyle nodded, as though she had fully expected that response. "So you ran away."

Was it *imperative* for her to be so damn blunt? "I wouldn't call it running away," Rebecca said stiffly.

Major Doyle glanced at her, then flipped her hamburgers. "What *would* you call it?"

Running away.

"It seems to me," Major Doyle started, then stopped as the telephone rang. She handed Rebecca the spatula. "Watch, but do *not* touch."

Yeah, yeah, yeah. Rebecca took her place at the stove, using the spatula to flatten each of the patties slightly. While she was at it, she — what the hell — sprinkled a little black pepper and garlic powder on them.

"Oh. Well, we *were*," she could hear Major Doyle saying, "but — something came up."

Someone wanting to know why she wasn't out on her date.

"*Chocolate*, of course," Major Doyle said, and then laughed. "Well, granted, but — *he* likes it, too."

She couldn't stand eavesdropping, although in this sort of situation, it was hard to avoid.

"He'll be over sometime in the afternoon," Major Doyle said. "Why don't I call you then, and maybe we'll take a ride over." She listened for a minute. "All right, I'll talk to you tomorrow." She hung up, and came back into the kitchen. "Did you touch anything?"

Rebecca shook her head.

"I'm overcome with relief," Major Doyle said, and reclaimed her spatula.

Once the hamburgers were ready, they didn't really talk during the meal — Rebecca unable to think of much to say, Major Doyle too busy eating.

"Um, how's Buddy?" Rebecca asked hesitantly.

Major Doyle took her time answering. "In Japan. He's trying to get them to send him back to his unit, but it sounds to me as though his injuries are too comprehensive."

She shouldn't have asked.

"On the other hand," Major Doyle said, now sounding more introspective than upset, "when he was a child, they didn't think he would ever *walk* again, forget play football and get through West Point."

Tough breed, the Doyles.

"Any word from *your* brother?" Major Doyle asked.

Rebecca nodded. "My father has a bunch of lawyers working on it. Negotiating."

"Well, I hope they can do something," Major Doyle said.

Rebecca nodded. Having Doug back would make things seem so much more — possible.

After dinner, they sat for a long time with coffee, a package of Oreos untouched in the middle of the table.

"Where are you going from here, Rebecca?" Major Doyle asked.

Rebecca shrugged, so tired that it was hard to sit up straight.

"If I thought you had come," Major Doyle said, looking at her with great intensity, "to try and make one last connection with someone before going off and killing yourself, I would *never* forgive you."

Was that what she was doing? "I don't know," Rebecca said. "Maybe I was hoping you'd throw me a rope over the side."

Major Doyle frowned at her. "Were I to extend your unfortunate choice of metaphors, I might point out that you are perfectly capable of *swimming*, Rebecca."

Jesus. Would it kill her to say something soothing? Rebecca shook her head, feeling her stomach start to knot up. "Well, I guess I kind of thought you might give me some advice," she said, very stiffly.

"That *is* my advice," Major Doyle said.

Sink or swim? Great.

Major Doyle sighed. "If I had a better idea, Rebecca, I would have shared it long ago."

Clearly, Maggie's only real interest here was in her going away as soon as possible. Preferably never to return. Rebecca set her jaw, fighting off the urge to slam her coffee cup across the room. Instead, she decided to take a shot of her own. "Is this the same advice you would have given Caity?" she asked.

"I rather suspect that it's the advice she would have given *me*," Major Doyle said quietly.

Rebecca hunched down now, feeling very ashamed of herself. "I'm sorry," she muttered. "That was a lousy thing to say."

Major Doyle's silence spoke lengthy volumes. "You know," she said finally, "you're not the only one who took a few hits over there."

Which made her feel twice as ashamed. "How come yours don't show?" she asked.

"Because I won't *let* them," Major Doyle said.

If only it were that easy.

Major Doyle leaned forward, looking at her with extreme concentration. "Rebecca, I've wasted half my life grieving, and not letting myself care about people, and — I'm not going to do it anymore. I *can't.*"

"So — " Had she missed something here? "Going to Vietnam made you *stop* grieving?"

Major Doyle shook her head. "No. Vietnam helped me relearn the messy business of getting close to someone."

Rebecca looked at her uncertainly. "Do you mean Jim McNulty?"

Major Doyle shook her head.

Oh.

"Look," Major Doyle said. "If I could wave a little wand, and grant you absolution, I would."

Rebecca had to grin. "So — that's not within your powers?"

Major Doyle grinned back. "Sorry."

It was late. Their coffee was very cold. Conversation aside, she still had all of the same problems she'd had this morning. She'd have them *tomorrow* morning, too. Rebecca looked around the kitchen, and then out at the living room, and all those books.

"Did you know that Emily Brontë had two sisters, Charlotte and Anne, who were *also* writers?" she asked.

Major Doyle laughed. "News to me," she said.

*   *   *

In the morning, after eating the gargantuan breakfast with which she was presented, Rebecca carried her duffel bag outside, stopping to pat the black-and-white cat, who was — again? *still?* — sitting on the front steps.

"I expect things to be better the next time I hear from you," Major Doyle said, finishing one last piece of toast.

"You mean, I can't stay?" Rebecca asked.

Major Doyle paused in the act of lighting her first cigarette of the day, looking alarmed.

Jesus. She should try developing a sense of humor. "I'm *kidding*," Rebecca said.

Major Doyle looked a little too relieved for her tastes. "Well — just drive carefully."

Right. "Get out of the Army," Rebecca said, gave her the fastest hug imaginable, and then climbed into the car.

She drove away from Washington, telling herself that she didn't know where she was going. That this was — random, nomadic travel. She was just a plain, ordinary American, on the road in a plain, old American car.

Emphasis on the old.

She made it as far as Dayton, Ohio, before she was so tired that she had to pull over. She checked into a little roadside motel, paying in cash and ignoring the blatantly lascivious demeanor of the rotund desk clerk. Then, she rode around until she found a McDonald's, and brought some food back to her room, moving the bureau in front of the door — just in case.

The next morning, she kept chugging down I-70 and into Indiana, still pretending to herself that she had no idea where she was going. That she was just cruising along the highway, admiring the great expanse that was the United States of America.

She had planned to stop in St. Louis, but when she got there, she was still wide-awake, so she kept going. Naturally, the car immediately overheated, but after hiking about a mile and a half to a service station, she got one of the kid attendants to drive her back, and pour water in the radiator for her.

"Going far?" the kid asked dubiously, when he was finished.

Not what she wanted to hear. "Yeah," she said. "Why?"

He just shook his head, wiped his hands off on his T-shirt, and closed the hood.

She drove about a hundred miles further, stopping in a town called Columbia, and found another small motel that had seen better days. The bathroom, however, was clean, and the television got two of the three network stations. She lay in bed, eating peanut butter and crackers, drinking a Coke, and then, like most of the rest of the country, fell asleep to Johnny Carson.

After checking out the next morning, she ate breakfast at a truck stop outside of Kansas City, feeling uncomfortable about the fact that a number of other diners seemed to be aware of the young woman with the bad haircut, sitting very much alone, with her poached egg and coffee. But, no one bothered her, and the stout, tired waitress was attentively solicitous. She spread out her increasingly wrinkled map, and studied where she had been. Where she possibly, might be, going.

Except she knew damned well where she was going. Out of all the roads, in all of the states, in all of the country, she had picked I-70. The quickest, straightest route to — Colorado.

Going there was probably going to be even stupider than going to see Maggie had been, but then again, her life was *already* a complete disaster. She might as well roll the dice.

Of course, there was one little problem here. She had no idea where he lived, and Colorado was *big*. So this was likely to be nothing more than a pathetic wild-goose chase. But, okay. On the assumption that she wasn't going to lose her nerve, turn around, and head back to New England at any given moment, what did she know?

Well, he had probably been evacuated to Fitzsimons Army Hospital, and odds were that she would know someone who knew someone there, and be able to get into the files, and see if she could find his address. But, red tape and confidentiality and Army intractability were going to get in her way.

So, what else did she know? He was definitely from Colorado. The Coors beer factory was in his town. His father owned a gas station. Well, how hard could *that* be?

Besides, she had not a single damn thing in the world to lose.

She drove through Kansas City — nothing looking noticeably up-to-date — and into the state of Kansas. It occurred to her that Coors was sold west of the Mississippi River, which she had crossed back near St. Louis, and so she started stopping approximately every fifty miles. She would stretch her legs, check the water level in her radiator, fill it if necessary, and then find the nearest liquor store, where she would examine their beer selection.

She struck it lucky in a place called Salina, where she found several six-packs in the refrigerator case. She carried one up to the cash register, submitted to being carded with good grace, then brought her treasure out to the car. She pulled one of the cans from the bag and studied the label. It was brewed from the finest malted barley, selected grains, and choicest hops, from pure Rocky Mountain spring water in — Golden, Colorado.

She felt a moment of extreme triumph — rock and roll! — and then unfolded her map, peering at Colorado. She couldn't find Golden, but so much the better — that meant that it was small, and the son of a man named Jennings who owned a gas station would be easy to find.

She hadn't had a drink since Friday — a new personal record of sorts — and she was going to open that very can to celebrate, but she went back into the liquor store and bought a bag of ice instead, since she was feeling pretty hyper and might as well knock off another hundred miles or so before she stopped for the night.

She checked into a roadside motel with a flickering vacancy sign, and then wandered around the nearby town until she found a drugstore where she was able to get a state map of Colorado. While she was at it, she picked up a couple of Milky Ways, a bottle of aspirin, and some magazines. She also went to a Dairy Queen, where she bought two hot dogs to go, with some french fries and a lime slush. She ate in the car, then went back to her motel room to look at her map, drink Coors, and watch *The Mod Squad*.

Golden was right outside of Denver, maybe ten miles off to the west. Less than three hundred miles from where she was now.

If she left bright and early tomorrow, she could be there by midafternoon.

Chapter Twenty-seven

At the state line, she almost turned back, and she reconsidered the idea every single time she passed an exit sign. This was dumb. This was embarrassing. This was pitiful.

Ill-conceived. Ill-considered. Ill-advised.

She felt exhausted, and nauseated, and afraid. Extremely so, in all three cases. It would be nonsensical to drive almost two thousand miles and then change her mind and go home, but who would be the wiser?

About halfway there, she stopped to eat two bites of a hamburger, and drink part of a Coke, her stomach rebelling with every swallow. Maybe she would get lucky, and her car would flat out die. Maybe *she* would flat out die. Maybe she should forget this whole imbecilic idea, and join the circus. Maybe — she threw away what was left of her lunch, and got back into the car.

It was almost two when she drove into the city limits. The map was hard to follow, and she was filled with nothing but dread, so she decided to drive by Fitzsimons, first. See what the place looked like.

It was big.

She pulled over near one of the main guard-posts — if they didn't like it, too bad — and looked at her map. There were a few stray protesters standing around with signs — one, two, three, four, we don't want your f-ing war — but she ignored them, too.

She was at the intersection of Peoria Street and Montview Boulevard. She — were she so inclined — wanted to be on Colfax Avenue, which would appear to lead straight to a Route 6, and Golden. She sent the approaching tight-lipped MP her best salute, and put the car into Drive.

Denver didn't look the way she expected. That is, not if Colfax was any indication. It was one long strip of traffic lights, car lots, and fast-food restaurants. Kind of — monotonous, and depressing.

For a while, she didn't even see any mountains — so much for the Mile-High City — but then she did, and she gulped. Jesus Christ, she was in *Colorado*. This was an epic mistake. She should flee, while there was still time.

There were signs for Golden now, and she had to keep swallowing. The only saving grace here was that no one else in her life would ever have to know that she had done this. She could tell them she had — gone driving around. Period.

Colfax turned into Route 40, which turned into Route 6. There were mountains all along her left, and up ahead. Gentle, naked-looking mountains. These days, when she thought of mountains, she pictured Vietnam and those lush, green-jungled peaks, but — these mountains were different. Browner. Less threatening.

She stopped at a red light, and squinted at the street signs. 19th Street. It looked like a main drag, so she turned right — and almost swerved off the road when she saw a gas station a few blocks away. Oh, Christ, it *couldn't* be, could it? She wasn't ready. Christ, he might *be* there, pumping gas on his prosthesis — and very unhappy to see her. She slowed down, greatly disturbing the guy in the pickup truck behind her, but the only two attendants she could see were both in their late twenties or early thirties.

Well, what the hell. She needed gas anyway. She turned in, her heart thumping loudly in her ears, gripping the steering wheel so hard that her hands cramped.

One of the men came over, cheery and grease-stained, a plain blue baseball cap pushed back on his head. "What can I do for you, miss?"

Jesus, what if Michael just suddenly walked *out*. What if — the guy was looking at her, and she gave him a trembling smile back.

"C-Could you fill it, please?" she asked.

He nodded, and unscrewed the gas cap, sticking the nozzle in the tank, and then picked up a squeegee to wash her windshield.

"Massachusetts, hunh?" he said, looking up from her license plate. "Pretty far from home."

She nodded, her stomach so nervous and jumpy that she was afraid to open her mouth.

"What brings you out to these parts?" he asked.

"Well, I, uh — " Her mind was blank. "I've never been here before," she said.

He was a little nonplussed, but he nodded. "Well, welcome to the West, miss." He tipped his cap, then winked at her. "We're mighty glad to have you."

She smiled, her hands clutching the wheel.

He topped off the tank, and then returned. "All set. Want me to take a look under the hood?" He grinned. "Sounds like it *needs* a look."

"No, thank you." She fished out enough money to pay him. "But, thank you."

He counted out a dollar fifty in change, and handed it back to her.

"Thank you," she said. Now or never. Sink or goddamn swim. "I, uh — " It would be unpleasant for all concerned if she threw up on him. "Is this — Jennings' gas station?"

The guy shook his head. "No, he's down by the factory."

Oh, Jesus. She really *was* in the right town.

"Look," the guy said. "Bert Jennings isn't the only one in town who does good work. I'd be happy to pull your car on in, and — "

She shook her head. "No, I was just — curious. He's, uh — the friend of a friend, and, uh — " She must sound like a lunatic. "Do you have a phone book I could borrow?"

The guy had, indeed, backed away from her, but he pointed to the small office near the repair bay, and she went over there, with him, uneasily, right behind her.

"Sure there isn't anything I can help you with?" he asked, watching as she flipped the skinny little book open, her hands shaking.

"No, thank you." She turned to the Js. "Just

checking something.'' There was no Bert Jennings, but there was an *Albert*, on 11th Street. If she was on 19th Street, that meant she was — eight blocks away. Slowly, she closed the book, then remembered that the guy was watching her. ''Thanks a lot.''

She was so nervous that she almost crashed into the pump as she pulled out — which would have *really* made him tense. She drove back up 19th Street, taking her first left and running into — 20th Street.

Okay. Start over. She turned around, and continued up 19th Street, taking her next right. Washington Street. Which was probably a main street, because she saw little stores on either side. A brown wooden sign spanned the street, with HOWDY, FOLKS! painted at the top, and a — golden — WELCOME TO GOLDEN painted below that. The whole scene was framed by cloud-shadowed mountains up ahead, and it was all so quaint and unfamiliar that she ran a stop sign, and had to jerk her attention back to her driving to keep from riding up onto the sidewalk. No one beeped at her, although a woman in a station wagon shook a stern finger, so it must be a pretty friendly place. In Boston, people got *killed* for less.

13th Street. 12th Street. She was homesick, suddenly, and somewhere between petrified and panic-stricken. She turned down 11th Street, with fields, a few distant buildings, and mountains off to her right, and houses to her left. She slowed down, looking so hard at the numbers on the houses, that when she saw the right one, she almost went off the road again.

Okay. Okay. Last chance to back out.

Aware that she was trembling pretty much uncontrollably, she closed her eyes for a few seconds, and then turned the car around, pulling up in front of the house.

Michael's house.

A nice house. Unassuming. Two stories, a dark brown wicker basket hanging by the side of the door instead of a mailbox. Small, well-kept yard, a couple of large trees shading the roof. Instead of a garage, there was a carport that was very crowded, but well organized, with an old Chevy that looked to be a work-in-progress parked on one side, and a station wagon parked behind it.

Okay. Now what.

She checked her reflection in the rearview mirror, and wasn't enchanted by what she saw. She looked sad, and tired, and her hair — what there was of it — had a sluggish and uncooperative quality. It would also be better if she were wearing a *dress*, and she considered driving back to that gas station to change in their ladies' room. Although that guy would probably close up when he saw her coming.

The longer she sat out here, the more likely it was that some member of Michael's family would come along and want to know just what the hell it was she was doing parked in front of their house.

Okay. Little to gain, but nothing to lose. Right? Right.

She opened the car door, wishing that she were less nauseated, and walked up to the front door. She could still change her mind. It wouldn't be too late until — as she stepped on the front porch, she heard a dog bark somewhere inside the house.

Otis.

Oh, God. Now, it was too late. She rang the bell, and when the door opened, she saw a very small middle-aged woman in a dark print dress smiling curiously at her.

"Yes?" the woman said, wiping her hands off with a dish towel, then setting it down on something unseen to her left. "May I help you?"

"I, uh — " Rebecca went blank again. The woman had a slight resemblance to Michael — alert, sharp features — but her smile and eyes were much more gentle. Kind. "Excuse me, I — I'm sorry to bother you, but — " She heard canine panting, and the sound of claws clicking against the floor as a medium-sized brown dog — mostly shepherd, and *completely* familiar — came trotting out to the hall, sticking his nose out around the woman's leg.

Otis. In the flesh. She felt tears come to her eyes, and promptly lowered her head. "I'm sorry to bother you, ma'am," she said. Mumbled, really. "I'm looking for — are you Mrs. Jennings?"

The woman nodded, an automatic hand reaching down to hold Otis's collar to keep him from pushing outside.

"I know I should have called first, but, um — " she was suffering from a near-total failure of nerve here — "Do you have a son named Michael?"

Mrs. Jennings nodded, her expression wary now.

"I don't mean to intrude like this, I — I just — "

She gritted her teeth. Spit it out! "I-I think we knew each other. In Vietnam, I mean."

Mrs. Jennings looked startled. Stunned, even.

"See, I think we were both stationed — " Yeah, right, she was just an old Army buddy. "I knew he lived somewhere near Denver, and, uh, I happened to be — " *just* happened to be — she stopped, shaking her head.

"You must be Rebecca," Mrs. Jennings said softly. Almost wonderingly.

Rebecca hesitated — God only knew what she had been told — but then nodded.

Mrs. Jennings stepped away from the door. "Please. Come in."

Rebecca took a deep breath, and followed her inside. The dog was still nosing around, and she patted him without thinking. "Hi, Otis. How you doing?" Then, she looked up, afraid that that might have seemed presumptuous. "Uh, Michael talked about him so much, I — I guess he seems familiar."

Mrs. Jennings nodded, and they exchanged rather timid smiles.

"Uh, how is he?" Rebecca asked. The house seemed *quiet*. "Is he — " okay — "home?"

Her mother nodded, with a certain strain in her expression. "Yes, of course. Come right this way."

Uh-oh.

"We're just so happy to have him back," Mrs. Jennings went on, "and I know he's going to be thrilled to see you. He's just been doing *wonderfully*."

The strain was evident in her *voice* now, but Rebecca nodded, following her down a dimly lit hallway towards the back of the house.

"Michael?" Mrs. Jennings called. "There's someone here to see you." She turned and went into a room on her left, pushing the door open. "Michael?"

Just as Rebecca was preparing a wide and happy smile, she heard a dull voice saying, "Tell them I'm asleep, okay, Mom? That I can't — " It was too late, and she was already standing in the doorway and they were staring at each other, Michael stretched out on a green couch and looking stupefied.

Aghast. Dismayed. Dumbfounded.

"Hi," Rebecca said, and tried to get her smile back — without success — and they just stared at each other. He looked thin, and pale, and his hair was *long*. Thick, wavy, and almost to his collar. Unrecognizable.

Mrs. Jennings broke the silence, her voice a little high. "Isn't this a wonderful surprise, Michael?"

"Who invited *you*?" Michael asked, his jaw rigid, and — yeah — his fists clenched.

"Well — " No one. "I was just — " In the neighborhood? Christ, she could do better than *that*. She forced a smile. "Did you know they don't sell Coors east of the Mississippi? It's — just criminal."

He didn't smile back.

"So, uh — " Damn it to hell. Why had she come? "While I was in Golden *anyway*, I thought I'd — " She, clearly, wasn't going to get a smile out of him, so she stopped trying, and shoved her hands — also clenched — into her pockets.

"Why don't you sit down, Rebecca," Mrs. Jennings said, "and I'll — "

Michael cut her off. "She's not staying."

Mrs. Jennings shot him a swift, motherly you-just-be-*quiet* look.

"What, I need her goddamn pity visit?" Michael asked. "I don't think so."

Okay. At least now, she knew. He hated her. "Well, it was worth a shot," she said, and bent to give Otis — whose tail was waving with appealing optimism — a quick pat. "You're a good dog, Otis. I'm sorry your owner's such a sulky, rotten, little son-of-a-bitch."

Mrs. Jennings looked as though she wished she were any other place in the *world.*

"Excuse me, ma'am," Rebecca said, very politely. "I'm sorry to have bothered you." She left the room, walking to the front door as fast as she could. She was going to cry, but she was *damned* if it would happen before she got outside.

She closed the door behind her, and stood on the porch, feeling her shoulders collapse. Okay. Okay. At least she wouldn't have to *wonder* anymore. He hated her, and — oh, hell. She covered her face with her hands, using enough pressure to try and *force* the tears back in. So she'd driven a long way, so what. She had nowhere to go, nothing to do — so what. Big deal. It didn't mean nothing. Not a goddamn thing. He wasn't *worth* her crying over. And certainly not worth falling apart.

She heard loud music — Hendrix — and adolescent male voices, and looked up to see a guy climbing out of a crowded T-Bird, yelling some sort of farewell, and barely glancing at the unfamiliar car parked in front of his house before jogging up the walk. He looked so much like a young, happy, two-legged Michael that her heart skipped. He paused when he saw her, his mouth dropping open.

Dennis. And here she was, a complete stranger, crying on his front porch.

"You all right, miss?" he asked. "You need help?"

She shook her head, brushing her sleeve across her eyes and putting on her sunglasses.

"You sure everything's okay?" he asked. "You want to come inside?"

That was about the *last* thing she wanted. "No, thank you." She walked briskly towards the car, and he came trailing along with her, then noticed the license plate.

"Whoa," he said, stopping short. "You're the *nurse*."

Lucky her. She kept walking.

"Stay here!" he said — ordered — and bounded up the walk and into the house, bellowing something she couldn't quite distinguish before the door swung shut.

She stood by her car, then realized that she had just let some *kid* tell her what to do, and took out her car keys. Purposefully. She was just getting inside, when a lower, gruffer voice said, "*Hey*," from the porch. Michael, of course, scowling in the doorway, balanced on a pair of well-worn crutches. He wasn't wearing a prothesis and someone — probably his mother — had pinned his left jeans leg up. Otis was peeking out from behind him, his head leaning against Michael's remaining leg. They stood, twenty-five feet apart, scowling at each other.

"Nice sight," he said, bitterly, "hunh?"

A sight she had waited a very long time to see. "Handsome as hell," he said.

Actually, even surly, and skinny, and disheveled, he *was*. She felt a grin coming, and fought it off. "You don't look so bad to me."

"*You* look terrible," he said.

And charming, too. She was the luckiest woman alive. She let out her breath, leaning forward with her arms resting on the roof of the car. "I'm going for a drive. You coming?"

He frowned. "Where I go, *Otis* goes."

She opened the back door, giving a little whistle. "Come here, Otis," she said, and he squirmed through the doorway, under Michael's stump, and galloped over to her. "Hop in."

Michael crutched down the walk, slow and self-conscious, and a legitimate example of someone being a shadow of his former self. Seeing her watching him, he looked angry and humiliated.

"Ashamed to be seen with me?" he asked.

"I don't know," she said. "I guess that depends on how you act."

He scowled, and paused to look over the car. "What's *this* supposed to be?"

He had a hell of a lot of nerve, trashing her like this. "It runs," she said.

"Yeah, well, it's a piece of shit," he said.

She was starting to have a hard time remembering ever liking him. But she didn't respond, coming over to open the door for him.

"I can do it," he said, slammed the door, and opened it for himself.

Right. She nodded, and walked back around to get in on her side. Then, they sat in utter silence, while Otis fussed and sniffed and turned around several times in the backseat to get comfortable.

"You aren't scared to be alone with me?" Michael asked. "Sometimes, us baby-killers go nuts — can't control ourselves."

She looked over. "So they tell me."

He nodded, and shoved his crutches so that they were in between them, then folded his arms across his chest, glaring out through the windshield.

Beyond charming.

"So, drive," he said.

Right. She put on her seat belt, struggling with the balky clasp. "Where should I go?"

He shrugged. "It's *your* crummy car. I'm just along for the ride."

"It's *your* crummy town," she said.

He didn't answer, slouching and glaring, with those folded arms.

"Okay," she said, started the car on the second try, and pulled out.

"Is this supposed to be good driving?" he asked, after they'd barely gone a block.

She stamped on the brakes, without looking in the rearview mirror first — pretty poor driving, actually — so that she could scowl over at him. "I'm going to end it all," she said, "and I've decided to take *you* with me."

He grumbled something, and slouched lower.

"Now it's *your* damn town," she said. "Where am I going?"

He looked at her, with his jaw jutting out, then sighed and pointed up at the next corner. "Take a right," he said.

Chapter Twenty-eight

He directed her, sullenly, back to 19th Street, and through the light.

She nodded up towards the mountain ahead of them, where a huge white *M* was displayed on the ground near the top. "What's that?"

"It's an *M*," he said.

Right. It would be nice if he could try being *less* of a bastard.

In the backseat, Otis was still engaged in canine querulousness, and she reached back with one hand to roll down the window a couple of inches, Otis sticking his nose out even before she was finished.

"I can take care of my own dog," Michael said, and unrolled the rear window on his side.

Yeah, yeah, yeah. Christ. She kept driving, the road curving up and to the right. *Way* up, it would appear.

She slowed down. "Do you want me to go up this mountain?"

Michael nodded.

"Well, uh — " she kept slightly more pressure on the accelerator than on the brake, to keep the car from stalling out — "I'm not sure my car can make it."

"Wouldn't be surprised," he said.

"So, isn't there someplace else we can go?" she asked.

He shook his head.

Fine. If he didn't care about them hurtling to their deaths, *she* didn't, either. She kept driving, shifting down to second gear as the car shuddered. Each long turn seemed steeper and more risky than the last, and she was clenching her teeth so fiercely that her jaw was starting to hurt.

"You're only making it worse by riding the brake," he said.

She ignored him, grinding away on her molars, waiting for the car to die. Then, the brakes would fail, and they would roll inexorably to the edge, powerless and doomed.

"If you're that nervous, ride up the middle," he said. "There's no one coming."

Yeah, go up the middle, and smash into a car speeding around one of the looping turns, and then *both* cars would sail off the side of the mountain, landing in a heap of flaming, crumpled metal.

Michael frowned at her. "Were you always this damn tense?"

Yes. She heard a strange, inhuman screeching outside, and cringed. "What's that?"

He looked bored. "Just deer."

Wow. She pressed harder on the brake so she could look out at the scrub brush to their left. "Real ones?"

"No," he said. "Disney's got a test lab here."

She spotted them, then — three *actual* deer, standing on the mountainside. She shoved the car into Park, and leaned over into the backseat, moving Otis out of the way so she could go through the drawstring bag she used as a pocketbook. She fished around inside until she found her camera, then opened the door.

"Oh, Christ," Michael said, and grabbed Otis's collar before he could go leaping out after her.

"I never saw real deer before," she said, and took several pictures of the animals cantering up the mountain in a panic. They probably wouldn't come out very well, but, what the hell. *She* knew they were there.

She got back into the car, put her camera away, and then shifted into Drive, the car rolling back with a sickening lurch before the gas kicked in. He seemed to want to go all the way to the top, so she grimly nosed the car around the curves. They were passing the big white *M* dug into the ground now, and she pointed with her elbow.

"What's the *M* for?" she asked.

"Michael," he said.

Right. Jerk.

They kept driving, up and up, the car's engine laboring.

"Okay," Michael said. "Here."

Yes, *sir*. Rebecca parked, well back from the edge.

"Buffalo Bill's buried up there," he said, pointing.

Yeah. So? She shrugged.

"And," he pointed down at the — admittedly spectacular — vista of the town spread out far below them, "that's the brewery, back there."

He had mistaken her for someone who *gave* a damn.

"We're on top of Lookout Mountain," he said.

A tour. How nice.

They sat, slouched, with their arms folded, staring out at the rolling mountains to their left, the small, cluttered town below, and stark plateaus beyond. Far in the distance, she *thought* she could see Denver, but it was too cloudy to be sure.

"So, what do you want?" he asked. "You get the impression I wanted to *see* you again?"

No. "I got the impression you wanted me to fall permanently from the face of the earth," she said.

Michael nodded. "Well, good. Had me worried there, for a minute."

What a son-of-a-bitch.

"This some kind of duty visit?" he asked. "Or just *pity*?"

"It was a mistake, is what it was," she said.

He nodded.

Fine. Next stop, New England.

"Your hair looks dumb," he said.

She touched it, flushing slightly. "So does yours."

He shrugged, pushing at the sagging door of the glove compartment, and frowning as it sagged more.

She wasn't going to give him the satisfaction of crying. She could save *that* for the long drive back home. And — she was just going to have to find some kind of future for herself. Join a religious order, maybe. Enter a mental hospital. Drive the hell off the side of this mountain.

In the meantime, she would inflict a little damage on *him*. "Snoopy was at the Evac.," she said.

Michael stiffened.

Good. She looked at him, expressionless.

"Was he — all right?" Michael asked.

She kept looking at him. "What do *you* care."

Michael didn't answer, but it was easy to see that he was upset.

Good.

"If you wanted to forget you ever met *me*, fine," she said, "but you goddamn well should have let *him* know that you were okay. He was your best friend, and you *owed* him that."

Michael took out a pack of cigarettes, and a dented Zippo lighter.

"He wasn't even sure if you were still alive," she said.

Michael shrugged, not looking at her.

Selfish jerk. "You care if *he* made it?" she asked.

He nodded, gripping the lighter.

Finally. Something resembling a normal reaction. "He did," she said. "He was stopping by on his way home. He figured — God knows why — that I might have heard from you."

Michael lit his cigarette, and dropped the Zippo back in his pocket.

"Anyway," she said, "I'll drive you home now, but if you have a *spark* of decency left, you'll take his address and damn well sit down and write him a letter to put his mind at ease." She paused. "Although why *any* of us ever wasted time caring about you is beyond me."

As she turned on the ignition, he reached over to cover her hand with his, turned the engine off, and then removed his hand.

"What about Hanson?" he asked.

"He was, uh — " thinking about Hanson still almost always made her grin — "on the mend."

"Meaning what?" Michael asked.

Did he want to hear about the kiss? Not likely. "That he was definitely going to survive, and the doctors' feeling was that the odds were better than even that he'd still have vision in the one eye," she said.

Michael nodded, and smoked.

Anyway. She moved her hand back to the ignition.

"So — that's why you came?" he asked. "To tell me to write Snoopy?"

She nodded.

He took a deep drag. "Helluva long drive."

If all else failed, she could attempt to retain her dignity. "Not really," she said. "I'm on my way to meet my boyfriend in Reno."

Michael nodded.

Reno. Christ, if she'd said Berkeley, or even L.A., he might have bought it. "He goes to Harvard," she said. "Third-year law school."

Michael knocked his ashes onto the floor in front of him. "Must be smart."

She nodded, enthusiastically. "I wouldn't waste my time with someone who wasn't."

Michael smoked.

Jesus, it didn't even *matter* to him. "He's also —" Michael was 5'8", tops — "*tall*," she said.

"Smart *and* tall?" Michael shook his head admiringly. "Well. Sounds like you're pretty lucky."

Yeah. Real lucky. Now she was sitting here feeling sorry for herself because there was no brawny, brainy Harvard man waiting for her in Reno. "Uh, yeah." She gave him a wide smile. "We might go ahead and get married while we're there, or wait until we go back East, so my parents can throw us a big reception at the Corinthian Yacht Club." No reaction to her right. "What about you?"

Michael shrugged. "Think I'll stay here. I'd probably be in the way in Reno."

Humor. Of all things. But, for some reason, instead of amusing her, this conversation was bringing more tears to her eyes. She focused straight ahead, hoping that he wouldn't be able to tell.

"Glad you found yourself a guy who can stand on his own two legs," Michael said. "Always knew you would."

Yeah, *right*. "I don't care about stupid *legs*," Rebecca said. "I just don't want a guy with a tencent head." Noticing that she was gripping the wheel the way her father did when he was angry, she dropped her hands into her lap.

Michael studied them. "No. Looks like you got a guy too cheap to buy an engagement ring."

This was an insanely irritating charade — and she was the one who had initiated it. "We're saving to buy a house," she said.

It was quiet for a few seconds, then he shook his head.

"Jesus, Rebecca," he said. "You never let up, do you."

No. It was one of her — many — tragic flaws.

"Might be," he looked at her, "you're bull-headed enough to stay with someone out of *guilt*."

"Yeah, well, *you'll* never know, will you," she said.

He shrugged again, stubbed out his cigarette on his crutch — Jesus — and lit another.

She shouldn't have come. She should have just gone somewhere and drunk herself into oblivion. "I just — " If she cried in front of him, it would be yet another reason *never* to forgive herself as long as she lived. "I was *stupid*, okay? I thought — I mean, for a while there, you were the reason I was getting through the *day*, and — " Damn it, damn it, damn it. She had to squeeze her eyes shut for a second before she could go on. "I know I was just — convenient — for you, and — it was a *war* thing, that's all." She looked down at her completely, devastatingly ringless hands. "We should have just had our five torrid little days in Tokyo, and then — see you later." Sayonara. Short and sweet.

"Sorry I went and got myself blown up," he said. "Ruined your vacation. But — you know us dumb grunts."

Yes, she was going to cry. Nonstop, forever.

"I hate Vietnam," he said, his voice as vicious as it was bitter. "I hate everything about it. And you *stink* of the place."

Precisely. She leaned forward against the steering wheel, pressing her face into the fold of her left elbow.

"*Shit,*" he said, gathered his crutches, and got out of the car, Otis jumping over the front seat and after him.

The next thing she heard — after the door slammed — was the hood going up. He seemed to be banging around under there, and — Christ. Was he trying to fix it, or tear it apart? Did it matter?

If she could still cry right, she would, but the tears just came streaming affectlessly out of her eyes, without any sobs, or shudders, or even a snuffle, to accompany them. She stunk of Vietnam. Yeah. She did, indeed. It had taken her over inside, and was now spewing out to cover everything, and everyone, around her. She was — fetid. Repellent.

She sat in the car for what seemed like a long time, unable even to cry after the first few minutes. There weren't any more sounds under the hood, but odds were, he wasn't making his way down the mountain on those crutches. She dragged herself out, feeling the need to lean on the car for support as she walked around to the front.

Michael was waiting for her, slouching back against the grill with his arms across his chest.

"I'm sorry," Rebecca said, not looking up. "That was embarrassing for both of us. Let me drive you home now, okay?"

He didn't say anything.

What, did he want her to cry again? "*Please,* Michael?" she asked. "Can we just go?"

He looked at the engine. "Do you *ever* have this thing tuned up?"

One-track mind. She shook her head.

He leaned over, checking the battery cables, and then indicating the darkly grease-encrusted battery itself. "If you pour a Coke over this, you can get a lot of that crud off."

She never gave her car battery any thought whatsoever.

"Your *car*, I can fix," he said.

"That all you're interested in?" she asked.

He pulled out the dipstick, wiped it on his sleeve, and checked the oil. "Maybe you *wanted* a dumb grunt," he said, examining the stick. "A guy you don't have to take too serious, because he'll die, like as not."

Oh, yeah. Described her to a T. She didn't say anything, not even patting Otis, who had come over to lean against her legs, wagging his tail. Much nicer than his owner.

"I'm a world-class fuck-up," Michael said. "You *know* that. The only way we would've met back in the World is if I gave you a ski lesson, and you tipped me a couple extra dollars maybe."

Maybe. But — they hadn't met in the World.

"I'm not the smartest guy who ever came along the pike," he said, "and I'm lazy, and I've got about a temper and a half. On top of which, I'm a god-damn *cripple*."

She watched Otis gambol away, in search of nothing in particular.

"So — go to Reno," Michael said, replacing the dipstick. "Move on. Do better."

Reno. "Yeah, well, unfortunately, I was dumb enough to fall in love with *you*, you stupid son-of-a-bitch," Rebecca said.

Michael straightened up so swiftly that she felt herself blush. She was definitely working without a net now.

"I said it," she said, blushing more, "okay? I know it isn't mutual, but that's how *I* feel." Help. "Okay? I feel like — " *Sex*, actually. Passion. Love. *Life*. And — well, good luck to her, and her damned baseball team. "The truth is — " she hunched over her arms so she wouldn't have to look at him — "I'd rather *fight* with you, than be happy with someone else."

There was a short silence.

"Hmmm," he said.

She frowned, too. Somehow, that last part hadn't come out quite right.

The silence continued.

"Jesus, Rebecca," he said, shook his head, and got back in the car.

Okay. Time to go. She pushed slowly away from the car to get in on the driver's side. For the last forty-five minutes or so, she had felt miserable, but *alive* — a nice change — and now, the familiar dead weight was returning to her back and shoulders.

It was going to be one hell of a long trip home. They drove back down the mountain without speaking, Otis sitting up front in between them. It was getting dark, and Rebecca drove very cautiously, alert for the possibility of carefree, if doltish, deer bolting across the road in front of her.

"You mind the dog?" Michael asked, his voice stiff.

She shook her head.

"Good," he said, and patted the top of Otis's head.

She wouldn't mind a pat like that, herself. Would *love* it, in fact.

When they got to the bottom of the mountain, it was such a relief that she couldn't help letting out her breath.

Michael looked over, cocking an eyebrow. "Got a little fear of heights there, Lieutenant?"

Big fear.

He pointed her back to 19th Street, and then back to his house, where the lights were on, and a pickup truck was parked in the driveway. His father, no doubt.

She didn't want to say good-bye — couldn't *bear* it — so she took her time parking, and turning off the engine. Michael didn't seem to be in any hurry, either, although Otis was standing on the seat and ready to go, wagging his tail in her face.

"Get in the back," Michael ordered — sounding strict enough for Rebecca to consider doing so herself. It appeared, however, that he had been talking to Otis, who jumped into the backseat.

She had *tried*. It was good that she had tried.

"Has it been as bad as you look?" Michael asked.

Worse. She nodded.

"Me, too," he said.

They both nodded, Rebecca wondering if her face could possibly be as haggard and exhausted as his was.

"Well," he said, abruptly, and opened his door. "My mother'll be waiting dinner."

So much for a lingering farewell. She felt like crying again — but what was the point? Better she should just smile, wish him luck with heartfelt sincerity, and leave it at that. Accept the outcome with her best imitation of grace.

Michael paused halfway out of the car to frown at her. "You coming, or what?"

She stared at him in complete confusion.

"Come on already," he said impatiently. "My mother'll be waiting on us."

Us? She blinked, then automatically checked her reflection, pushing her bangs away from her eyes and trying to remember where her brush was. Then, suddenly afraid that he might change his mind, she got out of the car with considerable haste.

He nodded, and started crutching up the walk.

"Is this really okay?" she asked. "I mean, is this what you want?"

He looked at her, and then sighed. "Damned if I know," he said.

Chapter Twenty-nine

Inside the house, his family was just sitting down to supper, and there was a little flurry of introductions, Rebecca hanging back shyly near the door. His father was stocky, with thinning, rumpled hair, and wearing an old, but clean, red flannel shirt and grey work pants. Carrie was small and dark-haired, like her mother, and looked about twelve with her big ponytail, but Rebecca was pretty sure she was a couple of years older than that.

There was only one extra place — Michael's — set on the table, but Mrs. Jennings was already up, swiftly taking another setting from the sideboard and putting it next to Carrie.

"Why don't you show Rebecca where she can wash up," she said to Michael, while motioning for Dennis to get another chair.

Michael nodded, crutching over to the stairs, Rebecca keeping her head down in case there were tearstains on her cheeks. Michael was trying to hurry ahead of her and, clumsy with his crutches, fell about halfway up the flight. Fell *hard*, and then stayed down, clearly mortified.

She knew — tempting, though it was — that helping the poor guys was contraindicated. That it only made them feel worse. "Lazy," she said, after a pause, "ill-tempered — and *slow*."

He didn't respond right away, but then he laughed, pushing himself up onto his hands and remaining knee.

"Hurry it up already, Mike," Dennis said from the table. "I'm starving."

Michael showed him his fist, before using it to grab the bannister, jumping up onto his right leg, and she handed him his crutches. He started to say something, but then just nodded and took them from her.

Once they were upstairs, he pointed her in the direction of the bathroom, and she was relieved to go inside and close the door. Be alone. Shiver a few times. Chew up two Rolaids. There were plenty of fresh towels, and she washed her face more than once. Her eyes were still a little red, and quite puffy, but the puffiness might also be the residue of her protracted drunken binge. In combination with her hideous hair, it made for a rather dissipated picture.

When she opened the door again, Michael was leaning against the wall on his crutches, waiting. He had, she noticed, changed into a fresh shirt — a plain white Oxford.

"I, uh, look like Ray Milland," she said.

"You look more like *The Lost Year*," he said.

No doubt, but she found herself grinning at him, anyway. A *big* grin.

He crutched around her, and into the bathroom. "Out in a minute."

She nodded, and sat down in a small, straight chair next to a telephone table. A well-mannered and courageous person would go down to the dinner table, but she decided to wait for him, instead. Otis came galloping upstairs, greeted her frantically, then skidded into one of the bedrooms off the hall — Michael's, presumably — before skidding back out in some bewilderment.

"In there," Rebecca said, as though the dog, perhaps, spoke fluent English.

Otis sat down on the long hall rug, and scratched what seemed to be an indeterminate itch, distracted only by the opening of the bathroom door, upon which he rolled instantly to his feet, wagging his tail.

Michael had dampened and combed his hair, although it was still unruly, and his shirt was tucked in. "You could have gone down," he said.

She nodded, her hands folded in her lap.

"Well." He flipped off the bathroom light. "They're waiting on us."

No doubt. She stood up, smoothing the front of her own shirt. She should have worn a damn *dress*. Done her best to look pretty. Regardless of that with which she had to work.

"Come on," Michael said impatiently.

Right. Dennis was starving. She nodded, putting her hands in her pockets — which was hardly pretty — and so, she took them back out.

"They already like you a whole lot," Michael said.

She looked up. "They don't even *know* me."

"Oh. Well — " his cheeks seemed to have reddened a little — "I guess I told them a bunch of stuff. I mean — well, you know."

So he *hadn't* come home and promptly erased her from his mind. Feeling more pleased than she maybe should, she followed him downstairs.

As Mrs. Jennings served them plates, Rebecca sat down next to Carrie, who gave her a shy smile. Dinner looked delicious — beef brisket, crisp potatoes, fresh peas, homemade biscuits — and there were so many little extra touches, like sprigs of parsley, and carrots carved into little curls, that either Michael's family habitually ate very well, or Mrs. Jennings had gone a little out of her way tonight.

"What would you like to drink, Rebecca?" she asked. "A glass of wine, or — ?"

Time to demonstrate some self-control. "Uh —" Rebecca looked around to see what everyone else was having — "this is fine, thank you," she said, lifting her already filled water glass.

"You want a beer?" Michael asked, sitting across from her.

Yes. She shook her head.

He reached for his crutches. "I'll get one for you." He shook his head as Mrs. Jennings started to stand up. "I'll do it, Mom."

"Could you get me a Coke instead, Mike?" Rebecca asked.

He nodded, and something about the way the rest of the family didn't quite exchange glances gave her the distinct impression that Michael hadn't been volunteering to help much recently.

In the little silence that fell, she heard the refrigerator door open, and then the sound of cans. He crutched back out, a can of Coke jammed in one front pocket, a Coors in the other.

"What'd she do, Mike?" Dennis asked. "Give you *Nice* pills?"

Michael just frowned at him, pausing by Rebecca's side of the table long enough to hand her the Coke before returning to his seat.

During the rest of the meal, Mrs. Jennings pretty much kept the conversational ball rolling by asking her lots of friendly questions, some of which she was even able to answer. Dennis contributed regular flippancy, while Carrie kept grinning at her, and Michael and his father ate. Mr. Jennings seemed nice though, since when they happened to meet eyes, he would smile warmly and nod at her, before going back to eating. A man of few words, it would seem.

"I guess you know a lot about makeup and hair and stuff," Carrie said, after they had finished clearing off the table and Mrs. Jennings was trying to shoo them out of the kitchen.

What could possibly have given her *that* idea? Rebecca checked her expression to make sure that she wasn't being sarcastic, checked Michael's to make sure he wasn't laughing, then shook her head. "Uh, no. I wouldn't say that."

Carrie looked disappointed, but then brightened. "Well — *I* can show you stuff."

Trading nail polish, and cutting each other's bangs. Rebecca had to laugh. "Sure. That would be nice."

"I want to be around to see *that*," Michael said.

Rebecca chose to ignore him, scraping and stacking plates.

"Hey, it's about to start," Carrie said, pointing at the clock.

It. Hmmm.

"*The King and I*," Michael said, seeing her expression.

Oh. Well — cool.

"Why don't you three go watch the beginning," Mrs. Jennings said, "while Dennis helps me in here."

Dennis straightened up from the open refrigerator, where he was — despite having just finished dinner — getting a snack. "*Me?*"

"You," his mother said, firmly.

Dennis sighed, with deep resignation, and picked up a dish towel. "Mike could help. *Mike* never does anything."

"You're the one who never does anything," Carrie said.

Dennis snapped the dish towel at her head. "Silence, oh, Ugly One."

Carrie kicked him, covertly, and Rebecca held back a grin, since it was the same sort of fight she and Doug had always had.

"I'm the only one Mom and Dad like, *anyway*," Dennis said.

Perhaps it would be wise to make an exit. "Um, thank you, Mrs. Jennings," Rebecca said. "Dinner was delicious."

Mrs. Jennings smiled at her. "Thank you, dear. Go enjoy your show now."

She followed Michael out to the hall, where she noticed a telephone by the stairs.

"Do you mind if I use your phone for a minute?" she asked.

He shrugged. "Go ahead. I'll be in the den."

She wasn't sure where the den was — but, okay. Once he was gone, she dialed home collect, her mother *very* eager to accept the charges.

"Where are you?" she asked, sounding nervous. "Is everything okay?"

Well, everything was *interesting*. "I'm fine," Rebecca said. "I'm — in Colorado."

There was a little pause. "Oh, that's *good*," her mother said.

Yeah. Rebecca nodded, even though she knew her mother couldn't see her. "I'm at his house, and — well, I thought I should — " She was in the Rocky Mountains; it was two hours earlier in New England. "Are you watching *The King and I*?"

"Yes," her mother said, sounding amused now. "We are, actually."

Rebecca grinned. "So are we."

After hanging up, she found Michael on the couch in the room where she had first seen him that afternoon, with Carrie and Otis. Deborah Kerr was already singing "I Whistle a Happy Tune," and she looked around, not sure where to sit. There was room on the couch, but she should probably choose one of the overstuffed easy chairs. Not push it.

Michael looked at her, then indicated the couch with a sideways jerk of his head, and she sat down in between Carrie and Otis, who wagged his tail, his head and front paws on Michael's lap. More accurately — on his *stump*.

Michael frowned at her. "What?"

Even though she knew better, she had been staring. Not with disgust, or aversion — just sadness. "He's a nice dog," she said, pretending that she hadn't been.

Michael nodded, patted him, and frowned at the television.

She should have just sat in one of the easy chairs. Here, on the couch, she felt intrusive.

Oh, hell, being at his house at *all* was intrusive.

"Do you have enough room?" Carrie asked.

Since she had a habit of sitting all folded in on herself, she never took *up* much room. So, she nodded, and smiled, and looked at the television. It was one of her favorite musicals — but she still couldn't seem to pay attention. She was here, with *Michael*, in his *house*, in *America*. If she reached out, she could *touch* him. Of course, he would probably scowl, and shrug her off, but — here she was.

It would be nice if he would hold her hand, but his body language was carefully angled *away* from her and — well, she should just take the hint. Watch the movie. Pretend that her entire being wasn't vacillating wildly between jubilation and the verge of stormy tears.

She must have sighed, because now he and Carrie were both looking at her. She flushed, shrugged, and folded her arms more tightly, upon which they both returned their attention to the movie.

"What'd I miss?" Dennis asked, coming in with an overloaded plate of cookies, which he dropped onto the coffee table, several of them spilling off. He squinted at the television. "Hey, *that* doesn't look like *Perry Mason*."

"Shut up," Michael said. "We're not watching any damn *Perry Mason*."

Dennis went over to change the channel. "Yeah, we are."

"Rebecca wants to watch *this*," Michael said.

Dennis stopped. "Oh, she does, *does* she."

"I want to watch whatever everyone else wants to watch," Rebecca said quickly.

"*Well*," Dennis said, and stepped over the coffee table, squeezing in between her and Carrie — which made for a tight fit. "We'll just see about *that*, young lady."

Michael leaned forward enough to glare at him. "We're trying to watch."

"Maybe you should only talk during the *commercial*, *Mike*," Dennis said, sternly, and he and Carrie both laughed.

Why didn't it come as a surprise that Michael was totally unreasonable when it came to his viewing habits?

"So." Dennis slung his arm around her. "Rebecca. Tell me all about yourself."

"Shut up," Michael said.

"You're a woman of the world," Dennis went on. "Tell me all the *really* intimate sexual details."

Michael didn't seem to be amused, but she was.

"Well," she said. "My past is so extensive that I don't know where to start."

Dennis looked thoughtful. "Just the highlights, then."

Michael scowled at him.

"The *low*lights?" Dennis suggested cheerfully.

"During the *commercial*," Michael said.

Christ, he was impossible. Rebecca grinned,

reached for a cookie, and broke off a bite for Otis — who snapped it right up.

"Did I say you could feed my dog?" Michael asked.

The guy gave curmudgeons a bad name. "Short men are *so* disagreeable," she said to Dennis, who laughed.

Michael looked past her. "You seen her car?"

Dennis nodded. "Gave me my laugh for the day."

"You should see the *inside*," Michael said.

"If you guys are going to talk, can I watch *Jonathan Winters*?" Carrie asked.

"No," Michael said. Barked, really.

Carrie didn't argue, leaning forward to get a cookie.

"*No*," Dennis said, and gave her hand a sharp little slap before she could pick one up, and Carrie quickly withdrew it.

Now it was Rebecca's turn to lean forward, so she could see past Dennis. "Are they always like this?"

Carrie nodded.

"Well — they're Neanderthals," Rebecca said. "You should smack them."

Carrie nodded.

"I'd *like* to see her try," Dennis said.

She had a brother; she knew how to play this game. Rebecca smacked him across the back of the head, and Carrie followed that by punching his arm.

Dennis grinned. "This one's tough, Mike."

Michael nodded. Didn't smile.

Great. Was Elizabeth tough? No, she was probably sweet, and ultra-feminine, and *gorgeous*. Pliant, demure, and presentable. All the things he must really *like* in a girl. Woman. Whatever.

Dennis nudged her. "I meant that, you know, in a good way."

So she must look as fretful as she felt. "Oh, yeah," she said, and nibbled her cookie. "Absolutely."

After a while, Mr. Jennings came in to collect Otis for a walk, and then Mrs. Jennings appeared with fresh cookies and glasses of milk. She sat down to watch the end of the movie, during which period everyone behaved, with the possible exception of Dennis, who kept making, "Hey, it's getting *hot* in here" remarks during the "Shall We Dance" scene.

During the commercial, Mrs. Jennings told her that she had made up Michael's room for her upstairs, and he would certainly be very happy to sleep down here on the couch, while Rebecca made polite noises about having passed a Holiday Inn just outside of town, and how she could easily — Mrs. Jennings would have none of that, and so Rebecca blushed, and thanked her, and avoided Michael's eyes again.

When the movie ended, the news came on, and Vietnam was the top story, with a bleak report about yet another nightmare battle, this one involving the 101st Airborne, who had been fighting so long, and so hard, and so pointlessly, that the place was being called Hamburger Hill. According to the anchorman, the objective had finally been achieved, the Communist menace routed, and "mopping up" operations were in place. MACV —

Military Assistance Command, Vietnam; more specifically, the idiots in charge — was pleased by the outcome — a ten-to-one kill ratio — and glossed over the fact that at least seventy GIs had been killed, and another four hundred or so wounded, explaining that "vital interests" had been protected. On a godforsaken hill out in the middle of the A Shau. The couple of grunts who were interviewed were dazed, bloody — and furious. And, on the homefront, Teddy Kennedy, among others, was speechifying on the Senate floor about how senseless it all was. Amazingly, this was being treated as *news.*

"That's good," Michael said through his teeth. "*Remind* the guys who left pieces of themselves up there what a waste it was."

No one else said anything — there wasn't much *to* say — and shortly thereafter, the rest of his family began making excuses to leave — Carrie, off to bed because she had school the next day; Dennis, to finish up some French vocabulary; Mrs. Jennings, to go "check something." Michael's father had already gone upstairs.

She and Michael watched the rest of the news — rain was likely the next day and, in sports, the Red Sox had won the first game of a doubleheader and were leading in the second. Actually, the sportscaster put much more emphasis on the Denver Bears — but she didn't pay attention to that part.

"You want to watch Carson?" Michael asked.

"Sure," she said, although she didn't care one way or the other.

He got up to change the channel, arranging the

crutches under his arms, his movements slow and unwieldy.

"Are you still having a lot of pain?" she asked, as he made his way back to the couch.

He lowered himself down. "Who gives a shit? Only *stupid* people go over there, anyway."

Right.

"What's another five hundred casualties," he said, "as long as we're going to have peace with *honor*."

She nodded, feeling very tired.

He looked tired, too. "I still feel my knee sometimes. I mean, it still hurts."

Phantom pains. "I'm sorry," she said.

He shrugged, staring at *The Tonight Show*.

"Not just the pain," she said. "About everything."

He shrugged.

This wasn't working out the way she would have guessed. Either, she shouldn't still be sitting here, or he should be *happy* that she was here. She sighed. "Michael, I — "

"I was thinking about you," he said, and looked at her, unblinking. "When it happened."

When it happened, not after. It would be cowardly to avoid his eyes, so she nodded, and looked back at him.

He let out his breath. "Viper always said not to think about anything but the *war*. Said it was the only way to make it. And — " He stopped, shaking his head.

"You can't help thinking," she said hesitantly.

"Yeah, but I took another guy *with* me," he said.

"A guy who thought about everything *but* himself — and I'm walking around out there with my head in my crotch."

Okay. She was no slouch at self-flagellation herself.

"Sometimes," Michael said, after a couple of minutes, "being able to think about you was the only reason I didn't crack up. And other times — it made me not do my job."

She couldn't criticize the cerebral major for not having enough advice when she didn't have any herself.

"I *meant* to, though," he said unhappily. "I mean — I *tried*. I really did."

So had she.

Chapter Thirty

They sat on the couch, well apart, Otis curled up on the floor by Michael's remaining foot. The house was quiet, except for the low volume on the television, and she assumed that everyone else had gone to bed.

"May I see it?" she asked.

Michael shook his head emphatically.

She thought about her ward at Walson, and those horrible first times when she would have to hold up a mirror for the kids with the reconstructed faces. "Have you let *anyone* see it?"

"Dennis," he said, after a pause.

Which surprised her. "Not your mother?" she asked.

He shook his head.

Okay. She reached her hand out far enough to touch his hair. "Why don't you wear your prosthesis?"

He shrugged. "Don't like it."

Okay. His hair — there was so *much* of it — was very thick, and she tried to smooth out a small tangle. ''Maybe it needs refitting,'' she said. ''We could ride out to Fitzsimons tomorrow, and have them take a look.''

''Doesn't matter if it's no good,'' he said. ''It's not like I *go* anywhere.''

Well — she could relate to that. She nodded. ''I feel like one of the walking dead, too.''

''Really?'' He glanced over. ''I'm one of the *lying down* dead.''

Her sense of humor might have been extinguished, but somehow, his was still alive and flickering. She smiled, letting her hand slide down to his neck, a little surprised by how warm his skin was. How smooth. She knew there was a long, jagged scar under his shirt, running across his collarbone, where he'd had the compound fracture, but from this perspective, his upper body seemed unscathed.

He was sitting very still and, feeling shy, she took her hand away. Back when he had been cock of the walk, *he* had been the one who made all the moves. In fact, it was possible that she had gone through her entire life without *ever* making a first move.

Why start now. Especially with someone who was so rigidly unresponsive.

''My arm is pretty awful,'' she said. ''Where I, uh, hurt it.''

He nodded.

''I showed my father, because — well, he's a *doctor*.'' She swallowed. ''It's ugly, but do you, um, want to see it?''

He nodded, very slowly.

Okay. The gutless way out — her usual way —

would be to roll up her sleeve, but she made herself unbutton her shirt, her hands shaking, and drew it off, too self-conscious to look over at him. She was sitting in the wrong direction, so she had to turn, and then lifted her elbow up so he could see. She wasn't quite sure how he was reacting, and when she felt his hand touch the scar, she flinched.

"I'm sorry." He pulled his fingers back. "Does it hurt?"

She shook her head, but felt herself trembling anyway.

"It's not so bad," he said.

No. But it certainly didn't help make her — beautiful.

His hand grazed her ribs, and she flinched again.

"Jesus, Rebecca," he said.

She thought he was talking about her being so jumpy, then saw that he was staring, not at her bra, or breasts, but at her ribs. Her skin looked very thin, and pale, the bones much too prominent. It occurred to her that she had spent the last couple of years staring, worriedly, at young men's bodies, but — with the exception of the occasional malnourished Vietnamese civilian — had never really thought about what women looked like. Or, anyway, what they were *supposed* to look like. She could see, glancing down, that her body was more delicate than she thought of it as being. Fragile. Pathetic.

Acutely embarrassed, she pulled her shirt back on, turning away from him to button it up.

"Becky," he said, and his hands came over to rest on her shoulders, easing her closer to him.

It felt *good*. "It's okay, Mike," she said shakily. "You don't have to — "

He kissed her, not with the eager passion she remembered, but soft, gentle kissing, as though he were kissing something very damaged. She kissed back, the same way, both of them with their eyes open and looking at each other. Careful, quiet kisses, their hands resting lightly on each other's shoulders and arms.

"Don't, Becky," he said, and kissed both of her cheeks. "Come on, don't."

She realized then that she was crying again, and trying to stop only made it worse.

"All right," he said. "It's all right. Come here, it's all right."

She needed to be held more than she needed *anything* else on earth, so she let him, hanging on tightly in return. "I'm sorry," she said. "I really am."

He moved her bangs back, and kissed her. "About what?"

Well, hell. "I can't think of anything I'm *not* sorry about," she said.

He nodded, stroking her hair, and she was relieved when he didn't say anything, because all she wanted to do was sit, and rest, and maybe try to learn how to relax again. The low, flickering television was very comforting, and she leaned against him, holding his free right hand with both of hers.

"I can sleep down here," she said, "if you want."

He hesitated. "Well — my father gets up really early."

She wasn't sure how that would affect her sleeping on the couch, but then figured it out. "Oh, I didn't mean — that is — "

The arm he had around her shoulders stiffened, and he pulled away. "You didn't mean *both* of us being down here?"

Well — no. She shook her head. "Not in your parents' house. I wouldn't want them to — that would be *furtive*."

"Furtive," he said.

He knew damned well what she meant. "Us," she said, "together on an old couch, in a frantic hurry because someone might walk in at any second."

He shrugged. "Doesn't sound so bad to me."

Actually, in the scheme of things, it didn't sound bad to her, either.

"And, you know, the couch isn't all *that* old," he said.

She grinned at him.

"Look." He pressed down on the cushions with one hand. "Lots of *bounce*."

She tested it out herself and found that yes, the cushions were quite bouncy.

"So," he said.

They weren't ready yet, and she suspected that he knew that as well as she did. "How about we each try to regain a little of *our* bounce, first," she said.

He shrugged. "I don't know. Seems like maybe — "

"Mike," she said, and rested her hand gently on his stump.

He nodded, looking away from her.

She gave his leg a little pat, then removed her hand, in case it was bothering him. "We need to get to know each other again."

He shook his head. "We never knew each other. You knew *me*, that's all."

In many ways — yeah.

"For Christ's sakes, you were keeping track of my *urine*," he said.

She sighed. His nurse, not his girlfriend. "That was my job, Michael. I just wanted to make sure you had the absolute best care, and it seemed —"

"I don't like us not being equal," he said. "I mean, I know you're older, and smarter, and all of *that*, but — I got enough problems feeling like a guy already."

She frowned at him. "An older woman driving two thousand miles to see you doesn't make you feel like a *guy*?"

"Well, yeah," he said, and grinned a little. "That was pretty okay."

To put it mildly. "My God," she said, "all *you* would have to do is give me a flower you found growing in the weeds — and I'd walk around smiling for a month."

He touched her cheek for a second. "Hard to picture, that."

A very sad bit of truth.

Otis got up and stretched, in apparent sudden need of affection, and Michael patted him, then motioned for him to lie down again. "That foxy major said it wasn't personal," he said. "That you were hard to get to know."

Had she now. "Well," Rebecca said, shortly, "she's the expert."

Michael shrugged, and leaned down to pat Otis.

Of course now her curiosity was piqued. "Um —" she shouldn't ask this, but — "what else did she say about me?"

He shrugged.

"I'm serious," she said. "I mean — curious." Seriously curious.

"I don't know." He dug an old tennis ball out from underneath the couch, and flicked it into the hall, Otis tearing after it. "That even when you were being infuriating, you were the most *genuine* person she'd ever known."

Hmmm. Rebecca moved her jaw. "Did she at least say it — fondly?"

He nodded. "Very fondly."

Well — okay. Maybe that wasn't so terrible. Infuriating, though. She would have hoped for — irksome — at best.

Michael looked at her. "She said she had never met anyone who was harder on herself. She said *God* would give himself more of a break."

Doyle hyperbole. "She's Irish," Rebecca said. "We're prone to effusion."

"Yeah," he said. "You're effusive as hell."

Amazing to think he had never known her before her conversion to catatonia. Mutism. "I was," she said quietly. "I hope to become so again."

He thought about that, then grinned. "I don't know. I'm not much for chatterboxes."

"You like *Dennis*," she said.

He laughed.

Snoopy was no slouch, either. Feeling herself about to yawn — exhaustion could only be put off so long — she covered her face with both hands for a few seconds until the urge passed.

"Long day," Michael said.

Jesus, yes.

"Come on." He squeezed her shoulder. "I'll show you where you're sleeping."

"That's okay," she said. "I mean, I'm not tired."

"Come on." He picked up his crutches. "We're both fried."

They took the stairs slowly, and he opened the first door on the left, balancing on one crutch while he flipped on the light switch. The room was very clean, and looked pretty much the way she would have expected, and she was especially pleased to see a couple of largish piles of books on the little wooden desk that also served as a bedside table.

"You're so neat," she said.

He shook his head wryly. "Think Mom's been in here shoveling out."

That made sense — unless he had picked up the art of perfect hospital corners at Fitzsimons.

"There's some towels," he said, pointing at the fluffy stack on the bureau, "and you know where the bathroom is."

She nodded.

"So, uh, I don't know," he said. "I guess that's it."

She nodded. "I really don't feel right kicking you out of your room, though, I — "

"Good night, Lieutenant," he said.

Wasn't he going to kiss her again? Or had that been a weak moment he now regretted? "Um, yeah," she said. "Good night."

He nodded, and turned himself around on his crutches to leave.

"Wait," she said, and went over to hug him, stretching up to give him a kiss on the cheek.

He turned his head to meet her mouth and, this time, kissed her exactly the way she remembered, letting his crutches fall, his hands running up and down her back. She wanted to concentrate only on kissing him, but he was off-balance on his leg, and so much of his weight was on her that she had to shift her position to support him — losing her own balance, both of them landing on the floor with a thud.

"*Shhh*," he whispered.

That's right — his entire family was asleep only feet away. They were twisted up together, and still kissing each other, Rebecca trying so hard to be quiet that she naturally started laughing.

"Next time you fall," he whispered, between kisses, "try and hit the bed, okay?"

She laughed, and pulled his head back down so they could keep kissing.

"And — laugh less," he said.

Which, of course, made her laugh more, especially when Otis came over to investigate all of this, sticking his head right between their faces.

"Go lie down," Michael said in his strict voice.

"Oh." Rebecca tried to get up. "Okay."

"I'm talking to the *dog*," he said.

Gee. Really? "Oh." Rebecca turned and gave Otis a little kiss on the muzzle. "You mean, I'm supposed to *kiss* the dog?"

"No," Michael said, and pushed Otis away. "Go lie down, damn it."

What a martinet. "So manly," she said.

"Yeah," he said, kissing her. "I'm really — "

A door opened somewhere out in the hall, and they froze. It was quiet, and then there was the sound of the bathroom light going on, and that door closing. As it did, she realized that *Michael's* door was wide open.

"My mother," Michael whispered. "And she'll come down and make sure you're all right, too."

They quickly moved apart, Michael fumbling for his crutches and Rebecca giving him a hand up, so that by the time his mother did, in fact, come down the hall and knock, they were standing up, pretending they barely knew each other.

Of course she just might notice that they were flushed and out of breath.

"I'm sorry," Mrs. Jennings said, wearing a plaid bathrobe. "Excuse me. Do you have everything you need, Rebecca?"

Rebecca nodded. "Yes, ma'am. Thank you." Her shirt felt a little funny, and she looked down, seeing that while she had managed to fasten the top two buttons, she had missed the next two, leaving a wide gap — and an intimate look at her taste in brassieres. She blushed, and buttoned them with as much casual swiftness as she could muster. One of them popped back open, and she had to rebutton it, blushing furiously.

"Smooth," Michael said, and while she knew she should just be embarrassed, she laughed — and then blushed all the more.

Mrs. Jennings must have decided to overlook

this entire exchange because she turned to Michael. "Are you all set downstairs, dear?"

He shook his head.

"Well, I'll make up the couch for you." She smiled at Rebecca. "Please let me know if there's anything else you need."

Rebecca nodded, and blushed. "Thank you."

"Night, Rebecca," Michael said, and winked at her before going after his mother.

Was there anyone on the *planet* less smooth than she was? She looked around for her duffel bag — and remembered that it was still out in the car. So, she went down after them, and Michael and his mother both waited on the front porch for her while she tried to open the car trunk, having to hit it a couple of times right above the lock to spring it loose. Then, she retrieved her duffel bag, using both hands to lug it over to the porch.

"Did you pay money for that car?" Michael asked.

Funny. "Good night, Michael," she said.

Once she was in his room with the door closed, having brushed her teeth and changed into a flannel nightgown, she looked around, feeling a little uncomfortable about going over and getting into his — empty — bed. The urge to poke through all of his stuff was also pretty strong, but that would be ill-bred, to say nothing of presumptuous, so she limited herself to a cursory glance.

Bed. Desk. Bureau. White painted bookcase. Closet door. Prosthesis on the floor in the corner.

Fresh white curtains, very pale blue wallpaper.

Nothing much on the walls, except for a poster of the Pacific Ocean, although there were marks and a couple of small picture hooks where other things must have hung.

A life-sized blowup of Elizabeth, perhaps? More likely, sports shots of skiers and other athletes he could no longer stand to see. Most of the books in the bookcase were car manuals, along with a couple of old textbooks, and books about baseball and dogs that he had probably been given when he was much younger. There were two dusty model airplanes on the shelves, and she pictured him, eight years old, but still stubborn, putting them together. She saw only one seam where glue had seeped out, leaving a tiny bump, so he must have been a very careful little boy.

There was a Golden High School yearbook, and it took every ounce of self-control she had not to open it. Resolutely, she walked over to the bed, pausing only to glance at the stacks of books on the desk, curious about what kind of literary interests he had.

Some mysteries, a few westerns, three or four more serious novels. Hardcover history books, most of them from the Jefferson County Library, about the Civil War, World Wars I and II, and thick biographies of Lincoln, FDR, and Kennedy.

History. Okay. Presumably his mother went to the library for him, often, hoping to keep him occupied during his recuperation. Was he planning to go back to school, or — was it any of her business? No.

She helped herself to one of the mysteries — a Dashiell Hammett she'd read before — and got into bed. It was nice and comfortable, the sheets cool. The pillow was softer than she liked, so she folded it in half before putting it behind her head.

She was in Michael's room, in his bed, reading his book.

Unbelievable.

Chapter Thirty-one

She was disoriented when she woke up — a strange room, with lots of sunshine coming in through the windows — but then she remembered, and relaxed. She would have guessed that it was about six-thirty or seven, but the little clock on his desk said eleven-fifteen.

She was still tired, but she jumped out of bed. His whole *family* was going to think she was utterly indolent. Shiftless. Slothful. She ran out to take a fast bath, scrubbed down the tub, and got dressed — a blue shirt, madras slacks, Keds. She probably looked too casual, but the inept, drunken choices she had made while packing her bag had, unfortunately, left her with very few fashion options. Her hair was wet and flat, but she fixed it as well as she could, peering into his small mirror, and then went timidly downstairs.

She found his mother sitting at the kitchen table, drinking a cup of coffee and writing a letter to someone. Seeing Rebecca, she smiled and stood up.

"Good morning," she said. "What would you like for breakfast?"

Lunch, more likely. "Oh, I'm fine, thank you," Rebecca said. "I'm sorry I slept so late." She located the coffee percolater, and walked over to it. "Do you mind if I — ?"

"Please do," Mrs. Jennings said.

She brought her cup back to the table, sitting down across from her. They both smiled, then Rebecca shyly sipped some coffee. It was good. Strong.

"You're sure you wouldn't like something to eat?" Mrs. Jennings asked.

Rebecca nodded. "I'm afraid it takes me a little while to wake up." Was Michael maybe still asleep, too? Lying in the den, mired in depression? Would it be overly familiar of her to ask? "Is, um, Michael awake?"'

Mrs. Jennings gestured towards the back door. "He's outside."

Throwing sticks for Otis, maybe? Taking in some sun while waiting for a very lazy nurse to arise? "I, uh — I really am sorry to have shown up so unexpectedly," she said, "and it was very nice of you to let me stay."

Mrs. Jennings looked at her, and Rebecca recognized something of her son's forceful stare. "I came down this morning," she said, "and he was *up*, and *dressed*, and eating breakfast with his father. Then, they went out to work on your car, and —" She shook her head. "I hope you stay forever."

Oh. Rebecca looked down, embarrassed, but also pleased.

"We've been at our wit's end," Mrs. Jennings said. "Watching him sit in the dark, drinking beer and smoking all those cigarettes. He hasn't been going anywhere, or seeing anyone — it's just broken my heart."

Which rang a few bells, and Rebecca thought guiltily about her own mother.

Mrs. Jennings looked at her with maternal concern. "I shouldn't say this, but you don't look very well, either."

Should she go for honesty, or prevarications? "I guess I haven't been, ma'am," Rebecca said.

Mrs. Jennings nodded. She had nice eyes. Dark, and intelligent, and serious, like Michael's.

"I — made a terrible mistake, in going over there," Rebecca said. "And since then, I haven't — well."

After a minute, Mrs. Jennings broke the silence. "It was different," she said, "when Bert came home."

"World War II?" Rebecca asked. Presumably.

Mrs. Jennings nodded. "He was in my class at school, and he joined up on his birthday. When he came home, wounded, a year and a half later, *everyone* we knew showed up at his parents' house. Casseroles, pies, cookies — he was our hero. And now — " She shook her head. "Half the people around here didn't even notice that he *went*, forget that they brought my boy back in — such shape." She looked very sad. "Some of the ladies from the church come by. Or a friend from school stops in — and stays five minutes. That's it."

Her mother certainly hadn't been inundated by neighborly offerings, either.

"I look at my sweet, shy boy, and it tears me up," Mrs. Jennings said.

Sweet. Shy. Michael? Well — okay. And, so far, this conversation would indicate that Elizabeth hadn't been a recent factor in his life. "Has he —" Smooth. Very smooth. Rebecca tried to come up with a better approach. "I mean, obviously, I don't expect — "

The back door opened, and Otis came barreling in, Michael crutching along behind him. He stopped and looked, ostentatiously, at the clock before looking back at her.

"Guess that pea we put under your mattress didn't bother you much," he said.

"I took it out," Rebecca said. "First thing."

He grinned, and started rinsing his grease-stained hands at the sink, using dishwashing liquid for soap. Then, he stopped and looked at his mother. "Sorry."

Mrs. Jennings smiled at him. "That's okay, dear."

"No, I'll go out back," he said, and turned the water off, leaving drips across the floor as he re-traced his crutch steps and went outside.

She and Mrs. Jennings both looked at the little trail of water, suds, and motor oil.

"If I left it there, they would all just walk right through it," Mrs. Jennings said.

Pre-nursing training, she would have, too. Locating the roll of paper towels, Rebecca ripped off a few and started cleaning up the mess.

"You don't have to do that, dear," Mrs. Jennings said quickly, also holding a handful of paper towelling.

It was nice to be called "dear." Rebecca finished with several long swipes. "No problem."

Mrs. Jennings watched her use the dampened towels to swab the sink and then throw them away in the red plastic wastebasket at the end of the counter, her expression hard to read.

"I, uh, guess I'm used to cleaning up on the ward," Rebecca said uneasily.

Mrs. Jennings nodded.

Pensive. She looked pensive. "I'm sorry," Rebecca said. "It was — rude — of me to — "

Mrs. Jennings smiled at her. "I guess I never expected him to meet someone *I* would like, too."

Oh. Rebecca smiled back.

Michael came in, cheerful and well-scrubbed, with water stains across an old grey Golden H.S. T-shirt. "Can we have lunch? I'm starved."

Mrs. Jennings nodded, already on her feet. "You just sit down, dear. It'll be ready in a jiffy. No, you sit down, too," she added, as Rebecca started to stand up.

Rebecca settled back, uncertainly, in her chair. Upon which, the obvious occurred to her, and she frowned at Michael. "What are you doing to my *car*? It runs fine."

He looked at her with great pity.

Well — it did. She drank some coffee, then put the cup down. "Did you come in and get my keys?"

He shook his head. "Didn't want to wake you up."

Which meant — what? She frowned. "So, how did you — ?" He hot-wired it. Never mind.

"She looks awful," Michael said to his mother. "I think she should eat some lunch, and go to bed."

Jesus, was he being salacious? No, because his mother was nodding.

"Okay?" Michael said, looking at her now.

Not to belabor the point, but — "I just got *up*," Rebecca said.

Michael shrugged. "So? When's the last time you went back to bed?"

Cold sober? She had no idea. "Over Christmas, maybe?"

He nodded. "Then, you're due."

Yeah, right. She was *really* going to take to her bed — *his* bed — after arriving entirely unanticipated and uninvited. She shook her head, forcing down some more coffee.

"Maybe I could take care of you a little, one time," Michael said, very quietly.

Okay. Maybe it wouldn't kill her to let him.

They ate grilled cheese sandwiches for lunch, with Michael forcing more milk or potato chips or pickles on her every other second. Mr. Jennings showed up to eat with them, which seemed to surprise both his wife and his son, and while he didn't have much to say, he did ask her if she had had a nice sleep, and also promised that they would have her car spinning like a top in no time. The literal prospect of that was an alarming image, but Rebecca smiled, and nodded, and ate her chips.

As soon as they were finished eating, and Mrs. Jennings had refused to allow her to help clean up, Michael escorted her upstairs to his room, where he leaned against the desk with his arms folded.

"I think you should put on your little night-gown," he said.

Self-respecting New Englanders liked to wear very *large* nightgowns. Year-round. "Are you going to stand there and watch?" she asked.

He glanced at the door. "Well — she might come up."

And a repeat of last night's scene would be a mistake. She went out to the bathroom to change, and when she came back, he was still leaning in the exact same place, but the bed was turned down, and his prosthesis had been moved to his desk chair.

Her nightgown suddenly seemed flimsy, and she was very aware of his eyes as she walked past him.

"That what they sleep in in convents?" he asked.

One man's perspective. "Yes," she said. "It was a gift from Sister Mary Matthew."

He nodded. "I figured."

She felt stupid getting into bed at one in the afternoon, and even stupider when he tucked in the loose end of the blanket, and then sat down on the edge of the mattress the way her father would have when she was little.

He looked at her for a minute without saying anything, then reached over towards his desk, lifting the prosthesis onto his lap. "You care if I put this on in front of you?"

Christ, no. She shook her head.

He nodded, and unzipped his jeans.

She had seen a lot of different guys, putting on a lot of different prostheses — but this was the first time she had ever held her breath while she was watching. He never once looked up, pulling down his pants, unpinning the extra cloth on the left side, adjusting his stump sock, and the like. She did her best to watch casually, but it was hard. Stumps always looked small, and pitiful. There were shrapnel scars on his remaining leg, but she was relieved to see that the muscle tone looked strong and healthy.

Once he had his jeans back on, he sat without moving and, not sure what else to do, she rested her hand on his knee. The fake one.

"I hate it," he said.

She had a lot more experience being a nurse than she did as a girlfriend. "On general principles, or because you're having discomfort?"

He frowned at her. "Because being crippled sucks."

Okay. That was specific.

He stood up, his first steps unwieldy, then turned around and came back with more confidence, stopping halfway to wait for her reaction.

If she just gave him a civilian-impressed *wow*, he wasn't going to buy it. "Trust it more," she said. "You don't have to swing your hip so much."

He scowled. "You know how many damn times I've fallen *down*?"

Too many.

"And don't tell me any stupid stuff about some guy who's way worse off, and still out there pitching," he said.

She grinned. "Even if it's a story that makes angels weep?"

"*Especially* then," he said.

Kindness would be more appropriate here than levity. "You look great," she said. "Your balance is excellent."

He shrugged unhappily. "What I look like, is a guy who should be carrying a tin cup."

Jesus, weren't they going to be able to help each other at *all*? "You look like a guy who's rising above it," she said.

"Oh, yeah," he said, but then winked at her. "Get some sleep, okay? I have a *really terrible* car to go fix."

She didn't think she was going to be able to fall asleep at all, but once she did, she slept endlessly. Every so often, she would hear a noise — someone on the stairs, the telephone ringing — and wake up, but then she would drop right off again. At one point, the door eased open, and a heavy furry body joined her on the bed, little bony legs digging into her back. She assumed it was *her* dog, Jack, remembered that it wasn't, mumbled, "Hi, Otis," and went back to sleep.

It was dark in the room when someone knocked, and the door opened. She woke herself up, blinking, and saw Michael silhouetted in the light from the hallway.

"You hungry?" he asked.

Jesus, what *time* was it? She sat up, almost knocking over the lamp on the desk before she managed to turn it on.

Michael came in, carrying a tray, careful on his prosthesis. He paused between each step, his full concentration on keeping whatever was on the tray from spilling. Otis trotted in, pushing right past his good leg, and Michael stook stock-still, gripping the tray. Once Otis had jumped back onto the bed, Michael moved forward again, lowering the tray onto her lap. Then, he straightened up, looking so pleased with himself that she wanted to cry.

"She only filled the milk partway," he said. "Just in case."

Nothing had spilled, except for a little bit of corn over the edge of the plate. "Did you carry it all the way up the stairs?" she asked.

He grinned. "Hell, yes."

Which made her feel even more like crying. But — happy tears.

He sat down on the edge of the bed. "It's probably pretty cold — I had to stop about ninety times."

"It looks wonderful," she said, and picked up her fork.

Michael stayed with her while she ate, helping himself to some of the chicken, and a couple of spoonfuls of mashed potatoes.

"It's almost time for Carson," he said. "You want to watch with me?"

She hesitated, since what she really wanted to do was go right back to sleep. "Well I — I kind of — "

"You're still tired," he said.

Extremely.

She did her best to be energetic the next day, but by eleven o'clock, Mrs. Jennings had caught her head nodding twice, and sent her back upstairs.

Rebecca went — and promptly slept some more, not sure if she were having a total breakdown, or just finally *relaxing*.

She got up for dinner, but only made it through half of *Ensign Pulver*. It was Friday night, and both Dennis and Carrie were out with friends, so she felt — a little — less stupid about going upstairs so early. Michael didn't say much, but he seemed more worried than annoyed.

She woke up again at about three in the morning, the house quiet and still. There was a small night-light in the hall, so she was able to find her way out to the bathroom without tripping and waking everyone up. She was tempted to go downstairs and see if Michael was awake — but most people weren't, in the middle to the night.

On the other hand, it couldn't hurt to check.

She found him lying on the couch in his underwear, smoking a cigarette and drinking Coors, while Otis slept on the floor by the fireplace. The television was on, and Errol Flynn was leaping around in the snow, trying to foil Nazis.

"So *that's* what you look like standing up," Michael said.

And now she knew what *he* looked like in boxer shorts. "Trouble sleeping?" she asked.

"*Now Voyager* is on in a little while," he said.

Bette Davis, playing a woman from Boston trying to make a new life for herself after suffering a nervous breakdown.

Swell.

"You want to watch?" he asked.

Why not. She sat down on the other end of the couch.

"Want a beer?" he asked.

Why not. She hadn't abused alcohol for almost a week now. "Thank you," she said.

He handed her one from what was left of the six-pack on the coffee table. "You have to sit way down there?"

She moved over, lifting his good leg up so she could sit with it across her lap, and rest her own legs on the coffee table.

"Better," he said.

Since he wasn't wearing a shirt, she could see the long scar across his right collarbone and she ran her hand along it.

"Doesn't really hurt anymore," he said.

She nodded. "Good." He was skinny, but his chest still looked strong, and his stomach had great, ridged muscles.

With all of her exposure to male bodies, she had not had *nearly* enough opportunities to touch and admire them in a nonprofessional way.

No time like the present.

"You go and make me crazy, and I'm not going to be able to pay attention to the movie," he said.

She lifted her hand. "Would that be so bad?"

He hesitated. "Well — it's kind of one of my favorites."

Oh, for Christ's sake. She sat back and drank some of her beer, using, without thinking, his stump for an armrest.

He hesitated again. "It really doesn't bother you?"

What? She followed his eyes. "No," she said, and he looked very happy.

Errol Flynn was gone now, and she settled back

to watch Bette Davis, reminded — upon Claude Rains's entrance as the kind-hearted psychiatrist — that it was actually one of her favorite movies, too.

"Does your family think I'm completely crazy?" she asked during the commercial.

He shook his head. "They've been dealing with me, so they're used to it."

Sounded like a mixed review.

"I yell when I'm sleeping, too," he said.

Oh, Christ, was she starting *that* again? She sighed. "Have I been doing it a lot?"

He shrugged. "I heard you once, and Mom and Carrie did a few times."

Terrific. She looked at him uneasily. "What did I yell?"

" 'Stop!' 'Don't!' " He shrugged again. "That kind of thing."

Don't shoot. Don't make *her* shoot. Damn. When she was at home, she would wake up to find her mother by the side of her bed, looking distressed, trying to calm her down and find out what, or who, it was that she so desperately wanted to stop. A couple of times, she had still been so nightmare-drugged that she had gulped out, "the *war*," but as a rule, she just shook her head and did her best to bring her heartbeat and breathing back under control.

"I yell 'Incoming!', mostly," Michael said.

Which pulled her out of herself, and she nodded. "All of the guys on the ward did." And most of the nurses in the hootches.

"You think it ever goes away?" he asked.

No.

Chapter Thirty-two

The movie was pretty romantic and by the time it was half over, they were curled up together. Michael was of the opinion that she looked a little overheated, and she was amused when he eased her nightgown off.

"Smooth," she said.

He nodded, and lit two cigarettes at once — the exact same way Paul Henreid kept doing it in the movie — and handed her one. She inhaled deeply, like Bette Davis, preparatory to blowing out a lingering cloud of smoke in response, but then destroyed the illusion by coughing.

"Smooth," Michael said.

Oh, yeah. Always.

They mostly only fooled around during the commercials — just enough time to get all hot and bothered; not *quite* enough time to lose control — and managed to find out a number of new anatomical facts about each other. She, personally, was not displeased.

When the movie ended, just after five-thirty,

they looked at each other for what seemed like a very long time, and then Michael let out his breath. Hard.

"My father'll be down here soon," he said. "I can hear the shower."

She nodded, reaching for her nightgown.

Their kiss good night lasted too long, and she had to wait for Mr. Jennings to go down the hall and into the kitchen before she could sneak out and run upstairs. It might not look convincing if she came bouncing right back down for breakfast, so she decided to wait about half an hour — and predictably fell asleep, not waking up until almost ten. Michael, it developed, had gone to the station with his father, and Mrs. Jennings insisted upon her sitting down and eating pancakes and bacon.

Afterwards, Rebecca was able to talk her way into doing the dishes, and then she carried a cup of coffee outside, where she could hear a radio blaring rock and roll. Might as well get some of that fresh mountain air. She stopped in the carport, and stared at the pieces of what had once been her Dodge Dart. Then, she stared at Dennis, who was cleaning something metal with a stained rag, a lot of elbow grease, and a pan of mysterious, strong-smelling solution. The carburetor, maybe? The fuel pump?

"What are you guys doing to my car?" she asked.

"*Major* work," Dennis said, rubbing away clots of old motor oil.

That much, she could see. She peered into what little was left of the engine. "How long is it going to take? I'm going to have to be getting home soon."

Dennis looked up. "What do you mean?"

"Well — " What did *he* mean? "Home," Rebecca said. "New England. Where I live."

Dennis nodded, shook some hair out of his eyes, and went back to scrubbing. "Does Mike know?"

Well — he had to, right? He couldn't think she was just moving in permanently — could he? "Well — " Hmmm. "I guess we haven't really talked about it yet," she said.

Dennis nodded.

She and Michael were going to *have* to talk. Soon.

"You want to help?" Dennis asked.

She liked *deft* tools, like tweezers, and hemostats, and scalpels. "I guess so," she said. Despite being, like her father, rather vain and cautious about her hands. "If you can think of something easy." Painless.

"Okay. I'll show you how to change the drive belts." Dennis looked at her outfit. "You might get dirty."

One of the few things in life about which she never worried. "No problem," she said.

"Cool," Dennis said cheerfully. "Mike's bringing new hoses back."

What wonderful news.

The job was easier, and more logical, than she had thought it would be, and it was fun listening to Dennis sing along with the radio. A guy who had been *born* to be wild.

"We'll do the fan belt next," he said.

Her strategy, exactly.

"Mony, Mony" came on, and they both sang,

alternating the "Yeah" parts, Dennis taking the lead.

Carrie came out from the kitchen. "Mom wants to know if you want anything to eat or — anything," she said hesitantly.

"Just to boogie," Rebecca said, holding a wrench in each hand — not that she was really planning to *use* either of them.

"Well, okay — " Carrie looked dubious — "I'll tell her."

When "Baby Love" came on, Rebecca was Diana Ross, while Dennis acted as his own unique, atonal version of the Supremes.

"You're not what I thought you'd be like," he said.

"Didn't expect me to be musically gifted?" Rebecca asked.

"No, I — " He paused to think. "I figured you'd be — I don't know — different."

Blonde. "Do I remind you of Elizabeth?" Rebecca asked.

Dennis laughed, going back under the hood. "Not hardly."

Right. No way a guy could get that lucky *twice*.

Dennis extended a hand behind his back. "Can I have that socket wrench?"

Rebecca looked down at the tools, took a guess, and gave him one.

"Thanks." He started loosening something. "Anyway, we were trying to decide if you were really quiet and, you know, shy — or just *polite*."

All of the above.

"But then," Dennis slipped off the old fan belt, "it seems like you're really friendly, too. I mean —

Carrie was saying she felt like she could talk to you, and you wouldn't tell her she was too young or stupid or whatever.''

"Well, I'll just have to go right inside, and change *that* impression," Rebecca said.

Dennis laughed, and picked up a new fan belt, putting it on and adjusting the tension.

Rebecca leaned on the edge of the car to watch him. "Are you going to college in the fall?"

He made a face. "Only if I *have* to."

"How are your grades?" she asked.

He made a worse face. "Depends on if I study."

So he was as capable of flunking out as Doug had been. "The war's not even close to ending," she said — Hamburger Hill, anyone? — "and you do *not* want to go there."

Dennis put down the socket wrench and wiped his arm across his face, leaving a long grease smear behind, not making eye contact with her. "Mike says your brother, uh, went away. Can't come back."

Rebecca nodded.

"I don't want to do that," Dennis said. "And I don't want to lose a whole bunch of weight, or act nuts, or pretend I like boys, or *any* of that."

Rebecca nodded, opting to listen, rather than comment. Always a good plan.

"I, uh," he glanced in the direction of the kitchen, "don't get along so great with teachers, and I heard if they don't like you, they grade extra hard to make sure you wash out, and — " He stopped, lowering his voice. "I *know* they're going to get me."

A nonacademic kid with a quick lip and a tendency to push his luck. Probably.

"And — don't tell Mike," he said, "but I'm not going over there. *No way*. People are getting wasted for *nothing*."

Rebecca nodded. "So you have to stay in school. As long as you can." Then she remembered seeing him squint at the television during *The King and I*. "How's your eyesight?"

He looked confused. "What do you mean? Fine."

Maybe. "Do you wear glasses?" she asked.

He glanced at the back door again, and the spectre of his mother beyond. "Well, I'm kind of supposed to, sometimes, like for the board, but — "

Good. "Okay, here's what you do," she said. "If they really *are* going to get you, try to join the Air Force, first. It's the safest."

"I thought the Coast Guard was," he said doubtfully.

She shook her head. "You could end up on river patrol — I've heard of guys who did. In the Air Force, without twenty-twenty vision, they'll never let you off the ground, so you'll probably end up as a mechanic or something. Plus, they've got the best food and hootches, and you're as likely to end up in Guam or Thailand as you are in-country."

Dennis frowned. "So — do I just join up right away this fall?"

Christ, he was young. Rebecca smiled at him. "Try getting good grades, first. It's easier."

He thought about that, then nodded a few times. Good.

He was explaining the fuel pump to her in numbing detail when the pickup truck pulled into the driveway and Michael swung down from the passenger's side, landing lightly on his good leg as Otis scrambled out after him. He saw her and grinned, reaching back inside and taking a bunch of flowers wrapped in green tissue paper from the front seat.

"Here." He tossed them to her. "I found these."

She caught the bouquet — carnations and baby's breath, with a few daisies — and grinned back at him. Widely.

"They were in a trash can," he said.

Her grin was veering towards foolish. "Thank you."

Mr. Jennings got out of the truck, carrying an armload of various hoses, nodding genially at her before bending over the Dart's engine to see what progress Dennis had made.

Michael retrieved his cane from the floor of the truck, using it for extra balance as he followed his father, pausing only long enough to touch her cheek where it was undoubtedly smudged.

"You okay?" Rebecca asked. "You must be tired — you didn't get any sleep."

Dennis perked up. "How do *you* know he was awake all night?"

Michael showed him his fist; Rebecca just frowned at him. Mr. Jennings gave no indication whatsoever that he had heard, although he must have.

Rebecca cleared her throat, hoping that her face wasn't as red as it felt. "I — think I'll go put these in some water," she said.

All three of them were occupied by the car now, and paying little or no attention.

"So — that's what I'll do," she said.

Dennis was talking at length about the carburetor, while Michael and his father nodded.

"Here I go," she said.

Michael grunted, his father nodded, and Dennis looked at her blankly.

Right. She opened the kitchen door and went inside.

There was much talk at lunch about the Dart's transmission and exhaust system. Rebecca, for one, had little to contribute. Michael and his father decided that they were going to have to take it down to the station, so they could use the hydraulic lift and *really* get down to serious work.

"You want to come?" Michael asked.

No. "Well," Rebecca said, and looked across the table, "I think maybe Carrie and I are going to make plans."

Carrie's face lit up. "Really? I mean — *yeah*."

"You don't want to watch me using heavy machinery?" Michael asked. "Sweating a lot?"

"If she wants to see *that*," Dennis said, not quite under his breath, "she should just — "

Rebecca cut him off. "Dennis, please pass me the mustard."

He smiled a sweetly wicked smile at her and passed the mustard.

After lunch, when everyone else was already clearing off the table, Michael put his hand on her arm to stop her from getting up.

"Um, tonight," he said. "I kind of thought — you want to go on a date?"

She laughed, stacking his plate on top of hers. "We've *never* been on a date."

"So we can give it a try," he said. "Just this once."

He was cute. "You mean, be seen in public together? Dress up?" she asked.

He nodded. "I'm not going to wear a damn tie, but, yeah."

Who could resist such an invitation. "Okay." She kissed him. "You paying?"

He nodded.

"Okay," she said, and grinned at him. "Wear a damn tie."

She and Carrie ended up at the local movie theater, eating popcorn, drinking Cokes, and watching a Tarzan and Frankenstein double feature. Altogether a pleasant afternoon, even if they were the only ones in the place over twelve.

Michael came home from the gas station rather testy, so she didn't push him on the damn tie. She knew he had to be tired, and suggested that they stay in, but he just shook his head and went upstairs to change, slouching on his crutches.

When he came back down, he was clean and neat in dark grey pants and a just-ironed striped shirt.

"You look nice," she said.

He nodded, exchanging his crutches for the cane.

He'd probably been overdoing it with the prosthesis. "Maybe you should stay with the crutches," she said.

He shook his head. "You ready to go?"

Despite his never having seen her in a dress, she was apparently not going to receive a compliment to that effect. "If you're sure you still *want* to go," she said.

He nodded, moving ahead of her to the front door.

Clearly, a fun evening lay ahead.

When they got outside, he wanted to walk, and she didn't argue, even though she knew he was in pain.

"Everything okay?" she asked.

He nodded shortly, lighting a cigarette.

Fine. If he wanted to limp and glower and court lung damage, that was his prerogative. *She* would just limp.

"I hear you're leaving," he said.

Ah. The plot thickened. Dennis had a big mouth.

He looked over at her. "You figuring on giving me a check for all the repair work, or just taking off?"

Ought she to point out that the damned car had been running fine?

"I guess your being here was just one long tease," he said, "right?"

She had developed an instant headache. Right between the eyes. "What did you expect? I figured I was just out here to track you down, get rejected, and head home."

"You acted like you were staying," he said sulkily.

What a nice, happy date this was. And now they were on the main street, Washington, so half the *town* would be able to walk by and enjoy their argument. "Yeah, well, I don't recall your asking me to," she said, and crossed the street without waiting for him, knowing full well that he couldn't walk as fast as she could. A childish tactic, no doubt.

Looking back, she could see that he was going to be even *more* childish, and not cross at all. Well, fine. There was a bench in front of a nearby shop, and she sat down on it, next to an old man in a green plaid shirt who was reading a newspaper and, of all things, wearing a weathered cowboy hat. How impressively Western. She knew Michael would give in first, and after a minute, he did, limping over on his cane.

"Well, hi, Mike," the old man said, lowering his paper. "How you doing?"

Michael nodded. "Fine, Mr. Ford. How are you?"

"Can't complain," the older man said. "This your girl?"

Rebecca was going to laugh, but instead, she looked at Michael with wide and ingenuous eyes.

"Are you?" he asked.

She turned to Mr. Ford. "I'm tormented by doubts, but he *did* give me flowers today."

Mr. Ford was a little flummoxed by this. "Well," he said, after a pause, "he's a good boy. Comes from a good family. Don't you listen to none a' them damn hippies."

"No, sir," Rebecca said.

Mr. Ford folded his newspaper and stood up. "You two kids have a good time now."

After he had ambled away, Rebecca stayed where she was on the bench, her legs crossed, hands clasped in her lap.

"Small town," Michael said.

Yes. She lived in one herself.

"I don't want you to go," he said, "okay?"

She sighed. "I kind of — " not kind of; *definitely* — "ran away from a lot of things." Her parents. Alcoholism. Adulthood. "And I can't put them off forever."

He nodded, stuffing his free hand into his pocket, the other gripping his cane. "So, where's that leave me?"

"Well, I guess we need to talk about that," she said.

He nodded, looking unhappy.

Christ. "What if I hadn't shown up, Mike?" she asked. "What would you be doing?"

He shrugged. "Lying on the couch, feeling sorry for myself."

"For the rest of your *life*?" she asked.

He shrugged again, and sat down next to her. "I don't know. I guess after a couple of years, I'd go out and try to find someone young, and sweet, and stupid."

Since she didn't fall into any of those categories.

"What were *you* going to do?" he asked. "If you didn't find me, or I told you to go to hell, or whatever."

Drink, and feel sorry for herself. "Use the GI Bill, I guess," she said. "I've been thinking about medical school."

He grinned. "Harvard, right?"

Well — yeah. What was wrong with that?

He lifted his arm, draping it around her shoulders. "Last I heard, there were schools here in *Colorado*."

No doubt, but — "I, uh, — " Hmmm. She didn't want to sound elitist. "If I were going to do it, I think I — " oh, hell, she *was* elitist — "I'm not sure I'd feel comfortable anyplace else."

His eyebrows went up. "You mean, you'd *only* go to Harvard?"

"Well — " Yeah. She frowned. "Yale, maybe."

He was still staring at her, but now he seemed amused. "Your parents must have *flipped out* when you went to Vietnam."

Still were.

"Bet they'd like it even better, seeing you with a crippled car jockey grunt," he said.

Would Michael and her father have anything to say to each other? Did *she* and her father have anything to say to each other? "As far as I can tell," she spoke slowly, "all they really want is for me to be happy."

"Think all *my* family wants is for me not to blow it with you," he said, and winked at her.

She was in agreement with his family.

"When you have to leave?" he asked.

It was beyond highly probable that he had seen *Mary Poppins*. "I shall stay until the wind changes," she said.

He grinned wryly.

Except she was trying to be less infuriating these days. "Or until you fix my muffler," she said.

He nodded, reached for his cane to ease himself up, and then paused. "Did I remember to tell you you have *great* legs?"

She shook her head.

"Oh." He slid his hand up underneath her dress and then back out. "Well, remind me to do that."

She was just plain crazy in love with this idiot. "Sure thing," she said.

Chapter Thirty-three

They ended up in a place called Dud's Cafe right near the movie theater, eating hamburgers and drinking — Cokes. Just about everyone there, from the hostess to the busboy to the other customers, seemed to know him, and they were either overly friendly or blatantly standoffish. It was also obvious that it had been a long time since any of them had seen him, and they all avoided looking down at his leg.

Neither of them said much during dinner — for her part, she was just happy to be in a safe, little local restaurant with him. To be on a date. To present the illusion of being a normal, ordinary, all-American girl.

After paying the check, Michael looked at his watch.

"Things get pretty quiet around here," he said, "but we could, I don't know, go over to the Ace-Hi and get a beer or something."

"I'm trying to retire from beer," she said.

He shrugged. "So we can head home. Sit down

somewhere and pretend we give a damn about looking up at the stars.''

Sounded good to her.

He held the door for her as they left, and they crossed Washington Street, walking away from what little Saturday night crowd there was wandering around.

"Is your stump okay?'' she asked. "You've really been giving it a workout, lately.''

He nodded. "It's fine.''

They walked down a quiet side street.

"Do you, um, still hear from Elizabeth?'' she asked.

He frowned at her. "What do you mean?''

"Well, Dennis was saying — '' She stopped. In addition to no longer being infuriating, she wanted to stop being a jerk.

"Dennis has a big mouth,'' Michael said.

That, she already knew.

"What brought *her* up?'' he asked.

An immature and jealous lieutenant. "Well, I — '' Yes, she felt, and sounded, like — a jerk. "You were saying you were going to look for someone young, and sweet, and stupid, and I — ''

"Who said she's *any* of those things?'' he asked.

No one. "Oh,'' Rebecca said, and flushed. "Well — I mean, I know she was really beautiful, and — ''

"I didn't say you weren't pretty,'' Michael said impatiently, "I said your hair was dumb.''

Which, until he reminded her, she had managed to forget. And it was going to take, what, at least six months to grow out?

"The day I met you," he said, "you weren't about to win Miss Massachusetts, know what I mean?'"

She knew. Throwing up had been a particularly glamorous moment.

"You shouldn't even have been alive," he said, "and there you were, all smart, and fierce, and making jokes." He shook his head. "I had no *idea* what you looked like — and I was already nuts for you."

He *sounded* so sure of himself. "Really?" she asked, worrying that he was maybe just being — kind.

"Christ, yes," he said, frowning at her. "What do you *think*? I'm letting you stay at my house — in my *room* — because I feel sorry for you?"

The thought had crossed her mind, so she grinned sheepishly at him.

"Jesus," he said, and shook his head.

His crankiness was reassuring, and she leaned up to kiss his cheek.

"We have to talk about it, though," he said, looking at her seriously.

She swallowed, already afraid. "Talk about what?"

"That day," he said. "Whatever happened."

Finally, the conversation that had been in the air between them from the first instant that they'd met. Whether she was ready for it or not.

"You already know," she said, "right?"

He nodded. "Only one way you end up with the other guy's gun."

Yeah. Law of the goddamn jungle. She swallowed harder, unable to look at him.

"Becky, it's there," he said. "We can't pretend it isn't."

Right. They were passing some little local museum, and her legs felt so leaden that she sat down on the bench out front, her arms tightly hugging her knees.

He had trouble getting his prosthesis to cooperate, but managed to sit down next to her, setting his cane aside.

"It was very personal," she said. "I was looking at him the entire time."

Michael nodded, reaching around her back to touch the scar on her arm. "Who shot first?"

Did it matter? "He did," Rebecca said. "But — " She was the one who walked away. She shuddered, remembering. "He was very *young*."

"*Doc* was young," Michael said. "And Jankowski, and LT, and a whole lot of *other* guys."

Yeah. She nodded, moving so that she was sitting even closer to him.

"You think you're the only one who ever did something terrible because you *had* to?" he asked.

She shook her head. Not that that had ever made it any easier to live with.

"Seems like if you judge yourself," he said quietly, "you judge me, and almost every other guy I knew over there."

The most inappropriate question *ever* to ask a veteran was, "Did you kill anyone?" Which was inevitably followed by, "How many?" "It's different," she said. "You all were supposed to — "

"So, you're better than me?" he said. "Maybe think I *wanted* to be out there shooting at people? Christ, I would never even *tap* Otis with a piece of newspaper, and I'm suddenly supposed to kill human beings? Jesus, Rebecca. Try thinking of yourself as a little less goddamned perfect, why don't you.''

Time to break the rules. ''Did *you* kill anyone, Mike?'' she asked.

He thought for a long time before he answered. ''I don't know. I mean, mostly — I almost never *saw* anyone. Like, maybe we'd see muzzle flashes, and we'd all shoot, but — how the hell do you know who did what? And if we went to look after, we might find some blood, or — a lot of times, I wasn't even sure if anyone had ever been there. It wasn't like we were standing around, waiting to see the whites of their eyes.''

Very different from sitting, looking at — and talking at — a boy for a good three or four hours before it happened. ''It wasn't like that for me,'' she said.

He massaged her arm, his hand warm and comforting.

''Did anyone else know?'' she asked. ''In the squad?''

''Well — '' he glanced at her uncertainly — ''all of us. I mean, it wasn't just you having that crummy old pistol, but — you had that weird, jumpy adrenaline going. All hopped up, like guys get after fire fights.''

And women, too, apparently. ''I figured you and Snoopy had talked about it,'' she said, ''but — Finnegan?'' Finnegan, who'd been so sweet to her at the hospital.

He nodded.

Jesus. ''*Hanson?*'' she asked.

Michael nodded. "Him, especially."

Jesus. All of this was starting to whirl around in her head, and she gave it a hard shake. "How about other guys? People not in your squad."

"What happens in the bush, stays in the bush," he said.

Which helped further explain why there had been no official repercussions. But still. "*Hanson?*" she said again. He had been so *nice* to her. Treated her — like a good person. "I would have expected him to think I was *terrible*."

Michael shrugged. "He knew better than anyone what it was like out there. Hell, there probably wasn't a guy in the platoon he didn't save at least *once*. Viper, too. And Finnegan, one time, when he was on slack, wasted a guy who was about to blast me away. I mean, half a second later, and I'm out of there."

Thank God for Finnegan.

"So, what's the deal," Michael said, folding his arms. "You sorry you're alive?"

Here, on this nice street, on this nice cool spring night, with — what the hell — all those nice stars up in the sky, above the black shadows of the mountains. With Michael sitting next to her, his hip pressing against hers. "I'm *overjoyed* to be alive," she said. "I feel like every new second is one I'm lucky as hell to have."

He shrugged. "Could've fooled me."

"What I hate," she said, "is that I feel this way while someone *else*, with an equally valid right to be alive — isn't."

He nodded. "Okay. I'll give you that."

Good of him.

"But, you want us all to hate you?" he asked. "So you'll feel better?"

The answer was a definite yes, but she shook her head.

"You think maybe that's why I got blown up?" he asked, expressionless. "Because I'm a really bad person?"

She shook her head, lightly touching his leg where his stump met the prosthesis.

"I don't, either," he said, then looked at her with very grave eyes. "That the only day that bothers you? Out of your whole damn tour?"

Christ, no.

"We'd walk around sometimes," he said, "two, three weeks without anything bad happening. A few guys'd get malaria, or dysentery, maybe."

She nodded. It was that grinding, everyday aspect of his war that she couldn't quite picture. She had had food to eat, water for a shower, a cot to sleep on.

"I was *in* your ER," he said. "And there was blood, and guts, and guys screaming and dying all over the place. Was it always like that?"

Yes. So, she nodded.

"And *that* doesn't screw you up inside?" he asked.

He was right. That was almost never what made her wake up shouting. "I don't think I've even gotten to that yet," she said. "All those poor — there were *so many*. And I can't — " Won't. "It was just — " Endless. Constant. Mind-numbing. "It's kind of all blurred in my head, and — " She couldn't — *wouldn't* — start dredging it up. Some horrors were best forgotten.

Michael nodded, and slouched back on his elbows to look up at the sky.

"You're right," she said. "I guess all I can handle so far is remembering the one bad day."

He nodded. "I kind of figured."

Which meant, what, that her entire being was going to churn around inside forever? That she would *always* be like this? She could feel him watching her, and tried to smile.

"I need you to talk to me," he said, seriously, "so I'll feel like I can talk to *you*."

She couldn't think of anything she *wouldn't* do for him — even that — so she nodded. Then, feeling lonely, she leaned her head against his shoulder, and he wrapped his arms around her.

"You really going to be a doctor?" he asked.

Was she? "I don't know," she said. "I'm not sure if I even have the nerve to try. But — I'd like to. Try, I mean."

He nodded, his chest feeling strong and solid against her face. "How long's it take, becoming a doctor?"

Years. She let out her breath. "I have some undergraduate credits to finish, and then, there's three years of medical school, your internship, and your residency." If she was lucky, she would be finished at some point in the — good God — late seventies.

Probably just in time to get drafted and sent over — as a doctor — to the goddamn war in Vietnam.

"Um, what about you?" she asked. "What do *you* want to do?"

He shrugged. "Hard to say. Being in *public's* still kind of new for me."

She nodded.

"I think my father's kind of hoping that I sign on with him down at the station," he said. "You know, permanently."

Was there a medical school, somewhere in Denver? There had to be.

"Are you pretty near the ocean, in Marblehead?" he asked.

She felt her breath catch somewhere inside. "It's right there. I mean, *right* there." Mere steps away.

He nodded, mulling that over. "I like the ocean. I mean, the only time I saw it was in-country, but — I liked it a lot."

She nodded, holding her breath.

"Think you already know where *I* go, Otis goes," he said.

This *had* to be heading where she thought it was, and she was too nervous to respond beyond a gulp, and a nod.

"So," he said, and grinned down at her. "When's the wind change?"

Which sounded like — a *yes*. "Monday?" she suggested, hearing her voice tremble slightly.

He thought about that, then nodded. "Works for me," he said.

When she called her parents the next day, they sounded tentatively delighted to hear that she was soon to arrive with a crippled car jockey and a small brown German shepherd mix in tow. *Michael's* family seemed to think that the whole thing was great, although she got the distinct impression that they thought New England was a fairly odd place to want to go, for any length of time. Typically, she and Michael had done very little talking about further specifics, beyond the notion that they were going to "take a ride." See what happened.

Monday morning, before school, Dennis and Carrie helped them pack up the car. Carrie, glumly, kept asking when they were going to be coming back, while Dennis was full of advice about their not doing anything *he* wouldn't do, and being certain not *ever* to drive on the left side of the road — even if it felt right. Michael kept telling him to shut up, but Rebecca thought he was funny. Otis, observing all of the activity, was beside himself with anxiety and excitement.

Once they were packed, they ended up down at the gas station with Michael's parents, so Michael could fill up the tank, and he and his father could give the engine one last going over. It took forever, so Rebecca went into the office, selecting a postcard from the dusty rack and politely leaving a nickel on the side of the cash register. Then, she went back outside, to use the car roof as a writing surface.

It was a very pretty postcard — if a bit prosaic — with a majestic picture of the Continental Divide, and she knew that the cerebral major would quite enjoy it.

"Hey." She leaned over to tap Michael on the back. "Do you say hi to Maggie?"

He frowned. "Who's Maggie?"

"Major Doyle," she said.

"Oh. Yeah." He went back under the hood. "Sure."

Michael says hi, she wrote. *More later.* — *R.*

She made the *R.* black and strong, tall and sloping, knowing that Maggie would, no doubt, both pick up on, and appreciate, the little du Maurier reference. And, if not, there were worse things than private jokes.

That taken care of, she opened the car door, setting the card on the dashboard and patting Otis, who was panting in the front seat.

"Look, we did what we could," she could hear Mr. Jennings saying, sounding very resigned.

"I'm making her get rid of it," Michael answered grimly. "Soon as possible."

Oh, he thought so, did he.

"If you two don't get going, you're still going to be here this time tomorrow," Mrs. Jennings said.

Rebecca nodded. "Yeah, come on, Mike. Enough already."

He made an impatient motion with his right hand, still fiddling around with some engine part with his left.

"Michael. Otis is *bored*," she said.

"Oh. *Well*," he said, and slammed the hood shut.

So predictable.

There was a round of prolonged good-bye hugs, during which Rebecca felt shy, and then Mr. Jennings went inside, coming out with still *more* maps for them to bring along, while they promised Michael's mother that they would be careful, and call a lot, and not stay away too long.

When they finally pulled away — after a brief argument about who was going to drive first, which Rebecca won — neither of them said anything for a few blocks, Rebecca wondering if he was feeling as overwhelmed by all of this as she was. He was very quiet — and maybe already a little homesick.

They came to a red light, and she stopped.

"So," she said. "Which musical would you like me to sing *first*?"

"Oh, Christ," Michael said, and fumbled around in the pockets of his battered field jacket for his cigarettes.

"I know *all* of them," she said.

"Run," he said to Otis, who was fussbudgeting around in the back. "Run for your life." Then, he lifted an eyebrow at her. "Do you know *No, No, Nanette*?"

"*Every single word*," Rebecca said.

He groaned, lit his cigarette, and snapped his Zippo shut. "You know how damned long a couple of thousand miles is?"

"I think," Rebecca said, pausing for significant effect, "I'll start with *Pajama Game*."

Michael groaned.

As they drove along Route 6 and then on to Colfax, Michael gave her many more directions than she wanted to hear, and they bickered a little about that, and how far they were going to go before they stopped, and whether they should have the radio on, or not — and if so, what station. Throughout which, Otis was restless and agitated.

Slowing down for yet another one of the interminable red lights, she looked at Michael slouching next to her, surly and adorable.

"Is this going to work, Mike?" she asked.

He shook his head. "Not a chance."

Oh. "Think we'll even make it as far as *Nebraska*?" she asked.

"Never happen," he said.

He was cute, and he was an idiot. "So — why are you here?" she asked.

He shrugged. "Nothing better to do today."

Right.

They were almost at the entrance to I-70, and she was beginning to find Otis's bouncing and scuffling around more than a little distracting.

"Tell your recalcitrant dog to sit," she said.

Michael shrugged. "*Our* recalcitrant dog."

Oh. She grinned at him, and was very happy to take the hand he held out.

"*Sit*, Otis," she said, and turned onto the highway heading east.

ABOUT THIS POINT SIGNATURE AUTHOR

ELLEN EMERSON WHITE has written several novels for young adults, among them *The President's Daughter, Life Without Friends*, and *Long Live the Queen*, which was named an ALA Best Book for Young Adults. She is also the author of the *Echo Company* series. While writing this series for Scholastic, Ellen White grew fascinated with the character of Rebecca Phillips and couldn't let her go. *The Road Home* brings closure to Rebecca's story.